HIGH PRESSURE
THE EXECUTIONER

HIGH PRESSURE THE EXECUTIONER

HAMMER-AXE SIX!

By

Robert Davis

iUniverse, Inc.
Bloomington

High Pressure the Executioner
Hammer-Axe Six!

iUniverse books may be ordered through booksellers or by contacting:

iUniverse
1663 Liberty Drive
Bloomington, IN 47403
www.iuniverse.com
1-800-Authors (1-800-288-4677)

ISBN: 978-1-4759-5631-3 (sc)
ISBN: 978-1-4759-5633-7 (hc)
ISBN: 978-1-4759-5632-0 (ebk)

Library of Congress Control Number: 2012919527

Printed in the United States of America

iUniverse rev. date: 11/26/2012

CHAPTER 1

The House of Ra was a large territory in the beautifully lush grasslands of central Africa, ruled by Queen Ramala, the Hayee Hellcat. One of her top Warlords, the Hayee, Ray found all three of his daughters, dead, early the next day, after a party held the night, before. His daughters were found, strewn across the road, a short distance from their family's compound.

All three were beheaded and had stab wounds on their torsos from machetes. No one knew who killed them. When the bodies were found several Warlords in the House of Ra reasoned it must have been the Hayee Hellcat, Ramala, or one of her two Hellcat cousins the Hayee, Tara and the Hayee, Wana.

The Warlords assumed Queen Ramala killed Shamika and her sisters, because of the sexual relationship between Ramala's King, Dan the Destroyer and Shamika. After several warnings from her Queen, to stop, Shamika continued having sex with the King. Most everyone thought that cost Shamika her life.

In retaliation, rebelling Warlords kidnapped Ramala's close cousin the Hayee Hellcat, Tara and her children. Their guards attempted to capture the Queen and her children. They failed. Queen Ramala's three daughters were the Ra, Ramala who was known as La, or the Number One Princess. The Ra, Ramashaya was called Shaya. The Ra, Danaaa was mostly called Baby by her siblings, was called High Pressure by Ramala, because of her non-stop aggressiveness.

Danaaa, with her extra ordinary sense of smell, combined with her uncanny hearing, detected guards sneaking through the palace attempting to ambush them. Danaaa alerted her sisters in time for them to get their axes and defend themselves, until their brothers and cousin arrived.

Queen Ramala's sons the Ra, Dan, the Ra, Don and the Ra, Ram arrived at their sister's room after thwarting an attempt by guards to capture them, also. Queen Ramala's six children, three sets of twins, a boy and girl in each set, and their cousin Yin would soon be known by all as the Hammer-Axe Six, even though there were seven of them.

All of the children raced through the halls, until they met their mother and father. They all moved to the entrance, where they saw rebelling Warlords and guards at the bottom steps of the palace. Queen Ramala's face was full of arrogant anger as she looked out at the guards. Before she could do, or say anything, Ramala's Warlord and cousin, Bantu, walked ahead of the guards. He looked at Ramala and said "We have Tara and her children." Shock and concern replaced the arrogant look on Ramala's face. Ramala angrily asked "Where is she?"

Bantu smiled and quickly said "I'm not going to say, just yet. However, she is having breakfast with some of our cousins. No harm has come to them. Just be careful not to make rash decisions that could affect everyone." Before Ramala could respond, everyone heard someone yell "Wait!" the crowd parted and Ramala saw her cousin the Hayee Hellcat, Wana.

Wana who was in charge of all Warlords and security of the House of Ra just arrived at Ramala's palace with the Butcher girls Ma and Syn, Jara. The Butcher girls were two of Ramala's top Executioners, called the Butchers. They were the only two Butchers in the main city, besides King Dan, who was also a Butcher. Butchers were killers who killed top rate killers and everyone less than that, on orders from their Queen.

Wana and the Butcher girls walked and stood on the palace stairs facing Ramala. Wana said "Allow me." Ramala gave a slight nod. Wana then turned to Bantu and asked "What's the meaning of this?" Bantu said "Ray's daughters have been killed." Ramala yelled "This is why you try and kill me and my family?!!" Wana warned "La!" Bantu face looked slightly confused when he said "That wasn't part of the plan!" Ramala quickly said "It looks like rebellion to me!" Wana turned to Ramala and said "La, I'm handling this!"

Ramala arrogantly raised her head, looking down her nose at Bantu, but said nothing. Wana turned back to Bantu. Bantu looked concerned when he said in a low voice to Wana "No one's planning on harming Tara and her children. However, we have a situation on our hands! We need help on this!" Bantu looked up at Ramala after saying that. Wana knew her cousin, Queen Ramala, would start taking heads once she knew Tara was out of harm's way.

Wana looked Bantu in his eyes and said "You let me handle La. Get these guards away from the palace. Stop this madness and let me investigate. I will find out what happened and bring the culprits to justice! I promise!" Bantu lowered his head to Wana and then to Ramala. He ordered all of the guards to leave. Wana watched until they were gone. She then walked up the palace stars. When Wana got to Ramala, she said "La, they have Tara. You let me handle this. Don't do anything, until you hear from me! Is that clear?!" Ramala stared at Wana for a moment and then said "Don't order me! Find Tara and bring her to safety. I won't do anything, until then." Wana, with concern and frustration in her voice, said "I'm just saying!" Wana looked at her nieces and nephews, before turning and leaving.

Shamika's killing was strange, because, in this day and age, killing was how you made a reputation for yourself. You wanted people to know you did it. In this case, someone didn't. That made this a murder mystery!

After conceding she would wait, until Wana finished her investigation, Queen Ramala ushered her children back into the palace. The Butcher girls, the Hayee, Ali, who was La's Warlord and La's Special guard, along with the Warlords, Elite Guards and regular guards that were loyal to Ramala made sure the Queen's palace was secured from the outside. No one except messengers could get close enough to mount another attack on the palace.

Once back into the palace, Ramala and her children walked to the room where they always had their first day's meal. The attacks that happened earlier in this day and the meeting with the Warlords put time past the first training session. Ramala was trying to make this day as less stressful on her children as possible, while trying to figure out how to get Tara to safety. First day's meal would help bring some normality to this day.

It was a silent walk through the halls of the palace. Somehow, things were different and everyone could tell. They all had the strange feeling of being compromised, finding themselves alert and on guard. They used to be relaxed, felling safe in their home, the palace.

In the eating hall, everyone took their seats at the large round wooden table. Queen Ramala looked around the table at each of her children and Yin. She could see the shock of what happened on their faces. Their shock was starting to give way to anger. Ramala could see their emotions transforming before her eyes.

Queen Ramala said "All of you listen to me. Don't let this day's events control your emotions and anger you. What happened this day was nothing. Some days will make this one seem pleasant. Keep your wits about you. That's how you deal with what's happened today."

Don curiously looked at Ramala and said "Mommy, what are wits?" Ramala said "It's what allows you to think and make the best decisions possible." Don had a curious look on his face as he was doing his best to place that firmly in his memory, knowing that his mother would expect him to remember.

Breakfast was served. None of the children said a word. They ate their food making little eye contact with each other. When they did look at each other, it was with measured anger.

After breakfast, Ramala said very little while her children sat and digested their food. A little later, it was time for training. Ramala told her children to go to their next training session. She watched as they all got up and left.

The children were walking through the halls when Danaaa, who was the youngest of Ramala's children, couldn't understand why guards weren't acting according to protocol. It irritated her that they weren't. At eight years old, protocol and rules were the only things that made this crazy world understandable to Danaaa. In a nastier tone than normal, Danaaa angrily yelled "Guards shouldn't to be in the palace, when first day comes! Everyone knows that!" The other children said nothing. After two more steps, Danaaa yelled "Guards shouldn't come in our room, when they think we're sleeping! Everybody knows that, too!"

This time all of the children looked at Danaaa with angry annoyed looks on their faces. After another two steps, Danaaa yelled "And they shouldn't to try and kill us! That's not what happens according to protocol!"

La quickly turned around, faced Danaaa and said in an angry, measured tone "Don't you think we already know that, Baby!?!" When La said that, the rest of the children, stopped, turned and looked at Danaaa. Danaaa stared at La and yelled "It's Jinn Eco!" While staring at Danaaa, La yelled "Alright, Jenny Co, calm down! We'll deal with this, later!" Danaaa sometimes called herself Jinn-Eco. To everyone it sounded like Danaaa was saying Jenny-Co.

Danaaa took a quick hop and was face to face with La. Both girls looked at each other. La was very close to taking her frustrations out on Danaaa. If Danaaa kept annoying her, that's what La was going to do.

Danaaa's eyes were angry and her lip hung crooked on one side. Danaaa poked out her chest and slowly yelled "Use your wits that Mommy was talking about, earlier and make a plan! Make a plan so everybody knows never to come in here when they're not suppose to! Make a plan, or there's going to be big trouble here and now!"

La and Danaaa locked eyes for only a second longer, before La turned, looked at Dan and then at everyone else. Even though La didn't like the way Danaaa said it, she knew Danaaa was right.

La knew they had to do something. She said "Everybody, follow me!"

The Ra children hustled down the long winding halls of the palace, until they came to one of the courtyards. They looked around, and then made a circle. La started talking. Dan joined in and added to the plan. Soon La and Dan had a complete plan. Danaaa was excited because Dan and La were using their wits.

The Ra children moved to an exit on the far end of the palace. As they were making their way out of the palace, Ali, a few Elite guard and most of their Special guard, met them. La and Dan stared at Ali. They wondered how Ali and the others knew where to find them.

Ali was La's Warlord. He was a tall, dark brown skinned, powerfully built man whose legs were longer than his torso. His muscles were chiseled, without being bulky. It was his job to protect La. Ali and his guards always guarded the exits, when La was in the palace. Ali looked at each member of the Hammer-Axe Six, before looking at La. Ali lowered his head and said "How can we help."

The Hammer-Axe Six consisted of Ramala's six Children and their cousin Yin. La was oldest and Hammer-Axe One, also known as Warlord Cut Faster. La's Butcher name was the Chop Era, Mesocyclone. La had the muscular body of a gymnast, but she wasn't short. She had medium brown skin and her eyes were golden brown. Her hair was jet black and always in a ponytail that came down to just below her calf. Her ponytail had a round metal ball on the end of it that was the size of a grapefruit. Her ruling cape that hung to her ankles covered her ponytail. La was extremely arrogant, cunning and smart. She wanted to control everything and everyone around her. She had a hot temper that could manifest itself at anytime.

Her twin brother Dan was Hammer-Axe Two, Warlord Faster Cut. He was the Butcher, Dan the Destroyer, the Chopper-Ra. Dan was tall, wiry, but very muscular. Dan's hair, skin and eyes were identical to his twin sister. His braided hair was in a ponytail and cut shoulder length. Dan was grounded, even-tempered and very smart. Dan loved to display his fighting skills.

Shaya was Hammer-Axe Three, the Pretty Girl, A Chop A. She was the Butcher Angry-Ax. Shaya was a very beautiful girl. Her brown skin was a shade darker than La's. Her eyes were that same golden brown. Shaya's ponytail reached down to her calf, with a metal ball on the end. Shaya was slightly thicker, shorter, than but just as muscular as La. She was, smart, but shy and submissive. She also liked things that were pleasing to her eyes. She was a pretty girl who liked pampering.

Don was Shaya's twin and Hammer-Axe Four, Warlord Ax-Angry, the Chop Chopper and he was the Meat Butcher. Don was wiry, muscular and shorter than Dan. He was identical to his twin sister and had the same golden eyes that all the Ra children, except for Ram. Don was the most handsome of the Ra boys and was attracted to the female body at a young age. Don had a happy go lucky attitude, unless he had to be serious.

Ram was Hammer-Axe Five, the Low Pressure Assassin, and Dirty Degenerate Butcher Eco-Jin. Ram was thicker than his brothers were and almost as tall as them. He had medium brown skin and was muscular, but not chiseled. Ram's eyes were a creepy shade of brownish grey. They had a deepness that made it look like someone, besides Ram, was also looking at you. Ram was quiet and very seldom spoke. He had an uncanny sense of smell and hearing, and was a hunter, killer, of humans. No one ever caught Ram in the act, although his brothers and sisters would catch him cleaning sculls, as if they were trophies. Because he was the Queen's son, Ram was the accepted serial killer in the House of Ra.

Danaaa was the Immaculate Degenerate, Dan Jinn-Eco, the High Pressure Executioner, Hammer-Axe Six! Danaaa was very healthy and thicker than her sisters were. She looked like the perfect mix of her two sisters. Her ponytail reached the ground and she hardly ever wore a metal ball on it. Danaaa had an aggressive attitude and non-stop energy. She was a child prodigy, when it came to fighting techniques. Danaaa was a smart girl, confused by simple things. Still, she was an expert at protocol.

All six were as deadly as described by their names. Even though Yin was part of the Hammer-Axe Six gang, he didn't have a designation. His father was the most ruthless killer of this time. Yin was named after him. Yin's name said spoke for itself. Yin was about the same size as Don. His eyes were dark brown and he had an evil grin like his father when he smiled. Yin had a volatile personality kept in check by his older cousins, La and Dan.

Dan looked at La and smiled. He told Ali how they all could help. After hearing Dan's plan, La stared at him for a moment in amazement that he could come up with something that would enhance their original plan. Dan said "Come on, we have to hurry, before someone figures out what we're doing!" La snapped back into reality.

Ali and the Ra children moved quickly to the dungeon. Shaya hated going to the dungeon. When they walked in the horrendous smell hit her nose. It was dimly lit, dirty and looked like a torture chamber. They passed several cells, with prisoners, before coming to Bo's cell.

Bo was a very dark brown-skinned man. He was medium height and at twenty-three years old was very muscular. For intentionally botching an interview with Ramala to become La's mate, Bo was here. Because of his fighting skills, Young Dan made Bo his Warlord, saving Bo from beheading. Bo had to serve time in the dungeon as punishment.

Ali and the Ra children released Bo and left the dungeon. Now, watched, the Ra made their way through the city. The guards on both sides of the conflict noticed this. Ali and the Ra children moved in front of Warlord Bantu's family compound. Shortly after that, their spies notified the rebelling Warlords, while Wana was notified by hers. Other Warlords started moving towards that area with their guards. If the Ra children did something as irrational as attack Bantu's family, who was one of Wana's biggest and most loyal allies that would be a disaster for the Hellcats. The Warlords knew at the very least, Tara would be dead. They would also capture, or kill all of the Ra children.

Earlier, after the Ra children left for their morning training session, Queen Ramala sat at the same table, in the eating hall, thinking of a way to get Tara back safely. She knew she couldn't just start taking heads. If she did that, Tara and her children might end up dead.

While Ramala was sitting there, bodyguards kept peeking in the doorway to see if she was safe. Each time they did, it startled Ramala slightly and she would stare suspiciously at them trying to read their intentions. She readied herself for attack, until the guards went back on patrol. Ramala realized she'd never reacted this way in her palace, before today. She didn't like not feeling completely safe in her palace.

The King of Ra Elder Dan, Syn and Ma walking into the room interrupted Ramala's thoughts. They all watched Ramala as they took seats at the table. Ma brushed some of the crumbs away from in front of her on the table. Two maids quickly came over with cloths in hand and wiped the whole table. Everyone at the table suspiciously watched the maids as they worked. That made the maids nervous. When they were done, the maids left as quickly as they'd come. Everyone was still on edge.

Dan, after watching the maids leave, turned to Ramala and paused, before asking "Have you thought of what you want done?" Ramala looked calmly at Dan for a moment without speaking. Then she said "I'm going to talk with Ray." Dan said "We'll go with you." Ramala stood up and said "You can escort me, but I'll be talking to Ray, alone." Dan questioned "Do you think that's wise?"

Ramala said "Wise? Probably not, but I do think it's the best thing to do, right now." Dan stared at Ramala. She already knew all the reasons he thought she shouldn't go. Dan was waiting on Ramala to tell him why she was going. Of course, she didn't.

Ramala smiled at Dan and said "Come on, let's get going before Wa tries to stop me." Dan got a little nervous when Ramala said 'tries to stop me' Dan's next thought was 'tries to stop you from what'? Dan knew he wasn't going to change Ramala's mind on this and he certainly wasn't going to argue with her. He was going to do what he always did. Dan was going to go with Ramala, watch her back and see where all of this was going.

Ramala's most trusted guards who were checking in on her from time to time, left the palace and patrolled the grounds while she was gone. Ramala didn't want anyone, in the palace while she was gone. The maids also couldn't stay. They were sent to their chambers, until Ramala returned.

Dan and the Butcher girls were the only ones Ramala allowed to go with her to Ray's compound. If they had left any earlier, they would have seen the royal children leaving the grounds of the palace. However, they didn't.

Word got to Ray, the other Warlords, as well as Wana, that Ramala was headed somewhere with her Butchers. Wana immediately left her meeting to find Ramala, before she did something irrational. Once Ray received word that Ramala was close and appeared headed towards his compound, he put his guards and family on alert.

When Ramala and her Butchers reached Ray's compound, Ramala told the Butchers to wait outside for her. They all protested, but Ramala was determined to do this her way.

Ramala walked up to the guards at the front of the compound. They wondered why she walked up by herself. Then, they remembered that this was still their Queen. They all got down on their knees, while peeking suspiciously at their Queen. After giving them permission to rise, Ramala told them to go and announce to Ray that she was here to see him and they should escort her to him.

Ramala was escorted to a large room where she saw Ray with his sons and about forty or so, of his best guards. Ramala looked at Ray.

His eyes were sad, yet strong. Ramala slightly lowered her head, without breaking eye contact with Ray, before raising her head to its arrogantly high normal level. Ramala looked at the guards, then back at Ray and said "I wish to confer with you in private."

Ray looked at Ramala, before motioning his guard to leave. His sons didn't leave until Ray directly ordered then to. He and Ramala both watched them all leave.

After they were gone, Ramala turned her attention to Ray. Ray was old, heavy set, but was in reasonably good shape. In a very soft and compassionate voice, Ramala said "You've suffered a terrible loss. I can't imagine what you're feeling. Even though Shamika and I had our differences, I assure you I didn't kill, or have her killed. If I had, you know I wouldn't hide it. You know that!"

Ramala paused and then said "We will find out who did this and deal with them." Ray said in an even measured tone, without looking directly at Ramala "They'll be dealt with, even if they are Ra?"

Ramala paused, because she knew Ray was indirectly saying that, at least, the murderous night stalker Ram was a possible suspect. Ramala didn't think it out of the realm of possibilities that her son could have killed Shamika. She said "You can be sure I'll make them suffer. Whatever I do to them will never reach the level of suffering you're going through."

Saddened by the loss of her uncle's daughters, Ramala's usually harsh sounding voice was sympathetic, with concern for Ray. Ray asked "What will happen to the men who were misguided by anger, causing them to do some irresponsible things, like entering your palace without permission."

Ramala realized negotiations were finally getting started. She said "Although, what they did can't be tolerated, I might see how emotions can sometimes get involved." Ramala paused, and then said "You're one of my most trusted Warlords in all of Ra. I want you to personally deal with these men and make sure they all understand that this kind of behavior is intolerable, regardless of the circumstances. The ones you can't make understand that, I expect to never see, again."

Ray knew that by Ramala putting the rebelling guards' fate in his hands, she had effectively pardoned them without saying so. Ray looked at Ramala for a few seconds, and then said "As you wish, my Queen."

Both Ray and Ramala looked at the entrance where two guards had just appeared. The guards looked panicked, and seemed to have something to say, but didn't want to interrupt. Ray said "Speak freely." The guard looked at Ramala, then said "The Ra children, along with Ali, Bo, their guards and the Special Guard were seen headed south through the city."

Ramala quickly looked from the guard to Ray. She stood up and said "Come on, we have to stop them before something regrettable happens!" Ramala and the Butchers, along with Ray and his guards, all boarded Elephants and hurried south on the main road to catch up with the Ra children. Ramala sent messengers to tell Wana.

Wana already knew and was on her way, too. She met Ramala's caravan just as it was stopping in front of Warlord Bantu's compound. Bantu had the most guards protecting the city of Ra. That made Wana slightly nervous. As she quickly made her way towards the Ra children's entourage, she sent her guards ahead of her to intercept them. Guards informed Wana the Ra children weren't here.

Wana turned just in time to see Ramala hurrying down the ramp on the elephant's back, followed by Dan, Ma and Syn. The second Ramala saw Wana and looked into her eyes, she knew her children weren't here. Still, Ramala headed towards Wana. Ray, along with his guards, made their way over to Wana, also.

Wana could see Ramala was angry, as well as upset. Before Ramala could say anything, Wana looked Ramala directly in her eyes and said "Stay calm." Wana's eyes scanned the distance, before looking back at Ramala. Wana said in a slightly frustrated, but calm voice "We'll figure out what they're up to . . . And when we do!" Ramala said "You don't have to tell me. They're in big trouble!" Wana said "Really big trouble if their actions cause Tara harm!" Ramala didn't say anything, but she gave Wana a hard stare. Wana said "I'm just saying!"

The Hayee Hellcats, Wana and Queen Ramala, were interrupted by several guards running up to Wana. Wana gave the guard permission to speak. The guard gathered himself, and nervously said "Something's happening at Warlord Benobu's place!! The Royal children were seen there fighting with guards!" Queen Ramala yelled "Careful, what you say about my children is the absolute truth!" The guard went down on his knees, looked at Ramala's feet and said "Of this I'm positive, my Queen!"

Wana turned to Ray and said "That's where most of the guards who infiltrated the palace, earlier, reside!" Wana paused for a second, before saying to the Warlord Ray "I want you to know that whatever the Ra children have done, I didn't support. That being said, I need you to locate Tara and make sure she's not harmed. I'll deal with the Royal children!"

Ray and Ramala had never heard Wana refer to her nieces and nephews as anything else but her nieces and nephews. They could see Wana was pissed. Wana quickly walked away, not waiting on Ramala. Ramala didn't want to yell to Wana, or look like she was racing Wana to Benobu's complex. Dan smiled to himself, while the Butcher girls tried to keep up with Ramala as she moved regally, but quickly, to her plat formed elephant, as only the Queen of Ra could.

CHAPTER 2

All Hayee resembled each other. Most Hayee were tall, medium brown to very dark skinned. They had long thick black hair, even though most men kept theirs reasonably short. Their faces were oblong, with slightly pointed noses. They also had intense eyes that made them look aggressive.

Still, within all the Hayee families, there were differences in certain features. The guards that attacked the palace all were medium brown skinned with less pronounced noses. That let the Royal children know the guards were from Warlord Benobu's clan. The Royal children decided to deal with those guards.

All of the Ra children had a role to play in La and Dan's plan. First, the Ra children took their royal capes and gave them to Special Guards that were equal in size. These same Special Guard were surrounded to the point of almost being hidden. They hustled to the home of Warlord Bantu. News of this spread quickly and everyone feared the worse. The plan was working, perfectly.

Dan, La, Danaaa and Ram were almost at the home of the warriors that attacked the palace, earlier. Don, Shaya and Yin followed a short distance behind. They all had their clothes covered with long peasant clothes that had hoods covering their heads. Dan and La told Ram and Danaaa that once they got to their destination, they wanted them to create a diversion so Dan and La could fight their way into the building the rebel guards lived in. That's when the youngest Ra twins would join their siblings inside the building.

Just as the Ra children were walking up, two warriors recognized them. La turned and looked at Ram and Danaaa to make sure they knew what to do. La was shocked when she didn't see Ram. Dan realized Ram was gone, just after La did.

Both Dan and La took a quick look around and didn't see him, anywhere. They turned back around, just in time to see Danaaa as she got to guards that joined guards, who had already spotted the Ra children. La and Dan took off running towards Danaaa and the guards, while pulling their axes.

When Dan and La told Danaaa what her part of the plan was, Danaaa gladly accepted it. It was like putting on a show every time Dan or La put her up to something. It didn't matter, to Danaaa, what it was. One of the most important things to Danaaa was executing the mission and putting on a good show. On top of that, Danaaa was still pissed about what happened, earlier. On the way to the warriors home Danaaa let her imagination take her thoughts.

As she was walking with her siblings, Danaaa couldn't understand why guards thought they could come into her room like that. Didn't they know, according to protocol that was forbidden? Yet, still, they did it, anyway. If they would do that, what else might they do? What if next time they succeeded? What would happen to her brothers, sisters, mother and others close to her? Danaaa couldn't answer any of those questions. Her eyes quickly darted in Dan and La's direction before looking ahead of her. Danaaa was sure she wasn't going to resolve this situation by using her wits. She just knew it!

Danaaa wits were never around when she really needed them. They liked to hide from her as if they weren't there. Using wits and answering questions like the ones Danaaa had, was something La, or Dan might be able to do. Danaaa resolved herself to that fact. Well, okay then! Danaaa knew something she could do. She could swing her axes really fast!

Danaaa never stopped moving forward when Dan and La looked at her for a second, after realizing the guards saw them. Danaaa never saw them stop walking and turn to look for Ram.

At the same time Dan and La turned to look for Ram, Danaaa was pulling her axes. She took off running towards the guards, full speed, with her axes pointing towards them. The guards barely had time to react, but got their weapons drawn. Just as Danaaa got to the group of guards, she angrily stared at one and headed towards him.

One step before she got to him she launched herself sideways, spinning, towards the guard to her left. The ax blade of the guard it looked like she was going to attack missed Danaaa, slicing through the air where she would have been if she had kept moving straight ahead.

Danaaa's ax split open the neck of the guard to her left, as the metal ball on the end of her swinging ponytail smashed into the side of the head of the guard who'd swung his ax. Danaaa landed with her axes pointed at the other guards. The guard she sliced across the neck was falling, holding his neck, trying to stop the blood from gushing out.

The guard the metal ball hit in the head was dazed, but now turning towards her. Danaaa quickly charged the other guards, swinging her axes at them, really fast. That put them on guard, training their axes on Danaaa. Danaaa turned her body, with blazing speed back towards the guard who'd been hit by her metal ball. Coming out of her turn, Danaaa jumped towards the guard, while jerking her head forward, slightly. The metal ball on the end of her ponytail came flying over her head at the guard with blazing speed.

Well, this time the guard decided he was going to deal with that ponytail better than the last time. He reached to block it with one axe, while he swung his other one where it would meet Danaaa's body flying towards him. He blocked the metal ball of the ponytail as Danaaa plowed her axes into both sides of his neck. In a fraction of that, second that Danaaa's axes drove into his neck the guard thought "There was no way her axes were moving as fast as mine! She should have been split open! Why wasn't she?'

Dan and La had arrived where the guards were. Dan took off the guard's arm at the shoulder when he saw him raise it to swing at Danaaa. Dan then plowed his ax through that same guard's back, just in case Danaaa's strikes weren't enough to bring him down.

La attacked the other guards using one of the most deadly techniques Queen Ramala taught her and told only to use when she, or her siblings lives were in danger. It was an offensive counter-attack move. This technique was called Taking Heads.

As soon as Dan turned to help Danaaa, by chopping off the guard's arm, La was running towards the other guards, full speed, just as Danaaa had, earlier. The guards positioned themselves to cut La to pieces if she tried the same thing Danaaa tried. This time two guards swung at La. One swung his ax at her neck and the other guard swung at her mid-section.

As the axes were coming at La, she jumped in the air, barely being missed. She flipped into a tight ball going up, extending her arms out away from her body with axes in hand and while spinning, her axes sliced clean through their necks, taking the heads of both guards. After landing, La quickly jumped in the air sideways, avoiding the next swing of an ax from another guard. While cart wheeling in the air she sent her ax through his neck taking his head. La took one more guard's head with that technique before the next guard positioned himself to strike her as she was coming out of the air. However, La's ax swings were so quick and accurate, he had to block her first swing and then her second one.

In the second that guard was about to release his axes from the blocks and cut La to shreds, the metal ball from her ponytail smashed into the top of his head full force. His legs gave way as he crashed onto his knees and then falling over sideways. La's metal ball attack was much more advanced and deadlier than her sisters were. The guard never noticed the subtle, but forceful movement of La's head that sent that metal ball on the end of her ponytail rocketing towards his skull.

As La landed on her feet this time, she could see guards all around her. Dan had just made it to her side. La and Dan didn't see Danaaa, anywhere. La only had a second to look for Danaaa before she had to attack the approaching guards with everything she had.

Dan was right at La's side fighting with her. He was swinging his axes, while occasionally ducking, just as La's ponytail with the metal ball would come whizzing over his head. Dan knew La's moves so well that every time the metal ball of her ponytail came flying towards his head, after ducking, he was standing back up, swinging his axes. Dan followed the metal ball with a powerful swing of his ax, slicing into the guard who was trying to avoid the metal ball so he could slice La with his ax. La quickly jumped into the air in a sideways cartwheel over Dan's head taking the head of the guard who saw an opening on Dan when he swung his ax, slicing open the guard who thought he was going to slice La.

Dan and La were covering each other offensively and defensively so well that they were destroying guards much older and more battle hardened. Dan and La were butchering these guards. Their battle was intense and went on for a short while. They both were so intensely into the battle that they had momentarily forgotten about Danaaa. That is until one of the guards came running out of the building, with his eyes blazing intensely, insanely screaming "It's Hell's Executioner!"

That this was a trained guard screaming this, instead of an old woman, or an old man shocked everyone to a slight pause, before they realized they were fighting for their lives, already. The guard's statement even hit La and Dan in the same peculiar way that it hit the guards. Everyone watched as that guard raced past them and down the road, occasionally looking back to make sure he wasn't being followed by the perceived threat. As I said, it was strange to all of them.

La and Dan fought their way to the front entrance as they heard yells from some of the guards as they were being slaughtered inside. They also saw several more guards running, even high-tailing it, from the building, not even attempting to join the battle outside, as they got there. The guards just bolted down the road, just as the others had.

Finally, Dan and La made it to the entrance. They knew Danaaa had been fighting, alone, for a while. That made them a little nervous. They ran through the entrance, on guard, ready to give the help they thought she would surely need. They stopped, looked around and couldn't believe what they saw, even though they were looking right at it.

After Dan and La arrived to help with the guards, Danaaa bolted through the entrance. A hail of spears greeted her. Danaaa squatted low and put both blades of her axes together at an angle in front of her, shielding her body and deflecting the spears.

Now that Danaaa was inside, many guards were moving towards her, quickly. Danaaa turned and ran away from the guards to a large support column. She jumped full speed onto the column, launching herself into a tight backwards flip back towards the guards. Danaaa, now in a tight spinning ball, put one blade of her ax over her head and the other blade at her feet. She sawed into two guards leaving them with gashing mortal wounds.

Several spears came flying at Danaaa just as she landed. She deflected them with the flat side of her blade, changing their trajectory, sending the spears right into the chest of several of the guards closest to her. As several more spears came at Danaaa, she deflected all of them into the torsos of guards close to her. Once the guards throwing the spears saw that Danaaa was using their spears as weapons against their own, they stopped throwing them.

Just as Danaaa thought she had a chance to regroup and plan her next attack, she felt someone moving quickly to attack her. Danaaa swung and stopped her axes a split second and inches from their target. Danaaa was met with a barrage of swings from a broom, by an angry determine old woman. This old woman swung her broom at Danaaa viciously with a fearless, reckless abandonment. Danaaa blocked all of the swings and tried to convey, with her eyes, to the old woman that she didn't want to kill her.

All of a sudden, Danaaa took one quick step and slammed the flat side of her blade into the old woman's shoulder, knocking the woman to the side. Almost in that same instant Ram's ax came flying past where the old woman's neck was. Danaaa turned, looked a stern warning to Ram, not to kill the old woman. She, then, quickly looked in the direction of the guards, before looking back at Ram.

Davis

That was all Ram needed to see. He ran towards the guards. Danaaa then gave the old woman a hard stare, while spinning her ax in one super-fast revolution and stopping it on a dime, pointed at some children who looked confused and were close to getting in the way of the battle. Danaaa then pointed her ax at the old woman and then to the open courtyard.

Danaaa took off towards the guards where Ram was chopping at their lower extremities, while avoiding the powerfully deadly swings the guards were taking at him. Even with that, almost every time they swung down on Ram he counter-attacked slicing their hands, arm, or legs, severely.

After looking in Danaaa's eyes and realizing she almost had her head taken by that silent little monster Ram, who was now attacking the guards, the old woman paused. She thought this was the last warning she'd probably get. The old woman took Danaaa's directions and quickly started yelling for and gathering all the children. She led them into the courtyard and made them get on their knees. She looked at the carnage going on inside, not believing what she was seeing, before she lowered her head, waiting on it all to end.

What the old woman saw was two, just before teenage, young children Butchering men. Ram was giving them hell with lightning strikes low, while Danaaa, like an acrobatic gymnast, flying through the air, was launching herself off pillars and walls, accurately chopping at the heads, necks and upper torsos of the guards. Ram and Danaaa were running and flying around with such speed it looked like two unruly children completely out of control. But as the guards were finding out, they weren't. Every one of their moves, although looking reckless, was precise. This was more than a massacre. This was the Hell of being cut to pieces, by two children.

That's what Dan and La saw as they both stood frozen staring at the entrance. They watched the carnage, until La snapped out of her daze when she saw that Danaaa and Ram had finished off the last guard fighting. Ram turned and was quickly on his way to the courtyard, where the old men, women and children were.

La yelled "Fat Boy! Get over here, now!!" Ram stopped, turned and looked at La, then looked into the courtyard, before looking at La, again. Ram then turned and started towards the courtyard, as he first planned.

Dan yelled "She said, NOW!!" Ram turned and looked at Dan, then at Danaaa. Danaaa had moved herself between Ran and the courtyard. After a moment, Ram twirled his axes one super fast revolution, in protest, and then slammed them in their holsters. He slowly walked over to La and Dan.

Danaaa had been watching Ram to see if she was going to have stop him from harming the women and children she sent to the courtyard. Danaaa would rarely ever confront Ram. Nevertheless, when it came to innocent women and children, well, that's where Danaaa drew the line. She was relieved when Ram put his axes, away. Still, Danaaa lightly scolded Ram, yelling "We don't kill innocent women and children! You know that!!" Ram peeked at Danaaa and turned back towards La.

A child about eleven years old startled the Ra children, seemingly jumping out of nowhere, swinging machetes at Danaaa. As the young man swung at Danaaa, she quickly moved just out of harm's way and smashed the hammer side of her ax into the knuckles on one of the hands holding the fast approaching machete, as she dodged it at the same time. She did the same to his other hand. Both of his machetes fell to the floor. The skin on both his knuckles was torn open from the force of Danaaa's hammer strikes.

Still, the young man had fire and hatred in his eyes as he stared at Danaaa, now without his machetes, building his courage for his next move. Danaaa yelled, while looking him in his eyes "All the women and children are out there! That's where you're supposed to be! Over there!"

The young man didn't like Danaaa calling him a child, even though he was. He'd had enough of Danaaa. He charged towards Danaaa, ready to tear her apart, with his bare hands. No sooner than he moved, Danaaa took a step towards him and launched herself, feet first, at him. Her knees went to her chest, before shooting out at the boy. Both of her feet landed in his chest and sent him flying backwards towards the courtyard. His back hit the ground hard, before he knew what happened. As he lay there on the ground holding his chest and trying to regain control of his breath, Danaaa, after landing on her feet, yelled, while looking down at him "But, I already told you, the women and children stay out over there!"

La looked from Danaaa to the women and children in the courtyard. She then looked at three Elder men of this clan. They were trapped in a corner of the room, guarded by the only ten remaining guards this family had here. La didn't know why Danaaa and especially Ram hadn't killed these Elders, but she was glad they didn't. That would have been impossible to explain to their mother.

La composed herself and looked angrily at the Elders. She said loudly, just short of yelling "This is what happens to those who attack me and my family! I spared your lives, even though I didn't have to. That was out of respect for the fact that you're Elders in my family. I choose to believe that you didn't have anything to do with the assault on the palace. It's best if you taught everyone that's left the proper respect and protocol on how to treat the royal family. If you don't, the rest of them will end up dead, too!"

La quickly turned and motioned for Danaaa to come to her. Danaaa turned away from the people La was talking to and walked towards Dan, La and Ram. She had blood spattered all over her clothes. None of it was hers. There was even blood on her face. Danaaa tried to wipe some of it off, with her forearm, as she made her way to her siblings. She only succeeded in smearing it all over her face.

When Danaaa got to La, La wiped more of the blood from Danaaa's face and said, excitedly "Baby, you can swing your axes really fast!" Danaaa yelled "But, you already know that!" La's face turned a little less excited, after Danaaa yelled in her face. La wasn't playing nice with Danaaa, anymore. She said "Come on Baby, it's time to go!" Then, La stopped. She, turned, curiously looked at Dan and asked "Where's Shaya?"

Earlier Shaya, Don and Yin were following a good distance behind La and Dan. They were supposed to arrive shortly after the fight and back the first Ra group up with Hammer throws and Yin's ax play. The plan was going along as scheduled, until Don patted Shaya on her shoulder and pointed at Yin. Shaya turned to see Yin walking in the opposite direction. Shaya instantly called to Yin, but Yin didn't answer. Shaya and Don ran up to Yin and after Shaya looked around to see who might be looking and was satisfied that no one was, Shaya sternly said "Yin, where do you think you're going?!" Yin half turned, without stopping and said "I'm going to find mommy and my sisters!" Shaya said "How are you going to find them, when you don't even know where they are!?"

Yin was beyond Shaya's reasoning. He said "That's why I'm going and looking this way!" Now Don and Shaya were walking with Yin, without realizing it, while Shaya was trying to talk some sense into Yin.

Without La, or Dan here to stop him, Yin decided Shaya and Don weren't enough to. He wasn't going to wait around wondering what was going on with his mother and sisters. Yin, much like his father, didn't have a plan. All he knew was that one way, or another he was going to find his family and save them.

After trying to convince Yin to stick with the plan, Shaya realized the plan was changing and she had to think of something quickly, before Yin got them discovered. Shaya jumped in front of, grabbed Yin by his shoulders and said "If we're going to find them, we have to think of the best place to look!"

Yin stopped and looked at Shaya. She now had his attention for the moment. Shaya said "Let's go and see if aunt Wana's guards can help us, first. If they can't, we'll start looking home to home, until we find them." Yin nodded in agreement.

Of course, Shaya was stalling Yin, while trying to think of a way to get word to La why she and the others weren't where they were supposed to be. Shaya suggested they take some of the less traveled back roads, as not to be seen. These roads were behind most of the buildings, homes, shops and palaces that faced the main roads. In addition, just as in times from then to now, the back roads were the most dangerous roads, anywhere. Even in the main city of Ra.

Yin, Shaya and Don walked between two buildings and were suddenly transported into what looked like another world. The Ra children had been on the back streets before. Only, those were the ones closest to the palaces. Those back streets were filled mostly with Ramala, Tara's and Wana's bodyguards. These people were different. They saw groups of men and women scattered in groups all down the road. They recognized a few of the men and a couple of the women as being outcast members of the Hayee family that most other Hayee looked down on because they didn't always act according to protocol within their own immediate families.

Although, the Hayee were forced to accept the Ra children and even some of them, over time generally liked them, most of the Hayee didn't like the Ra. They considered Ramala and Tara's children Degenerates.

A Degenerate was someone who had the pure blood of a family from one of the seven recognized Houses mixed with the blood of a so-called heathen. A heathen was someone not born from two parents from one of the original Seven Houses. Heathens were looked upon as human trash, fit only to serve. Degenerates were considered less than that and were mostly despised.

The Ra children could always tell how other Hayee felt about them by the way the Hayee looked at them. These Hayee had that distinct look that told the three Ra that they were not welcome here. All of the groups seemed to focus on the Ra children at the same time, putting Don and Yin on guard and making Shaya nervous.

Shaya, Yin and Don were startled when they heard someone yell in a thunderously loud, but deep voice "Wait!" It was Ram. He came running up to the three Ra children. The cloth that was supposed to be draped around him to conceal his identity was hanging only on his left shoulder, where he was holding it. Ram's whole body was exposed, as well as his weapons and you could definitely tell it was him. The Ra children half peeked at Ram, while still staying on guard against the people on the road.

All of the other people started moving backwards. They disappear between buildings, after seeing Ram come running up. The Ra children thought it strange that Ram had that effect on these people, even though they knew most everyone wanted no contact with Ram, if they could avoid him. Shaya saw that the danger was momentarily gone. She was relieved and happy to see Ram, but when she turned to Ram she half-heartedly scolded him, saying "What are you doing here?! Aren't you supposed to be with La?!"

Ram could see right through Shaya's attempt to act as if she was angry with him. He gave Shaya a sinister, but friendly smile, while shrugging his shoulders at the same time. Shaya was disarmed by the evilness and lovingness, all in the same smile. She half smiled at Ram and said "We're looking for Tara. Sniff the air and tell us where to go." Ram turned away from Shaya and did as ordered. Shaya and the other Ra boys curiously watched Ram as he turned this way and then that way.

After a moment, or two, Ram pointed. Shaya looked at Don and Yin and said "Alright, let's go get Yani and Aunt Tara. Don't mess things up! Listen to me and do exactly what I say."

As they started walking in the direction that Ram pointed, Shaya was proud of herself. She thought she sounded like La and her mother when she said that. The only difference was she didn't have to scream at people for them to listen to her.

While Shaya was high on her fantasy of controlling the situation, what she didn't know was that although the Ra boys heard what she said, they were going to do what they wanted to do. The Ra boys all thought the same thing, at the same time. 'Does Shaya think she's La?'

Shaya's group walked, until Ram pointed to the building where Tara was, supposedly. Shaya warned the others not to do anything hasty. That she would talk first and if they had to resort to action after that, so be it. Shaya gave Yin an extra warning in the form of a hard stare. She turned to do the same to Don and Ram. That's when she noticed Ram was gone. A flash of panic went through Shaya as she quickly turned and looked around. She didn't see Ram, anywhere. Shaya looked back at Don, then Yin. They looked determined to do this anyway. Shaya gave them a slight nod and the three of them headed towards the building.

The three Ra children saw that the guards at the back of the building were some of some of the toughest in the House of Ra. All were Hammer-Ax experts. The Ra children also saw some of the biggest axes they'd ever seen. The Ra children weren't scared, but they were very cautious.

When they got close, about twelve of the guards moved forward and fifteen to twenty of them moved back in front of the rear entrance. Shaya stopped in her tracks. She stared at the guards as an intense fear took hold of her. Shaya watched the guards closely to see if any of them would make one false move that would send her Hammers or a scream in their direction.

In her intense staring, she couldn't help, noticing the rippling muscles in one of the guard's arms and shoulders as he walked forward. She could also see the muscles in his legs flex, every time one of his feet hit the ground. Her eyes blinked slowly as she looked at the guard next to him, solely, to look at the same muscles on him, for comparison. Shaya's eyes weren't disappointed. This guard's muscles were larger and more defined than the previous ones were. Shaya's mouth slowly opened in wonderment, as she was awestricken, stuck staring at that guard's muscles. All of that happened in just a second.

That was a few seconds too long for Yin. He and Don didn't know why Shaya hadn't said anything, yet. They were clueless as to what was really going on with Shaya. Yin stepped forward and yelled "Is my mother in there?!"

The guards just stared at Yin as they slowly pulled their axes. That snapped Shaya out of her daydream. She moved her hands to within inches of her throwing Hammers. Someone from the behind the guards yelled "Hold it! Move aside! Let them through!"

It was the nephew of the Warlord of this complex. He also was a top captain of the Warlord. Upon receiving the order, the guards moved to the side, creating a path for the Ra children. Shaya, next to Yin, with Don walking backwards in between them, moved cautiously and suspiciously through the entrance, with their hands in a quick draw position next to their weapons. They were led down hallways, until they came into a dining room.

Once there, they saw Tara sitting with her youngest daughter, in her arms, at a table with several top Warlords. Tara-Yani, who was sitting next to her mother, baby sister, jumped out of her seat, and ran to meet her brother and cousins, excitedly yelling their names. The Ra children scanned the room for danger. There didn't seem to be any. Tara even smiled at them when she said "Come over here and show the proper respect."

When Tara-Yani reached the Ra children, she began to jump around in their faces, oblivious to her surroundings. The Ra children made their way over to Tara, still confused about the situation. They lowered their heads to everyone at the table, and then they lowered their heads to Tara, before raising them. Tara said "As you can see, I'm having first day's meal with my cousins. Much like you and your cousins do."

The Ra children were dumbfounded. They had no plan of action for this turn of events. Yin asked "How about if I stay here with you and then walk you back to the palace?" Tara said "That's fine with me. I'll be leaving in a little while."

Shaya, Yin and Don looked around again, before taking seats next to Tara. Yani climbed on to the same chair Shaya was on, asking her question after question about Danaaa's whereabouts, why she wasn't here and when she was coming. Shaya was patient with Yani and answered all her questions without really answering any of them.

It was a short time after that when guards came in and told of a massacre at Warlord Benobu's place. The guards said it was rumored that the Royal children were involved. They didn't want to directly accuse the Royal children in front of Tara. After the guard finished his report, everyone in the room looked at Shaya, Don and Yin, including Tara. Don, who was feeling the pressure of the silence and stares, said "We didn't do anything, accept for come here and look for you, Yani and Tammy."

When Don was younger, he used to be a repeater of everything that the Royal children did when he was under pressure. He'd gotten better at not doing it, but he wasn't completely cured of talking when under pressure. Shaya and Yin quickly looked at Don once he started talking. They were sure he would tell the whole plot. Yin interrupted Don, looking at him and saying "We didn't do anything, so you don't have to explain yourself."

Yin turned to Tara and said "Mommy, can we go home, now?" Tara looked at the Warlord who had brought her here. Once they were here, he told Tara that after she had breakfast with him and a short talk after that, she was free to go. He made it clear that he wasn't holding her against her will and that when she left, she should make that clear to Wana and Ramala. Even though the Warlord said she and her children weren't his prisoners, Tara knew they were. She knew the Warlord was negotiating with her, just in case things didn't go as, he and the others involved, planned. Tara agreed and had a very nice breakfast with several of the top Warlords in the city.

Tara, still looking at the Warlord, while talking to Yin said "In light of what the guard has said happened, I think it best we go home. That'll free your uncles here to go and investigate the situation." The Warlords all nodded in agreement. Maids helped Tara get ready and the Ra children, as well as guards escorted her back to her palace.

Shaya, Don and Yin followed Tara to her plat formed elephants wondering what La and the others had done. These three felt confident that they had gotten away clean, because they weren't there. That is, until they saw Ramala and Wana pass them going to Benobu's place. Ramala's caravan only stopped briefly to talk to Tara. Ramala ordered Shaya and Don to join her. Shaya and Don stared into Ramala's eyes. Even though she didn't say a word to either of them, they had a sinking feeling in the pit of their stomachs that said they were in big trouble.

Ordinarily, Yin would go with the Ra children, but this time he didn't. He wanted to make sure Tara and his sisters were safe. His father taught him to be very protective of Tara and his sisters. Tara was proud of Yin for that.

La, Dan and their two hell bound siblings, I mean Ram and Danaaa, were now walking back to the palace, tracing the path where they last saw Shaya and the others. They didn't get far before they saw a large caravan headed towards them. Panic set in on all of them. La said "Alright, it seems we're in trouble! Let me talk and see if I can explain things." The Ra children were happy that La was willing to stand between them and their mother's wrath.

As the caravan got to the Ra children, these Ra, just like Shaya and Don, stared into their mother's eyes to see her level of anger at what they'd done. The Ra boys also looked into their father's eyes, knowing they'd also be dealt with by him, more so than the girls would.

Upon seeing blood all over Danaaa's clothes, Ma jumped from her platform and ran to Danaaa. She frantically checked to make sure Danaaa was unharmed. Something that not even Ramala had done. After fussing over Danaaa and giving her a hug, Ma noticed everyone looking at her like she was crazy. Ma looked at the other Ra children as if she was disappointed in them. She then returned to the platform she was riding on.

After witnessing Ma's spectacle, Ramala motioned for La and the other Ra children to follow her, knowing they were going to Benobu's place. La saw Shaya and Don on the platform with Ramala. She wondered what they told Ramala. La started thinking what she was going to say when her mother questioned her about what they did.

CHAPTER 3

La reasoned that she was going to say that they went after the guards that assaulted the palace. La thought, if she chose her words carefully, that would be enough. Wana got to the entrance and looked in, while Ramala was still walking up. She turned to Ramala and shook her head slowly with a look of disgust on her face. Wana then looked at her nieces and nephews.

The Ra children walked with Ramala, as the Warlords passed the dead guards up to the entrance. When they walked through the entrance, they all froze. Ramala was mortified at the sight. As Ramala surveyed the carnage, her face contorted as a fierce anger built up in her. Shaya and Don stared in disbelief with their mouths hanging open, at what they saw. Ram just looked from Ramala to Elder Dan repeatedly, trying to gauge their moods. Elder Dan took one quick look and then stepped back and watched. He was going to let Ramala deal with this.

La was even shocked at seeing the scene for the second time. Because most of the bodies had bled out since last she was here, it seemed the entire floor was covered with blood, guts, bodies and body parts. La had never seen such a sight. La was scared out of her wits when Ramala slowly turned towards her with her face contorted in anger to the likes of which La had never seen before. La saw her mother's hand move in slow motion towards her. La was fear stricken when she took a quick step back from Ramala and yelled in a panic "Baby and Fat Boy did all of this, by themselves! Dan and me walked in just as they finished! That's what happened, I swear!"

Although, still extremely angry, Ramala realized that she'd never been able to put the fear of death in La like she saw in La's eyes now. Still, with that same contorted look of anger on her face, Ramala looked young Dan in his eyes for confirmation. Young Dan was no fool. He fearfully nodded his head, backing La's words. He thought it better that two of them faced his mother's wrath, than all of them.

After getting confirmation from young Dan, Ramala quickly turned and stared at Danaaa. Danaaa, while looking in Ramala's eyes saw La standing there terrified of their mother. In an instant Danaaa wondered why La didn't use her wits to come up with something better than telling on her? Danaaa thought that La's wits must sometimes hide from her, like Danaaa's wits did, because right now, they were nowhere to be found!

Danaaa decided at the moment that she didn't like wits. La just proved to her that wits were no good in high-pressure situations like this one. While still looking at her mother, Danaaa realized it was too late for that now.

Even though Danaaa was angry at La, she knew that would have to wait. Frustrated and still angry over this day's events, Danaaa took a deep breath, pointed inside Benobu's place, while looking at Ramala. She yelled "That's what happens to guards who come into the palace and try to get into my room! According to protocol, they're not supposed to do that! You know that! Now, guards better know that, too!"

There was an uncomfortable silence the moment after Danaaa yelled that. Ramala was offended by Danaaa's tone, as well as her choice of words. Ramala wanted to say something, but couldn't and wouldn't tell Danaaa that she was wrong for what she just said. Still, Ramala knew she had to be stern towards Danaaa in front of Ray.

Ray was just as uncomfortable as Ramala. He still couldn't believe Ramala's two youngest children did this by themselves. Ray had seen many battles and this ranked amongst some of the worse massacres he'd seen in his life. However, even he couldn't dispute Danaaa's words. She was within her rights doing what she'd done, according to protocol. Ray saw Ramala's hesitation and looked at

Wana. Wana sternly said to Ramala "The Royal children should be confined to the palace, until further notice." Ramala nodded in agreement.

Wana stayed and surveyed the damage. She also interviewed the survivors. To Wana, it sounded worse than it looked. She promised the Elders here that those left would be given favor for the hardship they endured. Wana left some of her guards to clean up. Wana knew she had a real mess on her hands.

Besides, Shamika and her sisters' deaths, the assaults on the palaces and the massacre afterwards, Wana knew that as soon as Warlord Hayee, Benobu received message about what happened to his family, he would return home to deal with the situation himself. Before that happened, Wana needed to clean things up here. She knew she had about a week before Benobu got word of the massacre and a week before he returned to the city of Ra, seeking justice. As she walked, Wana thought about Benobu.

The Warlord Hayee, Benobu started out as a bodyguard for the three Hellcats when they were pre-teen girls. For his service then, Mashaya, the Hellcats grandmother, promoted Benobu to Warlord in the House of Hayee. Although, Benobu was no longer bodyguard to the Hellcats, Wana still used Benobu to help her and her cousins bully other Hayee and build a coalition of guards. Benobu trained them and when they were ready, Wana asked Benobu to support her as her Warlord. Benobu consulted with Mashaya, without letting Wana know. Mashaya thought it amusing and allowed it. Benobu was one of the reasons that although the three Hellcats were young, they quickly gained power. Han, Ramala's Warlord was the other reason.

Benobu and most of his family that was old enough to be guards and warriors were with him in Yee province, helping Han. The men that were slaughtered at his compound in the city were the least proficient in their fighting skills. They were left behind to guard the compound and escort Benobu's Elders to functions given by the Queen. Being in the city of Ra, it was assumed their lack of fighting skill wouldn't be tested.

Ramala was so angry with what Danaaa and Ram had done that she put them, in cells, in the dungeon. She wasn't going to leave them there for long, but she wanted to show everyone that she was being tough on them. The rest of her children volunteered to stay and secure the dungeon with their Special Guard and young Dan's Warlord Bo, along with La's Warlord Ali and his guards.

Ramala agreed, but told Ali that her youngest twins were not to leave their cells, until she ordered it. That if any of her children disobeyed her orders, that he should get word to her, right away. She told Ali it was most important that her orders be carried out. Ali knew his life depended on the youngest twins staying in those cells, until Queen Ramala ordered, otherwise.

When Ramala returned to her palace, she found Tara there waiting on her with the Warlord and his guards who took Tara to breakfast. Upon seeing Ramala, the Warlord and his guards showed Ramala the proper respect by getting down on their knees. Ramala looked at Tara and saw that she was unharmed. Tara, seeing that Ramala was unsure of what was going on here, said "Warlord Hayee, Jon invited me to have breakfast with him, earlier, this day. We had pleasant conversation in which he expressed his unwavering loyalty to his Queen. When we heard the rumors of me and my children being taken by force, I came here to clear up those falsehoods. Hayee, Jon and his forces are here, only to serve their Queen and should be respected for doing so."

Ramala didn't believe any of that! She knew that somehow Tara and Jon had negotiated a reasonable solution to a situation that had gotten out of hand. Ramala nodded to Tara that she would respect her wishes. Ramala finally said "You may rise." It was an uncomfortable moment that lasted longer than the usual pause that Ramala took, before letting her subjects rise.

Ramala looked at Warlord Jon and said "As you know, it has been a very difficult day, so far. Anything you and your guards can do to make sure cooler heads prevail, your Queen would appreciate."

Jon acknowledged that he would. Ramala gave a slight smile, and then went into her palace, followed by Tara.

Earlier, Elder Dan walked into the dungeon just as Ramala was leaving, after having her two youngest twins put there. He wanted to let Ramala do her disciplining thing with their children. Dan didn't think Danaaa was totally wrong, although he didn't agree with what she'd done. Dan first noticed Danaaa staring angrily at La, from inside her cell, until she saw him.

Dan had the guard open Danaaa's cell. He walked over to Danaaa and gave her a reassuring rub on the head, before kneeling down and looking her in her eyes. Dan hugged Danaaa for a moment. He then held her back a little, looking into her eyes with a smile on his face. Dan said "What are we going to do with you?" Danaaa didn't have the slightest idea, so she shrugged her shoulders. Dan said "Be a good girl and stay here, until your mother sends for you. Right now, she's a little upset. She'll get over it, soon enough."

Danaaa gave Dan a hug and when she moved back a little, she gave him the biggest smile he'd ever seen from her. Danaaa watched as Dan went over to Ram and was much less affectionate with his reassurance of his youngest son. Danaaa felt special that her father came to visit her and didn't scold her. Elder Dan and Danaaa had some rough encounters in the past, but that was forgotten, for now.

After Elder Dan left the dungeon, Danaaa turned and looked at La. Danaaa immediately started forming an angry fantasy about what she perceived La had done to her.

Danaaa thought that if only La had used her wits, she wouldn't be here in this smelly, dirty dungeon. Maybe, La set this whole thing up from the start, knowing that it would get her in trouble. Yeah, it was La's fault that she was here! Why didn't La get into trouble? Danaaa thought it was probably because La used her wits to get herself out of trouble, instead of using them to help her.

Now Danaaa hated wits, because it seemed they hadn't done anything for her, so far. Danaaa was staring angrily at La, who was ordering the guards to clean up an area and bring food. When La turned around, she saw young Dan smiling, while he was looking at Danaaa. La curiously turned and looked at Danaaa. She saw

Danaaa staring at her with her lip hanging crooked on one side. Danaaa's lip started shaking where it hung crooked, a short moment after that Danaaa and La locked eyes. Baby was cross!

Danaaa couldn't think straight because she had worked herself into an angry state of mind. All she knew was La was going to pay dearly for this. When Danaaa got out of this cell, she was going to beat the wits out of La. She just knew it!

La knew her baby sister better than almost anyone and knew Danaaa was angry with her. La knew if she didn't do something quick, she and Danaaa would be fighting for days, if not weeks.

La walked up to Danaaa's cell, never breaking eye contact with Danaaa. When La got to the cell, she said "The plan worked perfectly!" Danaaa's eyes squinted, as she realized she was right about La purposely getting her in trouble.

La said "So what if you have to stay in the dungeon for a little while! We'll be here with you. I don't know why you're looking so angry, when you're the hero, here! You executed the mission, perfectly! After what you did, no guards would dare come into our room, ever again!"

Danaaa hadn't thought about being a hero, even though, at first, she thought she'd executed the plan perfectly, until she wound up in this smelly dungeon. Danaaa's eyes moved from La's eyes, to La's hand. La's hand reached into her vest pocket. She pulled out a cookie and extended her hand towards Danaaa. Danaaa's eyes went from the cookie to La's eyes, then slowly back to the cookie, as La said "Here, I saved this for you. Take it!"

Danaaa's hand took the cookie before she could decide whether she wanted to, or not. Then Danaaa's hand betrayed her once more by shoving the cookie into her mouth. That cookie was so good that Danaaa made a low yummy moaning sound, while staring into La's eyes. A happy smile came on Danaaa's face that said she and La were good, again.

La told Danaaa that guards were bringing food, blood and more cookies. As Danaaa looked at La, while La was talking, she realized that La beat her with wits and the help of a delicious cookie. Young Dan's excitement turned to disappointment once Danaaa's attitude changed.

Because there wasn't any clean places to eat in the dungeon, La ordered the guards to let Danaaa and Ram out of their cells. Ali reminded La of her mother's orders. La was still bothered by the fact that Danaaa stood up to their mother earlier, when she, herself didn't. La was caught off guard by Ramala and was embarrassed about it. The only way she knew to get over that was to openly defy her mother's wishes. Besides, if this was the worse that happened to Danaaa for what she did, how much trouble could she get in?

La thanked Ali for his diligence to follow his Queen's orders. She also told him how important it was to follow her orders. La said that they were only going a few buildings away, eat and get back to the dungeon. They wouldn't be gone, that long. No one would even notice they'd been gone.

Ali looked at La as if she was crazy. As soon as the Ra children left the dungeon, everyone would spot them. After all, they were the Royal children! Everyone noticed everything they did!

Ali was La's Warlord, so he motioned for the guards to let the two Royal children out of their cells. Young Dan looked a warning to La that this was going to get all of them in trouble. He saw that didn't matter to La.

Getting something to eat turned into an all-out party. A Dance Off started shortly after the meal and went on until Ali announced that the Queen's messenger sent word that all of her children return to the palace, at once.

La told everyone to let her do the talking. She was immediately hit with looks of suspicion from all of the Royal children. Young Dan said, unconvincingly "Yeah, right!" La quickly turned and gave Dan a hard stare. She then looked at Danaaa and said "You'll see, things will be different from now on!"

Dan still wasn't convinced, even though, La looked like she meant it. Dan at least knew things were going to get interesting when they got to the palace. He knew his mother would deal with La and Danaaa before she got to him. Dan hoped that would lessen his mother's anger towards him for his part in today's earlier events. Even though that had never happened in the past, Dan hoped this time it would. Young Dan was going to keep his mouth shut and see what happened. That was his best plan.

Dan was thirteen years old. This was the beginning of his teenage years. Being a young teenager, Dan was trapped in several worlds. Sometimes he was still that playful boy that found it hard to take things serious, unless his parents forced him. Dan had already lived a long full life as a child and at thirteen, he was an elder to those children younger than he was. Because he was still young like them and not too old that he couldn't relate to the immature ways of a young child's thinking, Dan was considered wise and someone to be looked up to, by children. That is, in the child world. I didn't make this up. That's protocol between children and young teenagers the world over.

Then there was the man in Dan that was ready to, let's just say, be a man. It started about a year ago. That's when Dan noticed that his personal urination device, located between his legs, would sometime stiffen up on him, from time to time. When it first started, it mostly happened at night when Dan was sleeping. Dan didn't know what to make of it and when he was trying to sleep, it was annoying, to say the least.

One day after training, Dan finally needed answers, so he questioned his father, Elder Dan. Elder Dan told his son that was a natural occurrence for a young man. It was part of becoming a man. Elder Dan said to young Dan that it would happen more often and at inopportune times. He said that young Dan would have to use his mind to calm his blood pressure and that would help. Still, that would only be after training at it for a good while. Elder Dan explained that sometimes even that wouldn't be enough to stop it. Young Dan asked "Do you have this same problem?"

Elder Dan responded "I did when I was your age. Now I'm a master of my blood flow. I control it, at will. You will eventually find out that what's happening to you isn't a problem. It's part of being a man."

Young Dan knew that it was imperative that he master this technique as soon as possible! Dan and the other Ra boys looked at Elder Dan in awe of the wisdom he was imparting on them. Well, they weren't picking up on all the wisdom part of what he was saying, right now.

The Ra boys all knew how helpful all of the techniques Elder Dan taught them in the past were. They all wanted to master the blood flow technique. Even though they didn't completely understand, they all wanted to work as hard as they had to in order to become blood flow masters!

When the children arrived back at the palace, they were escorted to Ramala's private outdoor courtyard. Elder Dan was sitting next to Ramala. All of the children lowered their heads and then walked over to their mother. Once they reached Ramala, they lined up in front of her. All of Ramala's children stared at her waiting to be instructed.

As La looked at her mother, she couldn't wait for Ramala to say something about her ordering guards to release Danaaa from her cell. La was willing to take whatever punishment Ramala would dish out, in order to prove to her siblings that she could be defiant in front of her mother.

Ramala could see an unusual amount of arrogance coming from La, as she looked at her. Ramala was sure she knew why. Ramala ordered La to step forward. La deliberately hesitated for a moment, all while staring directly into Ramala's eyes, before she stepped forward. Ramala didn't miss any of that.

It had already been a long day and Ramala didn't want to have to spend unnecessary energy on La. Ramala slowly stood up, never breaking eye contact with La as she did so. Ramala put her hands on both of La's shoulders and said "Calm yourself. Your father told me he ordered the guards to let Danaaa out of her cell so she could have a meal. So, there now, relax."

When reports came to Ramala that her youngest twins had been let out of their cells and all of the Ra children were partying in a nearby building, Elder Dan quickly told Ramala he gave them permission to do so. Upon hearing the guard's report about the

Royal children, Elder Dan was sure La gave the order. This was his way of protecting his precious La.

La quickly peeked at her father, before looking back at Ramala. La then said "I would have ordered them to, anyway, even if he hadn't. Baby and Fat Boy should have never been put there in the first place!"

All of a sudden, an uncomfortable silence engulfed the room. The kind that comes when everyone in the room focuses their attention, waiting, anticipating something's going to happen.

Even though La meant to say what she said, she hadn't planned to be as animated on her second sentence as she was. Still, right now La needed to be punished by Ramala, only because she didn't stand up to her, earlier.

La was disappointed that she didn't do better in that pressure situation. She decided she was going to create pressure now and see if she could do better this time. La was going to punish herself, using her mother to do it. Some girls are funny like that towards their parents. Especially, oldest daughters.

Ramala stared into her daughter's eyes. She still saw defiance in La even though she was doing her best to calm La. Still, staring at La, Ramala slowly said "Sometimes it's best to put on a good act, just to have a better advantage."

La still hadn't gotten Ramala to yell, or even look mean at her. That's when La announced "I'm the Number One Princess! When I decide to do something, it's going to be respected by everyone! I don't expect my own mother to throw my sister and brother into a dungeon, just to please some stupid Warlords! You can put on an act if you want to! To me, that's a sign of weakness!"

Ramala's hand left La's shoulder and went into an open hand slap across La's face. Ramala's hand went back to La's shoulder and the fingers from both Ramala's hands dug into La's shoulders. Ramala shook La roughly one good time. La, still defiant, but now a little angrier, was ready for some real punishment. She said "I don't care what you do to me! When you're done, I'm still going to do whatever I want to!"

La knew what was coming next. She braced herself for some physicality. La told herself, whatever her mother did next wouldn't last long. She was sure she could take it, no matter what it was.

Elder Dan, who was always protective of his oldest daughter, fought and forced himself not to interfere. Even he thought La was disrespectful and had gone, too far. Right now, Dan feared for La's safety, more than La, herself, seemed to.

Ramala roughly pulled La close to her. Then Ramala released the pressure of her fingers on La's shoulders, rubbing her hands around La's back and gently holding on to La. Ramala whispered into La's ear "My sweet little princess, I am not your enemy. Stay in your mind, not your emotions. That's how you do what's best. You're becoming a woman. For now, be a good girl for Mommy."

La was smarter than her mother, but Ramala had far more experience at being smart. Just as young Dan was a teenager and the man in him would come out, the woman in La would show herself, also. Ramala took pride in not letting any woman outsmart her.

Ramala quickly figured out that her daughter wanted her to get physical with her. Ramala knew if she gave La what La thought she needed, that would create this fantasy in La's mind that she had to keep challenging her mother like this in order to overcome a nonexistent roadblock her mother was putting before her.

Ramala wasn't going to battle physically with La, if she didn't have to. Ramala wanted the role of an adviser to La first and a mother and disciplinarian, when she needed to be.

Ramala gently released La, then looked at her other children, before looking back at La. Ramala calmly said "Alright, all of you, it's time to rest. Go prepare for sleep."

La was only confused for a second, before she realized that somehow, even though she didn't receive more physicality from her mother, she felt better, like she came out on top. La was very smart. She lowered her head to her mother and then to her father. La then turned to Shaya and Danaaa and said "Come on, let's go." The other Ra children showed their respects to Dan and Ramala, before leaving.

Once their children were gone, Dan turned to Ramala and curiously said "I thought you were going to kill her, for sure. Tell me, what did you say to her that changed both your attitudes?"

Ramala smiled at Dan and said "That's between me and your Number One Princess." Dan stared at Ramala waiting to see if she was going to give him a better answer than that. Once he saw she wasn't, Dan let it go.

In the hall, on the way to their rooms, Shaya asked La what all the Royal children wanted to know. Shaya asked "What did Mommy say to you?" La never looked at Shaya when she said "None of your business and don't ask me about it, again!"

None of the other Ra children asked La about that, again. Young Dan was just glad Shaya asked before he did. He knew he wouldn't have dealt well with La's nasty answer. Still, young Dan didn't like that La thought she had to be unpleasant to Shaya because La was scared of their mother. That was young Dan's interpretation of what just happened.

CHAPTER 4

When the Ra girls were younger and it was time to go to sleep, sometimes they would. Now, that La was a teenager and her sisters were pre-teens, they would always talk, until they fell asleep. La and Shaya did most of the talking, while they kept a watchful eye on Danaaa, making sure she didn't start any mischievousness. Most of the time Danaaa wasn't any trouble, because all of La and Shaya's talking bored her to sleep.

Tonight, Shaya and La were facing each other talking with Danaaa between them. Danaaa was on her back, eyes fixed on the ceiling, while looking at her sisters with field vision. Danaaa had excellent field vision that allowed her to see everything around her as clearly, as if she was looking right at it. Right in the middle of Shaya's conversation, La interrupted, saying "I think it's time to show people who's in charge. They're acting like they don't even know."

Danaaa said in her whispering voice "That's why we have to teach them. Just like I did today. If that's how I have to teach them, then I will. I can swing an ax real fast!"

Both La and Shaya looked at Danaaa. Danaaa whispered "If we don't teach them, how are they going to know what not to do?" La looked at Shaya, smiled, and then looked back at Danaaa.

La said "We'll teach them how to do what I say. That's the easy way, listening to me. The hard way, is you." Danaaa nodded in agreement. Shaya looked at La and said "You know Baby wants to teach them the hard way. That way she can swing her axes really fast!" all three girls giggled a bit and then talked themselves to sleep.

When next day came, after first day's training, the Ra boys got cleaned up and were headed to breakfast. They wrestled and played fighting with techniques they learned, earlier. Now, that young Dan was a teenager and his brothers and Yin were almost teenagers, their sparring would get very physical.

Young Dan would give Don, Yin and Ram individual beatings. All three Ra boys would then triple team Dan. That's when Dan would really show them that his skill level was much higher than theirs was. Still, the other Ra boys were smart. They knew they'd get less physicality collectively, than if they went one on one with Dan. The one thing the younger Ra boys knew was, just as at some point in the day they would have to fight with Danaaa, they also knew they were going to receive some physicality from Dan.

In the hall, on the way to breakfast, the Ra girls spotted the Ra boys. Shaya and Danaaa ran over to the boys. La walked. Dan watched, as Danaaa got closer. He moved to block her from getting to Yin. Most every time Danaaa saw Yin, she tried to fight him. Danaaa saw Dan and tried to move around him, but Dan was quick enough to stay in from of Danaaa. Everyone laughed. Danaaa, who was frustrated, yelled "But, I'm not doing anything, yet!"

Dan just laughed at her. When La got to where the other Royal children were, she could see that Danaaa was frustrated. La put her hand firmly on Danaaa's shoulder from behind. Danaaa quickly turned in one motion, knocking La's hand off her shoulder and was swinging her other fist. Danaaa stopped her fist, just inches from La's face.

La looked at Danaaa's fist, and then into Danaaa's eyes. Danaaa lowered her fist, while keeping her eyes locked on La. La said "Enough of this, let's go. It's time for first day's meal." Danaaa remembered that she was hungry. She nodded in agreement to La. All of the Ra children headed to first day's meal together. On the way, La had one of the guards get her messenger and tell him to meet her at the royal eating room.

The Royal eating room was a large room with high ceilings. The walls were bare, but large exotic plants lined all four walls. All of the tables were in the middle of the room, facing a large table where the Rulers ate.

The Royal children walked into the eating room, saw their Mother and father already there. They showed the proper respect to Elder Dan and Ramala. As they walked over to the table, La's personal messenger appeared in the entrance, looking submissively towards La. La quickly looked at Shaya and then walked toward the messenger. Shaya quickly followed La, followed by Danaaa. La had a short conversation with her messenger and then the Ra girls walked back and took their seats at the table.

Everyone ignored the messenger incident. Since it wasn't disrespectful or disruptive to first day's meal, Ramala overlooked it. It was when breakfast was over that Ramala got her first hint as to why the messenger came. La looked at Ramala and said "Mother, I would like to have a short meeting before my next training session." Ramala only looked at La for a moment, before saying "Be sure you don't miss any of your day's training." La acknowledged that she wouldn't.

That morning at breakfast, Ramala stressed to all of her children, especially Danaaa, how it was important not to kill their family members, unless necessary. They could severely beat, or wound them and make examples that would be just as effective. Ramala ordered her children not to do anymore killing, unless their lives were in danger, or ordered by their parents. All of the Ra children listened closely to Ramala's orders, while trying to find loopholes that would allow them to disobey her, if they had to.

La's messenger hustled and through a system of messengers under his charge, found and gave everyone that La wanted at this meeting that message. Once all of the Special Guard got word the Number One Princess ordered a meeting, they made their way to the meeting hall. The Hammer-Axe Six arrived shortly afterwards.

After the Royal children took their seats, they notice that the Hayee, Tania wasn't here. Danaaa kept looking at La, then at Tania's seat repeatedly, until she was sure La noticed it. La looked towards the entrance where her messenger was standing. He informed La that Tania wouldn't be here, because of a family situation.

Tania, over time had positioned herself as one of La's closest advisers. Tania could see that eventually La was going to be in control of most, if not all of, the House of Ra. Giving La the best advice she could think of and using her wits to help persuade her Hayee family members from plotting against the Ra, put Tania in good standings with the Ra girls.

Because Tania had been so helpful, La had her at all the meetings. La knew all the family Elders of La's Special Guard had to respect meeting requests from La. La wasn't sure whether Tania's family was disrespecting her, or not.

La addressed her Special Guard, telling them that she wasn't sure any of them were worth the titles they held as the next leaders in the House of Ra. La cited each of the incidents the day before, when the Special guard arrived just after the action was over. La told them that it was their jobs to know what's going and react, quickly.

La said "I'll see if you can do better next time, or see if you have to be replaced!" La looked around the room and then said "I need ten volunteers to go with me to have a talk with Tania, to see if she has a good reason for not being here."

Before La finished her sentence, all of her Special Guard were standing, ready to go. Dan smiled inwardly, even though he kept a straight face. He enjoyed the results of La's show of her power.

The Ra and their gang of Special Guard were on the move. Once seen, word quickly spread all over the city. This time the Hayee Hellcat, Wana was prepared. She caught up with the Royal children just as they reached Tania's family home. She stared at all the children, ending with La. Wana asked "What's going on here?" La said "That's what I'm going to find out." La explained that she was going to see Tania and why. Wana looked at La's Special Guard, then ordered "All of you, get to your next training, or whatever else you have to do!" None of them moved. La looked at Wana and said "They're only going to do what I tell them. After all, they are my Special Guard." Wana turned to La and said "I don't care who they are! I control what goes on here!"

La wasn't one to back down from a challenge, but she didn't want this fight. La looked at her Special Guard and said "I'm going to see Hayee, Tania. You can't go with me. So, I'll see you, later."

Bo and the other Special Guard started moving away, slowly. The other Ra stayed with La. After watching her guard leave, La turned to Wana and said "You can escort us, if you still don't trust me." La smiled. Wana said "Careful you don't get disrespectful towards me." La said sarcastically "I'm just saying."

Shaya and Danaaa giggled for a second, before they quickly got serious. After giving La a hard stare, Wana looked at all of the Royal children. She knew if she was there, she could stop anything La planned on doing. Wana smiled at La and then said "Alright, I'll go with you."

Hayee, Tania's family was already waiting on Wana and the Royal children when they arrive. They showed the proper respect to the Royal children and the Royal children did the same. The Hayee Elders granted the Ra an audience in one of their meeting rooms. Wana told the Elders of this house that she was only here to make sure the Royal children weren't disrespectful to anyone.

No sooner than all the formalities were over, La asked Tania to be brought in. La was told that Tania would be indisposed for a few days. None of the Ra children knew what the word indisposed meant, including La. All La knew was that she was told it would be a few days before she could see Tania. That wasn't good enough for La. La asked "Where is she?"

The Elders, again, said "Indisposed." La responded "Do you know who I am?" the Elder respectfully said "Of course, I do. You're the Number One Princess, but even still, you're in my home. Protocol says even you have to respect that."

La looked at Dan and then back to the Elder, before saying "You're right, about that. As the Number One Princess, I have to respect your home. Today, I'm Hammer-Axe One, Warlord Cut Faster. The Warlord Cut Faster doesn't really care about protocol. She does whatever she wants!"

Danaaa excitedly jumped forward and yelled to La "I want to be a Warlord, too!" Even Shaya had a glimmer of light in her eyes that hoped she could be a Warlord, also.

La stomped one foot and stared at Danaaa for a second. Danaaa stomped both her feet, one at a time, before angrily looking forward, again. Shaya was now back to concentrating on her hammers and her surroundings, realizing La had just stomped on her and Danaaa's dreams of having Warlord titles.

La looked back at the Elder and said "Take me to where ever indisposed is, so I can see Tania." Wana looked at Danaaa and then looked a warning to La to be careful how she proceeded.

The Elder seemed to be steadfast in his decision, when he said "Tania is with her mate. They'll not be disturbed this day, Warlord Cut Faster."

Danaaa's head quickly jerked towards La and then, just as quick, back to the Elder. Danaaa looked the Elder in his eyes. She did a quick nod of her head, up and then down, out of respect for the Elder. Danaaa then yelled "You don't tell us what to do!"

Danaaa pointed to La and yelled "That's why she's here! People around here need to start doing what they're told! If you're not going to take us to Tania, we'll find her ourselves!"

Wana stepped in front of the Royal children, followed closely by her guards. She sternly looked at them and said "You heard him, that's enough. Go back to the palace."

A commotion towards the back of the room caught everyone's attention. Three guards came in and announced La's Special Guard were at the back of the compound, making a disturbance. La smiled and said "We're not leaving, until we see Tania. End this nonsense and take us to Tania. If I have to, I'll have Baby sniff the air and then we'll go in that direction, until we find her."

Before the Elder had a chance to respond, he saw Danaaa sniffing the air. While staring at him, she yelled to La "She's somewhere in that direction!" as Danaaa pointed to her left.

That made some of Tania's Hayee male relatives move, blocking the path to the direction in which Danaaa pointed. Their movements put Danaaa on guard. She drew her axes, spinning them one super-fast revolution, before stopping them on a dime pointed at the Hayee. Danaaa yelled "This is why I get blamed for chopping people! It's because they think they can get in my way, instead of doing what they're told!" Wana yelled "Danaaa, shut your mouth!"

After seeing the Hayee looking unfavorably in Danaaa's direction, Young Dan knew the situation was quickly deteriorating. Knowing that, Dan didn't care. He was sick and tired of the Hayee not going along with the wishes of their soon to be leaders. Dan didn't want to be blamed for what was going to happen, even though he was going to make it happen. Dan instantly knew how to mix in the right ingredient to get maximum effect for this situation. Dan said "Hey, Stupid! Tell me again, you know, the story about your Kitty."

After the incident in which Danaaa killed a pride of lions, while befriending one of that pride's young lionesses, Dan would coax Danaaa into telling this story in her unusually loud voice, knowing it would upset his youngest sister, as she recalled one of her most painful memories.

Danaaa yelled "But, I already told you! You know the story! It was the day when I was forced to run away from home! A lot of things happened that day!" Danaaa's eyebrows furrowed, in confusion, as she recalled that day's events. Then she excitedly continued with "Then, I met kitty! When we first . . . .!"

Danaaa was interrupted by one of the Hayee men incredulously saying "No one wants to hear the story about that lion! Everyone already knows what happened!"

Dan smiled, just as Danaaa looked at the Hayee who spoke out. He didn't even ask permission to speak. Danaaa knew that if they didn't start making the Hayee adhere to protocol, the Hayee wouldn't do it on their own. Danaaa angrily yelled "I'm going to find Tania!"

Danaaa started walking angrily forward, with axes in hand. A group of Hayee came running up to intercept Danaaa. Danaaa saw that some of them had long pole hammers and some had long pole axes. Just as the Hayee with the long pole weapons came up,

Danaaa saw the Hayee who didn't care for her story about her Kitty. Danaaa could see he had a sort of happy smirk on his face. Danaaa moved to action.

She walked right into the swings of the long pole Hammers. Danaaa blocked and dodged the Hammers as she moved forward. Then the long pole axes made assaults on Danaaa, while the Hayee with the long pole hammers kept Danaaa trapped, bullying Danaaa in the center of the Hayee. Danaaa was busy defending herself in a battle the Hayee were controlling.

The Elder realized that Danaaa was trapped, the same time as the Ra children. He knew the other Ra children wouldn't stand by for much longer. The Elder was satisfied that this technique used by his family was capable of controlling the little monster, Danaaa. He didn't need to take things further. Just as La and Shaya were about to jump into action, the elder ordered "That's enough, I'll lead you to her!"

The Hayee guards moved back from Danaaa. Danaaa wasn't ready to stop. La saw that and said "Baby wait, they're taking us to see Tania!" All of the Royal children walked over to Danaaa. La and Shaya fixed Danaaa's clothes, which had become disheveled during her short skirmish. La gave Danaaa a serious look, and then said "You did good! Now, let's go see Tania." That seemed to calm Danaaa, for the moment.

The Elder led the Ra children, accompanied by Wana and her guards, to a small stone home on the compound. On the way there, it seemed this Elder was saying things, which could be construed as an alibi for himself and his family. That made La and Shaya a little nervous about what they would see. It didn't bother Danaaa, or the Ra boys, because they were too busy scanning the area for danger and frankly, they didn't care.

When they got to the small stone home a man who looked to be about thirty years of age came out and protested this intrusion, until he realized he didn't have any support from his Elders. He reluctantly moved out of the way of the Ra children, just as they were running out of patience with him.

The Ra children poured through the entrance looking for Tania. They walked into a back room and that's where they found Tania. She was on the floor. Her hands and ankles were tied to a sturdy wooden post. She was battered and bruised. The Ra children stared at Tania, shocked at what they were seeing, to the point that they were frozen at the sight of seeing her like this. They didn't snap out of their daze, until Tania stared at them and in a helpless, pitiful voice, almost crying, and begged "Help me, please! Help me!"

Shaya raced over to Tania and started untying her. La's face got angry. She took one look at Danaaa. For Danaaa, that was the last straw. La saw Danaaa's bottom lip was already crooked, hanging on one side and shaking where it hung crooked. A thin layer of moisture coated her eyes. Danaaa still didn't shed tears. One thing was certain to La and the only other person to see Danaaa's face, Young Dan, was that Baby was cross!

In that same second, Danaaa bolted out of the room and out of the stone house. La could have probably stopped Danaaa once she saw Danaaa was cross, by calling out to her, but she didn't. La didn't like what she just saw and was determined that even though she didn't know what Tania could have done to deserve this, it didn't matter.

The only person that was going to do this to one of La's Special Guard and get away with it was her, or her mother, or her siblings. Well, it was a very short list and that man, that she'd seen earlier, wasn't on it. La bolted out the door a few seconds after Danaaa did.

The rest of the Ra children turned to follow, until Dan turned back to them and ordered Don and Yin "Stay here and protect them!" as he pointed to Shaya and Tania. It was too late to say anything to Ram, because right after Danaaa ran out and before La did, somehow Ram had disappeared. Dan didn't have time to think about that. He ran out looking to see what La was getting into.

When Danaaa got outside of the stone house, she was confronted by the Hayee guards that used the long pole weapons to keep her in check, before. There were even a few more than before. All of them moved in position to do their part.

Danaaa saw that and instantly accessed every bit of information on how they trapped her before. Danaaa used quick, erratic movements, along with counter-attack moves to get past the Hayee that were everywhere. Ram magically appeared, slicing into the lower torsos of several of the Hayee before he had their attention. Then, as if that wasn't enough, La came running up like a mad woman, with her weighted ponytail and axes swinging at them with reckless abandonment.

Danaaa left that scene, locked in on the scent of the Hayee at the stone house and followed it to where he was. When Danaaa found him, he was with about twenty of his male cousins. They all heard about the rumors of the terrible things this young Ra girl had done. None of them could bring themselves to believe her that big a threat. Still, they were going to be careful that this young girl didn't make fools out of them.

After seeing the presumed guilty person, the second person Danaaa noticed was the Hayee who didn't care for her story about Kitty. Danaaa got sad for a second as she thought about her Kitty. Then she remembered that she was angry and had some unfinished business to handle.

Danaaa hoped that the other Hayee got in the way of her main objective, the Hayee who hurt Tania. Danaaa charged the group of Hayee and was met by some of the most vicious swings from axes and hammers that she'd ever witnessed, up until this point. The attack was so fierce that Danaaa couldn't avoid all of the swings. The ones she blocked came at her with so much force that Danaaa was knocked around pretty good, before La and young Dan arrived.

After catching up to Danaaa, the first thing both La and Dan saw was Danaaa blocking a powerful swing from one of the Hayee that sent her hard to the ground rolling out of the way of just being cut to pieces by another Hayee. That was all they needed to see. Dan and La attacked those Hayee with all they had. Before they knew it, they had severely wounded most of the Hayee, without killing them.

La stopped Dan and Danaaa, before they got to the rest of them. She backed them off the Hayee, without leaving an exit for them. There were only four Hayee left. They were in defensive stances, on guard against the three Ra. La stepped forward, pointed and then said "The three of you have nothing to do this. You can leave, or you can stay."

None of the Hayee moved. They would rather die than run. La could see that much. Still, she waited a moment, before turning her attention to the one Hayee that was with Tania. La said "Tell me, why Tania has been punished by the likes of you?"

The Hayee angrily looked at La and said "What I do with Tania is my business! You have no right to interfere!"

Danaaa quickly turned to La and yelled "Holler charge!" La put up her hand stopping Danaaa, without taking her eyes off the Hayee. La said "Evidently, you think you control what goes on around here and can say anything to me you like."

La took another step forward. She quickly twirled the axes in both her hands and then said "Best me in competition and I'll forgive you for your disrespect and I'll follow any order you give."

Danaaa looked at La. This was beyond her comprehension. Danaaa needed some clarification from La, saying she'd be taking orders from this Hayee. Danaaa incredulously yelled "But you're the Number One Princess! You're supposed to tell people what to do, not the other way around!" La smiled at the Hayee, but said to Danaaa "Don't worry, Baby. Just watch this, you'll see."

A young girl had just challenged this Hayee. His cousins with him now wouldn't move against La, unless he specifically asked them. In a situation like this, he being a thirty-year-old man, being challenged by a thirteen-year-old girl, asking for help would be considered a cowardly move. A perceived coward wouldn't last long in the Hayee clan.

So, with his eyes trained on La, he stepped forward, with his hands positioned to draw his Hammer-axes. He wasn't crazy enough to attack the Number One Princess. However, if she came at him, he'd rather die by the hands of Ramala, or Elder Dan, than to die by the hands of this young girl.

La concentrated her vision, making her aware of everything about this Hayee that she could use to her advantage. For La, this was a chance to use her Special techniques her mother taught her. Who better to use them on? The Hayee were going to find out why you don't become a problem for the Number One Princess!

La quickly moved her axes up, pointed at the Hayee. Then she took off as quickly as she could towards the Hayee. Still, that Hayee hadn't drawn his weapon, as he saw La coming right at him.

La, while running at Hayee, flipped in a cartwheel two revolution, before launching herself, spinning through the air in front of the Hayee. He saw La's axes close to her sides as she came spinning through the air at him. In that instant he drew his axes, bringing them up and blocking the coming strikes from La's axes. Almost too late, the Hayee saw the metal ball on the end of La's ponytail rocketing towards him.

He moved low and left of La avoiding the metal ball, still on guard against La's axes. He didn't have to wait. La struck with her ax, as the Hayee was moving low and away from her. He moved his ax up just in time to block La's strike. Just as he was about to swing that same ax at La, as she was spinning in the air past him, he was sliced on the forearm of that same arm, as he was moving his ax towards La, just missing her.

He didn't have time to think about that. He knew La was landing somewhere behind him, possibly ready to strike with her axes. He turned, while moving his axes in defense of his vital organs. He was right about La's axes. They clanged violently into his blocking axes. Just, as he was about to swing at La, came that metal ball rocketing towards him, again. This time he barely managed to move his head out of harm's way. The metal ball still smashed down onto the top of his shoulder.

It was hard enough to get his attention. Still, he was now focused on La, plotting his next attack. Wana, who had just arrived, watched as La attacked nonstop, forcing the Hayee to decided whether to be hit by the metal ball, or either get nicked and cut by La's axes. The Hayee was quick, but La was quicker. The Hayee took a thorough beating from La, in which he got a few consolation glancing blows in on La that left her unaffected. The Hayee fought valiantly, until La stopped.

The Hayee had cuts and deep, but non-life threatening slices of his skin missing from his arms and legs. He was bleeding from his wounds, already shaky on his feet and was putting up the best fight he could. Still, he wouldn't back down. He'd rather die, than to concede defeat to La. La decided it was time to finish this and moved forward to do just that.

Wana stepped in front of the Hayee, then motion for her guards to help him. While looking at the Hayee, as he was being carried away, La said "Don't ever touch Tania, again! I strictly forbid it! No one touches any of my Special guard, bodyguards, or my servants without asking my permission and receiving it! Otherwise, they get dealt with by me! I expect Tania to be taken care of and sent to my meeting hall, after training. If she's late, I'm not going to blame her, I'll just come back and start up with my axes again, until I get tired. And I never get tired!"

Wana said "Alright, you made your point! It's time to go."

Danaaa yelled to La "Not yet! Me and him still has to settle up, on account that he interrupted me when I was talking about my Kitty!"

Wana knew Kitty was a sore spot with Danaaa. Wana put one hand up at Danaaa and the other one up at the Hayee. Wana said "Hurry, tell your story. I'm sure he'll listen, this time." Danaaa told the story about Kitty again to everyone who had already heard it. The story became grander every time Danaaa told it. After she was done, Wana made the Ra children leave. When they were leaving, Wana whacked young Dan on the side of his head, for getting Danaaa so worked up. Dan looked at his aunt and received an angry stare from her.

Just as the Ra children were leaving, the Special Guard had just forced their way to them. La motioned for them to calm down. She looked at them as if she was still unimpressed that they got there when the action was already over. La was about to express her displeasure when young Dan put his hand on her shoulder, pulling her back, slightly. La looked at Dan as he said "They'll have another chance to see if they can do better, when next day comes. For now, let's get to our next training session. You know how mother gets when we don't train properly."

La stared at Dan for a couple of seconds, before she decided Dan was right. La looked at Shaya and Danaaa, without saying a word to her Special Guard. The Ra girls followed La and the Ra boys followed Dan. The Special Guard looked at each other, before leaving. They knew they had to impress their Queen, the Number One Princess, La before she decided they were useless to her.

CHAPTER 5

The next day, La's Bodyguards were waiting to see her after first day's training. Palace guards alerted Ramala and she had her guards have La's guards wait at the palace steps for her. They waited there, until La and her siblings finished breakfast. They escorted La to the meeting hall where she saw Tania.

Tania cleaned up pretty good, but you could still see scrapes and bruises on her face and arms. The Ra girls smiled at her, showing they were pleased that she was present. Tania smiled in appreciation at what La had done for her. The Ra girls had a private meeting with Tania. La reminded Tania that she would have been a slave, there for the bidding of her Hayee master, if they hadn't rescued her. Lastly, La said "Now, you know how far I'll go for you. I accept nothing less from you. You're very smart. I can see that. Use your wits for me and tell me what you see." Tania nodded her head that she would. That was the moment Tania officially became La's adviser.

Because of her new position, her family gave Tania special treatment. Her cousin, the Hayee who assaulted her and tried to make her his mate, was conveniently kept out of La and Tania's sight.

In the next two weeks, every day the Ra children went from compound to compound of all the largest Hayee families in the city of Ra, forcing them to comply to La's rules, mostly by beating into submission, anyone that resisted in any way. Still, they were respectful of the Elders of all the Hayee families, by not harming any of them.

With the Special Guard eager to impress La with their willingness to fight in her stead, fights broke out in all areas of the city. The Special Guard found themselves fighting their own family members, later, in support of La. Wana and her guards couldn't be in force, in enough places to stop all the fights. The city of Ra went into chaos.

Ramala forbid her children from leaving the palace, but that didn't work. They just snuck out after training sessions, or when Ramala wasn't with them. No matter the punishment, the Ra children continued to sneak out and cause trouble.

When the Ra children couldn't get out of the palace, La's Special Guard somehow got messages from her and still carried out disturbances all over the city. La even put her Special Guard in charge of their individual families and had them doing things according to the protocol of the Number One Princess, La, instead of their Queen, the Hayee, Ramala.

Elders from these families got word to the Hellcats letting them know what was happening. There was now suspicion on the Ra children for Shamika and her sisters' deaths.

Once Ramala heard this, she thanked the Elders and had a private meeting with Wana and Tara. The three Hellcats discussed how to deal with La and her siblings. After hearing her two cousins' suggestions, Ramala told them, what she thought was the best way to handle it. Tara and Wana stared at Ramala to see if she was serious. When they saw that she was, they reluctantly went along with Ramala's plan.

Ramala summoned her children to one of the meeting rooms at the palace. The Ra children knew that their actions hadn't gone unnoticed. Once they entered the meeting room, they knew they'd be punished, yet again. All of the Ra children looked suspiciously at their aunts and mothers, trying to get a hint of what might happen here.

After lowering their heads, out of respect, Ramala motioned for all of them to take their seats. Ramala had a calm, but all business demeanor. Even though the Royal children tried not to let it show, they were nervous.

Ramala looked at all the Ra children, one at a time, before staring at La. Looking into La's eyes, she said "Your behavior is getting out of hand. It seems to me you're trying to take control of the city, with protocol you set forth, even before mine. I can't have that. As long as I'm alive, or will it, things will be strictly run by the protocol set forth by me, the Queen."

Ramala paused a short moment, again looking at each of the Ra. The Royal children knew Ramala's next words would determine their fate.

Ramala, looking at La, said "I'm sending all of you to the Lower Houses of Ra. You will be the Ruling Warlords of that area. Under the Rule of your Queen, all of you will be responsible for holding that territory in my name. You can set forth protocol to get that done. There will be two moons of extra training before you leave. Not once will any of you leave without consulting me and getting my permission. In that time, no more disturbances by you, or your Special Guard. One more disturbance will be seen as a sign of serious disrespect to me and I'll blame all of you. I love all of you, because you're my children. Even with that, disrespect won't be tolerated. In the House of Ra, disrespect is punishable by death!"

All of the Ra children took a slow nervous swallow at what they just heard. They looked at Tara and Wana to see if they really heard what Ramala said. Danaaa turned and looked at La, trying to get a better understanding of what she thought she heard and if it meant just that, before looking back at her mother.

Ramala said "Now get out of here and go have a meeting with your Special Guard, or whatever you have to do to get this madness stopped!"

Without hesitation, La said "Yes, Mother."

All of the Ra children, stood up, lowered their heads and left. All Don, Shaya, and Yin got out of this was that they didn't get in trouble and they were going on a trip. Ram could hardly keep his composure, knowing that he would be away from his parents with only La and Dan supervising him. Dan couldn't wait to see the area he was in charge of. La tried to keep a straight face, knowing all of the Lower Houses would be doing things, according to protocol, that she set forth.

Danaaa walked along with her siblings, thinking about the last time they were at the first Lower House and how horribly they were treated, being attacked and all. Danaaa decided right then and there that if people didn't act according to the protocol that La set forth, she was going to teach them, by swinging her axes real fast.

In the next two moons, there wasn't one disturbance. La strictly forbid her Special Guard from doing anything except training as hard as they could for the upcoming expedition. The Ra children and the Special Guard trained hard with Wana going over security protocol.

Syn and Ma, who were already training the Royal girls, stepped their training to the highest level. Syn found great pleasure training the Ra girls. The Ra girls were advanced enough in their training that afternoon sessions were totally filled with training by the Syn, Jara. That time was mostly sparring sessions, split up between the three girls. Sometimes weapons were used, but this day they weren't.

The Ra girls trained in a private fenced in area. It resembled a large dirt field, with no grass and two weapons racks near the entrance. Hammer-Axes, Machetes, Gutting Knives and Long Poles were some of the weapons in the racks. There were no plant decorations, like most of the courtyards in the palace. This was the no frills training area.

La went first as usual. Shaya and Danaaa stretched on the sideline, got into their stance and watched. They took mental notes, until it was their turn.

Syn was average height for a woman. She was medium brown skinned and was muscular, without being thick. Syn waited on La in the middle of the courtyard. She watched as La smiled and then lowered her head. A second after La's head came up, the smile was gone from her face. La now had on her seriously intense kick-ass face. Syn had seen this face on Ramala and La many times, before.

Once La's head came up and Syn saw that serious look, she knew she would be attacked by La at any given time. La watched Syn for the slightest thing she could consider an advantage, even though she knew there was none. A moment after that, La attacked Syn, Jara.

La always used her ponytail with the weighted metal ball on the end, anytime she sparred without weapons. La jumped at Syn with a spinning kick that launched her ponytail into motion. Syn avoided the kick and was immediately assaulted by a barrage of four lightning fast punches, by La.

Syn moved slightly out of the way and then countered, swinging several times at La, backing her up. La twisted and turned her body, moving out of the way of every one of Syn's move. After twisting her body in an over exaggerated fashion, to avoid Syn, La moved lightning fast into a counter-attack. At the same time, La moved in swinging with her fist, the metal ball on the end of her ponytail came flying at Syn, continuously. It always amazed Syn how La could keep that metal ball whizzing at you, effortlessly, with pinpoint accuracy, while swinging her fist with deadly intentions. It was almost as if Syn was fighting two people at the same time!

Even with that, Syn wasn't going to be beaten by the likes of La, if she could help it. Syn stepped up her fighting to the next level. She avoided the metal ball and got close enough to La to administer several blows to La's midsection. La avoided all of Syn's strikes at her face, as Syn knew she would. Then, Syn placed a lightning fast kick to La's ribs and sent her fist to that same rib as her foot was leaving it. La seemed to over exaggerate the force of Syn's kick, but as soon as Syn's fist was about to connect with La's rib, La's ponytail wrapped around both Syn's leg and arm.

Because Syn's leg was going in the opposite direction of her arm, Syn's punch never made it to La's rib. La pulled her head back slightly, tightening the grip of her ponytail around Syn's arm and leg. Before La could completely tighten her hold on Syn, Syn pulled, yanking La towards her. La slammed her body into Syn as hard as she could and pushed even harder with her legs. Syn and La fell towards the ground. Before they hit the ground, Syn loosened La's ponytail, freeing her arm and leg. At the same time they were falling, La drove her fist as hard as she could into Syn's rib. As both of them hit the ground, they tucked and rolled into a standing position.

Syn's tuck and roll was faster than La's and when La came out of her tuck and roll, Syn's foot had stopped an inch from La's face. La froze in place, until Syn slowly moved her foot down, staring La in her eyes. The look in Syn's eyes said she could have taken La's head clean off with that kick. La, without breaking eye contact, took a step back and slightly lowered her head, before raising it.

Syn was surprised that La was able to wrap her arm and leg with that ponytail of hers. She was even more surprised when La plowed her fist into her ribs as they were falling to the ground. Syn could fell a slight soreness where La's fist connected. If La had more power, or even worse, if La had a hooked blade, Syn knew her ribs would have been split open. However, since that wasn't the case, Syn said "That was a pretty good punch, but it slowed down your response to defend yourself. If my kick had landed, you never would have recovered from it. You must practice coming out of your tuck and rolls faster. Also, you must be aware of where your enemy is in reference to where you are."

La nodded that she understood. Syn then said "Now, tuck that ponytail under your clothes and attack me without using it."

La did as she was told. She attacked Syn with everything she had. It wasn't enough. Syn punished La for about twenty minutes with some heavy shots to her midsection, because, although La was on defense, La wouldn't stop trying to counter-attack. However, after that twenty minute beating, La switched, completely to defense. Syn was still able to hit La from time to time, but because La was basically running now, Syn was only connecting, occasionally. After chasing La for another fifteen minutes, Syn decided that was enough.

La's offense was almost unstoppable, but Syn saw that La's defense, although good, needed more work if she ever hoped to be unbeatable. Right now, Syn was able to punish La because of that, explaining to La her defensive mistakes, afterwards.

Next was Shaya's turn. Syn could see in Shaya's eyes that this time was going to be much like all the other times she sparred with Shaya. Shaya was going to dance around and basically run from Syn, until Syn caught up with her. Syn wasn't having that today. She had a surprise for Shaya. Syn looked at Ma and motioned for her to come over. Shaya's face showed a quick second of curious surprise, before going back to the blank mask she always tried to portray.

Syn, while looking at Shaya, said "Since you like to run, see if you can run from me, while avoiding Ma." Shaya turned her body slightly in Ma's direction. She kept her eyes on Ma and Syn, while staying on guard against both of them.

Syn knew if she gave Shaya long enough to think, Shaya would figure out a way to run. Syn gave Ma one quick glance and they both attacked Shaya. Shaya was able to avoid both Syn and Ma for a few moments. Once they cut off her routes of escape, Shaya had to fight. But, even though she was fighting, she was negotiating the least amount of physicality that she could. Syn saw that, turned the heat up on Shaya, and punished her for about thirty minutes with some pretty good shots. After being hit with a few more solid shots, Shaya became angry.

One sure way to bring out Shaya's alter ego, the Angry-Axe, is to push her to anger. It happened in an instant. Shaya put a lightning fast potent attack on Syn that had Syn backing up a little, just to avoid being hit. Shaya ended her attack on Syn with a spinning kick that just missed. Syn knew she had a chance to counter-attack when Shaya landed back on her feet. But even faster than before, when Shaya's feet hit the ground, she went spinning backwards and landed a super-fast kick to the side of Ma's head. Ma, who was moving into position behind Shaya to strike, was caught completely off guard and stumbled a couple of steps from the force of Shaya's kick.

Before Ma had completed her stumbling steps, Shaya launched herself in the air towards Ma. Syn jumped at Shaya, at the same time Shaya launched herself at Ma. Syn grabbed both Shaya's arms, while wrapping her leg around Shaya's leg that was about to kick at Ma. Shaya did one hard struggle, until she heard Syn sternly say "Shaya, calm yourself!"

In that instant, Ma came into focus and Shaya realized what she'd done and what she was about to do. Shaya somehow loosened herself from Syn's grip and went straight down on her knees. She begged "Please, forgive me Aunt Ma! I'm so sorry!"

La took a strong step towards Shaya and then stopped in her tracks. She stared at Shaya, without saying anything. La's eyes shot over to Ma, before going back to Shaya's eyes.

Ma saw that even though La was conflicted about what Shaya had done, La was two seconds from screaming at Shaya about begging. Ma quickly said "I forgive you." Shaya's eyes quickly went to Ma's, before going to La's eyes. Shaya jumped to her feet, watching La the whole time. La and Shaya stared at each other.

Both were startled when Danaaa yelled "The one time when she deserves to be slapped, for what she did, YOU just stare at her, like you don't know if you should do it or not! But, why is that?!"

Not a half second later, La and Shaya erupted into laughter. Danaaa stomped one foot and then the other. She wrapped her arms about her chest in a huff. La and Shaya walked over to Danaaa and consoled her, letting her know everything was all right.

Shaya was excellent in her defensive moves, but Syn had to force Shaya to move offensively. Shaya's fighting was usually like a negotiation. She would evade her opponent as much as possible. If her opponent hit her or if she was angry is when you would see Shaya's offensive talents at their best. Syn would purposely hit Shaya with solid blows to make Shaya fight harder. That always worked and Syn got some great sparring sessions out of Shaya that way.

But of all the Ra girls, Syn would end up spending the most time sparring with Danaaa. Danaaa had crazy endurance and would push Syn, until Syn didn't want to go any longer, because she had other things to do, besides spend the whole day with Danaaa.

Syn would punish Danaaa with her best techniques, trying to wear Danaaa down. Danaaa would take everything Syn threw at her. That and the fact that Danaaa was very good at adapting to the fight at hand, usually left Syn spent after a long grueling sparring session with Danaaa. Even with that, Syn spent that extra time with Danaaa because she figured if a girl likes to fight as much as Danaaa did, that girl better be trained to her fullest potential.

Syn trained the Ra girls five out of seven days a week. After each training session with Syn, La would report everything that happened, first to Ramala and then to her top fighting instructor the Hayee, Deen. Both would give La insight on how she could do better against the Syn, Jara next time. And since Shaya and Danaaa were always present, they took in those instructions, too. Every night the Ra girls would test their training on the Ra boys, just to make sure they kept up to date on the latest training techniques.

Now that Wana had back control of the city, she could concentrate on more pressing issues. Her messengers told her that Benobu's caravan had just reached the lake and that he would be arriving in the main city within two days. Now that Wana had the city back under control, she wasn't going to let it turn into a war zone, again. Wana gathered some of Benobu's Elders and then she and her Elite Guards went to meet Benobu, along with the other two Hellcats, at one of Wana's security meeting halls to negotiate a peaceful settlement to the slaughter of his family members.

Benobu stipulated that he and the other Warlord families had just one other wish they wanted fulfilled and all would be forgiven. The negotiations took time, but once done Benobu got a nice piece of territory for his family to secure and run in the name of his Queen, the Hayee, Ramala. The territory was a large area just north of the lake. That was for his loss and his promise that he wouldn't wage war against the Royal children. The other Warlord families affected by the chaos the Ra children caused were also given special considerations. Benobu and the other families also got the special request they asked of the Hellcats. And just like that, the Benobu situation seemed to be under control.

When Wana got back to the main part of the city, she met with several of her captains, who said they had an update on the Shamika murders. The captains met with Wana and then escorted her to a heavily guarded location. Once there, she saw a young girl of about seven years of age. She was the Ra, Urianna. Urianna, Riana, or just Anne, was what she was usually called. All of the children born to Hayee family members in the House of Ra had the sir name of Ra. The royal Ra children always treated the new Ra slightly better than they always treated the Hayee. There were a lot of young Ra-Hayee in the House of Ra. Anne was a member of another one of Wana's top Warlord's family.

Anne was dark skinned and skinny. She had just lost her two front baby teeth. She sat in her chair, looking down, while nervously kicking her feet back and forth. When she saw Wana and her guards walk in the room, Anne looked up for a quick moment and then looked back down. Wana's guards took standing positions around the table, as Wana sat down opposite Anne. Wana gave the young girl a reassuring smile and said "Tell me what you know."

Anne looked up at Wana, then lowered her head and started talking. Wana listened as she heard Anne tell how she snuck out on the night of the gathering. She walked around the mostly empty streets, stealthily avoiding guards and other grownups.

Anne lost track of time and ended up staying out later than she expected. The Gathering let out and she knew she couldn't take the chance on racing her parents and other Elders to the family compound. Anne knew if she was discovered, she would be punished. She decided to hide, until everyone was sleep and then sneak back into the compound.

Anne sat in a darkened corner, on the side of a building right off the main road. She watched as people walked by, unaware of her being there. Anne watched as the large crowd thinned out to a few people here and there.

Just as she was about to leave she heard a commotion at the back of the building. Where she was, she couldn't see what was going on. Not wanting to be detected Anne slowly, carefully and quietly moved in the dark to get a better look. That took her a few minutes. By the time she got to a better vantage point, she saw Ram, just as he swung his ax down on the neck of one of three females on the ground. She watched as Ram chopped the heads off the other two bodies.

After Ram removed all of the heads, he picked them up by their hair, looked around and disappeared behind the building. Anne waited, until she was sure Ram was gone. As she slowly came out of the shadow, Anne cautiously peeked around the corner where she saw Ram disappear. When she didn't see him, she turned and walked over to the headless bodies.

Anne stared in horror at the bodies engulfed in pools of blood. After staring at the bodies for a while, Anne remembered she still had to sneak back into her home. She took one last look at the bodies and then turned to leave. That's when she saw Ram staring at her. He had axes in both hands.

Anne froze. She had never been more scared in her entire life. Her eyes quickly darted in both directions trying to determine if she could run in either direction. As Anne's eyes slowly moved back to Ram's eyes, she knew Ram was close enough to slice her up, if she made one false move. So, Anne stared at Ram with begging eyes, waiting to see if she would be his next victim.

Anne didn't have to wait long. Ram took a step towards Anne. Anne was so terrified that her legs got weak and her knees bent, while they were slightly shaking. When Ram got to Anne, he swung his axes very fast around her shoulders and head, before stopping the blade of his ax under Anne's chin, right at her throat. Anne hadn't moved an inch while Ram was putting the fear of death in her with his axes. Ram stared at Anne with his ax at her throat only for a few seconds, before removing his ax from her throat and pointing it at the road. Ram, in the deepest voice Anne had ever heard, said "Go."

She didn't have to be told twice. Anne ran as fast as she could, disappearing around the corner of the building. She managed to sneak back into her family's compound. Guards saw her, but since she was returning, they weren't going to report that she'd left and they only saw her when she returned. None of the guards needed the scrutiny that would surely follow.

Anne's family members noticed that she was acting strangely the next couple of days. Besides being very nervous, she wouldn't go outside of her family's home to play with the other young family members. After a few days of interrogation by elder women, Anne finally broke down and told what she saw.

Anne didn't tell her Elders that she always snuck out on a regular basis, exploring the city streets, alone. And although she had seen Ram on several occasions, Anne would hide and thought that Ram had never seen her. Also, Anne had never witnessed Ram taking heads before the night in question.

The older women made her tell them her story several more times to see if she was making it up. Once they were convinced she wasn't, they conferred with the male elders. They decided to let Wana hear this story before it spread throughout the city.

Wana had no trouble believing that her serial killing nephew had done what Anne said he did. She thanked the Elders of this compound and asked that they keep this information secret, until she decided her plan of action. Wana promised that no harm would come to Anne for the information she'd given. Wana put a large contingency of her Elite Guard around the compound. She even closed a couple of the road leading to the compound and placed even more of her best guards there. Even though Wana wanted to keep Anne a secret, most of the people in the city of Ra knew something was going on in that compound, because of the security, even though they didn't know what. Now, gossip and rumors were quickly spreading.

Because the heads were missing from the bodies, most people in the city already thought Ram was responsible for the murders. No one would dare accuse Ramala's son, unless multiple high-ranking witnesses caught him in the act.

La had spies everywhere. Even in the compound where Anne was being protected. They got word to La about Anne through her messengers. La figured Wana would probably be coming to interrogate Ram.

After the messenger left, La angrily looked at Ram and said "You never get caught! How is it that this time some girl saw you and lived to tell about it!?" Ram shrugged his shoulders, saying nothing, while looking at La. La said "That's just what you say when aunt Wana questions you, nothing! Did anyone else see you, besides that girl?"

Ram looked to the side, made a face as if he was checking his memory, and then shook his head no. La said "Good! I'll have that girl eliminated before next day comes, then we'll be done with this crazy rumor!" Ram's voice bellowed "Don't touch her!"

All of the Ra children turned and looked at Ram, confused as to why he would say that. Dan, who was lying on some cushions, quickly turned towards Ram and stared at Ram. Dan smiled as it suddenly dawned on him. Dan looked at La and said "So that's why he didn't kill her that night! He likes her!"

Ram turned and gave Dan an angry look. Dan and the other Royal children had absolutely no fear of Ram's murderous ways. He was their baby brother. Dan knew Ram was subject to whatever Dan decided, or Ram would take a beating from him. Now with the other Ra children looking at Ram, Dan asked "If we don't have her eliminated, what should we do with her?"

Ram took a step towards Dan and said "Leave her alone!" Dan could see he had his youngest brother riled up. All he had to do was push a little harder and he could have a good wrestling match with Ram.

La saw what Dan was up to and didn't want everyone to lose sight of the situation. La walked over to Ram and said "We won't do anything, for now. You don't say anything. If Mommy or Daddy forces you to talk, just say you didn't do it. We'll be leaving for the Lower Houses very soon. Once we're gone, they won't be able to blame you when peoples' heads are missing."

Everyone quickly turned and looked at La, baffled at what she'd said. La's last sentence was said to convince Ram that everything was going to be all right. It only confused the other Ra children. They couldn't figure out how people's heads were still going to be disappearing around the city, if Ram wasn't here to take them!

Wana came to the palace and met with Tara and Ramala, before summoning Ram. Ram walked in with all of his siblings. The Hellcats looked at all of the children. When they looked at La, she looked guilty of something.

Wana and Ramala question and threatened Ram, but still he wouldn't talk. Just as Ramala stood up and was about to get physical with Ram, Tara lightly put her hand on Ramala's arm stopping her. Ramala looked at Tara for an explanation. Tara looked at Ramala and said "I don't think he did it. Evidently, that young girl must have heard all the past rumors about Ram. Just to get some attention, she fabricated a complete lie. I say that girl is the guilty one and should be punished severely!"

Ram's eyes got fearful, as he looked away wondering what would happen to the girl. The other two Hellcats could see that Tara had broken Ram with words. Wana yelled "Good work Tara! Guards have that girl brought to the dungeon! I want the truth beaten out of her!"

The fearful look in Ram's eyes turned to anger, as he said in his booming bass voice "Leave her alone!" The guards and everyone else stopped in their tracks, shocked by Ram's voice. Tara looked at Ram and said "I'll not have some snot nosed brat making false accusations about my nephew. She has to be punished!" Ram looked at Tara for a moment and then said "She's telling the truth! I chopped their heads off."

La looked at her aunts and then at her mother. She didn't like the way they tricked Ram into confessing. Ramala was beside herself. She couldn't understand Ram's murderous ways. Frustrated, Ramala yelled "After all I've taught you, you turn around and do this! Is this what you think I brought you into this world to do?" Ram opened his mouth to answer, but Ramala yelled "Silence! Don't you dare say a word, unless I order it!"

Now Ram was confused. He was in no man's land. If he answered a question he wasn't supposed to, he could receive some physicality from his mother. If he didn't answer, Ram could still suffer the same fate. So, he did what he, his father and brothers always did in these situations. He kept his mouth shut.

Ramala was angrier with Ram for what he'd done, than at who he did it to. She talked and yelled at Ram for a good while, then fed him and sent him to the dungeon, saying "If you're going to act like a murderous heathen, then that's how I'm going to treat you!"

Of course, Ramala only made Ram stay in the dungeon for a short period, before giving the order to have him released. She threatened him that if he kept up with this kind of behavior, she'd be forced to commit him to the dungeon for the rest of his life.

Still, Ram was home in time for dinner. Wana personally escorted Ram. On the way, Ram was lectured and questioned by Wana. The only question Ram answered was when Wana asked "Why did you pick them to kill, knowing they were daughters to my top Warlord?" Ram looked up at Wana and said "I never said I killed them, I just said I chopped off their heads. The girl didn't kill them, either. She came after I did."

Wana was shocked. She stopped and quickly asked "Did you see who did it?" Ram shook his head no. Wana's mind was now racing. Right now, it seemed to Wana that the killer or killers might still be on the loose.

CHAPTER 6

On the eve before the Ra children were to leave for the Lower Houses of Ra, Ramala talked to them about everything she thought would make them successful. She also told them something that would be required of them on this journey. All of the Ra children listened carefully. When next day came, they got to see just what they were dealing with.

Just before everyone was ready to board their designated plat-formed elephant, the Hammer-Axe Six stood looking at the precious cargo they were forced to take with them. The Ra children looked at twelve children to young teenagers, which they had never seen before.

All of these children were Ra, even though their parents were Hayee. In the House of Ra, it was an unspoken truth that Ra children were expected to be treated better than most Hayee, because they were considered the future. That also caused a population boom in the House of Ra because all of the Hayee here wanted favor by having children with the name Ra. Even La and Dan treated all children with the Ra name better than their older Hayee siblings.

After looking at all twelve of them, their attention settled on a humongous, just teen-age male. He had a sack of food that he was continuously scooping out of with a hand that looked like bear paw. He was shoveling food into his mouth with machine like efficiency, while holding the sack covered by a tree truck of an arm, defensively shielding it against attack.

His name was Jumbo. He stared at the Royal children as if they were a threat to his food. The Ra children stared back. All the while suspicious of them, he never stopped shoveling food into his mouth. The Ra were snapped back into reality when they saw the Hayee, Chusee, one of Ramala's best messengers, spraying his good-bye to his son and daughter. Chusee had two extremely large buckteeth that pointed almost straight at you out of his mouth and when he talked, saliva would spray out of his mouth with almost every word.

His children had the same affliction, only worse. His daughter had choppers that assured no man would ever kiss her in this lifetime. In addition, if any man was bold, or desperate enough to dare to kiss her, he was sure to get his lips cut to shreds by her ferociously protruding teeth.

Her brother's teeth were even worse. Even though he had pretty big lips, because his teeth were even bigger and protruded outward, he couldn't completely close his mouth. He constantly had to lick his teeth and lips to keep them from drying out on him. Even still, his tongue wasn't long enough to lick his teeth all the way up to his gums. The Ra girls had never seen such a ghastly sight in their entire lives. The Ra children watched in horror as father and children sprayed each other with an emotional farewell.

None of the Ra children had the exceptionally keen sense of smell like Ram and Danaaa had. Ram and Danaaa could distinguish different smells from a good distance away with the greatest of ease. Nevertheless, the other Ra didn't need that special skill to smell one of the girls standing a little ways from the others. She smelled to high hell, as if she'd smeared shit all over herself and had been left in an underground dungeon to ferment in a vat of rotting flesh.

Everyone kept their distance from this girl for obvious reasons. Those were just the ones that caught the Ra children's attention, right off the bat. Still, the others had problems that they would soon discover.

After seeing all of them, the Ra children all but knew these were twelve of the most worthless, unproductive, non-achieving young Ra that the top Hayee Warlords of Ra could produce. These youngsters were all embarrassments to their family in one way, or another. They were usually kept out of the public eye. But since they were Ra, they still commanded a certain level of respect.

Normally when the Hayee had such children, they would lead them out into the bush, leave them there and let the lions, hyenas and other predators deal with them. When they saw that Ramala wouldn't do that to her two youngest murderous monsters, most families stopped doing it to their own.

Still, something had to be done about these children, considered unworthy of any positions of importance. When the Warlords found out that Ramala was banishing her children, I mean sending them away on a learning expedition, the Warlords figured they had found a way to get rid of their undesirable children, too.

The Hellcats agreed to this request and that the Hammer-axe Six were to deal as best as they could with these children. Protocol says that since these children were under the charge of the Ra children, the Ra children had to protect and supervise their training, as well as teach them proper etiquette. Elder instructors would do that, since the Hammer-Axe Six were children, themselves. The females from the Warlords families said their good-byes, as if they never expected to see these children, again.

The trip was uneventful. The caravan arrived at the first Lower House of Ra and was given a respectful greeting under the suspiciously watchful eyes of the Ra children. The Ra children hadn't forgot the beating they took the last time they were here. Whatever happened, they were determined they'd do better this time.

The First Lower House of Ra was more developed than the last time the Royal Ra were here. It wasn't as large as the main city, but there were many huts and houses, surrounding the public courtyards and social buildings. It also had areas with elephants and livestock in the northern part of the city, away from the jungle.

The royal Ra children were given a large stone house and a couple of smaller ones for personal use. Their Special Guard and bodyguards were put in housing, nearby, that was less plush. Ali requested that he and his guards use all of the housing surrounding the houses the Ra children were staying. After negotiating, the Elders gave in. The twelve undesirable Ra children were secured in housing and were watched by bodyguards and guards of this Lower House.

After everyone settled in, the Ra children spent most of the day meeting with the Elders and Warlords of the First Lower House, learning protocol. Each of the Six Lower Houses had protocol that was specific to that House. Protocol not only was followed by the members of that House, but also by any guest visiting.

The Hammer-Axe Six and their Special Guard were told how important it was that they respect these protocols, by the Hellcats. They listened closely to the Elders and Warlords, while trying to find loopholes in the protocol being told to them. The Ra children spent the better part of two weeks visiting and meeting with all the Elders of the Six Lower Houses, receiving protocol on how all six were run.

After that, Young Dan called a meeting of all the top Elders from the Six Lower Houses, along with their top advisers. Ramala taught Young Dan that as Warlord of this territory, according to protocol, he could do that anytime he wanted to.

The Elders knew their position and the advantages it gave them in protocol when dealing with the Ra. They also knew Dan's position. Besides being Warlord over this Ra territory, he was also first in line to be the first-born King of Ra, if he made it that far. Therefore, even though the Elders had control over protocol in their individual Houses, Dan controlled all of the territory their Houses occupied.

The meeting was held in a large courtyard, in the First Lower House where the Warlord Dan resided. A throne area with seven lavishly styled chairs faced all the attendees, who sat in chairs that made a half circle facing the throne area.

The Hayee first watched as the Special Guard walked in and posted up around the throne area. Dan's Warlord Bo, was now playing the role of Dan's top general, now that Dan had the role of Warlord. That didn't mean Bo had any less rank than a Warlord did, it just meant that was the capacity in which he had to serve, now that Dan was the Ruling Warlord. Ali came in next and had his guards post up in strategic areas around the courtyard. La's Executioner, Hoban, along with Tania, walked in next with Bo. The three looked at the crowd. Bo yelled "Rise and then get down for your King and Queen!"

This hadn't happened in the earlier meeting with these Elders. They hesitated for a moment. When they realized Bo was serious, they reluctantly complied, even though they had Bodyguards with them. When the Elders got down on their knees, so did their Bodyguards.

Seconds later the Ra children walked onto the throne area and took their seats. All seven of them looked out at the Hayee. La ordered "You may rise and take your seats."

Everyone did as La ordered. It surprised these Hayee Elders when it was Dan, instead of La, who stood to address them. Dan looked at the Elders and said "As Warlord of the territory in which all of you reside, it's my order to serve your Queen Hayee, Ramala, by making this area most productive to her wishes. That means I'll need complete cooperation from everyone here. If I don't get it, there are going to be repercussions I'm sure none of you are going to like."

The Hayee Elders looked at Dan as he talked. Dan was only thirteen, but he was calm and straight to the point. His voice wasn't loud and offensive, like his mother and sisters. Dan was saying "The Royal Ra here with me are my top generals, here to enforce protocol. If anyone has a dispute, don't take matters into your own hands. As of now, any disputes, or concerns about protocol will be referred to me, for resolution. Now, you will be addressed by my sister, Warlord Cut Faster, the Chop-Era Butcher MesoCyclone, Young Queen Ramala, the Number One Princess."

The reason Dan spoke off all of La's titles was that each title came with certain power levels of protocol control. The more titles you had, the more things you could do according to protocol. If you couldn't do it under one of your titles, you possibly could under another one.

La stood up and said in her normal, arrogantly, loud voice "I' d like to thank the Warlord of this territory, Young Dan the Destroyer, The Hammer-Ax Champion, Warlord Faster Cut, the Butcher Chopper Ra and First Born King of Ra for having your young Queen Ramala as his guest."

Dan had many important titles, too. La continued with "While here, I will set forth protocol for the whole of this territory. That protocol will be strictly enforced by Warlord Dan the Faster Cut and his top generals, along with my Special Guard. Remember this, because it's important and I'll only say it once. I accept nothing less than total cooperation from all of you. I won't hesitate to take heads, if I have to. Disrespect won't be tolerated!"

It looked to La as if several Elders had questions. Therefore, La said "If you have questions, ask them."

One of the Elders stood up, lowered his head, raised it and said "We have many young family members. We can't be held responsible for each and every one of their actions, can we?"

La looked over the crowd of Elders, before settling in on the one who spoke and saying "Of course you can't. Even still, they will be held responsible for their actions and possibly might get dealt with by my Executioner Hoban. If need be, I'll involve my protocol enforcer and Top General, the Immaculate Degenerate Jenny-Co, Warlord I Chop I, High Pressure the Executioner! It's best for everyone if she doesn't get involved."

The titles of Executioner was only given to the members of a Warlord's staff, whose sole purpose was to Execute, or eliminate anyone the Warlord deemed disrespectful to protocol that Warlord set forth. In other words, an Executioner was a Butcher, Hell bent of enforcing the protocol of death, when ordered by their Warlord.

All of the Elders and most Hayee had heard stories about Danaaa. Looking at Danaaa and never seeing her in action, made it hard for grown men to see this eight year old as a serious threat, let alone an Executioner. To them, Danaaa just had the look and attitude of an eight-year-old brat, although she was remarkably well behaved as her older siblings spoke. She sat in her chair, kicking her legs, seemingly not paying attention, even though they could see she was. Still, they thought, against their best, she wouldn't last very long.

After a few more threats, La ended the meeting with the Elders. She then had a meeting with her siblings and her Special Guard. La told her Special Guard that she had a mission for them. That it was most important that they succeeded. Dan helped them make a plan. The Special Guard practiced the plan for five days. They left on their mission two days, later.

La and Dan purposely sent La's Special guard back to the main city of Ra. They tried to send La's Warlords Ali, Hoban and Dan's Warlord Bo, but they all refused to leave the Royal children here with very little protection.

The Ra Warlords were allowed to stay and had to have their guards patrol the grounds where the Ra children lived here. They also were to guard the twelve undesirable Ra children that were under Dan and La's charge. Although they were responsible for these children, La didn't want to deal with them. She pawned them off on her Warlords. She had strict training regiments set for them.

La and Dan had a reason for sending the Special Guard to the city of Ra on a mission and limiting Bo and Ali to just guarding their residence. They wanted to test the members of this Lower House to see if they would do anything the Royal Ra could interpret as disrespectful.

Now that the formalities were mostly over, the Ra children settled into their training routines. Starting early, training, eating and resting took up the better part of their day. The Ra girls screamed in private pits for at least two hours every other day.

It was late afternoon before the Ra children could be addressed by anyone, unless it was an emergency. Food was brought to them and in the evenings, the Ra children kept to themselves and stayed at their small compound, plotting strategies.

It was now the forth evening after the Special Guard left on their mission. It was a few hour before dark. The Ra children told their Warlords that they would be going for a walk by themselves, but that they should be on alert, just in case they were needed. Tania, La's personal adviser, was to stay behind, also. Tania protested to no avail.

After arming themselves to the teeth, the Hammer-Axe Six left the compound. As they were leaving out, they saw the huge Ra teenager with his usual sack of food, shoveling food into his mouth, with a slight look of worry for the Royal children, as he watched them leave.

From the time La first saw that teenager, until now, she always saw him eating. Right after they passed him, La said "Does he ever stop eating?!" Shaya took a quick glance at him, before saying "Probably not. He looks and eats like an elephant." Everyone laughed.

Danaaa tried to understand why he was like that. She yelled "Maybe his mommy didn't feed him when he was little, so now he has to eat as much as he can to make up for that!"

La looked at Danaaa. She couldn't believe Danaaa said something so stupid. Dan laughed and said "That's the most stupid thing you've said yet, Stupid!"

Danaaa yelled in her whining voice "But, it could have happened! When you don't eat, it makes you hungrier and then there's no telling what you'll do! Now, he just can't stop eating!"

Shaya looked at Danaaa and said "You don't get that big by missing any meals, at all." again, everyone laughed. Danaaa wanted her point to be taken more seriously, so she yelled her best explanation in support of her argument, saying "After not being fed for so long, once he got some food, he trained himself really hard at eating! He told himself that he was going to eat as much as he could, just in case, ever a time came that he couldn't eat! Now he gets stared at, when all he's doing is training himself for the greatest battle of his life!"

All the Ra children were laughing, except La. La couldn't believe what she heard coming from Baby. Unlike Dan, who loved to hear Danaaa's stupid tirades, La was sickened by Danaaa's ability to make something up so unreasonably impossible.

La turned quickly and stood right in front of Danaaa, taking a deep angry breath. She sternly said "I've had enough of this nonsense! We have more important things to do than to talk about someone's eating habits!" La and Danaaa stared at each other, until Shaya put her hand on both their shoulders and said in her calm, begging voice "Come on, let's go!" Danaaa, while still looking in La's eyes said, to Shaya, in her whispering voice "She sounds just like mommy!"

Shaya pulled Danaaa closer to her and said "I know." Shaya looked at La and then pushed past her, walking with Danaaa. La yelled "Hold it!" Shaya and Danaaa stopped, quickly turned and looked at La. La walked up to and in front of them and said "You know I always walk in front!" Shaya and Danaaa looked at each other, smiled and then followed La, as usual.

By now, everyone was watching the Ra children make their way down the main road of this Lower House. They saw guards posted outside of a huge courtyard. They could hear the racing beat of drums. The closer they got, it looked like a feast was going on. Dan and La looked at each other, before heading in that direction.

When the Ra walked up, the guards showed the proper respect by lowering their heads and moving aside. La and Dan were surprised by this level of cooperation. Still cautious, they walked on to the courtyard. Food and other stands were on one side, while seats around tables filled the other half. It was a party like feast, with dancers and others performances going on in the center. All that stopped when the Ra walked on to the courtyard. It was dead silence as everyone lowered their heads and stared no higher than the chest of the Ra children.

After being caught off guard once, La was ready this time. She calmly, but loud enough for everyone to hear, yelled "As you were!"

Everyone sort of went back to doing what they were, before. Only now, most of their attention was on the Royal children. A man and two teenage girls came running over to the Ra children. Danaaa and Ram's hands moved quickly to a draw position close to their axes. La and Dan weren't worried, they just watched as the three ran over. All three lowered their heads. The man meekly asked "We have special seating for you and these girls can get whatever you want to eat and drink. What can we do to make you visit more pleasant?"

While the man was speaking, Don was checking out the girls. He examined them from head to toe, stopping for a moment at each area that was most pleasing to his eyes. Even though the girls were looking down, they could feel Don's eyes looking them over pretty good. These girls felt that same stare from older men and knew what it meant. It made the girls very nervous, even though right now, Don's intentions weren't that of a grown man. Don was just satisfying his fascination with the female body, by staring at it and touching it when he could.

Once the Ra reached the First Lower House, Don found that he didn't have to peek at the women and girls around him, fearful that his mother would catch and scold him for staring. Now he could look without reservation. At first, Don employed the technique his father taught him. Look and then look away. If you have to look again, that's alright. Just don't stare!

However, as an adolescent, Don soon forgot that technique and reverted to outright staring. Now Don was staring at most every girl he came across. Don's siblings, as well as everyone else, noticed this increasing behavior.

Dan and La didn't make a big deal out of it because Don did what they told him to do. If fact, even though Don was younger than Dan, Don now had Dan looking more and more at females than he would have on his own. Sometimes, Dan would find Don's behavior funny and it would tickle him to laughter. Other times Dan would find himself caught up in a web of mystery and intrigue staring at the same girls, or women that he saw Don staring at.

The man who had been talking was somewhat distracted by Don's staring at these girls. The man smiled, looked at Don and then at Dan. He said "And for you . . ." as he waved his hand, displaying the two girls next to him, said "They would be happy to serve you in any way you like and there are many, many more girls that would do the same."

Don looked at the man and then back at the girls. He took a slow lustful gulping swallow, not believing the good fortune that had just fallen into his hands. Because La wasn't that sexually aware, it took her a moment to realize this man wasn't talking about these girls serving Don with food, or drink. Suddenly, she realized he was talking about these girls serving Don some boom boom! (Boom boom was sex.)

La was instantly offended. She yelled "How dare you imply that my brothers would be interested in such things at their age! That's not what they're here for!" the man nervously said "But I just thought . . ." La yelled "Who told you to think!?" La's hand moved towards her ax handle, as she said "I am offen . . . !"

Dan interrupted La with "I'll handle this!" Dan looked from La to the man and said "Don't ever speak of such things around my sisters. If you have any questions about how, or what you want to impress me with, see my Warlord Bo. He will see me and I will decide whether to give audience to your suggestions. Now, show us where we can be seated and enjoy these festivities."

La gave Dan a peculiar look why he stopped her, but she didn't interfere. Dan thought that La telling this man that he and Don weren't interested in girls was going, too far. Whatever he and Don thought about women was none of La's concern!

As the man led the Ra to a sitting area that had the best view of the entire courtyard, Dan whispered to La "He was just trying to be helpful. You know mommy said the ones that are being helpful, we have to give a chance. There will be plenty of people to make examples of."

La didn't think she needed a lecture. She was already cooperating with Dan. Didn't he know that? La said "He'll get the chance to serve you, if that's what you want. If he offends me, just once more, I'll have his head!" Dan peeked at La and let it go. He knew La meant for him to keep this man as far away from her as possible.

Most all the people in the courtyard were standing and conversing. They were watching the Royal Ra, while trying to look like they weren't staring.

The Ra were given front row seats. The Ra children stood by their seats, but didn't sit down. They watched everyone in the courtyard. Shaya stood close to La, leaning on her shoulder. Danaaa was close, in front, and between them. La held Danaaa's ponytail, keeping her in check. La and Shaya, besides watching the crowd, had to keep an eye on Danaaa.

The Ra boys stood next to each other, just not as close as the girls did. Dan, Don and Yin had the task of keeping up with Ram. However, since he always got away from them, they didn't waste time putting much energy into stopping him.

Then, the drums started up with a strong, racy, beat. Danaaa jumped away from La, turning and facing her, all in one motion. La could see excitement written all over Danaaa's face. She let go of Danaaa's ponytail. La was going to let Danaaa have fun, as long as she didn't get out of control.

Danaaa knew La just like La knew Danaaa. Danaaa realized when La let go of her ponytail, she could do what she wanted. She also knew La trusted her not to get out of control. Danaaa was going to use everything within her to make sure that didn't happen.

No sooner than she jumped, turned and looked at La for a second, Danaaa started moving to the beat of the music. She had a big silly smile on her face, as she did so. Next to fighting, Danaaa loved to dance. As she danced in front of her two sisters, her eyes beckoned them to join her. La and Shaya loved to dance, just as much as Danaaa, so they couldn't resist joining her. All three girls took off their weapons belts and threw them on the ground near the Ra boys. La looked in their direction without looking directly at anyone in specific and said "Watch these for me."

Now the Ra girls were ready. As they walked towards Danaaa, Danaaa backed up making sure all three girls had enough room. The Ra girls would spend hours before bed dancing on their own, or either practicing a team routine for Dance Off competitions.

The Ra girls looked at each other and instantly they decided to do their best routine.

La looked over at the band for a second, motioning for a quicker beat. The bands of this day and time consisted of several drummers with many different sized drums, a man who would put two reeds up to his mouth, blowing through them, making a buzzing sound, somewhat softer than a horn. There was also a man who had a cowbell like instrument, in which he would beat real fast with two sticks. Last, but not least, you had several men chanting a guttural bass like chorus, just barely audible under the beats of the other instruments. Trust me, this was the music that got everyone, especially the females of all ages, pumped up with adrenaline.

Once the beat of the music quickened, all three girls settled into river-dance styled feet movements, while gyrating their hips, with a jump to it at every seventh or eighth step. That was followed by all three of them moving forward one step to their right, then back, doing the river dance-like step and hop, and then moving a step forward to their left, and then back, again. They repeated those movement to the beat so fast and accurate that everyone one in the courtyard was trying to get a better vantage points to see the artistic dance routine the Ra girls were putting on.

But, the Ra girls weren't done, yet. La and Shaya quickly moved closer to each other doing the same move, while in the same instant Danaaa who was in between them, launched herself straight up in the air, with her feet landing one foot on La's shoulder and the other on Shaya's shoulder. Danaaa proceeded, doing the same dance as her sisters, but now doing it, while standing on their shoulders. The Ra girls did these moves, effortlessly, not missing a beat.

Then, just as quickly as they'd done before, La and Shaya moved to the side, letting Danaaa fall back in place between them, while still doing the same dance step. As La and Shaya kept the dance movement going, Danaaa sprinted into a tumbling routine, cart wheeling and flipping across the courtyard. She stopped and then in the same sprinting tumbling routine, bolted back towards her sisters. Just as Danaaa reached them, she jumped, flipping straight up into the air. As she was flipping coming down, La and Shaya flipped one revolution backwards in sync with Danaaa. All three girls landed at the same time, leaning backwards and balancing themselves in a triangle at the shoulders. All three girls, now looking up towards the sky with their backs arched and balanced by each other's shoulders, raised both of the arms and hands towards the sky, while taking one step at a time to the left, moving slowly in a circular motion.

The movements were so precise that not only was the routine spectacular, it was damn near erotic. If it had not been for the fact that the Ra girls were so young, it would have been taken as just that. Still, by some, it was.

That last move his sisters were doing, and seeing how everyone was looking at them, especially the men, made Dan uncomfortable. He looked at the band and once he had their attention, motioned for them to stop the music.

Once the music stopped, the Ra girls stood up and saw a mesmerized crowd staring at them. There was a moment of silence, before the crowd erupted into a chorus of claps and favorable cheers. This went on for several moments. The Ra girls took it all in, smiling and waving to the crowd, turning and waving to even more cheering spectators.

The Ra girls made their way over to the Ra boys. They smiled and looked at Dan for some measure of appreciation for their performance. They got none. Dan just stared at La with a slight displeased look in his eyes.

La was confused by this. It wasn't even in her, or her sisters' minds that what they had just done might have been taken as sexual. They just came up with the best complicated set of dance movements that couldn't be beat by any other groups of girls. And they were right. There were no challenges to the Ra girls, even though there were many dance groups there. No one could, nor were they willing to try to compete with the routine they'd just seen. They would try to come up with something, just as spectacular to challenge the Ra girls, another day.

Therefore, La couldn't figure out the motives behind Dan's look. Right now, she didn't want to. She looked and didn't see Ram, or Yin. La turned back to Dan and asked in a less than normally arrogant voice "Where are they?"

Dan, with a hint of frustration in his voice said "How should I know where they went?" Shaya quickly looked at La to help her understand Dan's attitude. La and Danaaa just stared at Dan for a moment, until La said "What's wrong? What has happened that you would act this way?"

La looked from Dan to Don to see if he knew something. Don didn't know that it was Dan's brotherly protectiveness kicking in. Don's protectiveness only kicked in when he perceived trouble, or harm coming towards his sisters. Right now, he didn't see that.

Dan, while still looking displeased, said "We already have enough trouble around here, without you dancing like that!" Dan quickly turned from La, walked to his seat, looked at some servers and yelled "Get me some food and drink!"

La was floored by what Dan said. She tried to think of anything she'd done, while dancing, that would cause him to react like that. He'd seen her dance many times, like that, before and never reacted this way. She couldn't think of anything that was offensive. La picked up her weapons holster and quickly made her way over to Dan, followed by Shaya. La needed some clarification on this, right away!

Since La couldn't think of what she might have done, she said "What's wrong with you? We were only dancing! We do it all the time!" Dan didn't look at La when he calmly said "You do whatever you want. What do I care?"

La stared at Dan, now pissed off that he would make an issue out of something she was so proud about having just done. La didn't care about ruling protocol, or that she was in public. She was about to explode on Dan and give him a piece of her mind and a fight after that. That's when Shaya tapped La on her shoulder. La quickly turned and yelled "What!" Shaya looked La in her eyes. She then turned and pointed out onto the courtyard.

Earlier, when the Ra girls first started their routine, Ram slowly moved away from the other Ra. This time Dan saw Ram out of the corner of his eye. Dan sternly said "Where are you going?" Ram with both palms open shrugged his shoulders. Before Dan could say anything else to Ram, Yin said "I'll go with him and keep an eye on him."

Dan took his gaze off those creepy eyes of Ram, turned to Yin and said "Alright, but don't go too far." then he turned back and looked a quick warning to Ram. Ram and Yin walked off, while Dan and Don watched the crowd and their sisters.

Ram never really talked that much. Therefore, whenever the Ra children were around him, they'd have to hold the conversation for themselves, as well as Ram. Yin knew his cousin and the protocol when it came to dealing with Ram. As the two of them were walking, Yin looked over at Ram and said "I'm not here to watch you. I just said that so we could get away from Dan. I don't care where we go, or what we do." Those few short sentences told Ram all he needed to know, just as Yin intended.

Yin followed Ram through the crowd, knowing better than to ask, the always quiet Ram, where they were going. To Yin, half the fun of following Ram was finding out what Ram was up to. The other half was dealing with it, when they got there.

Since Ram's reputation was already notorious, with everyone, he was watched everywhere he went. Ram led Yin to a building right at the edge of the courtyard where the cooks were bringing the food. Ram pointed up at a sturdy awning that overhung the entrance of that building. Ram had a devilish smile on his face, before climbing onto the awning. Yin followed, climbing up, also.

Once they sat down, Yin could see they had a perfect vantage point overlooking the entire courtyard. They could see everything and was close enough to get back to the other Ra, if there was trouble. Yin looked at Ram for a second, in wonderment, at how he knew this place even existed. That wonderment only lasted a few seconds. Yin turned and watched all the happenings going on all over the courtyard. Now Yin was watching the crowd with his cousin, the predator Ram.

When La looked to where Shaya was pointing, she saw Danaaa in the middle of the courtyard. She had her weapons belt back around her waist. La watched as Danaaa took her axes out of their holsters, got down on her knees and put them on the ground in front of her. La knew Baby was about to put on a show, in which she would amaze everyone, by swinging her axes really fast. However, since La never saw Baby start a show this way, La momentarily forgot about what she was going to say, or do to Dan. She was stuck, looking at Baby, wondering what she was going to do next.

When the Ra girls walked over, after finishing the best dance routine they'd ever done, so far, Danaaa stared at Dan not understanding the change in his attitude. Because she didn't understand many things, Danaaa wasn't going to waste time on that. She was still high on the attention she and her sisters received from their performance. Danaaa knew she could do even better than that. She looked at La and Shaya and knew that Dan had dragged them into something they couldn't get away from, right now.

Danaaa was determined that Dan wasn't going to trap her and take away her happiness, as he'd done to La and Shaya. Danaaa decided she was going to put on another show. She was going to put on the best show ever!

Danaaa was now on her knees, looking down at her axes, which were on the ground in front of her. With her knees spread apart, Danaaa extended her arms out over her axes. She then started slowly lowering and raising her open hands, palms facing down, over her axes, as if she was trying to raise them, without touching them. Danaaa's movements were slow and deliberate. It looked like she was moving to a beat that no one could hear but her.

The drummers picked up on the slow cadence of her movements and started a slow drumbeat in rhythm with Danaaa's movements. The crowd was now as mesmerized, with Danaaa's movements, as they were earlier with the routine all three Ra girls had performed.

When Danaaa heard the drum beat start, she stepped up her movements by raising and lowering her torso, in conjunction with the raising and lowering of her arms and hands over her axes. Then, to the amazement of the crowd, Danaaa incorporated lifting herself up off her knees, almost on her toes, then back down again, slowly arching her back, while still doing all of the previous movements.

La was snapped out of her amazement by how provocatively Danaaa was moving. La scanned the crowd and could see how all the males were looking at her eight-year-old sister. La looked at Dan to see if he saw what she saw. She just saw him looking at Danaaa like he was enjoying another one of her stupid shows.

Dan saw La looking at him out of the corner of his eye. He didn't have time for that, now. Dan didn't see Danaaa in the same light as he saw La and Shaya. La and Shaya were young teenagers with developing breast and ass-sets to match. That made Dan protective of them when he saw other males looking at those two.

But Danaaa was undeveloped and had the muscular body of a boy. There was nothing feminine about Danaaa, except for her pretty face. Males weren't looking at Danaaa's body, they were avoiding her so as not to have to fight her, because of her aggressive attitude. Dan was just enjoying another stupid show being put on by youngest sister, who he referred to as, Stupid.

La was pissed that Dan wasn't treating Danaaa as he'd treated her, earlier. La had had enough of this. She stepped forward to go and stop Danaaa. That's when Shaya stepped to La and put her hand gently, but firmly on La's shoulder, stopping her. La looked at Shaya, who had a smile on her face that said Danaaa was just putting on a show like the ones she always did. La only looked at Shaya for a moment, before looking back at Danaaa. If Danaaa got any more provocative than she was now, La was going to put an end to Danaaa's stupid show.

After rising up off her knees and lowering herself back down on them a couple more times, Danaaa saw La jump up out of the corner of her eye. Danaaa knew she had the crowd hanging on her every move, but didn't want La to interfere with her show. So Danaaa raised herself once more and this time she stood up and slowly started walking in a circle around her axes, dragging each foot slowly and rhythmically as she walked.

Ram and Yin were still sitting on the awning. Danaaa's movements enthralled Yin. He'd never seen Danaaa move like this. Yin was so wrapped up in Danaaa's show that he couldn't see anything, besides her.

On the other hand, Ram was watching the crowd. The predator in Ram told him that with everyone watching Danaaa, this would be the perfect time for someone to kill someone and get away with it, if they wanted to. Ram searched the crowd and made scenarios how he would kill certain individuals in the crowd and not get caught. From time to time, he would look at Danaaa and his other siblings, just to see what they were doing.

After slowly walking around her axes for three revolutions, Danaaa jumped straight up into a flip. She came down hands first grabbing her axe handles that were on the ground and then going into a tuck and roll movement, coming up to a standing position in which she was swinging her axes, really fast!

Danaaa was swinging her axes fast around her body, while she walked to the slow beat of the drums. The crowd moved back and to the sides, out of her way, with eyes fixated on Danaaa. Danaaa quickly put her axes back in their holsters, then after one step she pulled them out, twirled them one super-fast revolution and put them back, before she took her next step. She repeated that same movement, this time twirling them two revolutions before putting them back in their holsters, then twirling them three, then four time, putting them back in their holsters, each time before taking her next step. The crowd was so amazed by what they were seeing that the only sound you could hear was the low whirling sound of Danaaa's axes as they sliced through air.

After astounding the crowd by drawing and twirling her axes four revolutions and putting them back between steps, Danaaa left her axes in their holsters, still slow walking, dragging her feet as she walked to the slow beat of the drums. Her hands were at a quick draw position, next to her axes. Everyone watched in anticipation of what Danaaa would do next.

Now Danaaa was almost drunk, high on the attentive energy the crowd was giving her. This show wasn't over, yet. Danaaa had more to show this crowd. Still moving to the slow beat of the drums, Danaaa waltzed right up to a table that seated six large, not so friendly looking Hayee men, armed with Hammer-Axes.

They watched Danaaa closely as she smiled at them, while making her way to their table. When Danaaa got to the table, she put an even sillier smile on her face, as she bent down, lowering her head just under the table, then jumping up to where her eyes were looking over the tabletop at these men. She then slowly lowered her head under the table again, before popping up with just her eyes looking over the tabletop at these men, again.

Just as she slowly lowered her head for the third time, the two men closest to Danaaa, at the table, sent their axes flying in the direction in which they anticipated Danaaa's head to reappear.

The crowd, as well as the men at the table, was surprised to see one of the men who had swung his axes at Danaaa, falling over towards the ground as Danaaa's axes were, with swift precision, slicing him on his way to the ground. The other men at the table quickly stood up and smashed the table with their axes, in order to get a better line on their target. Danaaa had just avoided being sliced in half by the other Hayee who first swung his axe at her. As she was just being attacked by the other four men, one of the men closest to Danaaa had his neck split, nearly from one side to the other, courtesy of Ram flying through the air past him.

Once Ram saw that Danaaa was being attack, he took a running jump from the awning and struck the Hayee closest to Danaaa, with his axe. Yin snapped out of his daze and followed closely behind Ram. As soon as Shaya and Don got within striking range, Hammers started flying at the men that were left. Don's Hammer throws were good enough that they had to be blocked, or dodged by those Hayee. Shaya was so astoundingly fast and accurate that she hit every one of the men she threw her Hammers at. The Ra children made short work of the six Hayee so fast that no one in the crowd had a chance to help these Hayee.

Bo, Hoban and Ali suddenly appeared out of nowhere, roughly tying up five of the six Hayee. All of the attacking Hayee men survived, except for the one who got his neck sliced open by Ram. Although, the Hayee that Danaaa sliced up was badly injured, he would survive his wounds. La ordered these men be put in the dungeon and heavily guarded.

The Hammer-Axe Six went to the dungeon the next day, after training. Dan and La did a short interrogation of the five remaining Hayee. None of them said a word. It didn't matter. The Ra children already knew that these men were from Hayee, Benobu's clan because of their striking resemblance to that part of the Hayee family.

La had four of them beheaded, leaving the one Danaaa had badly wounded to go back and tell what happened. La left this Hayee alive because she knew he would be no more than a cripple, incapable of ever fighting again. La sent him back with the four heads of his comrades and a message to Benobu that if assassins continued to harass the Ra, she was going to hold him accountable. La and Dan also sent messengers telling the Hellcats what they'd done and why.

It was very important that Dan and La give very clear explanations on any drastic actions that the Hellcats would surely hear about. Dan and La had a strong fear of being called back home and branded as not being able to control their territory, according to protocol. If the Hellcats thought that the Ra children were purposely mistreating Ramala's subjects, or not ruling according to protocol, that's exactly what would happen. Although, La was doing whatever she wanted, she always sent messengers with a good explanation of why she did it.

CHAPTER 7

La had very little tolerance for others now that Ramala wasn't around every day reinforcing that she should be. One of the reasons the Ra children were being treated with more respect, than the last time they were here, was because of the threat of being beheaded on orders from La.

La was very intolerant of what she considered disrespectful behavior and she was getting worse as time went on. If she was in a good mood, you at the very least had to be very respectful around her. If La was in a foul mood, someone was going to be blamed for something, whether they were guilty, or not.

La's Special Guard and her Bodyguards learned not to hesitate when La ordered punishment for disrespect. Dan, Shaya and sometimes Tania were the only ones who could dissuade La from dishing out cruel punishment. La was very unforgiving of everyone here. La was still upset over the beatings she and her siblings had taken here, when they were younger.

In the first month that she was here, La had ten guard and six local men beheaded. Now everyone was on their best behavior. No guards from this House ever questioned her when she came somewhere, unannounced. They just moved out of the way, while sending someone to announce she was there.

La was also bothered that assassins were sent to do her and her siblings harm. La had a lot of plans and didn't need the distraction of assassins harassing her.

La had a meeting with Dan to discuss what could be done. They'd already sent Benobu a warning with the heads of his assassins. It was time to send warnings to everyone else that would stop them from sending assassins.

Dan and La thought of the best plan to deal with this problem. They decided to send Danaaa to tell the members of Yee and Wa provinces not to send assassins. And any request from the young King of Ra and the Number One Princess should be done, without pause. Dan suggested they take a few Shinmushee heads and drop them off on each visit. Dan told La he was sure that would make a strong point to everyone. La smiled deviously at Dan and said they should send Ram with Danaaa. She was sure he could help. Dan nodded in agreement.

La and Dan told Danaaa and Ram their mission. They gave them food, water, cookies and blood for the journey. Ram and Danaaa were told to resupply at Ra checkpoints along the way. Ram barely paid attention, while Danaaa listened intently. Danaaa was all about completing every mission, successfully.

Shaya nervously fussed over Danaaa's clothes and weapons. Shaya made sure everything was in place. Shaya turned and looked at La and Dan. With concern in her voice, Shaya said "I'm not sure about this! What if something happens to Baby?"

Dan gave Shaya a reassuring look and said "You know what she did to Benobu's guards and his assassins. Don't worry, she can handle herself." Dan turned and looked at Danaaa. He said "Isn't that right, Stupid?" Danaaa quickly nodded her head in agreement. Dan turned back to Shaya. Shaya smiled nervously, still concerned about Danaaa.

The rest of the Hammer-Axe Six watched as Ram and Danaaa boarded the elephant they would be traveling on. La and Dan were just under fourteen years of age. They had no idea the danger they were putting Ram and Danaaa in. All they knew was that Ram and Danaaa were killing machines. They were going to get as much use out of them as possible.

There were three plat formed elephants in the small caravan. Two elephants carried four Elite guards each. Ram and Danaaa sat on a platform on the elephant's back, along with two Elite guards. One Elite guard guided the elephant, while the other scouted the area ahead. After traveling a short while, Ram pulled his sack of cookies from his vest pocket. Danaaa watched closely as Ram start gobbling down cookies. Danaaa said "We're supposed to wait and eat them, later, when we get hungry!" Ram paused long enough to smile at Danaaa. He quickly went back to eating cookies.

Danaaa stared angrily at Ram. La specifically told them to save their cookies and only eat them when they needed to. Danaaa angrily grabbed her sack of cookies. Ram was forcing her to break the protocol that La set forth. Ram watched as Danaaa moved the cookie towards her mouth. When Danaaa saw Ram looking at her, she angrily said "What are we going to do when all our cookies are gone?!"

Ram shrugged his shoulders and grabbed another cookie. Danaaa was disgusted with Ram. It was like he didn't care! Danaaa angrily stuffed a cookie into her mouth. After chewing on the cookie several times, Danaaa began to make a low yummy moaning sound. She stuffed another cookie into her mouth and then one after another. She stared into Ram's eyes, thinking he somehow tricked her into eating her cookies when she didn't want to.

Ram and Danaaa didn't stop, until all of their cookies were gone. Danaaa angrily said "All of our cookies are gone! Now, what are we going to do?" Ram reached for his container of blood and started drinking from it. Danaaa was appalled. She grabbed her container and drank, also. They both drank until they could drink no more. Ram put away his container and fell back on the floor of the platform, looking up at the sky.

Danaaa put away her container and then got on her back like Ram. They both looked up at the power blue sky, which had a few puffy clouds slowly passing by. Ram said "A tree." Danaaa looked over at Ram and saw he was looking up at the sky. Danaaa looked up and she saw a cloud that looked like a tree. She looked at another cloud. Danaaa said "Rhino!" because that's what that cloud looked like to her.

Ram and Danaaa played the cloud game, until Danaaa fell asleep. When Ram saw that Danaaa was sleep, he pulled her ruling cape over her head to shield her from the sun. He'd seen Dan do that to his sisters on many occasions. Ram pulled his cape over his head and fell asleep after that.

A few hours into the journey the caravan stopped. The Ra twins were awakened by that. Ram and Danaaa stood up and looked around. They could see a large group of Shinmushee warriors off in the distance. The Elite guard with them said "When they pass, we'll continue." Danaaa looked at the guard and said "Wait here! Watch the food and water, until we get back!"

The Shinmushee warriors, that the Ra caravan spotted, were a group of attack scouts. The roamed the plains looking for small groups of Ra guards they could capture, torture and kill. They would avoid the larger groups of Ra guards and report the position of the Ra guards to their superiors.

The Shinmushee attack scouts spotted the small Ra caravan, before the Ra guards spotted them. Several of the Shinmushee warriors stealthily hid behind bushes and trees, making their way towards the Ra caravan from different angles. The first Shinmushee warriors to get to the Ra caravan would attack, while the others moved in from all sides, trapping them.

As Ram and Danaaa were walking towards the main group of Shinmushee guards they heard and smelled the Shinmushee guards sneaking closer to where they were. Ram and Danaaa looked at each other, acknowledging what they both realized. In his deep bellowing bass voice, Ram said "You go!" Danaaa only looked at Ram for a second longer, before she started walking forward. Ram disappeared behind some bushes, heading towards the Shinmushee scouts.

Danaaa walked quickly, until she got to the Shinmushee scouts. They watched her as she stopped a short, but safe distance from them. All of them stared at Danaaa, examining her closely. Before any of them spoke, Danaaa raised her hand with her fingers extended towards the Shinmushee. She then said "I need this many of your heads to take with me! If you can't decide who, I'll choose myself!"

Several of the Shinmushee laughed. One of the ones who didn't said "Normally, I don't kill little girls. I'm going to make an exception in your case!" Danaaa said "I'll start with your head! I can swing an ax real fast! I Chop I!"

Several Shinmushee warriors moved towards Danaaa. The one who spoke put up his hand stopping them. He sneered at Danaaa and said "I'll handle this Shit faced Ra brat!" Danaaa had been called a brat before. That didn't bother her. But for this Shinmushee to think her face looked like it had shit on it was too much to take! Danaaa was offended!

The Shinmushee warrior walked towards Danaaa, measuring her with his axes. When he was in range, he attacked. Danaaa carved up that Shinmushee within three swings of his axes. All of the Shinmushee warriors were shocked, silently staring at this young girl in astonishment and disbelief. That is, until she looked at them and said "But, I already told you! I can swing an ax real fast!"

Then came horrific screams from the distance. It sounded like their Shinmushee brothers were being slaughtered. Danaaa said "My brother can swing an ax fast, too!" Right after Danaaa said that, all of these Shinmushee warriors attacked her with everything they had. This day, it wasn't enough. Danaaa carved up thirty-one Shinmushee warriors inside of ten minutes. Ram killed the other nine that were going to attack the caravan.

Ram walked to where Danaaa was and started removing heads from the dead bodies, just as Danaaa finished off the last warrior. Ran was already dragging the heads, by their hair, which he'd already removed. Danaaa turned and saw Ram. She said "That's more than enough! Let's go!"

Ram turned and gave Danaaa a sinister stare. Although being twins, Ram was the oldest. Ram would do what La and Dan told him, but he wasn't going to be told what to do by his younger sister. Ram turned from Danaaa and continued removing heads. Danaaa put her hands on her hips in protest and watched as Ram removed all of the heads from the bodies. When Ram was done, Danaaa yelled "Are you satisfied?!!" Ram only looked at Danaaa for a moment, before walking towards their caravan, dragging the heads with him.

Ram and Danaaa delivered half the head to the Warlords in Wa province and half to the Warlords Han and Chi in Yee province. Danaaa couldn't remember what La told her to tell the Warlords when they delivered the heads. So with the always quiet Ram at her side, Danaaa made up something close. In her normally loud and harsh voice, she said to the Warlords "These Shitmushee heads are a gift from the Number One Princess! Do what she says, or I'll be dragging your heads back to Lar! I mean La!"

All the Warlords got the message loud and clear. They fed the two Ra twins, gave them food, cookies, blood and water for their journey. The Warlords also sent messengers to La giving their support.

While Ram and Danaaa waited on their caravan to be resupplied, they were watched closely by Chi and his spies. The young Ra twins ran around the courtyard and played with the other children here. Chi saw that when Ram and Danaaa were eating cookies, they seemed to be less focused on their surroundings. So much so that one of the boys that Danaaa had roughed up earlier was able to sneak up on her and hit her with his toy ax. Danaaa barely paid attention to him, as she continued to eat cookies. Chi, always looking for an advantage, placed that in his memory. Other than that, Chi noticed when these two weren't killing, they mostly acted like children their age. After that, the young Ra twins' caravan quickly made it back to the Lower house of Ra.

When Ram and Danaaa made it back, La had Danaaa tell everything that happened. Dan, La and Shaya got a good picture thanks to Danaaa. Danaaa made sure she told La that Ram didn't listen to her and did whatever he wanted. La and Dan didn't care about that. They smiled deviously at each other, knowing they had two special weapons they could use at will.

The next day the Hammer-Axe Six were having breakfast when guards told them their Special Guard were back and had successfully completed their mission. La and Dan hadn't told the other Royal children what the mission was that they sent the Special Guard on. La ordered the Special guard to come to her. When the Special guard walked in, they carried a terrified

Urianna, all tied up, with them. They put her down standing up in front of the Ra. This shocked the Ra that they didn't know about it. None more than Ram.

La and Dan smiled deviously at each other that their plan had worked. La turned and looked at Anne and said "Did you think I would sit idly by and let you spout lies about my brother?" La paused, but really wasn't looking for an answer. She looked at Anne as if she was insignificant and then said "I just wanted to see the look on your face, before my henchman takes your head!"

Ram immediately stood up and walked over to Anne. The Special Guards standing next to Anne moved a step back from her when Ram put his hands in a draw position next to his axes. Ram looked into Anne's eyes as he drew his ax, spun it one super-fast revolution, slicing down through the ropes that wrapped around Anne's body. The next spin of Ram's ax, just as fast as the first, sliced through the rope tied around her wrist.

La yelled to Ram in a slow angry voice "What are you doing!?!" Ram bellowed "Touch her and I start chopping!"

A whole sentence from the Ra who rarely talked, made everyone, including La, pause for a second. After that second La stood up and said, while staring at Anne "We'll see about that! Guards!"

Dan interrupted, ordering "Hold it!" The guards stopped in their tracks, waiting on words from Dan, the Warlord in charge. Dan calmly said "No one touches this girl on orders from me." La angrily turned to Dan and yelled "WHAT?!"

Dan looked at La with a reassuring smile and said "Don't worry about her. Can't you see he's protective of her? We'll keep her here. When he tires of her, you can take her head. Until then, she has favor with me."

La wanted to say something, but didn't. Dan had more rank than she did in this matter. There wasn't anything La could do. La gave Anne a sinister look and said "Alright, we'll do it your way." La waved off the guards, who were relieved that they wouldn't have to go against Ram, knowing the other Ra would take his side in battle.

Anne stood there, not knowing what to do. She was still terrified, knowing that the look she got from La meant that it was only a matter of time, before she was eventually killed.

Ram stood there staring at La. He'd seen the look she gave Anne, before. Ram didn't know whether La was trying to get him to lower his guard so she could kill Anne, or not. So, Ram just stood there, on guard against attack.

Dan smiled at Ram and said "Tania, take this girl and get her cleaned up. She is to be treated as if she is one of my sisters. Teach her, her position according to the protocol I've just set forth. Remember, don't mistreat my youngest sister."

Everyone in the room was shocked at Dan's words. Now, La was fuming. Was Dan purposely trying to make her look like a fool? La couldn't figure out why he was doing this. So now, seething with anger, La's eyes slowly moved from Anne to Tania. La stared at Tania liked if she took one step, she was dead. Tania saw La and didn't move. La's eyes slowly moved back to Anne, wondering what Dan and Ram would do if she killed Anne right here and now.

Dan could see La was furious to the point of action. Dan put his arm gently, but firmly around La's shoulders, whispering in her ear, that only she would hear "Look at Ram, who would kill for you at a moment's notice. Now he stands ready to do what he has to, to defend this girl, against you. You know you're not your smartest when you get angry. That's why I'm here. Now stop being angry, so you can be smart enough to see that you're still in charge and you'll still get to do what you want to her, eventually. So start cooperating!"

La was angry and didn't want to cooperate. Still, she knew she could wait, until Dan and Ram weren't around and kill this girl. What could they do after it was done? They would only stay angry with her for so long. After all, she was their sister.

La looked away from Anne, forced a cooperative smile, on her face, that was half crooked with bitterness and looked at Tania. That let Tania know it was alright to do what Dan ordered. Tania moved, quickly. She hustled Anne out of the room and down the hall. Once Tania got Anne out of the building, she began to talk to Anne.

Tania told Anne that even though Dan had given her favor and no one would dare harm her, La was going to have her killed the first chance she got. Anne looked up at Tania with fear in her eyes and said "What should I do?" Tania gave Anne a serious look and said "Exactly what I tell you to."

Right now Anne was in a bad position and didn't have a plan of her own. If Tania was willing to help her, she would do whatever it took to stay alive. Anne was going to do what Tania told her, until she could think of something, better.

Anne's mind went back to when she saw Ram coming at her. When he sliced the ropes from around her and stood at her side, although she was still terrified, she somehow knew she was safe. Anne was glad Ram was there, otherwise she thought she would have been killed. Tania was still talking and noticed that Anne had zoned out. Tania yelled Anne's name and that brought Anne back to the seriousness of the situation.

Dan later came to Tania and told her that he was holding her responsible for Anne's safety and training. Dan told Tania to use whatever resources available to make this girl presentable to La. Tania knew the only way to keep Anne alive was to keep her out of La's sight. Therefore, that's what Tania did.

Tania put Anne on a strict training schedule that kept her out of the Ra's sight. The first thing Tania taught Anne was to do her best, learning, to get La to accept her. Secondly, she told Anne that she had to keep Ram's attention. If Ram lost interest in her, La would have her killed soon after that. Anne didn't know how to do either, but Tania told her she would teach her.

When Ram wasn't busy, he would spy on Anne to see if she was being treated well. Sometimes Anne would see him, sometimes she wouldn't. Once Ram was satisfied that Anne was all right, he went back to whatever else he was doing. Other than that, Ram didn't show much interest in Anne. Ram's lack of interest made Tania worried that Anne wouldn't live for much longer.

Tania wanted Anne to live, because besides being an adviser to La, Tania knew if she controlled Anne and could get Anne to control Ram, that would give her power and leverage with the Ra. Tania and everyone else knew that it would only be a matter of time before the young Ra ruled all of the House of Ra. Tania was a Hayee and had ambitions of having power. So, it was important to her for this girl to stay alive, for now.

After delicate negotiations with Dan and La, Tania got permission to have Elder females supervise meetings between Ram and Anne. These meetings consisted of the two of them having a snack together and sitting for a short while. This was to see how the two reacted around each other. The older women watched and took mental notes.

Ram never said a word. He would sit and eat his snacks, which usually consisted of cookies. After he was done eating, Ram would watch the older women, who were watching him. He would only look at Anne from time to time, just to see what she was doing.

Anne would eat her cookies and watch Ram. She never said a word, because Ram didn't. She felt awkward in this setting. Anne noticed two things about Ram, right away. One was that he didn't say much, if anything. The other was he really liked cookies, by the way he ate them. Anne liked cookies, but they weren't that big a deal. Ram would always eat all of his cookies before Anne was done with hers. Then he would watch Anne eat hers. After she ate her cookies, Ram didn't pay much attention to Anne.

Anne, like most girls, after watching a man, will learn him. Anne picked up on Ram's tendencies. After the third meeting, in which Ram finished his cookies and was watching Anne eat hers, Anne extended her hand, giving Ram her last cookie. Ram almost snatched the cookie out of Anne's hand and shoved it into his mouth. Anne stared at Ram as he did so. When Ram finished that cookie, he smiled at Anne, until he noticed the older women looking at him. Ram took the smile off his face, while looking at the women. When he turned and looked back at Anne, she was smiling at him.

Anne was smiling at Ram because that was the first time she'd seen him smile. Even though Ram had his usual stone look on his face, Anne was happy she was able to make him smile.

Anne said "You like cookies, a lot, don't you?" Ram nodded his head in agreement. Anne said "You don't talk much, either. Why is that?" Ram raised both his hands, palms up and shrugged his shoulders. Anne smiled as she said "That's okay, sometimes I don't like to talk, either, but sometimes I do. You don't mind if I talk, sometimes, do you?" Again, Ram shrugged his shoulders. Anne took that as yes, you can talk anytime you like. So that's what she did.

It was a month, before Tania brought Anne around La. The Ra girls watched Anne, closely. La watched for any little thing she could consider disrespectful that would allow her to supersede Dan's orders not to harm Anne. However, Anne played her role perfectly. Anne showed the utmost respect for all of the Ra, especially La. La could see that Tania had done a great job training Anne in protocol. Still, that didn't matter to La. La was going to play nice, until Ram tired of Anne. Once that happen, Anne was dead. That's what La agreed to and she was sticking to that plan.

Benobu and his cousins didn't like that La killed his assassins, sending their heads back to him. In addition, although the Hellcats didn't say a word to Benobu about it, they knew he'd sent the assassins. Ramala told both her cousins that the Ra were a more powerful fighting force than her original Butchers. It was just that people didn't know it, yet. Ramala told her cousins that soon enough, everyone would find out that you don't attack the Ra.

However, the Hayee, Benobu and his clan hadn't figured that out, so they sent seven more hardened assassins. Even though they didn't like La and the other Ra, the main goal was to kill Danaaa for what she'd done.

The plan went like this. Information was given to the seven assassins from members of the first Lower House, who also wanted the Ra dead. They will remain nameless, for now. The assassins were told the time of day that Danaaa was usually alone training, while the other Ra were exploring different areas of the city.

La and Dan made Danaaa train longer so she wouldn't give them as much trouble. They would let her join them after her extra two hours a day of training. The assassins also figured she would be tired, spent from her all day training routine and probably her most vulnerable. They had heard the many stories about this young girl and her reputation for killing. Although, not afraid to face her in a fair fight, that wasn't their goal. Their mission was to kill her. The best chance to succeed and to get out of the Lower House alive was to catch her at her weakest. That was the plan.

The night before the attempt on Danaaa's life, the seven assassins were camped out in the thick brush close to the first Lower House. They were having dinner, going over their plans. They were going to leave at daybreak and enter the city while all the Ra were in training. They would hold up in a house that was close to where Danaaa's late training session was. Every day, after that training session, Danaaa would go to the main compound of the Ra and clean herself. The Ra girls would always meet her shortly after she was cleaned up. The assassins were going to kill Danaaa the second she walked out of that training session.

They all agreed the plan was perfect. Then they heard the snap of someone stepping lightly on a branch. They all jumped to attention, grabbing their weapons. That's when they saw Danaaa entering the light of the fire they had going. The assassins saw a young girl with nightclothes on. They also saw that she had a weapons holster around her waist with two Hammer-Axes in it.

One of the assassins said "Who in the hell are you?!" Danaaa yelled "I'm the bad girl! You know the one you're looking for!"

One of the assassins, who knew what Danaaa looked like, said, "It's her! That's the Ra, Danaaa!" All of the men moved slowly and cautiously, spreading out, while keeping their eyes on Danaaa. Another assassin, who'd never seen Danaaa, said, "So you're that degenerate heathen they call Danaaa."

Danaaa's face was serious when she yelled, "It's Dan Jinn-Eco!" All of the men stared at Danaaa. One of them said "Alright Danaaa Jenny-Co, where's the other Ra?" as the rest of them looked around the perimeter of their camp.

Danaaa stood on guard. Her hands were in a draw position next to her axes. The men moved, cautiously, closer to her. Danaaa quickly drew her axes, putting one down at her side, just behind her, while bringing the other ax in front of her, just below eye level, with the blade pointing out at the assassins.

Danaaa answered, yelling "But, I don't need the Ra to deal with you, you worthless, less than ant shit, humans! Why do you think she came here all by herself!?! It was because she didn't want to bring shame upon your families for what's about to happen here! It's best that all of you suffer this humiliation in private, where no one can see! I can swing an axe real fast! I Chop I!"

The only reason Danaaa got to say that much was because the assassins were shocked that this young girl, by herself, would have the nerve to talk to them this way and think she'd live. Now, they were over that. It was time to kill this smart mouthed brat.

Danaaa was surrounded. Two of the assassins attacked her, one in front and one from behind Danaaa. Danaaa watched the axes coming at her. It looked like the axes and everything around her was moving in slow motion. Danaaa thought that if they were going to move this slowly, they'd never hit her. Danaaa decided she wasn't going to move slowly like everyone else. Instead, she was going to move as fast as she could, while swinging her axes.

Danaaa moved herself out of harm's way, just before the axes got to her. Then she saw two spears coming at her. The spears were flying through the air just as slow as everything else was moving. They seemed to take forever to get to her, before she changed their trajectory with the flat side of her blade, sending the spears through the chest of two of the assassins. To Danaaa, it seemed the assassin weren't even trying that hard to kill her. Didn't they know she was for real, even if they weren't?

After that, all of the assassins attacked Danaaa at once. The precision, in which these assassins normally swung their axes, always hitting their mark, wasn't good enough this night. It seemed to them that the young girl was miraculously moving, effortlessly, just out of the way of each one of their strikes. It seemed that every time they missed, one of them was severely sliced by one of her axes.

It was a fierce fight with these assassins swinging furiously at Danaaa with their axes. They gave everything they had, until they fell mortally wounded by Danaaa's axes. Danaaa sliced open the last assassin, who was struggling, trying to get up, so he could have one more chance to kill her. Danaaa looked at him from a safe enough distance, twirling her axes one super-fast revolution and then slamming them back into their holsters. Danaaa yelled at him "But, I already told you! I can swing an axe real fast! I Chop I!" Then, she walked away, disappearing into the darkness, just past the campfire light. That last assassin fell over, dead, right after Danaaa disappeared into the darkness.

On the way back, Danaaa thought about what happened earlier, this day. She'd slept most of the day, in between and after training sessions. La made everyone let Danaaa sleep, because it meant less trouble from her.

That night, when La and Shaya were asleep, a voice inside Danaaa's head, which she perceived to be her own, strongly suggested she sneak out of bed. Danaaa tried to ignore the voice, by trying to get some sleep. That wasn't working because she'd slept most of the day.

Finally, Danaaa gave in. She slowly and quietly maneuvered herself from in between her sisters. Once she'd done that, Danaaa got her weapons and made her way down the hallway. She saw Ali with the most trusted Ra guards, outside. Danaaa marched up to Ali and motioned for him to come, closer. Danaaa said in her whispering voice to Ali, "I have to go and deal with some enemies of the Ra. Keep your guards here and protect them. Follow me not, for there will be no witnesses to what I will do. If you, or any of your guards, follow me, for them, it will be the wrong place, wrong time. If the Ra awaken and ask if you saw Danaaa, say, not, that you saw her."

Ali was baffled by the way Danaaa was talking, but understood what she meant. Because Danaaa could be big trouble if she wanted, Ali cooperated.

Even stranger to Danaaa was the fact that she was telling herself where to go, even though she didn't know where she was going. Danaaa listened to herself, because most of the time she listened to her older sibling and did what they said. Danaaa thought it was about time she was finally telling herself something to do, even though she didn't know where it would lead.

When Danaaa got to the camp of the would-be assassins, her instincts told her, right away, these men were dangerous. That's when the other voice inside Danaaa's head, which she identified as Jinn Eco, told Danaaa to follow its direction exactly and she would leave here, without a scratch.

Danaaa agreed she would and as soon as she did, a strange feeling came over Danaaa. Everything started moving in slow motion and Jinn Eco used Danaaa's mouth to talk. Danaaa thought what Jinn Eco said was very funny and she wanted to laugh, but couldn't. It was as if she was in a dream, watching what was going on.

Danaaa had to concentrate very hard just to follow the commands of the Jinn Eco as she was being attacked. Even though everything was moving at its regular speed, Jinn Eco moved Danaaa's awareness right between the realm of the spirit world and the present. Since spirits live in the past, present and future, it seemed to Danaaa that everything was moving in slow motion. So, even though she was in a dream like state, Danaaa was coherent enough to execute orders to the letter. Danaaa was always all about executing the mission, no matter what it was.

After all the assassins were dead, or dying, Danaaa walked back the way she came. She noticed Jinn Eco was gone, but even though Danaaa didn't remember the way she came, she knew which way to go. All of this seemed strange to Danaaa. The only sense she could make out of it, was that she was lucky to find those assassins, who were clearly going to try and do harm to her siblings.

As Danaaa was walking and thinking to herself, she was oblivious to her surroundings. It was the dead of night and every predator was out on their nightly prowl. Not one of them came near Danaaa. That's because the spirit of the Jinn Eco was with Danaaa.

Jinn Eco Jin is a supremely powerful Jinn under the command of the Ruler of all Jinns, Be-Est, or Best the Jinn. Between Heaven and Hell is where Best the Jinn rules. So Danaaa couldn't be harmed with Jinn Eco's protection. Jinn is unbeatable.

Best a Jinn?

Be it, How?

It's the Jinn Eco Jin!

Best here and Best beyond!

Danaaa got back just as La and Shaya came running out of the building looking for her. They were shocked to see her axes bloody, with small shreds of flesh glued to them, by the drying blood. They could see blood splatters all over Danaaa's nightclothes. Shaya and La ran up to Danaaa, checking her body to see if she was wounded. As they stared in horror, they slowly came to the realization that Danaaa was unharmed. Shaya looked at La with relief in her eyes and voice, when she said excitedly "She's unharmed!"

Now, La was a little angry and upset that Danaaa had snuck out without herself, or Shaya realizing it, even though Danaaa was resting between them.

La yelled "Don't you know how dangerous it is, going out by yourself at night? Where were you!?"

Danaaa took a deep breath, stared La in her eyes and yelled, "I had to kill some assassins, who were probably going to try to kill you! Now help me get cleaned up so I can get some sleep! I'mmmmm tired!!"

La didn't like when Baby yelled at her from close range and it showed on her face. Shaya jumped between La and Danaaa, facing Danaaa. Shaya lightly scolded Danaaa, saying, "You know me and La worry when we can't find you! You shouldn't have gone out by yourself!"

Shaya loosened the weapons holster from around Danaaa's waist and let it drop to the ground at Danaaa's feet. She grabbed Danaaa by her shoulders and said, "Come, let's get you cleaned up so you can get some rest."

Shaya then turned, with her face now serious, to the guards and ordered, "Get her axes cleaned and sharpened, first thing, when day comes! I expect she should have them back before first day's meal is over!"

The guards got down on their knees and waited for the Ra girls to get far enough away from Danaaa's axes to approach and get them. Shaya turned and gave La a look like La should have done what she did, instead of getting angry with Danaaa. Then Shaya smiled at La. With her arm around Danaaa's shoulder, Shaya reached for La's arm and pulled her close. La didn't resist and all three girls walked inside. Shaya excitedly said to Danaaa "Now tell us everything that happened and don't leave out any details!"

More than a dozen more groups of assassins were sent to kill Danaaa in the next two months. These were some of the best killers the Hayee could come up with. None of them succeeded. Danaaa would meet them before they got inside the First Lower House of Ra and viciously slaughter them, with the help of Jinn-Eco.

That's when Danaaa earned the title of High Pressure, the Executioner of Assassins. That name was shortened to just High Pressure the Executioner, the same name Dan and La made up for her. Now, no one was that eager to challenge the Executioner, High Pressure, or Jenny Co, as Danaaa was also called.

Ram, who was instructed by the voice in his head, Eco Jin, the other half of the Jinn Eco Jin, to stalk and assassinate ring leaders that plotted to harm the Ra. Although, Ram killed most of the ringleaders, plotting against the Ra, Ram didn't kill any of the Hellcats Warlords, including the Warlord Benobu, who had unleashed several groups of assassins.

Best the Jinn had plans for the Ra, so it fiercely protected the Ra, using its Jinn Eco Jin, which was evenly split between the twins, Ram and Danaaa. Danaaa having the powers of Jinn Eco, pronounced Jenny-Co. Ram having the powers of the Eco Jin, pronounced E-Co Jin.

That made the Hayee less willing to plot against the Ra, knowing that the Low Pressure Assassin Ram would somehow figure out whom the ringleaders were and murder them in the middle of the night. That and the fact that the other Ra were always protected and near unbeatable, allowed Dan and La to run this territory without any opposition, after just four months.

Ramala sent the top training teacher Hayee, Deen to supervise the training rituals of the Hammer-Axe Six. She also sent her father, the Hayee, Roe to advise the Ra children and be a voice of reason to Dan and La in dealing with their Hayee family in this territory.

Now that everyone was in line and with the Hayee, Roe there advising the Ra children, the Six Lower Houses of Ra were a very pleasant, prosperous and safe place to live, as long as you abided by the protocol set forth by the Warlord Dan and his sister, the Number One Princess, La.

CHAPTER 8

The Queen of the Northern Houses Japha, Jania Jett had complete control over all of the territory her and her brother King Japha, San ruled over. After forcing everyone in the remaining Northern Houses to change their sir name to Japha, San and Jan created one army for the whole of their territory. Most all of the members from the House of Hayee, including Ramala's father the Hayee, Roe, moved south to join their relatives in the House of Ra, rather than change their name to Japha. Japha, Jan allowed it because they were Ramala's family. The Hayee Hellcat, Ramala, Queen of the House of Ra and being Jan's most powerful ally is the only reason Jan allowed the Hayee to move south, without retribution.

The King and Queen of the Northern Houses made another move soon after changing all the inhabitants in their territory's names to Japha. They changed the name of their territory from the Northern Houses, with each House having their family name as their House title, to all of the Houses being called by one name, the House of Japha. The capitol city of their territory was the city of San-Jania where the King and Queen resided.

San and Jan's older brother Japha, Jett 2 spent all of his time in the former Houses of the North searching for opposition to the Rulers of Japha and stamping it out, ferociously. Jett 2, along with his other brothers, who tried to have San and Jan killed, was the only one of his brother to survive that botched attempt. He was now doing everything in his power to insure his brother and sister would stay in power.

Jett 2's power was in the military. He had control of the city of Japha, the former capitol of the House of Japha. He also had control of twenty-five percent of the military. San controlled forty percent of the military and Jan controlled the other thirty-five percent through their top Warlords. So even if Jett 2 tried another attempt, he wouldn't have enough power to succeed.

Jan Jett was also confident that the surviving members of the Tat clan, who had amazing mental abilities, would alert her to any plots against herself and San. That was the promise the Tat made in order to keep their name and way of life in a sanctuary built for them by Jan. The Tat kept their promise to Jan. They gave her information about threats to her kingdom. Jan gave orders to Jett 2 to eliminate those threats, immediately.

Things were going well for the Rulers of Japha. King Japha San now had four children. The two oldest were boys and the two youngest were girls. From oldest to youngest were San-Jett who was ten years of age and just months older than Ramala's second set of twins. Then, there was his younger brother Jeb, named after his great uncle. Teesana was the oldest girl. Teesana was mostly called little Tee, or just Tee. The youngest girl was Sania-Tana. Sania-Tana was called Sanny.

All of San and Tee's children were about two years apart. Just like Ramala, Tee had her hands full dealing with four children, even though she had many maids helping. San and Tee kept a tight rein on their boys, grooming them to become the next Rulers of Japha. However, San spoiled his girls and that made them trouble for Tee and her staff of maids. Tee's two girls were very troublesome and eventually were named the Terrible Two by Jan and her closest relatives.

Jan and Ramala corresponded through messengers. Jan learned that Tara's youngest girls were also the Terrible Two. Both thought it a strange coincident. Jan loved to hear the stories about Ramala's children, especially Danaaa.

Jan loved the story of Danaaa and her Kitty, the young lioness Danaaa befriended that was killed by Ra guards, sending Danaaa into a fit of rage. That was Jan's favorite story about Ramala's children. She went into sidesplitting laughter when the messengers told her that story.

Still, Jan and Ramala were only willing to share certain stories through messengers. They couldn't share things that they would talk to each other about in person. That made them miss each other's company. Both promised they would visit when time permitted. Ramala was excited and wished Jan would make the trip south to visit her. Jan was a little less enthusiastic about Ramala and her army marching north through the House of Japha.

Jan convinced San to come with her and bring his young family to visit Ramala in the south. San made Jan promise that she would return with him, after a short visit. San didn't want Jan to get south and end up having a prolonged stay. Jan agreed she wouldn't stay, too long. Jan sent messengers telling Ramala that she would like to visit her. Of course, Ramala gave Jan permission to visit as soon as she could.

Jan and San were asked to meet with the council of Elders of the House of Japha, who resided in the city of Japha. The twin's father Japha, Jett 1 was on the council. The meeting was very cordial, at first. Then, it turned serious, bordering on tumultuous, with the twin Rulers asked to take care of some unfinished family business that they had been avoiding for some time. All of the Elders on the council were getting older and demanded that they take care of this business, before they passed on.

Jan and San knew that they couldn't put this off any longer. The Elders had been very cooperative in helping the twins assume power. They also didn't cause trouble for the new Rulers. San and Jan knew that if they didn't take care of this business, the Elders would find a way to do it themselves, no matter what the cost. Neither San, nor Jan wanted that. So, they promised the Elders that they would take care of this matter personally and that this should be kept confidential, until it was taken care of. The council agreed.

Five months before Ramala received message that Jan would be visiting, she was getting messages from her spies in the Lower Houses telling her of her children's progress. It seemed that they were doing very well controlling the territory. Ramala was very proud of them.

After sending her children away, the city of Ra settled back into its normal routine. More Hayee were streaming into the city from the former House of Hayee, which was now part of the expanding House of Japha. The older, more established Hayee were allowed to stay in the main city as guest of the Hellcats. The young to middle-aged Hayee men and some of the women without children were sent west to Wa and north to Yee provinces, to train in service providing. The most unruly Hayee young men and teenagers were sent south to be trained, by La and Dan in how to strictly adhere to protocol.

Ramala had a lot of time to herself, with her children gone. She spent her time training herself with the Butcher girls, her Hellcat cousins and Dan. Ramala still had it in her mind that she could beat Syn, Jara in a one on one fight. Something she had yet to do. That one thing would bother her from time to time. The other thing that bothered Ramala was the fact that she hadn't taken control of the Southern jungle.

Ramala was still annoyed with Dan when she sent him to take over the Southern jungle. Instead of taking the jungle, he succeeded in agitating the Shinmushee and stirring up a hornet's nest of thousands of warriors. The war with the Shinmushee cost the House of Ra many casualties. With depleted forces, the Hayee Hellcat, Wana was happy with the stalemate in the war with the Shinmushee. As leader of the Ra army, Wana knew she needed time to train younger, less talented warriors to replace the dead and crippled ones she'd already lost.

Even though Wana explained this to Ramala repeatedly, Ramala still pressed Wana on when the Ra army would be ready to take the Southern jungle. Wana had to get the other Hayee Hellcat, Tara, along with Dan to help her convince Ramala to wait, until the younger warriors developed into the killing machines she needed to move into the jungle. The only thing that kept Ramala from ordering Wana to invade the Southern jungle was the fact that Wana told Ramala if they did invade and the war went on for a prolonged period of time, casualties would deplete the Ra forces to the point that they might not be able to defend the city of Ra.

Wana said that if the city of Ra had to be evacuated, the Hellcats would have three choices. One would be to fight to the death in hellish battles, trying to defend what was left of the House of Ra, which they would eventually lose. The other would be to beg for help from the King and Queen of the northern Houses. The last option would be to head north to the House of Japha and seek asylum.

They would then have to rely on Japha, Jan to give them, at least some of their old ancestral home that use to be the House of Hayee. Wana impressed upon Ramala that at that point they would be at the mercy of whatever level of help the Japha deemed appropriate.

That put a halt to Ramala's plans for the moment. Now, she was pressing Wana to get the Ra army back to top preparedness. To Wana that meant that Ramala was giving her time to train and increase the army, so she could send them into the Southern jungle.

Wana enlisted every young man and even young women who looked like they had potential to become a killer and sent them to train with the top fighting teachers in the House of Ra.

Wana also still had the question in her mind about who really killed the Hayee, Shamika and her sisters, if not Ram. Even though everyone now thought that Ram had done it because of the testimony of the Ra Hayee, Anne, Wana was still putting together the whereabouts of everyone on that night. Her investigation was so intense that she even questioned the other two Hellcats on where they were for the time that she wasn't with them and couldn't account for. To Wana, it seemed everyone had some missing time at some point, or another, that night.

Now, that Wana was charged with increasing the skill of her army, she ordered the halt of the operations that were harassing the Shinmushee. That meant she wanted the outpost outside of Yee province and the outpost outside of Wa province shut down. Wana didn't want the Shinmushee to get agitated into starting an all-out war. Wana was going to start the war with the Shinmushee on her terms, when her army was in peak condition.

The outpost outside of Yee Province was shut down, immediately. Han was to hold extra training sessions for his forces north of Yee, so that the Shinmushee couldn't see what they were doing. Wana's messengers told Han that Wana expected his warriors and Warlords to be at their best and ready for action, at a moment's notice. After receiving the message, Han knew he and his forces would be going to war.

Han, his Captains and all of his warriors had a big feast that night. The next day Han put his forces on an extra heavy training regiment, north of Yee Province. Han knew how important it was to impress Ramala. Han also knew that even though he had never lost Yee Province in all the wars, Wana needed to be continuously impressed, too.

Yin was at his outpost, just outside of Wa province. Yin had a series of five buildings he used to slaughter the Shinmushee every time he provoked them to attack. Each of these buildings had short hallways that lead to several rooms. Each of the rooms had secret passageways that allowed Yin and his forces to attack, make hasty getaways and counter attacks on the Shinmushee warriors. It was house to house guerilla warfare at its finest.

At first, the Shinmushee thought they could over run Yin's outpost, by flooding it with Warriors. They succeeded in doing so, but caught hell trying to take control of the five buildings. Yin, Kiki and the rest of Yin's forces butchered every Shinmushee that entered those buildings. They even butchered a few of the Shinmushee Butchers. That's when the Shinmushee decided they needed to come up with a better plan to attack Yin's outpost. So they waited and made up a plan to destroy the Ra outpost, which the Shinmushee called Yin's Houses of Hell.

When Wana's messengers gave Yin the order to head back to the main city of Ra, Yin ignored them. Several more messengers went and at Wana's request, insisted Yin return to the main city. This time, Yin sent word to Wana that he had the Shinmushee right where he wanted them and as soon as he completed his mission, he would return with news of a great victory over the Shinmushee.

Wana viewed Yin's message as nothing more than him disobeying a direct order. Wana's next messenger told Yin that this was the last messenger telling him to return to the main city. The messenger said that if he disobeyed this order, he would be removed from the outpost by force.

Since Yin had come to his outpost he felt more alive than ever, before. He was in control of this and forced the action against the Shinmushee, whenever he wanted. It also was an extra bonus for Yin when the Shinmushee made surprise attacks on him. It was a super charged atmosphere, where the heat of the battle was always at hand. Yin was having the time of his life. There was no way he was going back to the boredom and safety of the main city. Yin told Kiki and the others to leave. Some of them left. Kiki and a few hardened adrenaline junkies stayed. Yin sent the messenger back without a response.

If Yin had been anyone else, besides Tara's mate and the father of Wana's nieces and nephew, she would have had him killed, immediately, for disobeying her orders. Now Wana found herself arguing with Tara over the Yin issue. Tara begging Wana was the only reason Wana had put up with Yin this long. Wana looked to Ramala to help her convince Tara that Yin was a lost cause, but Ramala was no help.

Yin's three children, Yin, Tara-Yani and Tammy were favorites of Ramala's. Ramala didn't want to be a part of giving the order to have their father killed, so she told Wana to do what she thought was best. Ramala also didn't help Wana with her arguments against Tara on this. Without Ramala helping Wana against Tara, Tara was able to keep Wana from having Yin killed. Still, Tara knew if something wasn't done to get Yin away from that outpost, it would only be a matter of time before Wana dealt with Yin.

Finally, after some time passed, Tara negotiated a compromise with Wana. Tara wanted to send Ma along with Dan to try to convince Yin it was in his best interest to come home and visit his children. That he could return to the outpost after a short rest. Tara said Yin would come home to see his children and her. While he was gone, they would destroy the outpost. Even if he went back, there would be nothing there and he wouldn't have the protection of those buildings. If he decided to stay after that, Tara said she wouldn't try to stop anything Wana deemed necessary to protect the House of Ra.

Wana agreed she would go with this strategy, but warned Tara that if this didn't work, she should prepare not to ever see Yin alive, again. Tara agreed. Tara knew that when she got Yin back here, it was imperative that she convince him to stay. Tara was going to do everything she could think of and things she hadn't thought of, yet, to keep Yin here in the main city.

Jan sent word to Ramala that she forced San to bring his family so she could meet his children. Ramala was excited about that and thought it a good opportunity for her children to meet San's children, who would surely Rule the House of Japha one day. Ramala ordered her children to come back to the main city for a visit and that Dan should ready himself for the annual Hammer-Axe Championship Tournament. When young Dan got word of that, he knew what his mother expected. Dan trained as hard as he could, until it was time to go visit the main city.

A large contingency of the Japha army escorted San and Jan's caravan right up to the fringes of Ra territory. Because Ramala and Jan were close allies, there was a soft border of about two to four miles. Both armies could roam that area and not be seen a threat for invading.

The Japha army made camp in this area and were to wait here, until their King and Queen returned. San said it would be about close to fourteen days, but Jan was going to make it a little longer, if she could.

Now that the caravan was in Ra territory it was smaller than it first was. San only had two Warlords and a little over two hundred top guards and bodyguards protecting him, Jan and his family.

When the Japha made it to the first checkpoint, they were surprised to see a large number of Wana's guards there. These guards joined the Japha caravan and escorted it to Yee province. Now, the caravan looked like an army, again. San talked to the Warlord in charge of Ra forces. San asked "Is Rebel and Shinmushee activity such that we need this much protection?"

The Warlord smiled at San and said, "No, it's not. I'm here to make sure you can relax and enjoy your visit to the south, completely free of any thoughts of attack. That's the wishes of my Queen Ramala and the Hellcat Hayee, Wana. Enjoy your journey and rest assured that you and your guards will see not one rebel, or Shinmushee, unless you see us dragging their bodies out of the way of the caravan. And since we have so many guards on alert ahead of us, I doubt that you would even see that."

The Japha made it to Yee Province where they rested for one day and were re-supplied. Han made their visit most enjoyable. Even the Japha guards enjoyed the stay in Yee province. They especially enjoyed the Spot, a very popular night entertainment spot.

From there the caravan made its way to Wa province. Wa province was now the most heavily guarded area of Ra territory, after the main city of Ra, because of Yin's activities. After the Warlord in charge of protecting them and the Warlord in charge of Wa province cautioned against it, San and Jan insisted on calling Yin for a visit. When the Warlord explained that Yin was now acting on his own against the Shinmushee, San, and Jan said they would settle for nothing less than a short visit with Yin.

Yin was alerted that a large caravan was coming to his outpost. Yin was in bed with Kiki when he received the news. Kiki was still laying half on Yin even after hearing the news of the coming caravan. She was exhausted from the work she and Yin had put in on each other, just a few hours ago.

Yin lifted his leg and forced Kiki off him. Yin sat up. Kiki said jokingly "Tara has finally sent Wana to come get you and bring you to her!" Kiki started laughing. That comment annoyed Yin. He said, "Shut the Hell up! Anyway, if it is Wana, I hope you don't think she plans of keeping any of us alive!"

Kiki stopped laughing and looked at Yin to see if he was serious. Even if he wasn't, that was enough to sober Kiki up. She jumped up on her knees and said, "What are we going to do?" Kiki looked at Yin, as Yin tried to think of the best way to deal with what he knew would be a pissed off Wana.

Yin was relieved, but still suspicious when he found out it was the Japha twins. He watched closely as Jan ran up to him and gave him a big hug. She seemed genuinely happy to see him. As Jan was talking and fawning over Yin, he watched as San walked up. San slapped Yin on the shoulder and said "Somehow, this is where I envisioned you'd be."

San smiled. Yin did after that. San extended his arm and said, "These are my children." Yin looked and saw four children standing next to Tee. Tee smiled at Yin, while her four children looked suspiciously at him. Yin looked back at San and said, "They look good. We don't have accommodations suitable for them." San interrupted Yin, saying, "Don't worry about them. Have a meal with me and Jan at our caravan. I'm sure you could use a good meal, couldn't you?"

Yin didn't want to, but San and Jan were bringing him out of his kill at will mode, by treating him like family. Yin told himself that he would have a meal with the Japha and enjoy their company. Soon they would be gone and he would be back to doing what he did best.

At dinner, Yin could see that San was softened by the life of ruling and raising children. Yin asked San "When was the last time either of you saw some real action?" Jan answered before San, saying, "We still train hard." Yin said, "That's not like the real thing, you know that." Jan said, "We don't have a need to do battle, if that's what you mean."

Yin could see in San's eyes that what Jan said wasn't completely true. Still, Yin didn't press the issue. He enjoyed his meal, while watching Tee and San's children run around playing. That made Yin think of his children. A luxury he couldn't afford out here.

Yin and Kiki spent a restful night, and then got up to see Jan and San when next day came. The Japha were already packed and ready to leave for the city of Ra. Kiki and Yin noticed that San and his bodyguards weren't aboard their elephants. Yin looked up at Jan, who didn't seem very happy. Jan motioned for the caravan to start moving.

Yin looked back at San. San said, "Jan and Tee are going to visit Ramala and her children. I'm sure they have a lot of catching up to do. These days, it's not often I get to be out in the field. I was hoping for a little action, before going to the city of Ra, if you know what I mean." San smiled Yin. Yin smiled back. He knew exactly what San meant.

CHAPTER 9

Ramala's children had been gone for the better part of a year. They arrived the afternoon three days before Jan and her caravan did. Ramala was with her two Hellcat cousins, along with the Terrible Two, Yani and Tami.

The Ra children were very poised as they walked down the ramps and lined up in front of the Hellcats. Ramala's father the Hayee, Roe and the number one trainer of the Ra children Hayee, Deen lined up behind the Ra children. The Special guard lined up behind them, following the Ra children. They all got down on their knees in front of the Hellcats, except for Roe and Deen, who lowered their heads out of respect.

Ramala proudly peeked at her two Hellcats cousins, with a proud look at how well behaved her children were, according to protocol. After that, Ramala motioned for everyone to rise. After they'd done so, the Ra girls went to Ramala and hugged her.

The Ra girls looked around and then La asked, "Where's daddy?" Ramala's happy face had a look of reflective confusion on it when she said, unenthusiastically "He's in there, somewhere." as she pointed to the palace. The Ra girls curiously looked at Ramala, because of her attitude, and then they took off running into the palace.

Ramala's boys stood there, until Ramala walked over and hugged them. It was the same with Yin. After his two younger sisters ran over and started clawing at him, Yin still didn't move towards his mother. Tara only thought about that for a moment. She walked over and grabbed Yin, hugging and kissing on him, embarrassing him in front of his peers. Tara was amused, in the same way Ramala was, at the Ra boys discomfort with their mother's overt affection.

After a short reunion at the dock of the palace, everyone went to reunite with their families. The Terrible Two, Yani and Tammy were very fond of Ramala. Ramala would spoil these girls, while giving them tough training and instructing them in female protocol.

Even though Tara wasn't as tough on the Terrible Two as Ramala was, Tara would have to chase, wrestle and fight with her daughters to get them to do things that they would willingly do for Ramala. That pissed Tara off and made her sterner with her daughters. So today, when The Terrible Two pestered Tara, because they wanted to go with Ramala, Tara decided she would visit for a while and let her girls burn off some energy, before taking them home.

The Ra girls found Dan in his training courtyard. Shaya and Danaaa ran up to Dan, hugging him, while wrestling each other for more attention. Shaya didn't realize how much she missed her father, until she saw him. Danaaa took in her father's scent and was never happier to smell him, even though she always thought he needed a bath.

Dan looked over and saw La slowly walking towards him with a disappointed look on her face. La stopped a short distance from Dan and folded her arms, staring at him, showing him that she was not happy.

La was fourteen years of age and looked just like Ramala did when Dan first met her. The difference was La was thinner than and not as developed as Ramala was, back then. Dan also could see that his little La was now a young woman. For a moment that startled Dan, before he realized why La hadn't come over to him. Dan smiled at La and said, "I'm not always going to come running to you every time you show up. You're not a baby, anymore. It's time you start acting like the young woman you are. Now get over her and give me a hug!"

At first, La was angry that Dan hadn't come to greet her. After he said that, she was just happy to see him. La still wanted her father to know that she wasn't happy about him not meeting her. So, La slowly walked to Dan and didn't hug him, until he wrapped his arms around her. That was the best protest La could muster, after not seeing her daddy for close to a year.

The Ra girls talked Dan's ears off and pulled on him, clinging to his arms. La's voice was loud and aggressive. Shaya's voice was loud, soft and whinny as she negotiated for talking time. Danaaa's voice was harshly loud and had a cadence that would startle you with an even louder boom, occasionally.

All three girls settled into an ignoring each other, while yelling their adventures to Dan at the same time. It was nerve racking, to say the least, for Dan. Dan tried to get them to talk one at a time. After that failed he put up with it, because he missed his daughters.

Dan knew he wouldn't be able to complete his training. After a half hour of non-stop talking from his girls, a messenger came in and said that Ramala requested them for a meal. Dan told his girls he was going to get cleaned up and he would meet them in the eating room. The Ra girls walked Dan to his cleaning room, before going on their way.

When Dan was cleaned up and walked into the hall, he saw his three daughters sitting on a bench smiling at him. He smiled at them. They then jumped up and continued to talk his ears off on the way to the eating hall.

Tara's oldest daughter Tara-Yani was five and a half years of age and looked like both her parents. Yani liked to pester people. She would find out what bothered you and do it, until Tara stopped her. Yani also had a bad temper that usually manifested itself, whenever Tara had to stop Yani from pestering someone. Just as Danaaa liked to fight and you knew she would be fighting someone at some point in the day, you also knew Yani would be pestering someone.

Tammy looked more like Tara than her siblings did. She was the instigating force that always fueled Yani's pestering into trouble for these two. Tammy was smart mouthed and at four and a half years of age would talk back to most anyone at the drop of a dime. She looked up to Yani and thought that Yani could do no wrong. Tammy was the perfect sidekick to her pestering sister.

When Dan walked into the eating hall with his daughters, Yani and Tami raced up to Dan and hugged his legs. The Terrible Two liked Dan. La lightly pushed Yani with her elbow, letting her know she was invading La's personal space, next to her father. Yani caught La off guard with a viscous elbow to her stomach, which was more of an annoyance, than anything else was. Tammy busted into laughter, saying, "She taught you a lesson you won't soon forget, will you?"

Tammy erupted into laughter, again. La was more annoyed with Tammy, than she was with Yani's elbow. Shaya saw La was annoyed and said in a pleasant voice to Yani "That's not nice. Little girls shouldn't . . . ." then Shaya screamed out in pain and hopped around on one foot. Yani had stomped as hard as she could on Shaya's foot. Tammy was howling in laughter, beside herself, stopping just long enough to say to Shaya "Look at you! You look like an idiot!" Tammy was more offensive with words than Yani was with pestering.

Danaaa could see what was going on here, as Yani looked her square in her eyes. Before Yani could move, Danaaa plowed her foot into Yani's stomach. As Yani was moving back from the force of the kick, Danaaa grabbed two hands full of Yani's hair and pulled Yani's head back towards her, twisting Yani's head and taking her hard to the ground. Danaaa quickly got on Yani's back while pulling her head upwards by her hair.

Tammy, shocked by the violent nature in which her sister was thrown to the ground, ran up and pointed her finger in Danaaa's face, yelling, "You let her go, now!"

Tammy had no idea the danger she put herself in. Before she knew what happened Danaaa yanked her by the arm that her finger was pointing and slammed her to the ground. Danaaa, in one quick movement, wrapped her legs around both girls' necks, pinning them to the floor. Yani struggled to get loose, while Tammy screamed for her mommy.

Ramala was about to say something, but Tara stopped her. Tara was tired of this behavior from her daughters and was glad Danaaa was teaching them a lesson.

Danaaa, while away from home, had dealt with some of the most deadly assassins and unruly Hayee, wasn't about to take any crap from her two younger cousins. Danaaa, while squeezing a little harder with her legs to make her point, yelled to them "If you keep acting like this, I'm going to put a serious beating on you! Do you understand me?!" Tammy yelled for Tara's help one more time. Tara just said, "I told you this would happen if you kept up this behavior. Now, you'll have to deal with it as best you can."

Danaaa now knew she had a free pass to teach these two a lesson. She squeezed her legs a little tighter, then yelled "I said, do you understand me?!" both girls cried in unison "Yes! Yes, we understand! Please, let go of us, please!"

Danaaa held then down another moment, just to make sure her point got through and then she let them up. Both girls ran over to Ramala for some babying that they knew they wouldn't get from Tara. Ramala soothed both girls with some calming rubs.

The Ra girls, satisfied that Danaaa had done enough for all of them, went over to the table. The Terrible Two stayed close to Ramala nervously watching Danaaa, making sure she didn't get close enough to them to make another one of those lightning fast moves they never saw coming.

Dan saw his sons standing near their mother. When they saw him, they walked over and lined up. After inspecting them, Dan walked over, mussed their hair, and wrestled them a bit. Dan could tell that his sons were much stronger than they were letting on.

When the Ra girls took off their Ruling capes their ponytails dropped behind them. Ramala noticed that at least two of her girls' hair hadn't been cut at the proper length, which was just below the calf. La's was at that exact length, but Shaya's was just above her ankles and Danaaa's was dragging on the ground, with more to spare.

La was the only one of Ramala's daughters who had the metal ball attached to her ponytail. La knew that ball on the end of her tail was one of her most powerful weapons, so she always had it attached.

The Ra girls saw Ramala looking at their hair. That's when Ramala said "It's time that all of you get your hair cut to proper length. I expect it to be done by next day's end."

Danaaa looked at Ramala, pulled her ponytail up, wrapped it around one of her shoulders, and then wrapped it around the other shoulder, letting the rest of the tail fall in front of her, just above her waist.

La smiled at Danaaa and then looked at Ramala. La said, "That's how Baby likes to where her tail, wrapped around her body, just like that."

Ramala said, "I never taught her that. It has to be cut. Besides, it's too long to be properly manipulated as a weapon." La looked at and then smiled at Shaya, saying, "Baby doesn't need her tail as a weapon. She can swing her axes really fast!"

Ramala looked at La for a second, before looking back at Danaaa's hair and saying "So, I've heard. Still, a young girl has to have every advantage she can. What if you can't get to your axes? Wouldn't it be best if you had your hair as an extra weapon?"

Danaaa looked at Ramala and then looked at La. Danaaa yelled "But, I like my hair the way it is! That's why it hasn't been cut! Why do I have to get my hair cut?!" Ramala had almost forgotten how nasty and disrespectful Danaaa's voice could sound. Ramala didn't know whether Danaaa was making it sound that way on purpose, or not.

Ramala was fed up with this conversation, so she looked Danaaa in her eyes and said, "You're getting your hair cut to proper length and that's final!" Danaaa looked in Ramala's eyes for a moment, trying to find a compromise. When Danaaa did not see that, she turned and looked angrily at La, while yelling, "That's why we shouldn't have come back, because she's going to make us do whatever she wants us to! When we leave, I'm going to let my hair grow longer than this, if it can!"

There was a moment of silence in which La looked a warning to Danaaa not to say another word. Danaaa wasn't trying to be disrespectful. She just didn't hold thoughts in her head. They would come out through her mouth, before she could stop them. Right after La gave her a stern look, was when Danaaa figured she probably should have kept that thought in her head. It was too late for that. Right now, Ramala felt Danaaa was being openly defiant.

Ramala sternly said, "So, you've been gone for a while and now that you're back, you think you can talk to me any way you like?" Danaaa looked at Ramala not knowing whether that was a statement, or a question. Since Ramala kept staring at her, Danaaa figured it was a question.

Then, it seemed, just in the nick of time, Danaaa's wits showed up. Normally, Danaaa didn't like hers, or anyone else's wits. Nevertheless, looking in her mother's eyes, Danaaa was going to give her wits a chance to make up for lost time. Danaaa's wits told her what to say. Danaaa thought it was better than saying nothing.

Danaaa's eyes darted to La's eyes, and then to Ramala's eyes and back to La's. Danaaa then yelled, "I wasn't talking to you, I was talking to Lar! I mean La!"

Danaaa felt good about the fact that she corrected her own diction, before her mother did. Ramala yell "Well, who are you talking to now!?!" Danaaa's could see her wits were nervous and shaky, but they still came up with a sufficient answer, she thought. Danaaa yelled "But, I already told you, I'm talking to La, not you!"

There were so many flaws in that statement that it was even clear to Ram that Danaaa was in big trouble. Elder Dan and young Dan both stared at Ramala, as did everyone in the room. Her face went from annoyed to angry. Elder Dan shook his head, knowing Danaaa was in big trouble. Young Dan smiled inwardly because he realized the same thing his father did.

In Ramala's entire life, there were only two people that could get her this angry at the drop of a dime. One was Elder Dan and the other was Danaaa. Ramala said in a slow angry voice "Come to me, this instant!"

Danaaa immediately looked around in her mind and saw that her wits were gone. That sneaky bastard! Now Danaaa was here, facing her mother all by herself. Danaaa thought that the next time her wits showed up she was going to beat the hell out of wits. Danaaa confused herself, wondering how she was going to do that. Then she snapped back into the reality of her mother waiting for her to come to her.

Danaaa slowly got out of her chair, never taking her eyes off Ramala's eyes. She stood next to her chair, frustrated, and yelled "Am I going to get hit!?!"

Ramala said, "If that's what I choose to do!" Danaaa nervously yelled in her whining voice "But, I don't want that!" Ramala stood up with her eyes blazing, as she moved towards Danaaa, saying, "It's not about what you want! You should have thought about that, before you opened that smart mouth of yours!"

Danaaa thought it wasn't her smart mouth that told her to say that, it was her wits. Still, they weren't anywhere around to save her. Just as Danaaa all but gave up hope, guess who showed up? It was her old pal survival instinct, saying just one word to her. That word was run. It sounded like a good idea, so Danaaa listened to her old pal. Just as Danaaa looked at the door, Ramala saw her. Ramala moved quickly, while threatening in a slow angry voice "Don't you dare!"

It was too late. Danaaa bolted out of that door it seemed to everyone, before Ramala took her next step. Before Ramala took another step, both Shaya and La were on their knees, clinging, one to each of Ramala's legs begging her not to harm Danaaa.

Shaya pleaded, "Mother please, don't get yourself worked up chasing Baby! You know she's too fast, to catch! That will only make you, angrier. Let us go find her and bring her back to you. Then you can punish her, if you like."

All while Shaya and La were pleading with Ramala, Ramala was trying to move her legs. She realized the strength her two daughters had when she could barely move. Ramala grabbed both girls by their hair and yanked up hard, trying to move them. However, it seemed that all the hair strengthening training made her effort fruitless. Their heads didn't move an inch from her thighs.

Ramala let go of their hair. Frustrated, she said, "Alright, go get her and bring her to me! I don't care if you have to tie her from head to toe, just bring her back alive, so I can get my hands on her!" Both Shaya and La chorused "Yes, Mother!"

Young Dan stuffed some more food in his mouth and quickly washed it down with some blood from his cup. He looked at La and then ordered the Ra boys "Come on, you heard mommy! We have to go find Stupid!" Ramala turned and gave Dan an angry look when he said that. Dan quickly said, "I mean, Baby."

The Ra boys were trying to stuff food in their mouths, too. Dan angrily looked at them and said, "I said, come on!" the Ra boys got up and followed Dan to the door, where Shaya and La were waiting on them. Yani and Tammy jumped up and started heading towards the door. Tara stopped them by yelling "You two are not going, anywhere. Come here!" The Terrible Two heard in their mother's voice that she was dead serious, so they turned and slowly walked towards her. Tammy said, while looking at Tara "Mommy, why is big Baby such a bad girl?"

Tara wasn't ready to agree with the label of bad girl for Danaaa, so she said "Don't you worry about her. You just make sure you do what I tell you to do!"

Ma forced Syn, Jara to come to Ramala's palace to see the Ra children, once she found out they were home. Syn knew Ma just wanted to see Danaaa, most of all. When they arrived at the steps of the palace, they saw Danaaa racing towards them with a look of desperation on her face. Ma jumped in front of Danaaa, who was in full stride and was almost knocked over by her. Ma asked, a still struggling, Danaaa "What's wrong?" Danaaa yelled, "If she catches me, she'll kill me! I have to get away!" Ma asked "Who?" Danaaa said, while looking back up the palace stairs "Mommy, who else!?"

Syn burst into laughter, saying, "I guess some things will never change!" Ma took a good long look at Danaaa. She was taller and still thick. Ma smiled proudly at Danaaa, who kept looking back at the palace to see if Ramala would show, so she could take off, again. The only reason Danaaa didn't evade, or try to get away from Ma was the bond she had with Ma.

Even though Ma didn't want their reunion to end so quickly, she had a worried smile on her face when she said to Danaaa "I don't know what happened, but I'm sure it was just a misunderstanding." Ma looked up and saw the other Ra children running down the stairs. She said, "Maybe it's best if Ramala doesn't see you for a while."

Danaaa nodded her head in agreement. Just then, Shaya and La reached Danaaa. They could see Danaaa was already in flight mode. La looked seriously at Danaaa and said, "Wait! Don't run! All we want to do is to make sure nothing happens to you! Follow me! We'll find somewhere to go, until it's time to have dinner. By that time, I'll have figured out something."

Danaaa watched all of her siblings closely to see if they were trying to trick her and take her back inside. Ma said, "Right, now get out of here before your mother sees you!" La, leading the way said, "Come on Baby! You know if mommy catches you, you're in big trouble!"

Danaaa already knew that much. She could see everyone's wits, except her own, working to help her. Danaaa wished her wits were like everyone else's, but she knew deep down inside they weren't. Danaaa decided that wits weren't bad all the time. It was mostly just hers. Shaya snapped Danaaa back into reality by pulling on her and frantically, saying "Come on! We have to go, now!"

Danaaa let herself be hustled away by her sisters, followed by the Ra boys. Ma looked at Syn, smiled and shook her head at the Ra children's antics. Now there was no need to visit Ramala's palace. The two Butcher girls turned and went to find some other way to occupy their time.

La kept Danaaa away from Ramala by visiting relatives they hadn't seen since they were last here, until dinnertime. She then had Danaaa go to their mother by herself and beg for forgiveness, saying not one word after that. La told Danaaa not to answer any questions their mother might ask. She told Danaaa that would do more harm than good. La told Danaaa if her mother asked her a question to just look as pitiful and confused as possible, without saying any words.

Danaaa was all about executing the mission and pulled it off, perfectly. Ramala was charmed back into showing favor for her youngest daughter, who she thought somehow, didn't have the understanding of her other children. After that, Danaaa mostly kept her mouth shut around Ramala, just like La told her to and everything seemed to go a lot smoother. Even though Danaaa couldn't find her own wits, she was glad La's wits were always around.

Ramala was now spending her days checking her children's skill level. It seemed to her that Roe and Deen had increased her children's skills and tightened up their fighting techniques. Elder Dan tested Young Dan's skills and gave him points in which he thought his son could do better. Other than that, Elder Dan didn't try to change any techniques Young Dan was comfortable with so close to the competition. Still, Ramala pushed Dan hard for the Hammer-Axe Championships that were being held in a few days. She let him rest his body two days before the event.

Jan and the Na, Tee arrived at the main city of Ra to festive cheers. This was the first time the soon to be Rulers of Ra were meeting the future Rulers of the Japha.

The Hellcat, Butchers, Ra children and Hayee, watched as the Queen of Japha and her Royal court walked down ramps from the platforms on the elephant's backs. Once on the ground, Jan lowered her head slightly, while all of her Royal court got down on their knees. Tee's children had to be told to do it, because the only people they had ever gotten on their knees for were the Elder council of Japha. Even with that, Tee's oldest son San Jett asked, "Why do we have to get down on our knees for them?" Tee slapped San Jett on his head and gave him a motherly stare that made him get on his knees. Then the Japha court stood up as

Jan motioned her hand for them to do so after a short respectful moment.

The Hellcats, Dan and the Ra children all lowered their heads, while everyone else on the Ra side got down on their knees. San Jett, upon seeing the Ra children not getting down on their knees, yelled to Tee "Why didn't they get down on their knees, like I had to do?!"

Again, Tee smacked San Jett across the top of his head and told him to be quiet. San Jett's attitude caught the attention of everyone, none more so than the Ra children. After a respectful moment, Ramala had her side stand. That's when Ramala and Jan ran to meet each other. They hugged and fussed over each other, until everyone else joined in. All of the children on both sides were introduced. They still looked at each other suspiciously as children, that don't know each other, do.

Shaya played peacemaker among the children, talking to the Japha, inviting and engaging them in conversation with the Ra. After seeing that the children were at least cordial to each other, the grownups migrated a short distance away, catching up on old times and time lost.

To San Jett and his sibling, most everyone was beneath them in rank, just like with the Ra children. It still bothered San Jett that he had to get down on his knees and the Ra children didn't. His immaturity led San Jett to want to let the Ra children know just how important he was.

San Jett pointed to La and said "You there, quickly, step and fetch me something to drink. I'm thirsty!"

(This was probably the origins of the arrogantly racist term 'step and fetch' which in layman's terms means hurry your steps and get me what I ordered, you lowlife slave subordinate of mine. Okay, now you get the same picture that the Ra children got.)

Yani and Tammy giggled right after San-Jett said that. All of the Ra children were offended. La wasn't a servant, or a maid. Those Japha were already told that she was the Number One Princess. Danaaa angrily moved towards San Jett, until La pulled on her ponytail. That stopped Danaaa. When the Ra girls were in public

La would hold on to Danaaa's ponytail. She would pull hard on it to let Danaaa know to wait and see what La would do.

The Japha, Teesana, who was just as arrogant as her brother was, said, "You heard him! Chop, chop, hurry it up and get to it!" the Japha's, Jeb and Sania laughed. Tee's motherly hearing heard Teesana, even though she was a ways away with the other grownups. Tee said "Tee, be respectful how you talk to people!"

La smiled at the Japha Na, Tee and said "They're just thirsty. I'll have the maids bring drinks for them." San-Jett pointed to La and ordered in a nasty tone "I told you to do it!"

Tee quickly yelled "San-Jett, mind your manners! Otherwise, I'll make you come and stand next to me!" San-Jett didn't want that, so he looked at Tee as if he would calm himself and be respectful.

Seeing San-Jett talk to La like that had Yani and Tammy looking at San-Jett as if he was a God. They could never talk to La like that, without La having Danaaa administer severe physicality to them. They liked the boldness of this Japha, San-Jett!

Maids brought drinks to the young Japha and La was very nice to them. Once Shaya saw that La wasn't bothered by San-Jett's disrespect, she joined La, being nice to the Japha. La had to pull hard on Danaaa's ponytail several times to keep her from doing something harsh to the Japha children. In Danaaa's mind, disrespect was not to be tolerated. Danaaa decided she didn't like these young Japha.

After a short period the young Japha, La and Shaya begged Tee to let them tour some of the city. Tee was apprehensive, because her children were unfamiliar with their surroundings. Nevertheless, La begged that they would be safe. La said her Special Guard would be with them and the Ra guards were everywhere. Ramala and Wana reassured Tee that security was tight and everyone knew they were special guest of the Hellcats. Tee said her two oldest children could go, but Tee's Terrible Two begged their way into going. Tee asked that La have her children back in time for dinner. La smiled and said that she would. Tara's Terrible Two asked, but weren't allowed to go. Tara knew her daughters were troublesome and didn't want Danaaa to beat the crap out of them.

San-Jett and his brother Jeb were in excellent fighting condition for their ages. Elder San and the toughest fighting instructors the House of Japha had to offer gave them the toughest training. They were always armed with machetes and axes, like the Ra children. The young Japha girls just had machetes in their waist holsters and a small knife hidden, strapped to their thigh like most girls of this day had.

Once out of the sight of his mother, San-Jett got a little bolder. He said, "Normally, I walk out in front and everyone follows me. I guess, since I don't know where we're going, it's alright if you lead the way, just this once."

La smiled at San-Jett and said "Thanks. Follow me, I'm going to show you some places around the city I think you'll like." La's voice was light and soothing to San-Jett's ears, as she pointed and showed him places that they walked by. La seemed to be paying extra attention to San-Jett as she showed the Japha around. San-Jett thought that once he let the Ra know how important he was, they weren't bad to be around, at all. San-Jett liked the teenage Ra everyone called La.

When they walked up to the dungeon, La explained what it was. She said she would take them inside to see if someone was getting their head chopped off, but she didn't think their mother would approve. San-Jett didn't need his mother's approval. He told La that his mother didn't have to know about everything he did. La looked at San-Jett's sisters as if they might tell. San-Jett made his sisters promise that they wouldn't. That's when La reluctantly gave in. She led the young Japha into the dungeon.

As soon as they walked into the dungeon, La and Dan rushed San-Jett taking him to the ground hard, while Don and Shaya did the same to Jeb. The Terrible Two were shocked by this and easily subdued, one each by Danaaa and Ram.

La had her Special Guard tie the Japha boys up and hang them upside down in a cell, while she had the two Japha girls tied to a post with their mouths covered, because they wouldn't stop screaming for their parents.

Once everyone was secured, La walked over to San-Jett and stared at him for a moment before saying "You thought you could come here and talk to me anyway you like. Now, look at the trouble your mouth has gotten you into. Do you know who I am!?"

As if on cue, Danaaa incredulously yelled "She's the Number One Princess!" La responded, "That's right! I don't care who you are, or where you come from. You're going to show me the proper respect!" San-Jett, although shaken by the unexpected turn of events, tried to put up a brave front when he said, "You'll never get away with this!"

La slapped San-Jett, hard and fast, three times across his upside down face. She then plowed her fist hard into his stomach. San-Jett gasped for air, as La's fist hit his stomach, unexpectedly.

La paused for a second and then slapped him twice more. She then hit San-Jett two more times in his stomach, before turning her back to him. This time the punches didn't hurt as much, because San saw it coming and tightened his stomach muscles. La smiled at her siblings, before turning back to San, with a serious face and saying "You're so stupid, you keep talking when you should fear for your life!"

Danaaa interrupted La, by turning to her and yelling "But how can he be Stupid, when I'm Stupid!?!" Dan, who normally liked Danaaa's stupid tirades, wanted to see where La was going with this, so he yelled to Danaaa "Shut up and quit being stupid, Stupid!" Danaaa looked at Dan for a moment. She could shut up, but she didn't know how to quit being Stupid, because that's who she was.

San-Jett, still defiant, but now a little scared, pulled out his ace in the whole and said, "Wait until aunt Jan finds out what you've done! You're going to be in big trouble!"

Once La saw that Danaaa was back under control, she pulled out her machete, placed the point of it on San-Jett's forehead and pushed slightly. La said, "How's she going to find out if all of you are dead and we feed your bodies to the hyenas."

La looked into San-Jett's eyes, letting her words sink in. San-Jett had never thought of that possibility and now feeling the point of La's machete pressing on his forehead, he was done with being defiant. He was now in a very cooperative mood.

Although, begging for his own life, but not wanting to seem like he was, San said, "Please, just let my sisters and brother go! Please, I won't say a word to anyone, about this!" La looked at San as if she didn't believe him. She reared back with her machete, paused for a moment and swung it at San-Jett's neck, stopping it just before it touched his skin. Then La let the blade touch San's neck, without cutting him.

Everyone was startled by Teesana, who had chewed the cover from around her mouth, just enough to scream "Please, don't kill my brother, please! He's telling the truth! He won't say anything! I can tell when he's telling the truth! And he really is! Don't kill him, please! Please! Please!" then Teesana broke down crying, uncontrollably.

That was enough for Shaya to give La a worried look that said this was enough, already. To Young Dan this was priceless. He wanted to see how far La could push these brat Japha. San-Jett looked upside down over at his sister, before looking in La's eyes with a great deal of sincerity. He begged, "I promise we won't say anything. We'll act right. Please, just let us go!"

La looked over at Dan, with her machete still at San's throat and said, "What do you think?" Dan, who was leaning against one of the cells, stood up and walked towards San with his hand moving to the handle of his Hammer-Axe. San didn't miss that hand movement. Dan walked up to San and looked him in his eye, letting San know that he and his siblings could indeed be killed and fed to the hyenas. Dan said "You know who I am, don't you?" San did, because he was told by his aunt Jan. San said, "You're the Hammer-Axe Champion, Warlord Faster Cut."

Dan said, "That's right! Remember that I'm a faster cut than anyone you know. Don't ever disrespect me, or my family, again. Is that clear?"

San answered with a strong and believable "Yes!" Dan said, "Let them loose." no, sooner than Dan said that, La lowered her machete and motion to the guards, saying, "Right, then, you heard him!"

The guards cut the two Japha boys down and untied them, while other guards untied the Japha girls. Once San-Jett was on his feet, Dan plowed his fist into San's stomach. San bent over and gasped for air from the force of the punch. Dan's punch was much more powerful than La's. When he stood up, San looked at Dan wondering what that punch was for. Dan pointed his finger at San and said, "That was just a reminder. Don't say a word about this to anyone."

The terrible Two ran over to San and hugged him, clinging on to him for dear life. They were terrified and panicked. They didn't know what the Ra would next do to them. San and Jeb calmed them, warning them not to say anything to their mother, or aunt.

Once the Japha composed themselves, La led them out of the dungeon. The Japha got in line behind the Ra without saying one word. Danaaa and Ram walked beside the Japha, because La gave them their weapons back. That insured that San and his brother Jeb wouldn't try anything with their axes. The two Japha girls were too shaken up to try, or be a part of anything other than what they were told to do. They just wanted to get back to the safety of their mother.

Once the young Japha got back, the two girls raced to their mother. Although panicked, when questioned they said nothing. Japha Na, Tee and Jan knew the Japha children had been through a terrible ordeal, by the red slightly swollen marks on San's face and the prick on his forehead from La's blade, coupled with the Japha girls clinging to Tee.

Tee and Jan were upset by this and although it showed on Tee's face, it didn't show on Jan's. Jan knew it was a good thing that the future Rulers of Japha learned firsthand about their counter-parts in the South.

It surprised both Tee and Jan, the next day, when the Japha boys begged to go and spend the day with the Ra boys. After constant badgering, Tee finally gave in to her boys. After that, Tee's boys spent the rest of the visit with the Ra boys.

Tee's girls wanted nothing to do with the older Ra girls, at first. They stayed and mostly spent time with their counter-parts, Tara's Terrible Two. When all four of these girls got together, they seemed to feed off each other and created all sorts of mayhem for the maids and servants. Since Tara and Tee only intervened when their girls were completely out of control, for the maids and servants, these girls were the Terrible Two, times two!

CHAPTER 10

The Hammer-Axe Championships were held during a seven-day period, with La's Executioner the Hayee, Hoban winning the strength competition, while young Dan's Warlord the Hayee, Bo won the power competition. Young Dan won the speed, agility, offensive, defensive and sparring competitions. That made him this year's sole Hammer-Axe Champion.

That evening, there was a big feast honoring Young Dan's victory. Japha, San and his bodyguards were just arriving from their visit with Yin. Jan, Ramala and Wana met them. After a brief meeting with San, Wana called a meeting with the Butchers.

The meeting was held at Wana's palace in a private room. The Ra children weren't invited. The Hellcats, along with Jan and San were already present when Dan arrived with the Butchers. After everyone was seated, San stood up, looked at each of the Butchers, lastly looking at Ma and saying "We were ambushed by the Shinmushee three days, ago. The Butcher Yin was killed, along with Kiki."

Ma immediately jumped up out of her seat, eyes blazing, yelling to San "No, it can't be! Tell me, it's not true!"

San said, "They made an early morning raid on us, just as Yin was taking us out to see if there was anything going on south of his position. We fought them for over four hours straight, before Kiki was killed. That left us unprotected on our right side. The enemy took advantage of it, immediately. My bodyguards and I were separated from Yin. We fought hard to get back to him. We got there just in time to see it happen." San looked down after saying that.

Ma saw tears flowing down Tara's face. Ma turned and stared at San. She was still in shock. Ma's eyes filled with tears as she shook her head in disbelief, saying "No! He can't be dead! He just can't be! Where's my brother!?!"

Wana motioned to the guards at the doorway. They had two guards bring in Yin's headless body on a stretcher like cot. Ma ran over to Yin's bloated, close to decomposing body. The smell almost made her vomit. As Ma searched the body for birthmarks she knew Yin had, in a panic, Ma yelled, "Where's his head!"

San replied, "His head was chopped off and they took it away. I would have hunted them down and retrieved it, if only I had more men."

Syn and Dan went over and grabbed Ma, just as she identified marks on Yin's body. Ma started screaming Yin's name. She passed out and was taken to Syn's place.

Tara walked over and looked at Yin's body. Her voice was choked up when she said, "Yin and his sisters don't need to see their father like this. Get rid of his body. I'll think of something to tell them." Wana motioned and the guards took Yin's body away.

On the morning Jan's caravan left for the city of Ra, San and Yin had breakfast at San's caravan. They were talking about old times, letting their food digest. Yin was going to take San to some of the hot spots, hoping for a few battles with the Shinmushee, before San headed to the city of Ra.

They didn't know that the Wa rebels, along with the Shinmushee planned an ambush. Everything was set, they but noticed a large caravan moving towards Yin's position. The Shinmushee waited to see what was going on. The next day they watched as the larger part of the caravan headed south, leaving only a few men behind.

After making sure the caravan going south wouldn't be able to get back in time, they decided to continue their mission of killing all the Butchers at Yin's House of Hell.

Yin, Kiki, San and his bodyguards were given a good lead by the few Ra guards in the area. Yin had the guards stay back so the Shinmushee would think they had an advantage. Yin and San were talking, making their way towards a thick Forrest, with tall trees, bushes and thick undergrowth. Yin knew this area was a good place to hide a lot of Shinmushee. He was right and San noticed Shinmushee hiding in the upcoming Forrest. San covertly let Yin know. Yin had already seen them and moved briskly ahead, while San cautiously followed.

The Shinmushee waited, until Yin was at edge of the Forrest. That's when they attacked. Yin swung his Hammer-Axes, immediately carving up Shinmushee. San and Kiki took up positions next to Yin and held their ground. San's bodyguards moved to protect their backs, just as more Shinmushee poured out of bushes surrounding them.

The battle raged on in the same area, until Yin started pushing the fight into the Forrest. San reluctantly backed Yin up, even though he knew they would be at a disadvantage there. San had to fight, while stepping over large plant and avoiding hitting trees with his axes. He let Yin know, without breaking concentration on his battle, that they should move back, outside the Forrest.

However, it seemed Yin was hell bent on pursuing the enemy, as if Yin had the larger force. San kept backing Yin up, getting himself deeper and deeper into the Forrest. San wanted some action and it seemed the deeper they got into the Forrest, the more intense the battles got. San looked for a quick second and couldn't see Kiki. He couldn't worry about that, because the Shinmushee were attacking, waiting for San to make one mistake they could take advantage of.

San's bodyguards had their hands full trying to protect San's back, while keeping a path out of the Forrest. Yin pushed further into thicker parts of the Forrest. This time San didn't follow. San didn't have a death wish, but it seemed Yin did. San fought hard from where he was for a little over an hour. Just when he was about to retreat out of the Forrest, the Shinmushee faded away into the thicker parts of the jungle.

San and his bodyguards surveyed the area looking for Yin. About five minutes later Yin appeared. Yin looked wild eyed and a little winded, but he was unharmed. He laughed at San while jokingly saying, "Living in a palace has made you a little reluctant to keep the enemy backing up! Don't worry about it though, by tomorrow I'll have you chasing them, just like me!"

Yin walked briskly past San, out of the Forrest and noticed he didn't see Kiki. As he was about to turn and ask San where she might be, Yin realized that San's bodyguards were moving close to him with their axes still in hand. Yin's instincts were still on high alert and he was just about to dismiss it, when San's bodyguards attacked him. Yin blocked several powerful swings from San's bodyguards when he realized San was behind him.

In that instant, Yin remembered all the Japha he had killed during the war with the Northern Houses. San interrupted Yin's thoughts by saying, "Hold it!"

San's guards disengaged Yin and slowly moved backwards with their axes on guard against Yin. Yin quickly turned sideways, so he could watch San and San's bodyguards at the same time. Yin had his evil grin on his face when he said "What's this!?!"

San looked conflicted when he said, "I've come to take your head back to the Japha Elders. I wish there was a better way, but there's not." Yin said, "That's not going to be easy, you know."

San said, "I know. But since this is for your head, hopefully it's the greatest battle of your life." San motioned for his guards to move back even further, allowing more room for himself and Yin. San pulled both his axes. Yin said "It'll have to be." then he raised his axes on guard against San. That's when San attacked.

San found out right away that even though Yin was wild and crazy, the real reason Yin hadn't been killed yet was that this was what he was best at. Yin was just that good. Yin's axes came at San from all angles. Even with that, San couldn't get a clean shot at Yin. They both went hard at each other for close to forty minutes before pausing, while circling each other, plotting their next attack. Yin still had his evil grin on his face when he said, "If that's the best you can do, you'd better get your guards to join you."

San smiled and said, "What makes you thing that was my best?" This time Yin attacked first. San's concentration was superb. Just like the first time, San blocked, or dodged all swings by Yin. It was different this time when San went on the offensive. Before Yin blocked and avoided San. This time Yin mounted a strong counter-attack. It was potent enough that Yin drew first blood as his ax got a glancing slice that caught San, going upward on the left side of his chest all the way to his shoulder.

San reacted instantly by turning the heat up on Yin and slicing Yin three times before San and Yin backed away from each other. Just like San's wound, Yin's were non-lethal. San was all business as they slowly circled each other this time. Yin, still with his evil grin, taunted San, saying, "I can do this all day and all night! Don't you know I'm Yin?!"

Yin attacked right after that. He was putting some real heat on San this time. He sliced San twice more, before having a shot clean at San's neck. San sold out with everything he had not to get his head taken off. Yin was surprised he missed, but knew he now had a chance at San that wouldn't miss, no matter what San did.

However, Yin had to bring his axes up to protect his own neck. San's bodyguards had snuck into a striking position on Yin. Yin blocked a barrage of lethal blows coming from the two bodyguards.

Yin needed to make a defensive move so he could turn and protect himself from San. But it was too late. Before Yin could react, San took his head clean off with just one powerful swing of his Hammer-Axe.

Yin's head flipped up and then fell to the ground, rolling a couple of times, before stopping. His body fell to the ground like a sack of potatoes, while his limbs twitched, a few times, before not moving at all. San stood and watched for a moment. He thought Yin deserved better than that. San then turned and stared at his two bodyguards.

San was angry that they interfered, even though they saved his life. He wanted to kill them for doing what they were supposed to do. The two bodyguards saw that in San's eyes and went down on their knees, lowering their heads and waiting on San's judgment. San knew what he had to do. He reluctantly said "Good work! Both of you have proven why you're worthy of you positions. Rise and let's find the others."

Once San and his two bodyguards got to where his other bodyguards were San ordered five of them to take ten guards and take Yin's head back to the city of San-Jania and wait with it, until his return.

One of the guards who had Yin's head by the hair, asked, "What do you want us to do with the girl?" as the guard pointed towards Kiki. San looked where the guard was pointing. He saw Kiki's body slumped over near a tree. The other bodyguards surprised her with an attack earlier and killed her. All the Butchers here helping Yin were also killed. San looked at the guard and said, nonchalantly "Leave her here. We got what we came for."

San turned and walked towards his caravan. Jan had pleaded with San not to tell that they planned the ambush and death of Yin. Being the King of the House of Japha, even though San didn't want to kill Yin, he didn't see why he had to lie about it. After all, Yin was just a heathen. The Hellcats wouldn't confront San about Yin's death, especially since they would understand why San had to do it. However, it seemed to San that Jan didn't want to have to kill Ma and risk a confrontation with the Syn, Jara. San decided to make up a simple lie that everyone would have no problem believing, knowing Yin's mentality. San took one last look around, before wondering what Jan and his family were doing in the city of Ra, before heading back to his small caravan.

Although Tara was putting on a good face, she was hurting over Yin's death. Tara often told herself that Yin would end up in a hellish death of his own making. She tried to prepare herself for that eventuality. Now that it was here, Tara was dealing with it as best she could. Tara asked Wana that Yin's death not be announced, until after the feast and festivities tonight. The Hellcats agreed.

After meeting with the Hellcats, San and Jan met in private. San told Jan everything that happened. Upon hearing, everything

San had to say, Jan walked over to the door and ordered her guard to see if she could meet the Hellcats in private. San waited until she was done then asked, "What are you planning?" Jan turned and looked at San. She smiled and said, "I'm going to do what's best for me, you and the House of Japha." San gave Jan a suspicious look, and then said, "What's that?" Jan said, "You'll see, because you're coming with me."

It was a meeting with just the Hellcats and the Japha twins held in one of Wana's private meeting rooms. The Hellcats were curious and let Jan start as soon as she and San showed up.

Jan looked at all three Hellcats, before looking back at Ramala and saying "Sister, I want you to listen very carefully to what I have to say. Although I came to visit you, San and I had another mission. The Elders and many Japha families who had members killed by Yin demanded justice."

Tara realizing where this was going stared in disbelief as Jan told the entire story about how San took Yin's head and had his guards take it North to Japha as proof of Yin's death. Yin was an enemy of the Japha. Jan explained that if they hadn't taken care of this, members of the Japha army would have moved into Ra territory seeking Yin. That could have led to another war.

San was uncomfortable that Jan put him in a situation like this. To San, Jan seemed to trust that the Hellcats wouldn't take this as disrespect towards them. San was on guard, without trying to look like he was. If things went bad, he knew he had to find a way to get himself and Jan out of here.

Jan ended with "I tell you this because I want no secrets between us that you might find out about, later." Jan looked at Tara and said, "We had to do this to keep peace. Believe me, there was no other way."

Tara, while looking at Jan, said with attitude in her voice "So, now my children have to grow up without a father, because you decided it was best for everyone that he be killed!"

Jan paused, before saying in a conciliatory manner, "Your children are loved by all, including the Japha. They will have favor in all of Japha and will be treated that way according to protocol."

Tara turned her head away from Jan and San, when she said, "I wonder who else, in the House of Ra, is next on your death list!" Jan, with a concerned look on her face, looked away from Tara and turned to Ramala for help.

Ramala knew this was a delicate situation. Ramala didn't care that Yin was dead. He had become reckless, unruly and wouldn't follow Wana's orders. If it were a few years ago, she would have dealt with Yin, herself. Still, Tara was grieving and Ramala knew she had to seem sensitive to Tara's feeling for Yin.

Wana went over to Tara, got down on her knees and held Tara's hands in support. Ramala looked at Jan, stood up and moved behind Tara, putting her hands on Tara's shoulders, rubbing them gently, as she said "My cousin's frustrations with her loss is very understandable. She might be very difficult during this time. Bear with her and show her the proper respect as she mourns."

Ramala looked at both San and Jan as she spoke, letting them know that they would have to put up with Tara's attitude, if they didn't want Yin's death to become a major issue.

Jan already knew that. Even though San didn't think it was best to say what he'd done, Jan knew it was best they didn't lie to the Hellcats and have them find out about it, later. Jan was also confident that the bond between herself and Ramala was strong enough to endure this and stay strong.

Jan was sure of that because she consulted the Tat on this matter. The House of Tat was once one of the original seven Houses. Their family members had mental skills that allowed them to see into the future and also read the thoughts in other's minds and manipulate those thoughts with telepathic suggestions. They lived and enjoyed a peaceful life, until the mountain they lived on blew up, imploding upon itself. Several of the Tat left days before the mountain blew up and were the only known surviving Tat.

After their homeland was destroyed, the remaining Tat visited the House of Japha. Jan quickly embraced them and offered to build them a sanctuary where they could continue to live, undisturbed, according to the Tat protocols. The Tat agreed and for Jan's generosity, she persuaded the Tat to give her any insights that could help her. The Tat told Jan that she and San would have a little trouble on their trip, but nothing they couldn't handle. That was enough to make Jan confident that she could tell the Hellcats the truth about Yin's death.

As Wana consoled Tara, she was glad that San killed Yin. Wana wanted Yin dead and was formulating a plan to get it done. Now she and Tara wouldn't have to be divided over this issue. Wana could support Tara, relieved that Yin wasn't a problem for her, anymore.

San stood up and got down on one knee. Still a safe distance from Tara, San said, "The King of the House of Japha gives his greatest sympathy for the pain he has caused you. There are no words that I can say that can convey my regrets that this had to happen. Know that I am in dept to you and your children. That you have great favor in the eyes of the King of Japha and favor in all of Japha."

When San was done talking, he meekly walked over to Tara, went done on one knee again and reached for her hand, not looking up at Tara. For a King to do this was unprecedented. Kings never get lower than their subjects, or anyone else, let alone get on their knees.

Tara looked at San for a moment. She wanted to quickly pull her machete and take his head. Tara knew Jan would have to be killed right after that and the Hellcats would be at war with the North. With Ramala gently pushing on Tara's shoulders, letting her know what she needed to do, Tara slowly extended her hand out to San. San gently took Tara's hand and while caressing it with his hands, he slowly kissed it.

After his lips left Tara's hand, San looked up into Tara's eyes. Tara could see that San had regret over what he'd done. Tara put her hand on San's face as her eyes filled with tears and the tears rolled down her face. Tara looked at San only a moment before she turned away. San was now aware of the pain Tara was feeling, just as she wanted. San stood up, walked over and took his seat next to Jan.

Wana could see that Tara was temporarily disarmed by San's show of respect to her. Wana took advantage by ending the meeting. Just as everyone was getting ready to leave, Tara said, "San, if you're serious about me having favor with you, come to my palace and discuss with me what might make this hardship easier on me. My guards will let you know when I'm available." San hesitated, so Jan said, "You just let us know when and we'll be there."

Tara quickly said, "San will come by himself to hear me out." Everyone in the room looked at Tara. Jan looked confused, until San put his hand on her shoulder and said, "I'll go. Don't worry about me, we'll be just fine."

After San and Jan left, Ramala and Wana questioned Tara as to what she was up to. Tara said, as a matter of fact "If San wants to offer up something to appease me, I'm going to see just how much he's willing to give." Ramala excitedly said, "We'll come and help you!"

Tara said "No, if either of you are there San will see this as manipulation by the three of us, when really, it will just be by me." All three Hellcats smiled deviously at each other.

Tara hadn't told Yin that his father had been killed. She wanted to think of something that wouldn't leave a bad memory for any of her children. Tara certainly wasn't going to tell her children that the Japha killed their father. That would create a generation of warfare between the North and the South. Since Young Dan was being honored with a feast for winning his second Hammer-Axe Championship this evening, Tara decided she wouldn't tell Yin, until after that.

CHAPTER 11

Everyone in the House of Ra knew who was in control, after their Queen, the Hayee, Ramala. It was the Number One Princess Ra, Ramala, or La. La made sure that everyone knew she would soon be the Queen of Ra, so they should start treating her like that, now, if they wanted favor with her when she actually became Queen. So, looking for favor with La, the guards who handled Yin's body personally asked for an audience with the Number One Princess, alone. La said she would grant it, but her brother Dan would be present. La didn't trust any of the Hayee and after the Hayee's failed assault of Ramala's palace.

The guards met with and told La about Elder Yin's death and where his body was being disposed of. La and Dan instructed the guards not to say a word about Yin's death to anyone else and to take them to Yin's body. They got there on the far end of the city, just as Yin's body was being prepared to be burned.

Dan and La looked around and wondered why no one was here to show respect for their uncle Yin. They stood there and watched as the body was about to be burned. After a few minutes, Shaya showed up with Yin, Don, Danaaa and Ram. Shaya threatened the guards to take her where La was, even though La told Shaya and the others to stay at the palace, until she and Dan returned. La turned and stared at Shaya for a moment, before turning back and staring at the flames that were just getting started. All of the children were aware that this was a funeral flame of a burning body.

Shaya asked, "Who was that?" La said in a low solemn voice, without breaking her gaze on the fire "One of the great heroes of

Ra." Shaya not thinking La knew exactly what she meant asked, "What's their name?" La said, "This is not the time for questions, it's the time when you show respect."

Shaya knew this person had to be important if La and Dan were here. She looked from La to the flames and said "Then we should get down out of respect for what this great hero has done for the House of Ra, shouldn't we?"

Without answering, La and Dan got down on their knees, still watching the flames. The other Ra children did so after they saw the oldest two do so. The guards also got down on their knees, more so because Dan and La had done so.

No one said a word as they felt the heat of the bright flames on their faces. La and Dan were affected, knowing this was their uncle Yin. They watched, until the flames were almost gone. The Hammer-Axe Six and the guards there were the only ones to pay tribute to Yin's burning body.

La and Dan looked at each other and decided it was time to go. They didn't know how to tell Yin his father was dead, so they didn't. Without saying a word to each other, Dan and La thought it best if they told Yin about his father, later.

Shaya still had many questions that hadn't been answered. First, she couldn't figure out why La and Dan wouldn't let her and the others come. Secondly, who was this great hero? If he was so great, why weren't more people here to show this hero respect?

No one was talking on the way back, so Shaya thought it a good time and asked, "Who was that?"

Neither La, nor Dan answered Shaya. Shaya was annoyed that she was being ignored. She decided that someone was going to give her an answer. Shaya asked, a little more animated than before "I said, who was that?!"

La and Dan didn't say a word. Just as Shaya started moving closer to La, so she could yell her question, Danaaa bumped Shaya hard and yelled "But, she already told you! It was a great Hero of Ra! Weren't you listening!?! Even, I heard that much!!"

There was a second of silence and then Don erupted into laughter. Everyone else joined in after that, laughing uncontrollably.

High Pressure the Executioner

The only one who wasn't laughing was Shaya. She didn't find this funny. Shaya still didn't know who that great Hero was. Only now, she refused to ask, because she didn't want to be a laughingstock, again.

Shaya had attitude with La, up until just before the feast, when La promised Shaya she would tell her when they were in bed, just before sleep. Since the Ra girls always talked before they went to sleep, Shaya was willing to wait.

Everyone showed up for the feast. There were so many people from the Hayee clan that the feast not only filled the largest courtyard in the city, but the party was in most of the streets throughout the city.

Dancers entertained, until the teenage girls started the Dance Offs. All of these teenage girls knew how good the Ra girls were and were upping their own skills to compete. This dance off was the most fiercely contested one to date, with all of the girls involved putting everything they had into it. There were many uncomfortable fathers in the audience watching their daughters do things that they would normally enjoy, if it were any other women, besides their daughters. Even Elder Dan was enthralled by the dancing these teenagers were doing, until his three daughters got on the floor.

At first Elder Dan couldn't believe how synchronized and accurately his daughters were with their movements to the beats. Soon though, Dan was annoyed, then outright offended by the looks the other men were giving to the moves he deemed overly provocative. Elder Dan endured as much as he could before he stood up and was about to put an end to this madness his daughters were calling dancing. However, it seemed just as he was about to do just that, his girls put an astounding end to their routine. The crowd immediately erupted with applauds and favorable chants. Dan stared at his daughters in frustration as he angrily wiped the sweat that had accumulated on his forehead.

Ramala saw Dan go through the torture of watching his daughters shake it up in their dance routine and enjoyed every second of Dan's suffering. Ramala, without looking at Dan, said as a matter of fact, "You better not scold them when they get over here. They did a great routine out there. You didn't think they would be babies forever, did you?"

Elder Dan didn't respond to Ramala. These two hadn't been getting along that well, but were putting up a good front for their children's sake. Still, the children noticed the difference in the way their parents interacted with each other. It was different, but since there were no big fights between their parents, like in the past, the Ra children perceived the change as not bad.

All three Ra girls ran over to Elder Dan after being congratulated by the crowd that had gathered around. Dan hugged his daughters, pretending he wasn't uncomfortable with their performance. After a few moments with Dan, the Ra girls got bored with him and moved on, looking for something more exciting to occupy their time.

Elder Dan decided to walk around and inconspicuously see which females might give him a good time, later. As he was moving through the crowd, because of who he was, everyone moved out of his way, making a path. Dan was walking through the crowd when four of Ramala's bodyguards slowly crossed his path, blocking his way for a moment.

All four looked at Dan. Crossing the path of someone of higher ranked than you was a serious sign of disrespect and considered a challenge. Dan wasn't bothered by that, figuring it wasn't done on purpose, until one of the bodyguards, the Hayee, Monty stopped and stared at Dan. He looked at Dan, with an arrogant smirk on his face, as if Dan was worthless. Although, Dan always had his Axes with him, he became instantly aware that Monty and the other bodyguards had theirs, also. At that moment, the tension in the air was so thick, you could only cut it with an Ax.

Monty was Ramala's personal bodyguard and the only other man Ramala had sex with, besides Dan. Dan never found out and even though it was only one time and meant nothing to Ramala, it left an impression on Monty. Monty thought that Ramala would have given him another chance by now, but she hadn't.

Every time Monty saw Dan, he thought Dan was why Ramala wouldn't risk being with him again. Over time, Monty's resentment towards Dan grew. Tonight, that resentment manifested itself in the form of an unspoken challenge.

Before anyone made a move, Young Dan and his brothers were at their father's side, with the Ra girls quickly moving closer. Young Dan stared at Monty and ordered "On your knees, at once!"

Now, Young Dan had dared Monty not to back down to his normally subservient position, or get cut to pieces by the Hammer-Axe Champion and his siblings.

La, on guard, came right up to Young Dan, staring at Monty and the other bodyguards, before saying to Dan "What's going on here!?!"

Monty and the other bodyguards moved back, got down on their knees and lowered their heads. Dan, while still watching Monty closely, said to La "Nothing."

La suspiciously looked at Dan and then back at Monty and the other guards. She looked at her father and lastly at young Dan, again. Elder Dan walked away, leaving his children with Ramala's guards. La said to young Dan "Are you sure, it's nothing?" Young Dan said, "Nothing we can't handle, later, if we choose to."

That was a direct threat to Monty and the others that they would be dealt with by young Dan if they got out of line, again. After young Dan was sure Monty and the other guards now understood their place, he ordered, "Get back to your post!"

Now, angry and humiliated, trying not to let it show, Monty and the other guards left. As they were leaving, Danaaa took one deep sniff of all four men. Danaaa pulled La's arm towards her, putting her lips to La's ear, while peeking forward. She said in her whispering voice, "They smell like trouble to me!" La peered at the guards. She looked around the room, before grabbing Danaaa's ponytail, pulling it and saying "Come on, this show is over!"

The Ra girls went over to Ramala, who was talking to Japha, Jan, Na, Tee and some high-ranking Hayee women. La watched as her father mingled with some of the female dancers. To La, her father a saint. La told herself that part of being the King was getting to know everyone, even if he mostly just got to know the females.

La was a daddy's girl and even though she was a young teenager and wasn't always holding her father's hand, or demanding he pick her up, as she did in the past, she was very protective when it came to him.

La only saw the guards standing in front of her father, after she saw young Dan and her brothers' move to her father's side. Still, that was enough for La to see that some sort of disrespect had happened, even though young Dan handled the situation.

What La couldn't figure out was why her mother hadn't reprimanded those guards, immediately. La peeked at her mother a couple of times, and then she said, while not looking directly at Ramala "Your bodyguards are getting a little too disrespectful for my liking. They need to be taught a lesson."

Ramala, not thinking La should be telling her how to treat her bodyguards, especially in public, said, "You let me worry about my guards. Besides, if your father is going to start relying on his children to fight his battles, he'll lose any respect he has."

La didn't like that answer. Before she could stop herself, La quickly looked at Ramala, before turning back towards the crowd. Ramala, upon seeing that, said, "La, calm yourself. That incident was nothing to concern yourself with. I've always told you not to wrap your mind around unimportant things."

La sternly pulled on Danaaa's ponytail without saying a word. Shaya saw that and knew it was time to go. All three girls turned back to Ramala, lowered their heads, and then walked away. Na, Tee's daughters the Terrible Two, whom after getting over being put in their place, followed the Ra girls everywhere they went. Therefore, it didn't surprise Tee when they followed the Ra girls this time. It was the same with Tee's two sons always being wherever the Ra boys were.

The Ra girls mingled with the crowd. They were very popular among the young Ra and the Hayee that were older than La, but not yet grown-ups. Young Dan walked over and had a few words with La.

Ramala was now enjoying conversation with some of the high-ranking females and males in the Hayee clan, along with her self-proclaimed sister Japha, Jan. Wana was there, also, enjoying pleasant conversation.

As Ramala scanned the room, she didn't see Elder Dan. She knew he probably found a few girls to whore around with. She told herself that when he returned to the palace, she would punish Dan verbally and then sexually well into the next day to teach him a lesson about being a whore that he wouldn't soon forget.

Ramala looked around the room again and didn't see Ram. That made her a little nervous, as it always did. She scanned the room to see if she could get Young Dan to look for his brother before someone came up missing. However, to Ramala's surprise she didn't see young Dan, either. She didn't see any of her children. She relaxed a little, telling herself and hoping that Ram was with his brothers and sisters. Ramala went back to enjoying conversation with Jan and her cousins.

Earlier, just before the feast, Tara sent messengers to let San know to meet her at her palace. The messenger said they would meet for a while and then join everyone at the feast. San agreed. Before San went to meet with Tara, Jan talked San's ear off, telling him how smart Tara was and that he should be very careful negotiating with her. Jan told San that whatever he agreed to, to make sure it was beneficial to the Japha, as well as the Ra. She said that the alliance with the Hellcats was most important and his decisions should be based on protecting that. San listened to Jan. He knew she couldn't help herself and was mostly talking for her own benefit.

San wasn't worried about this meeting in the least, bit. Whatever Tara had to say, he knew she wouldn't be stupid enough to make an attempt on his life. He also knew Ramala wouldn't let Tara go as far as to harm Jan, or his family. Anything short of that, San knew he could deal with.

His bodyguards escorted San to Tara's palace. Tara's guards stopped San's guards and said they would have to wait outside the palace. No guards were allowed inside. San looked at his guards and told them to wait for him outside. San's guards posted up at the bottom steps of Tara's palace, while San was escorted up the steps and into the palace. Maids met San at the entrance to Tara's palace. Not even Tara's guards were allowed to enter Tara's palace, without Tara's permission. The maids took San to a large room that had a table with food on it and a sitting area off to the left where Tara was lounging.

This was the first time San was in Tara's palace. It was just as lavish as Ramala's. Plants and small trees lined both sides of the halls, as well as the borders of the large room he was in. San was impressed!

Tara watched San as he walked in. San was dressed as if he was attending a military meeting. He had his Hammer-Axes on his back harnesses and machetes on his weapons holster. After entering the room, San lowered his head, out of respect to Tara and then raised it to eye level.

Tara smiled at San and said, "You look like you're ready for war. I hope I didn't give the impression that you'd need your weapons."

San said, "You didn't, but I'm a King. A King should never be without his weapons."

Tara said, "Would a King bring weapons, while having a meal with one of his closest allies?" Tara made her way to the table with food on it. San said "With most allies, yes. But not with you."

San only looked at Tara for a moment, before he took off his weapons and put them on the floor near the table. Tara waved her hand, presenting the chair next to her, saying "Please." San sat next to Tara and they had a short meal. Tara made light conversation in between eating, so as to keep the atmosphere comfortable.

After the meal, Tara stood up and said, "Come, let's walk and converse in my garden. It's much less formal than in here." Tara led San through the halls of her palace.

They came through a doorway and were in one of Tara's private gardens. Tara stopped walking and gave San a chance to look around. The garden was large and very impressive. Torches around the perimeter lit the garden. Chairs, benches and tables were strategically placed around the garden. The deep blue star lit sky gave a beautiful backdrop.

While San was taking in the beauty of the garden, Tara started talking. She said "When Japha, Jan told me what happened to Yin I was so angry, I wanted kill you."

San was startled by that statement and although he thought Tara might have felt that way, he never expected her to say it. Tara was within arm's reach of San. He took all of that in and watched her every movement, without being obvious. San remained calm and continued to listen to Tara.

Tara turned facing San and said, "Since then, I've had time to calm myself to somewhere less than that. Right now, I'm very hurt. I don't want to do anything that would cause war between the House of Japha and the House of Ra."

Tara paused to let San know the significance of what she just said and that she indeed had the power to cause war if she chose to. None of this was lost on San. San knew Tara was letting him know she had an advantage in this negotiation process. San was now ready to hear what Tara's demands were, so he asked, "What can the King of Japha offer that would help ease the burden of your loss and help you in your healing process?"

San had opened the door to serious negotiations. Tara moved close to San, put her lips right at his ears, and whispered as if she didn't want anyone to hear but San, even though there was no one around. Tara whispered, "I'm very emotional over what has happened. I'm afraid that I might do, or say something very irrational, that I might regret later. I need to be consoled."

San was already aware of Tara's breast, flat stomach and hips pressing up against him. He listened as Tara's soft voice lightly vibrated his eardrums to a subtle level of excitement. As soon as Tara said her last word, her hands moved slowly around San's waist and up his back, while her lips moved from San's ear, just barely touching his face, as they slowly made their way to San's lips.

San knew that his reaction to Tara would affect everyone, whether it be positively, or negatively. So when Tara's lips reached San's, she had San's full cooperation.

After a very passionate kiss, it seemed to San that Tara's whole body was vibrating against his. The only other time San had ever experienced that was during very intense sex.

Tara arched her back, while still kissing and keeping her lips and tongue locked on San's. With her back arched Tara started clawing at San's shirt from the front, trying to get it off. San, wanting to be helpful, started maneuvering his body and arms to help Tara achieve her goal. Tara's passion was bordering on being forceful, but Tara had a soft way about her forcefulness that made it pleasurable to San.

San's shirt was now off and his pants were hanging around his knees. He couldn't get them completely off, because Tara had posted and pressed him up against the wall and was kissing him while manipulating him, with her hands, to a rock hard stiffness.

Tara took a quick step back from San and looked down at his stick, which was pointing up towards the sky. Tara then looked into San's eyes for a moment, before she started ripping her clothes off. San saw the urgency in which Tara was moving and decided to use this opportunity to get his pants completely off.

No sooner than he'd done so, Tara was back on San, climbing up onto his body. San lifted Tara by her thighs all the way up to his chest, before letting her slowly slide down on him. Tara reached around San and put his member where she needed it to be. San supported Tara, letting her ride him at whatever pace she deemed necessary. San leaned his shoulders, arching back against the wall, while keeping his legs and feet in a solid stance he was sure could withstand Tara's passionate, thrusting, ride she was already putting on him.

San felt so good inside Tara that, coupled with the stress of Yin's death, had Tara's body and mind completely out of control. She had one arm clawed onto the back of San's neck and her leg on the same side of her body wrapped around and behind San's leg. Tara used her other arm to give her leverage while she pushed herself up and down with her hand off San's chest. Tara's other leg was pushing her foot off the wall, behind San, giving Tara the power and positioning, along with maneuverability, to ride the hell out of San!

San was aware that the skin on the top of his back and shoulders was being grated like cheese by the wall behind him from Tara's relentless riding, but he didn't care because of the pleasure he was receiving. Just when San had stabilized his mind and body to put up with what Tara was doing, Tara slowed down a little, putting both her hands on San's chest. Now, slowly grinding on San, and looking into his eyes with a sex drunken madness in her eye, Tara wrapped her other leg around San's leg.

With both her legs wrapped around and behind San's, Tara leaned backwards placing her hands on the ground next to San's feet. That bent San's stick down and almost parallel to his thighs.

Tara then proceeded to push and pull herself to and from San's body just enough to ride him from that position. Even though Tara was riding San, she could barely take it herself.

While riding him from that position, her body quivered in a long continuous orgasm that had Tara going from a loud moaning to an all-out scream. She could no longer support herself on her very unstable hands. Tara reached up with her hands and tried to pull herself up with her stomach muscle and legs. She struggled with that because her stomach muscles were still quivering from the powerful orgasm she had just experienced.

San saw this as an opportunity and grabbed Tara's wrist, forcing her back down and locking the inside of her elbows, just outside of his knees, while holding on to Tara's wrist, San started thrusting his hips between Tara's legs. Because Tara was slightly swollen and very sensitive in her private area, so soon after that orgasm, her sensitivity to San's thrusting had Tara howling and jerking, struggling to get away, while at the same time, with each thrust of San's hips, Tara was being charged and drained of her energy. Her head would jerk up in rebellion, and then fall back in defeat, taking everything San was dishing out to her. San had Tara revved up at a high level of sexual activity that she'd never experienced before.

San then pulled Tara up by her arms. He put his forearms back under the back of her knees and started bouncing her up and down. Tara reacted immediately, screaming, while clawing at the back of San's neck. She was holding on for dear life, while bounce, bounce, bouncing!

After rapidly bouncing Tara for a while, San's legs gave way and as his back slid down the wall to the floor, he let go of Tara's wrist. Tara's body jerked forward and she clinched her arms under the back of San's shoulders and dug her fingernails deep into his skin. Tara's body had recuperated enough to where she started riding San from on top of him, while in a close clinching position. San reached around Tara and tried to wipe the sweat that was now burning his eyes. San struggled because Tara was getting busy and refused to move.

As Tara rode San, her body kept vibrating. It quivered in and jerked even more when she was experiencing an orgasm. All of this was giving San one of the most pleasurable sexual experiences he'd ever had. Tara rode San, until she rode him into a humongous orgasm that had her unstably crawling off San on hands and knees, only to fall and roll over on her back, looking up at the stars in the sky. Her eyes were glassy and her body was weak. She desperately tried to take control of her breathing, which was as shaky and unsteady as her heartbeat was.

While Tara was doing that, San got on top of her. Tara was unsteady and unable to fight off San. She begged, between breaths, saying "Please, ... give me . . . . a moment!"

San wasn't having that. He lifted her legs close to her shoulders, entered Tara and started riding her, putting everything he had into each thrusting movement he made. Tara's body was so sensitive now that all she could do was howl, yelp, yip, yap and scream with every thrust San made, while her body jerked out of control. San came to a roaring orgasm with Tara clawing his back, with her legs wrapped around him just above his shoulders. Tara held on to San, as San tried to make his way to the ground. San was on his back, only for a minute, before Tara started manipulating his stick in various ways. Now, San was the sensitive one and Tara took full advantage, while San jerked, jumped and tried to deal with the waves of sensitivity. Finally, sensitivity gave way to stiffness. Tara jumped back on San and started riding him, again. These two took turns on each other, until finally after San got off Tara one last time, leaving her herking and jerking on the grass, as he rolled over on his back next to Tara.

San peeked over at Tara, not knowing if she was going to use this opportunity to her advantage. However, he saw she was spent, with her eyes glossed over, as if she was in a trance. San thought it a good idea to go get his clothes and get out of here, seeing that most of the night was already gone. First, San decided to catch his breath for a moment. He blinked once, and then he blinked his eyes, again. The second time he left them closed. It felt so good he decided that it wouldn't hurt anything if he left them closed for another minute. That was all San remembered. He didn't wake up, until the sun was burning his naked body and the side of his face. San looked around for Tara and didn't see her, anywhere. San thought that the least she could have done was wake him, before she left!

CHAPTER 12

Earlier, in that same night, all of the Ra children had stealthy moved out of the festive gathering on to the side of the main road. La gave Dan a serious look, before looking at the other and saying "Follow me, we have something important to discuss."

Even though the other Ra children didn't know, La was planning to tell Yin about his father. As they were walking, they looked down the pathway that led to the back of the place where the gathering was being held. There, they saw Monty and his fellow guards.

Upon seeing them, La turned and walked towards them. The Ra girls turned when La did and followed her down the path. Dan and the Ra boys hesitated for a second, and then followed.

Monty saw the Ra children approaching. He looked at the other guards. They turned and faced the Ra children, hoping these youngsters wouldn't push them into a fight. These men had already been embarrassed in public. In this pathway, with no one around, there would be no witnesses, if things got out of hand.

The Ra children were now close enough to see the faces of the guards. The guards just stared at the Ra. The guards weren't down on their knees out of respect, either. All of the Ra noticed that. When the Ra children stopped at a safe distance, La said in the nastiest tone she could muster "You stand before me, disrespectfully, the worthless Hayee less than ant shit, you are! I am offended at the sight of you! Draw you weapons, so that you can, at least, die with respect!"

La and her sibling pulled their Hammer-Axes, right after La's last word. The guards quickly did the same, immediately going on guard. Ali raced up with his guards. Bo and Hoban, along with several others in La's Special Guard, also showed up. They all quickly lowered their heads before raising them, while pulling their weapons. Ali asked, "My Queen, how may we help?"

La yelled, "I want them dead! All except for one!" then La pointed at Monty and yelled, "Start with him, first!" Ali and La's Special Guard attacked Monty and the others. Bo hesitated, because Monty was a, not so distant, cousin of his. Bo's first instinct told him to help Monty, after seeing Ali and the others attacking Monty. Bo knew his efforts would be fruitless. Bo knew he couldn't stand there and do nothing, so he turned and attacked one of the other guards.

Monty and the guards fought hard, fighting with their backs to each other and not letting anyone breach their fighting perimeter. Monty and the other three guards were some the best the House of Ra had to offer. That's why they were Ramala's personal bodyguards. The fight raged on and after ten minutes, the noise of the clanging axes was attracting attention. La knew it would only be a matter of time before Ramala found out what was going on and came out to put a stop to this.

La looked at Shaya and then at Shaya's hammers. Shaya knew what La wanted her to do. Then, La looked at Danaaa. Danaaa didn't have to be told twice, or looked at twice. Both girls watched La to see what technique she would use.

La took off running towards Monty, with Danaaa closely following her. Monty saw this and prepared himself for the oncoming attack. Just before La got into striking range of Monty's Axes, she slowed herself, squatted, then stood up quickly, launching Danaaa, who had jumped onto La's shoulders, spinning in the air, with her axes, like a saw blade upwards, then down towards Monty's head. Immediately, after launching Danaaa into the air, La jerked her neck violently in a circle. While bending backwards and taking a step forward, she swung her head forward as hard as she could, landing on her knees in front of Monty with her ponytail rocketing at Monty's head.

Although, La was now in striking range of his Axes, Monty had to use his Axes against Danaaa who was now coming down fast and was just about to chop open the back of his skull. Even still, Monty kicked his left leg, with his foot aimed at La's face. La leaned slightly to the side, barely avoiding that kick.

Monty then moved one of his Axes to protect the back of his skull, successfully blocking both swings of Danaaa's axes, while blocking the rocketing ball on the end of La's ponytail that was headed towards his skull, with his other ax.

Just as Monty's Ax was moving La's ball to the side and at the same time, planning on bringing his Ax down to split La wide open, he was hit square in his nose with a hammer. As his head moved back a little from the force of that hammer throw, he was instantly hit on his fore head with another hammer. In that same instance, Danaaa chopped her Axes through both of Monty's hamstrings.

La, while still low and after the second hammer whizzed over her head, anchored her Ax on her shoulder for leverage. She then pushed up with her legs, plowing her ax into Monty's midsection, driving the Ax upwards threw his chest, with her shoulders and pushing with the force of her legs.

Monty was split open from the bottom of his stomach up through his chest. He fell backwards on to the ground, with his guts spilling out on the ground beside him. He gurgled a couple of times, before not moving. Ali and the others finally finished off the other guards, leaving one alive, just as La ordered.

The crowd that had gathered parted as Ramala, Wana, the Butcher girls, Jan and others came rushing up to see what happened. They saw Monty and the other guards dead. The guard, still alive, was on the ground, holding one of his knees that were busted from hammer blows. His ankles, shoulder and one elbow had also been smashed with hammers.

Ramala and Wana looked sternly at La for an explanation. La, being in charge and full of herself, said, "I won't be disrespected by guards, or anyone else! This is what happens when someone disrespects me! If you need further explanations, ask him!"

La pointed at the crippled guard on the ground. When everyone looked at the guard on the ground, La quickly walked away. Ramala turned to see her children, quickly, fleeing the scene of the crime. Ramala could see that Wana was about to move to action. Ramala quickly grabbed Wana's arm, looking at her, letting Wana know that she would deal with La and the others, later. Wana gave Ramala a stern look, and then she ordered her guards to clear the bodies and clean up the mess.

The Ra children were now moving fast away from the scene of the crime, with Ali and their special Guard. In all of the times, before this that fights broke out La's Special guard would arrive after everything was over. This was the first time they were there in time to take immediate action. Both La and Dan were pleased. The Ra children were escorted to Ramala's palace. La dismissed everyone, telling them she would meet them when next day came. They all got down on their knees and then left.

Upon entering the palace, La kept looking at Dan and at Yin. Once Dan was on board, knowing what La was about to do, he moved closer to Yin. All of a sudden, La and Dan grabbed Yin. Yin didn't know what was going on, so he struggled. All three fell to the ground. Shaya and Danaaa helped keep Yin pinned to the floor, even though they didn't know what was going on.

Ram stood back. He was confused and wanted to keep the other Ra from harming his cousin Yin. Ram didn't think Yin had done anything to deserve this. Ram reached for his axes, just as La had maneuvered herself on top of Yin. La said, "We're not trying to harm you! I just have something very important to tell you, so try to stay calm! That hero we paid respect to earlier was your father, uncle Yin!"

Yin looked at La and then at Dan to see if they were serious. Once he realized they were, Yin's face got angry and sad at the same time. Ram put his axes back in their holsters, relieved he didn't have to cut Dan and the others, in order to save Yin. Since they hadn't noticed Ram, they never knew he would have.

While still holding Yin down, Dan said, "You can be sure we're going to find who ever did it and make them pay! We'll make a plan and everyone will stick to it. We have to be very careful. Whoever killed uncle Yin has to be very skilled. We want to be able to kill whoever did this, without getting any of us killed. So don't try to do anything by yourself! We're going to do this together. Tonight you stay here with us. I'm sure mommy and Aunt Tara won't mind."

La and Dan released their grip on Yin. Everyone got off the floor. They all looked at Yin with anger, mixed with sorrow. Yin thought about all the good time and the bad time he had with his father. Yin was sad that he wouldn't see his father. He was also angry that someone took his father's life. Still, Yin wasn't as upset as he thought he would be. He wondered why he wasn't. Yin told himself that maybe it was because he was getting older. After all, he was a young man at the ripe old age of eleven and a half.

The Ra boys went to Dan's room and the Ra girls went to La's. Dan kept his ears alert and didn't fall asleep, until he was sure Yin had. Because Dan didn't see a lot of emotion out of Yin, he wasn't sure what Yin might do. One thing Dan was sure of was that they were going to make the person or persons responsible for his uncle's death, pay. Dan drifted off to sleep shortly after having those thoughts.

The Ra girls changed, got cleaned up and into bed. They talked, until they fell asleep, like always. It had been a long day with the festival, learning of their uncle's death and the fight in the alley. The Ra girls talked about how well they executed the triple team maneuver they used on Monty and how effective it was. The Ra girls were proud of themselves.

That was only one of many triple team techniques Ramala taught her daughters. The Ra girls were also practicing techniques they created themselves. They wouldn't use the ones they made up in a real battle, until they were absolutely sure they would work as well as the ones their mother taught them. After seeing how well that one worked, the Ra girls could hardly wait, until they could use another one. All three girls wanted to use the next technique on whoever killed their uncle Yin.

When next day came, La and her sisters whispered to each other about what, they thought, their mother would do to them. They got up early and had first day's training. They hadn't seen their mother yet, but knew they couldn't avoid her at first day's meal. So, after training, they slowly walked to the eating hall where they knew their mother would be waiting.

Ramala purposely didn't go see her daughters when next day first came. She wanted them to sweat thinking about what she might do. Ramala hadn't heard from Tara, since a little after noon, the day before. Tara's messengers told Ramala that she would be having breakfast with her. Ramala couldn't wait, until breakfast was over so she could interrogate Tara on what she and San talked about the night, before. It also was the last day of the Japha twins visit. Ramala sent messengers to Tara, as well as others, letting them know that breakfast was being held in the great hall of her palace.

Everyone filed into the great eating hall. It was a huge formal dining room that had several very large tables that could seat up to twenty people each. Those tables were facing two very large tables where the Royal family ate.

Today, because it was the Hellcats, Butchers and the Japha, all the grown-ups sat at one table, while the youngsters sat at the other one. After everyone was situated, breakfast was served.

When Tara looked into Yin's eyes, they looked very sad. She realized he knew about his father's death. Tara went over to Yin and apologized for not telling him when she first found out. Yin tried to put on a good face, but today he was affected more than last night.

It was quiet all through breakfast, mostly, because of two reasons. The first was the Ra children didn't want to do, or say anything that might bring up last night's events. The second was that all of the grown-ups knew, or just found out that San spent the entire night at Tara's palace.

Ramala and Wana, along with everyone else at the table that didn't know what happened, looked in the faces of everyone else, trying to get clues as to what happened. Tara was the only one at the table who wasn't, at least, slightly uncomfortable.

The Na, Tee was upset, even though she tried not to let it show. Tee watched San after he returned from being with Tara the entire night. San said nothing about why his meeting took all night and Tee didn't ask. Talking about it would make it worse.

San told Jan what happened. Jan told San that even though it was tough facing Tee, this day, he did the right thing. In addition, even though Jan thought San did the right thing, she wondered why Tara would do such a thing. Jan told herself if a night with San was all it took to get Tara's forgiveness she could live with that. Besides, they would be leaving some time, after noon.

Still, Tara's unusually happy attitude had most everyone on the Japha side uncomfortable. Ramala and Wana just wanted first day's meal to be over so they could grill Tara on every little detail.

Tara looked around the table during breakfast and would look at Tee a little longer than anyone else would. Tee noticed and refused to look at Tara. Once Tara saw that, she decided to make a game of it by constantly looking at Tee from time to time.

Now, everyone wanted breakfast to end, as soon as possible. Tee was doing very well, not looking at Tara. It was working, until Tee's eyes betrayed her and she looked at Tara. They locked eyes for a moment and in that moment Tara said "Last night San showed me first hand why you and Jan love him so much."

Everyone was shocked at Tara's words. Ramala wanted to warn Tara not to say anything else, but knew if she did, Tara might just say something, out of spite. Everyone was very uncomfortable, as they watched Tee staring in anger at Tara and Tara smiling at Tee, as if she was unaffected.

Wana moved closer to Tara and touched her shoulder softly, but firmly, letting Tara know not to take this any further. While still looking at Tee, Tara said, "Oh, don't worry Wa, as good as he was, and he was good, they can have him. He's now, at the very least, just sloppy thirds."

Ramala yelled "Enough!" as she stared at Tara, daring her to say anything, else. Tara didn't say anything, but she smiled at Ramala, knowing that Ramala really couldn't stop her from saying whatever she wanted to.

All of the Ra and Japha children jumped to attention when they heard Ramala yell, thinking one of them had done something. Now, the children were watching everyone at the grown-up's table, wondering what was going on.

Japha, Jan was offended by Tara's words and could see that Na, Tee was at the edge of her ability to control herself. Jan also could see that San tried to look as if he was unaffected by Tara's words. Jan stood up and lowered her head to Tara and then to Wana and lastly to Ramala, before saying "The Hellcats have been gracious host, making our stay here most pleasant and pleasurable. Unfortunately, we must prepare for our journey home."

Jan paused for a second. She looked at Tara and said, "Sister, I know this has been very hard on you. Even with that, you have been most gracious. I would be more than pleased if you ever decide to come north and visit."

Tara stared at Jan, without saying a word, until she heard La say "Is there any news on who killed uncle Yin?" Tara looked at Yin, while everyone else looked at La.

Wana said "Don't worry about that, I'll take care of it." La stood up and said, "I'm not going to worry about it, I'm going to do something about it. We're going to find the rebel trash that killed our uncle Yin. If there are any leads you can give us, I'd appreciate it. If not, we leave for Wa province when next moon comes. We're going to kill every rebel and Shitmushee, until we get the heads of uncle Yin's killers and bring them back to Aunt Tara. We won't rest, until that's done!"

La went down on her knees. The rest of the Hammer-Axe Six stood up and went down on their knees, except for Yin. Yin lowered his head to his mother and said, "Mother, we'll take care of this."

La and her sibling stood up after Yin said that. Tara looked at her nieces and nephews, before lastly looking at Yin and saying "I know you will."

Ramala hoped that Tara wouldn't say anything that might give the children the slightest clue who killed Elder Yin. Things would get complicated, really fast, if she did that. Still, Tara hadn't said anything, yet. Ramala needed to end this before Tara changed her mind.

Ramala looked at La and the other Ra children and said, "Where are your manners! We have guest! Although, these are very trying times, we must adhere to protocol! This is a topic for a more private setting. Rest assured we'll have a conversation about what happened to Hayee, Montezuma and my other bodyguards, after your training. Now show your respect and then take your leave!"

All of the Ra children lowered their heads to the Japha, to Tara and Wana, before lowering their heads to Ramala. Ramala said, "You may leave." The Ra children left, heading to their next day's training session.

After the children left, Ramala escorted the Japha twins out of the palace. Ramala assured them that Tara was just venting and that she would never jeopardize the alliance with the House of Japha by saying anything about Yin's death to anyone, including Yin and the other Ra children. She said she would meet them before their caravan left.

Ramala went back to find Tara readying herself and her girls to go back to her palace. Wana was with her. Ramala looked at Wana, then at Tara's girls. That let Wana know that Ramala wanted her to take Tara's girls, so she could have a private conversation with Tara. Wana took the girls for a walk to the front of the palace.

After they were gone, Ramala checked to make sure none of her servants were around. Ramala then turned her attention to Tara, who had been watching her the entire time. Before Ramala could say anything, Tara said "Don't worry, I'm not going to say anything! I just wanted to see those Japha squirm and sweat, wondering if I would. I was just having fun at their expense. Even with that, how long do you expect it will be before La and her spies find out the truth?" Ramala stared at Tara and said, "Until, everyone that knows about it has passed away. Tara, none of us will ever speak of it."

Tara angrily said "I said I wouldn't, didn't I!?!" Ramala smiled and said, "Alright, I'm just saying!" Tara smiled a little at hearing Ramala joke, saying one of Wana's favorite sayings. Tara said, "I'm just saying, too!" Ramala knew Tara was back on board, after that.

Ramala got a curious smile on her face, and then said, "You had sex with San?" This was both a question and a statement, because from what Tara said earlier, Ramala knew she had. Tara said nothing. She just smiled at Ramala. Ramala said "Tell me everything that happened and don't leave out anything!" Tara only made Ramala wait for a moment while she gathered her thoughts. Once she'd done that, Tara proceeded to tell Ramala everything, leaving out nothing.

After talking to Tara, Ramala went to meet with Wana. She wanted to make sure the Japha caravan was well supplied for its journey home. They suggested that Tara not accompany them and told her as much. Tara was good with that. She already had her fill of the Japha and didn't care to ever see them, again. Tara decided to have a light training session in one of her private courtyards, so she could conveniently miss personally bidding farewell to the Japha. She had her maids take her daughters to Ramala's palace to visit with their cousins, for a while.

Tara did her warm ups and stretches, before she started her workout. About twenty minutes in, one of Tara's servants told her, she had a visitor and told her whom it was. Tara gave permission to bring the visitor to her. Tara smiled to herself. Not three minutes later, Tara's visitor walked onto the courtyard. It was the Na, Tee.

From the moment, San got back to her and she knew he had been with Tara for the night, Tee tried to control her emotions over the situation. She was doing fairly well, until Tara all but threw it in her face, taunting her, at first day's meal.

The Na, Tee was seething with anger, but tried not to let it show. Tee told herself that she would soon be going home and all of this would just be a bad memory she was sure she could forget, over time.

However, as time went on, this situation with Tara brought back the painful truth that not only had Tara used her King as her personal whore, but so was Jan. Jan was there with Tee helping her get the children ready for the trip home. Looking at Jan only fueled Tee's anger. Tee thought to herself that one day she was going to deal with Jan in private over this matter. That day wasn't now. Tee decided that she was going to deal with Tara, this day.

Tee stopped what she was doing, looked at Jan and said, "I need you to make up something to tell San why I'm out." Jan asked, "Where are you going?"

Tee said "To have a little talk with Tara." With a concerned look on her face, Jan questioned "Do you think it's wise, to do that?" Tee said, as a matter of fact, "Wise has nothing to do with this." Jan looked at Tee for a moment, before saying "I don't think you should go. It will be very dangerous. You might even be killed."

Tee sarcastically said, "In that case, maybe I'll see you later, or maybe I won't." Jan said "You be very careful." Tee only looked at Jan for a moment, before leaving.

After Tee left, the look of concern on Jan's face turned into a devious smile. Jan thought that if Tee went to Tara's palace, beat the hell out of Tara, and somehow made it back, that would be retribution for what Tara had done, earlier. Jan thought Tara, at least, deserved a beating for that. If Tee was killed, it would be no loss to Jan and San couldn't blame her for Tee's death. Either way this turned out Jan didn't see how she could lose.

Meanwhile, Tee was at the entrance to the courtyard. She looked around at the servants, before settling her stare on Tara. Without taking her eyes off Tee, Tara ordered her servants to leave and had them tell her staff of maids and other servants that she was not to be disturbed.

The servants looked at Na, Tee and then did as they were told. They also went and told guards what they witnessed. The guards let the other two Hellcats know what they thought was about to happen.

After the servant left, Tara smiled at Tee and said, "I couldn't have hoped for a better ending to your visit." Tee was all business, walking towards Tara, when she said in a calm, but angry voice, "You already know what it is!"

Nothing more needed to be said between these two. Tee cautiously walked towards Tara. Once Tee reached Tara, she threw every combination of punches and kicks she had in her arsenal, at Tara.

Tara, still upset over Yin's death, let all of her frustrations pour out through a series of potent kicks and punches. Both women seemed to throw defense out the window, determined to punish each other, despite the cost to themselves.

That lasted for about twenty minutes, until Tara, although administering severe punishment to Tee, decided that she'd taken enough punishment, for her liking. Tara started mixing a healthy dose of defense, to compliment her offense. However, it seemed that Tee hadn't changed her strategy. Tee was still willing to take as much punishment from Tara, just to stay close enough to Tara to keep doing serious damage.

Both women were taking a good beating from each other. The only difference was Tara couldn't match the emotional fury coming from Tee. Tee was taking her beating in stride, because of the emotional adrenaline that was pumping through her body. Tara's emotional fury was subsiding, somewhat and she was starting to feel the pain from some of the blows she was taking from Tee. It was starting to take its toll on Tara. Tara, refusing to readily take blows from Tee, was now mostly on defense. However, Tee was furiously forcing the action and still getting a few punches in, through Tara's defense.

Tara was in a dogfight she knew she was losing. Still, she couldn't get enough separation between her and Tee, so she could take in enough air to get out a scream. Besides that, she needed a breath, just to control her breathing enough to take in air.

The accumulation of blows from Tee was taking effect on Tara. Tara was dazed by several shot from Tee and lost control of her arms and legs. Tara was barely conscious as she fell to the ground. Tee was so angry that when Tara was dazed and her arms dropped, Tee got off a couple more punches in on Tara.

Tee was about to unmercifully beat Tara, when she received a powerful flying kick to the side of her head from Wana. Tee was dazed, but turned and fought hard against Wana, with the same fury, as she'd done with Tara. But, Wana wasn't Tara. Wana was much better than Tara was and instantly started administering a severe beating to Tee.

San, Jan and Ramala, who came in right after Wana and thought Wana rushed over to stop the fight, were all surprised at seeing Wana beating the Hell out of Tee, for what she'd seen Tee doing to Tara.

Ramala knew her guard wouldn't move to stop Wana from fighting. Ramala certainly wasn't going to fight Wana, trying to stop her, after seeing what Tee had just done to Tara. San was ready to move into action to break up the fight. Both Jan and Ramala knew that would just escalate the fighting. Jan looked at Ramala and Ramala knew what had to be done. Jan grabbed San's arm stopping him from moving forward, while Ramala took in air. Ramala screamed and froze Wana and Tee. Tee was already dazed, taking a beating from Wana. When Ramala screamed, both girls fell, off balance to the ground.

Ramala ran over to Tara to see if she was all right. San and Jan ran over to Tee to make sure she was all right. Wana's guards ran over to her and tried to move her to a more comfortable position.

Because Tara wasn't in the direct path of Ramala's scream, she was shocked and mostly shaking off the cobwebs of being clobbered by Tee.

Everyone was startled when San yelled, "She's not breathing! Help me get her to start breathing!" Ramala thought San was overreacting, so when she saw that Tara was all right, Ramala went to help with Tee. Just as Ramala knelt to help rub the back of Tee's neck, in order to help Te regain movement, her eyes rolled up, behind her eyelids, as San held her in his arms. He body then went limp. After seeing that, Ramala checked Tee for a pulse. Everyone froze for a moment, realizing Tee was dead.

Ramala couldn't understand how that scream could do that much damage to Tee and not to Wana, or Tara. Ramala knew she hadn't put that much into the scream. She only screamed enough to barely freeze them.

However, what Ramala hadn't taken into account was that Tee was dazed and was close to losing consciousness from the blows she was taking from Wana. That and the fact that she had used up a lot of energy fighting, both Tara and Wana, left Tee without enough strength to fight and hold her vibrating spirit in her body. San stood up with Tee's limp body in his arms. His face was angry, sad and hurt, all at the same time. He carried Tee out of Tara's palace, without saying a word, followed by Jan and Ramala.

Ramala ordered her guards to clear everyone from the roads all the way to the Japha caravan. Once there, Ramala asked if there was anything she could do. Jan said there wasn't. Jan said she had to attend to San's children, before they saw their mother like this.

Ramala apologized for not realizing the affect her scream would have on Tee. Jan looked Ramala in her eyes and in a low voice that only Ramala could hear said, "Don't blame yourself for this. I'm more at fault here, than anyone." Jan paused, while both women looked at each other. Jan whispered to Ramala "Don't worry, I'll clean up the mess I made on this end. You just make sure you clean things up here."

Jan pulled Ramala close and gave her a hug. Jan whispered in Ramala's ear, saying, "Sister, just like you told me when we were younger, as long as we back each other, we can do anything we want and everyone will be powerless to stop us." Jan pulled back a little, smiled at Ramala, then changed the look on her face to concern as she turned around, facing the guards.

Ramala was shocked. She was now realizing that Jan was just as cunning as she was. It bothered Ramala, realizing how smart Jan really was. Ramala thought back to when she and Jan first made their alliance. Ramala always thought she was in control, helping Jan. She used Jan to control the North, while she herself, took over the South. Now, Ramala was reevaluating things.

It was starting to look like to Ramala that she was taking all the risk, even though she was reaping rewards. She saw that Jan took very little risk and was reaping rewards.

Ramala was the one who eliminated Jan's brothers, who were intent on killing Jan and San. Ramala took all the risk in warring with the North, while Jan sat in the background, only backing Ramala when needed, which was rarely.

That war made Ramala and the Butchers enemies in the North and South, while Jan gained a Kingdom and very few enemies. Jan came South under the impression that she missed Ramala. Later, only after the deed was done, Jan reveals that she and San were on a mission to take Yin's head back to the Elders of Japha.

Now, Tee was dead. Ramala wondered would San blame her and Tara for Tee's death, after he mourned. Jan never really liked Tee, because Jan was in love with her twin brother, but had to publicly share him with Tee. That was one of the reasons Tee was dead. Jan could have stopped Tee from going to Tara's palace, but she didn't. Still, there was no implication that Jan had anything to do with it.

Ramala knew Jan had the Tat and the use of their mental abilities helping her, even if Jan didn't admit it. Every time Ramala asked about the Tat, she got very little information from Jan. Ramala wondered where she fit in Jan's ultimate plan.

When the Hammer-Axe Six heard Ramala's scream, they raced from their training session. The boys met the girls and they arrived just in time to see the Japha San putting Tee's body on a phant. They were shocked, so they turned and looked for an explanation from Ramala and Wana. Both Hellcats gave them a stern look that said be respectful and don't ask questions. Ramala said, "Return to your training. Midday meal will be served, shortly." Ramala looked at Yin, who started walking towards Tara's palace. She sternly said, "That means you too, Yin!" Yin stopped and looked at Ramala. She looked serious, so Yin moved back towards his cousins.

La and her sisters looked around at all of the guards and servants in the immediate area, while the boys watched the Japha move towards their caravan. La pulled on Danaaa's ponytail. That let Danaaa, as well as Shaya, know it was time to leave. Dan saw La leaving and took one last look around, before looking at Yin and his brothers and then leaving.

La was sure someone knew what happened here. La had spies everywhere. They knew how important it was to keep the Number One Princess informed on everything going on in the House of Ra. If her mother wasn't going to tell her what happened at Tara's palace, with the help of her spies, someone would!

Right after training and just before the midday meal a messenger, to meet the Hellcats and bid farewell to the Japha, summoned the Ra children. Several of her spies had approached La, earlier. They told her all they knew of what happened at Tara's palace, this day and the night before. La and Shaya looked at each other. It looked like Tee got herself killed in a jealous rage over San spending the night with Tara. They couldn't figure out why their uncle San would purposely cause this trouble. Both girls discussed it, but still had unanswered questions.

Danaaa didn't care. She didn't have the need to know every little detail, like La and Shaya. She thought La and Shaya had already talked too much about something they couldn't do anything about.

The farewell was heartfelt amongst the young Japha and the Ra. The Japha children were sad and distracted by the loss of their mother. The Ra children consoled them as much as possible.

Through all that, they'd gone through, the Ra children and the Japha children created a bond with each other, just as their Elders hoped they would. However, as all of the children noticed, the grown-ups weren't as animated in their farewells as they were when they first met at the beginning of the Japha visit. They thought it must be because of Tee's death. The Ra watched as the Japha caravan moved north, until it slowly disappeared from sight.

After midday meal and just before the next training session, La and her sisters went to go see their aunt Tara. The Ra girls were always followed by La's Warlord Ali and her Executioner Hoban, along with the Elite bodyguards assigned to the Ra girls. Tania was there, along with a few of La's Special guards, who weren't in training sessions. When they walked up to the palace steps, one of Tara's guards announced that Tara was indisposed and wouldn't be receiving guest.

La stared at the guard. She hated when people used words she couldn't remember the meaning of. The two words La couldn't remember the meaning of were desire and indisposed. Probably, because La never desired for anything, as far as she knew. In addition, you could never be indisposed when the Number One Princess came calling!

La pointed to the guard who said Tara was indisposed and motioned for him to come to her. Once there, La gave him a lightning fast backhand and a returning open hand slap. Before the guard could think, Hoban and one of La's Elite bodyguards grabbed the guard by his arms and wrestled him to his knees.

La's other bodyguards and Special Guards turned towards Tara's other guards, daring them to move. Tara's guards weren't afraid of La's bodyguards, but they were no fools. They knew how much trouble La could be and she was already showing it. Tara's guards all took a step back.

After seeing that Tara's other guards knew their place, La looked back down at the guard and said in an arrogantly nasty tone "I Don't care about indisposed! When I show up somewhere, I expect to be announced, not told about such things as indisposed! When something goes on in the House of Ra, I expect all of you to find a way to get word to me about it! It's always important to impress you next Queen. Remember these lessons! I'll not teach them, again!"

La looked at Hoban and her bodyguard and then motioned with her hand, for them to remove the guard from her path. They tossed him, unceremoniously, to the side. Several of Tara's other guards, not wanting to offend the Number One Princess, hustled over to the entrance of the palace and told servants to alert Tara that her nieces were on their way to see her. La told Hoban and everyone else to wait on her, at the bottom of the palace steps, until she returned.

Shaya and Danaaa followed La into Tara's palace, unaffected by La's arrogant tirade. They were use to La's arrogance and expected she would act this way all day, every day, if things weren't to her liking.

Maids led the Ra girls to where Tara was resting. Tara was alerted that La had bullied her way into the palace. Tara was waiting on the Ra girls when they arrived.

After all three Ra girls lowered their heads, out of respect to Tara, Tara looked at La and asked, "What was so important that my rest has been interrupted?"

The Ra girls could see that their aunt Tara was roughed up, pretty good. La knew she had to be very respectful of her favorite aunt, Tara. La lowered her head, again and said with concern in her voice "How are you feeling?" Tara responded "I've been better." then she looked at La to continue. La said, "There have been strange going ons here in the past days. Please, explain them to me, so that I don't do something rash. If not, I'll find out on my own and chances are I will react unreasonably."

Tara looked at La for a moment. She still couldn't believe how much La looked, sounded and acted like Ramala. Sometimes it would shock Tara to silence. After thinking for a second, or two, Tara said, "Send for Yin and your brothers. When they get here, I'll tell you everything."

La sent for the Ra boys, telling them it was urgent that they meet her at Tara's palace. Because the messenger used the word urgent, the Ra boys were there in no time flat, armed to the teeth. They saw Hoban, Ali and the others waiting outside. Dan had his Warlord Bo and his bodyguards wait there with the others.

Once the Ra boys were inside, Tara told them how Elder Yin made enemies, by ruthlessly killing, sometimes for no good reasons. She told them how Elder Yin had gotten to the point, in which he wouldn't follow orders and was putting the security of the House of Ra in jeopardy. Also, that Wana was probably making a plan to have Yin killed, when the Japha San took Yin's head, in battle, for killing important members of the Japha family.

Tara said that she and San debated deep into the night, negotiating a way to a reasonable settlement. Also, that Tee came to the palace and was very unreasonable and disrespectful. Tara said that cost Tee her life. She told the Ra children that it was very regrettable what happened to both Yin and Tee. That both sides lost someone they loved, dearly. Tara said that the Japha were willing to forgive her for Tee's death, so they should forgive San for Yin's death. That as hard as it might be, it's what's best for everyone involved.

Once La humiliated Tara's guards, one of them got word to Wana's guards, who let her know that La was up to something at Tara's palace. Wana sent word to Ramala, who was watching Tara's two girls that they should meet at Tara's palace, immediately. Wana arrived in time to hear the last of Tara's explanation. Wana didn't interrupt, because she didn't hear anything in Tara's explanation that she deemed inflammatory. Ramala arrived just after it was over. Upon seeing all of the Ra children at Tara's palace, Ramala feared that Tara was spewing venom towards the Japha. Wana looked at Ramala letting her know that things were under control.

After Tara was done, all three Hellcats watched the Ra children closely, trying to see their reaction to what Tara just said. They could see La and Dan were already formulating a plan of action. Ramala decided it was time to find a way to occupy her children's time, before they started more mischievous behavior. She told them what she expected of them, under the threat of losing their rank as Warlords. Neither of them wanted that. The Hammer-Axe Six were told that they would be nothing more than bodyguards for the next two moons, for what they had done the night before. They would learn all the techniques and protocol for being a Ra bodyguard.

They were also told that it would be a good learning experience. Since they had no choice in the matter, for now, La and Dan had to make a plan to deal with what Ramala had planned for them.

CHAPTER 13

The trip back for the Japha was hard and troubling, to say the least. San, along with his children were devastated from the loss of the Na, Tee. All of the memories that San had since the first time he met Tee were flooding into his mind, in sort of a continuous daydream. He also couldn't forget when he saw her take her last breath. San was so much in and out of a daze that he could barely hear his children.

San's boys were visibly shaken and waves of sorrow would bring them to tears. After composing themselves, San's boys would repeat this behavior over and over, again.

However, Tee's Terrible Two were the hardest to deal with. They yelled, cried and begged San and Jan for their mother. Jan had to deal with Tee's girls, because San really wasn't up to it.

Jan decided that on the second day of the journey home, the caravan would have a day's rest, and then proceed north. San didn't see the need, but didn't protest. It also seemed strange to San that Jan had an early morning training session. San saw that Jan was trying to get back into a normal routine, hoping that would lessen the stress of the situation. San thought the only thing that would lessen his stress, was if he could kill Tara with his bare hands. He put that out of his mind. At this point, that wouldn't solve anything, except for his personal gratification.

San had to admit, watching Jan's sparring session and seeing her doing all of the intricate moves, took his mind off of Tee, if only for that session. San smiled at Jan, letting her know that he appreciated her efforts.

The Japha Rulers had a light meal and were relaxing, when some of their guards reported that they had been attacked. San was puzzled by this, because they were still in the main city of Ra, although, just past the lake. San stood up, but was stopped by Jan, when she said, "Guards, move the children a safe distance and lead the attackers here."

The guards quickly moved on Jan's orders. Once they'd left, Jan looked at San with a huge smile on her face. She said, "It seems we'll get an opportunity to take out our frustrations. I don't think we could have a better way to do that, than showcasing our skills, can you?" San was down with this. If he couldn't kill Tara, whoever this was would do, for now.

For a brief moment, San allowed himself to think that Tara might just be stupid enough to come here and attack his caravan. San also knew that if Tara was here, at least one other Hellcat would be with her, if not all three. Right now, San didn't care if he had to kill all three Hellcats. After all, he'd never made an alliance with any of them. That was all Jan's doing.

San was snapped out of his daydream by guards running up. San already had his Hammer-Axes with him. He was ready for battle. Then he saw Ma walk up and look at him with hatred in her eyes and two bloody baby Hammer-Axes in hand. San wondered why someone would tell Ma what happened, unless they wanted her dead.

After finding out about Yin's death, but not knowing the truth of what happened, Ma went into seclusion, only getting information about things going on around the city, from Syn.

Syn forced Ma to see Japha, Jan, before the Japha left the city. Ma didn't know why, but when San wasn't with Jan, she didn't feel the need to go searching for him, just to say good-bye. Ma wondered if she felt a little more distant from San, because he was the one who brought her the news of Yin's death.

When next day came, after the Japha had gone, Ma was lounging around, still not feeling up to getting back into her regular routine. She reasoned to herself that she would force herself to in a day, or so.

Soon after that, Ma heard a familiar voice. She smiled and watched the entrance to her room, until she saw Danaaa enter. As soon as Danaaa spotted Ma, she ran, jumped and landed on cushions right next to Ma. Danaaa immediately started launching a barrage of punches close to Ma, trying to bait Ma into a play fight.

Danaaa realized, right away, that Ma wasn't in a play fighting mood. Looking into Ma's eyes, Danaaa yelled, "You don't look happy! Are you still sad over uncle Yin's death?!"

Even though Ma was use to hearing Danaaa yell, at close range, today Danaaa's voice seemed particularly loud to Ma. Ma smiled at Danaaa and said, "Yes, I am. But, I'll be better, soon." Ma saw Danaaa's eyes light up with a thought, so Ma said "Please, Danaaa, whatever you say next, use your whispering voice."

Danaaa gave Ma a strange look, wondering why everyone always wanted to hear her whispering voice. Danaaa thought that everyone must really like her whispering voice. So, Danaaa replaced the strange look with a smile and whispered to Ma "But, I still don't understand why uncle San had to chop off uncle Yin's head and send it to some old Japha, I mean, Elder Japha, just so they wouldn't start a war. Couldn't they find a better way not to go to war, even if uncle Yin did kill a lot of Japha a long time, ago?"

Halfway through Danaaa's first sentence, Ma was hit with such shock that her hands dug deep into the cushions she was laying on. After Danaaa's question, Ma asked, "Who told you this?"

Danaaa whispered, "Aunt Tara told me, La and Shaya. Then La had her spies find out more details. After that, La pestered mommy, until she told us what she knew. After mommy told us, I knew it had to be true. La and mommy told me not to say a word to anybody about it. You're not just anybody. Besides, I thought you already knew!"

Ma smiled at Danaaa and whispered "Thanks."

Just then, Syn walked into the room and suspiciously asked, "What are you two doing?"

Before Danaaa could answer, Ma tickled and wrestled her. After a brief moment, Ma looked at Syn and said, "What we always do, when we're together. We're having fun!" then Ma went back to tickling Danaaa.

Elder Dan had already told Syn what really happened to Elder Yin. So, Syn watched Ma closely to see if she thought Danaaa had said anything about Yin. However, it seemed to Syn that Danaaa's visit had lifted Ma's spirits. Syn was happy these two had their special bond and decided she would leave them alone and check on Ma, later.

Ma didn't let on that she knew anything. That entire day she looked into the eyes of everyone she was sure knew the truth about her twin brother and didn't tell her. That included Syn. Ma saw how nervous Syn was when she saw her alone with Danaaa. For now, Ma decided to let everyone think whatever they wanted.

Ma told Syn that Danaaa's visit lifted her spirits so much, that she'd asked Ramala if Danaaa could spend the night with her. Ma told Syn that she hoped Syn would understand that she wanted to spend the night alone with Danaaa. Syn smiled in agreement, thinking that might just bring Ma back to normalcy. Ma left the city of Ra, shortly after dark.

When next day came, Syn couldn't find Ma anywhere. She raced to Ramala's palace and pleaded for the guards to get Dan.

When Ma caught up with the Japha caravan, she saw that scouts spotted her, right away. Ma trotted at a steady, but fast pace. She didn't know how many guards she would have to fight to get to San. That didn't matter to Ma. Today, it was going to be, first come, first served!

It wasn't long before about twenty guards approached Ma. They saw she was on guard. The Japha guards knew Ma from missions in the past. One of them stepped forward and said "Come, we'll take you to see Jan."

Ma nodded in agreement and started walking with the guards. As Ma was walking, she noticed the guards, even though, not being obvious, were moving on all sides of her. Ma had been in enough battles to know that you don't let that happen, if you can help it.

Whether this threat was real, or imagined, Ma wasn't going to take any chances. All in one move, Ma drew both her Baby

Hammer-Axes and drove them into two guards closest to her. Ma then went on a frenzied attack, killing all but two of the guards. The last two thought it might be a good idea to get away and let Jan and San know what was going on.

Ma saw other guards keeping their distance, while leading her right up to the Japha caravan. She walked past a couple of elephants, and then she saw Jan, with San standing a little further back.

Jan saw Ma looking past her at San, so she asked, "Why have you come here, this day?" Ma still moving forward with Baby-Axes in hand said, "You know why I'm here. I've come for San's head!"

Jan turned to one of her guards and looked at him. The guard threw Jan's golden staff to her. Jan caught the staff, without taking her eyes off Ma. Jan said "Wrong answer!"

Jan immediately started twirling her golden staff around her body, while moving closer to Ma. Ma had seen Jan use that golden staff, only one time, with devastating results.

There was no time to think about that now. Ma charged Jan and ferociously attacked her. Jan's golden staff blocked every one of Ma's swings. After blocking, at least twenty swings from Ma, Jan was finally in position to strike. She did so with astounding speed and accuracy.

Jan, after a block, swung her staff back at Ma, smashing into Ma's arm, just above the elbow. In the split second that Ma felt the pain in her arm, Jan had twirled her staff one revolution over her head, then letting it slam full force into Ma's shoulder of the same arm that was just hit. Ma's arm dropped a little after that blow and she jerked her body to the side, barely avoiding being slammed in the side of the head by Jan's staff. Ma jumped backwards, to get some distance, so she could regroup.

However, Jan wasn't having that. She closed the distance, swinging her staff at Ma, who managed to block it with her ax. Jan slid her staff down off the block, crashing it hard into Ma's knee, then spinning around and catching Ma with a powerful blow to her back.

Ma felt extreme pain in the knee that Jan's staff smashed. She couldn't put any weight on that leg. Ma quickly hopped on her good leg, turning back towards Jan with her axes up in a blocking position. Jan's staff clanged violently off of Ma's axes, only to return several more times, trying to break through Ma's defense. Ma was severely wounded by Jan's staff. She was defending herself, with everything she had, not to take another blow from that staff. Ma knew the next blow could possibly lead to her death.

Jan knew she had the upper hand and was going to keep high heat on Ma, until she finished her off.

After forcing the action hard and heavy, Jan swung her staff at Ma's head. Ma had to block, or get out of the way. There was no time to get out of the way, so Ma moved her ax up bracing it, against the force of the staff. However, the staff never came. Jan faked that move and when Ma committed to the block, Jan reversed her swing to the other side, low and into Ma's legs knocking her off her feet. Ma's back hit the ground hard.

Jan jumped in the air towards Ma, with the point of her staff aimed at Ma's chest. Just inches from Ma's chest, Jan's staff was pushed out of the way enough to slam it into the ground next to Ma. Jan brought her staff up with lightning speed and swung it several revolutions in defense of herself, before sending the staff back at Ma's chest. Again, it was blocked.

Now, Jan was completely aware that Syn had blocked her efforts to finish Ma off. Right off of the second block from Syn, Jan was attacking Syn with her staff. Jan ferociously attacked Syn, who had two Baby Hammer-Axes. Syn blocked everything Jan threw at her, while standing over Ma, not giving one inch. Jan moved back from Syn, while spinning her staff around her body. Once Jan was sure she was at a safe enough distance from Syn's axes, she slammed her staff into the ground, parallel to her body. With her hand still holding the staff, Jan looked around.

Syn hadn't advanced on her and Jan could see Dan, Mangler and a few of Dan's best guards. She also saw that San and his bodyguards were between her and Dan's people. Jan couldn't imagine how Syn had gotten pass San and his guard to where she was fighting Ma. Before she made her next move, Jan had to know, so she asked "What's going on here?! Where are the Hellcats? Do they know you're here?"

Syn said, "They know nothing about what we're doing. We don't want trouble. We just came to get Ma, that's all."

Jan looked at Ma and said, "She came here looking for trouble. She found it. When I'm done with her, you can have what's left!"

Ma winced in pain, as she tried to get up, but couldn't. Her leg was busted up pretty good, amongst other things, but still, she yelled, "Go to Hell! And take that shitty excuse of a worthless brother with you!"

San looked down at Ma. He said, "Say what you will, while you can. It won't be long, before you'll be joining your brother." San looked at Syn and then he looked at Dan. San said, "Now's not the time to test me, seeing what's happened with Tee. You two should leave now, or I'll be forced to do something I might regret, later."

Dan thought that sounded like a threat. He got straight to the point, looking San in the eyes and saying, "We're taking Ma with us. Whatever happens in that process might be something you'll regret, later."

San's face instantly became angry, after Dan's mocking. Jan saw San's hands moving towards his Hammer-Axes. She yelled, "Hold it, San!"

Everyone turned as a Japha guard came running up and got down on his knees. Jan ordered "Speak!" The Japha guard said that Ra guards were surrounding the Japha caravan, but staying their distance. Jan looked at Dan, who now had a smile on his face.

Jan was serious when she said, "Dan, this is not a game. Ma made an attempt on the lives of the Rulers of Japha. Protocol says she dies for that. Ramala would never approve of something like this, knowing that if a Japha made an attempt on her life, or any of the Hellcats, they would be dead. Be smart and consider carefully what you're doing. Something like this could possibly lead to an unnecessary war, all over this heathen!"

Syn pleaded with Jan, saying "But you've already crippled her! Can't you forgive her for all the service she has done for you?"

Ma said in a nasty tone "Don't beg for me! I'll deal with them myself!" Syn, while still on guard, yelled to Ma "Shut up! You're not helping!" Jan said, "Dan, you're the King of Ra. You would war with me over a heathen?"

Dan said "That heathen Ma belongs to the House of Ra. You can be sure she'll be punished for this." Jan blurted out "I want her dead! Why would you deny me that?! You know Ramala wouldn't!"

Dan said, "She's not here." San said, "You know he's not smart enough to make decisions without the help of his Queen."

Jan yelled "San!"

Dan said, "He's right. No more talking! We're taking Ma back to the city."

Jan paused, while looking at Dan. She calmly said "Alright, Dan. If that's what you want." then Jan turned her head to the side and yelled "Don't bother with them, just kill Ma!"

Jan's bodyguards moved into position in front of her, while other Japha guards poured in from all sides, surrounding Syn and Ma. Syn looked at Jan like 'Are we really going to do this?'

No sooner than Jan looked from Syn, to Ma, a barrage of spears came flying at Ma and Syn. Ma blocked them from the ground, while Syn did the same, from a standing position. After that, the Japha guards attacked, trying to get to Ma. Syn masterfully defended Ma by dancing back and forth over Ma's body, blocking and chopping up the guards that posed the greatest threat.

Dan, Mangler and the Ra guards moved to help Syn protect Ma, but were attacked by Japha guards. San and Jan stood back and watched the battles. Dan and Mangler fought their way to Syn forming a perimeter around Ma.

The battle raged on for close to an hour before San ordered his guards back. That's when the six remaining Ra guards ran over and joined the Butchers. Jan said, "Give us Ma and we can end this nonsense!" Dan said, "I hope you didn't think that was enough to convince us. We can do this all day. Besides, how long do you think it will be before the Ra army realizes their King is being attacked?"

San said "Right, then, some more convincing!" San waved his hand and twelve, just short of brute sized warriors walked up. All of them were muscular, without an ounce of fat on them. They had large Hammer-Axes. That was the second thing the Butchers noticed, after the size of these men. Dan could read eyes, well. He saw these men were head collectors of the nastiest kind. Even though Mangler and Syn couldn't read eyes as well, they saw that, too.

The twelve brute warriors surrounded Dan's group. San smiled and said, "Let's see if you can protect her and yourselves, at the same time!" San sternly ordered, "Kill her!"

The sound of clanging axes instantly filled the air. These men were instant heat on the three Butchers. What made this battle extremely tough was the fact that the Butchers couldn't spread out and maneuver around to avoid the powerful swings of the axes. The six Ra guards stood guard over Ma, only fighting, or blocking when they had to. There was very little room to fight because of the pressure from the Japha Hammer-Axe experts. At first, all the Butchers could do was block everything these brutes threw at them. That made it tough on Dan and Mangler, but they were strong enough to hold their own against the pounding of the Hammer-Axes.

However, blocking giant Hammer-Axes wasn't one of Syn's strongest skills. Normally, she would avoid the swings as much as possible, counter-attacking off them. She couldn't do that, right away, knowing if she moved out of position and one of those brutes got past the Ra guards Ma would be dead.

After a few more blocks that sent pain through her arm and shoulder, Syn knew she had to change her strategy, or she would be injured to the point of being useless.

Syn quickly moved behind Dan, who had created a little space between himself and Ma. That left the Ra guards to defend against the Japha where Syn had been. Syn took two running steps, jumped on to the shoulders of one of the Ra guards and launched herself up and over the Japha brutes, landing behind them.

Two of the four she had been fighting, quickly turned and attacked her. Now Syn had space to maneuver and was counter-attacking off every swing of the large Hammer-Axes. Both Japha swung their Axes, one at Syn's neck, the other at Syn's mid-section. Syn flipped in the air, barely avoiding the swings, while extending her arms and slicing one in the bicep and the other across his forearm.

That barely slowed them down because when Syn landed, she had to instantly go into a tuck and roll, as the blade of one of the axes came whizzing past, just missing her head. While in her roll, the other Japha jumped over her, landing on the other side of Syn, cutting off her route of escape, while being in the perfect position to split her wide open.

Syn saw that and while still low, she sliced her axes through the upper inside of both his thighs, before diving out of the way of powerful swings from him and the other Japha she was fighting.

Blood poured out of the gaping wounds on his thighs as he tried to stabilize himself enough to attack. He didn't have time, because Syn quickly moved on him, staying and attacking him from his side. He couldn't move fast enough to front himself and get a good swing at Syn. Syn carved him up, while she ran and avoided swings from the second Japha. Finally, the loss of blood and the accumulative chops caught up with him. The wounded Japha fell to his knees, only to have Syn's Ax slice three quarter of the way though his thick neck, sending his head flopping downwards, hanging only by the partial flesh of his neck. He awkwardly fell sideways onto the ground. Syn didn't stop moving for a second, once her blade went through his neck. She was dancing and swinging her axes, putting high heat on the other Japha.

Some of the other brute Japha saw, out of the corner of their eyes, when Syn killed their comrade. They also saw the high heat she was putting on the other Japha. They broke away from their main mission of killing Ma, just as Syn finished off the second Japha she was fighting.

Now it wasn't about Ma, anymore. Syn had killed two Japha and now, she was the main target. She saw the other Japha charging at her and ran in an all-out sprint towards them. Syn avoided the swings of three of them, while slicing and mortally wounding two, as she ran past them.

Dan and Mangler turned to help Syn. Now, it seemed, the brute Japha were surrounded. Jan saw this and ordered "Enough! Back away from them, now!"

The Japha only fought for another moment, before begrudgingly disengaging from the battle. The look of anger in their eyes let the Butchers know they had enemies for life.

The three Butchers quickly moved back to defensive positions around Ma, looking at Jan. San slowly walked over to Jan. Guards drug away the dead bodies, while the two brutes Dan and Mangler had severely wounded were helped away.

Once that was done, Jan looked directly at Syn and said, "Killing those Japha wasn't very smart! What did you think would come of that?"

Syn said, "That's not something I think about." Jan said, "Come hitherward, if you dare! I have something for you to think about!"

Syn calmly said, "I'm not here to fight you. We just want to get Ma out of here." Jan said, "That's not going to happen. You'll have to get through me to do that. So, let's quit fooling around and get to it!"

Dan yelled "Jan, no good will come of this!" Jan said, "You should have thought about that, before spilling Japha blood!"

Syn peeked at Dan and said, "I'll give her what she wants."

Syn stepped forward, on guard against Jan. She watched as Jan twirled her staff, while quickly moving towards her. Jan was so fast, swinging her staff at Syn that Syn had to respect it and was instantly on defense. Jan swung her staff with such speed and accuracy that there wasn't enough of an opening for Syn to go on offense, or counter-attack.

After about fifteen minutes of an all-out attack from Jan, Syn decided it was time to put an end to this. Syn quickly moved inside of a powerful swing of Jan's staff. She swung both her axes.

One at Jan's chest, the other at her neck, knowing Jan could only block one of them.

Jan blocked down hard on the axe aimed at her chest, while just moving her neck out of harms way. Syn swung again at Jan's neck with the ax that missed the first time. Jan lifted herself up on her staff, catapulting herself up over and behind Syn, thrusting her staff behind her at Syn's spine. Syn barely avoided the staff and dived over Jan, swinging her axes down as she went flying over Jan. Jan got low, but still had to raise her staff blocking those axes coning at her head. After blocking, Jan quickly swung her staff at Syn trying to catch Syn before she landed solidly. However, as soon as Syn landed, she flipped over the staff coming at her, back towards Jan.

Now, right next to Jan, Syn swung each of her axes at Jan's hands holding on to the staff. Jan let go of the staff with one hand avoiding the blade that sliced past where her wrist would have been, while moving the staff and herself, out of the way of the second ax. Before Jan could make another move, Syn smashed the hammer side of her ax into Jan's midsection, instantly followed by the other hammer of Syn's second ax, hitting Jan in the same spot. Jan fell to one knee, supported only by the staff in one hand, holding on to her ribs with the other hand.

Syn took a step back from Jan, just as San came flying through the air, at her. Syn did a tuck and roll, barely avoiding having her head taken off by San's Hammer-Ax. After landing and just missing Syn's neck, San measured where Syn would come out of her tuck and roll. He moved with lightning speed, diving and closing the distance between himself and Syn. Before Syn could see where San was, his Ax was flying towards her unprotected neck.

Ma had been watching from the ground. She saw San had a clear shot at Syn's neck and it was too late for Syn to react. Ma's mind flashed back to when she saw her best friend, Catismallianne's head being chopped off. Ma yelled "JARA!!!"

The blade of San's Hammer-Axe was violently forced downward, slicing into the dirt, by the hammer side of Dan's ax. San swung down on Dan with his other ax. Dan blocked it and lunged his other ax at San's mid-section. San moved backwards out of the way. That gave Dan just enough time to regroup, before San started swinging his axes masterfully at Dan.

As Dan and San went at each other with everything they had, the Japha guards moved quickly on Syn. Mangler joined in, helping Syn with the Japha guards. Syn saw that the Japha guards had their hands full with Mangler, so she moved to check on Ma. The Re guards were helping Mangler, while several of them still had a perimeter around Ma.

Jan hadn't moved from where she was kneeling. She was fighting the pain of her injuries. Jan took a deep breath, when, all in one violent movement, she coughed and blood splattered on the ground in front of her. She breathed heavily for a few seconds and then coughed up more blood.

Once Syn saw that Ma was protected and before Jan knew what happened, Syn was at her side wrapping cloth she got from one of the dead guards around Jan's ribs. Several of the Japha guards had a clean shot at Syn, but Jan motioned them to move back.

Syn wasn't as unprotected as the guards thought she was. Syn only looked at them for a second before turning back to Jan. Syn said, "This is going to hurt. I have to wrap this as tightly as possible to keep you from breathing heavily. That's what's causing the convulsions."

Jan's words were painfully measure when she said, "Why would you help me, after trying to kill me?" Syn stopped for a second, looked in Jan's eyes and said, as a matter of fact "If I were trying to kill you, you'd be dead. I just would have sliced you with the ax side, instead of hitting you with the Hammers. I had to stop you from swinging that deadly staff of yours, at me."

Jan, while looking Syn in her eyes, realized Syn could have killed her. Jan winced in pain and said, "You've proven, once again, you're the best." Syn said "Don't talk too much, that'll only make it hurt worse." Jan still couldn't believe Syn was caring for her, after she, herself, was doing her best to kill Syn, Jara.

San and Dan were fighting so violently with their Hammer-Axes that no one dared come close enough to help either of them. Their battle raged on, even after Jan made a weak attempt to call San off. San hadn't heard her. Jan's voice wasn't loud enough to stop the Japha guards from fighting.

After another forty minutes of all out warfare, everyone heard loud singing to the likes of which they'd never heard. The melodic tone of the voices instantly enchanted the emotions of everyone within earshot. In less than a minute's time, all of the men fighting were powerless to raise their weapons. The singing got louder and louder, until a group of women appeared. They continued to sing, until all of the men were rendered useless. Even though San and Dan held out the longest, they too were shedding tears at an uncomfortable rate, which made fighting impossible. Between tears, they laughed at seeing each other crying, while trying to shake off the embarrassment of crying themselves.

The women pushed the tones of their voices to a crescendo that put some of the men on their knees. When they stopped, Ramala walked between them and made her way over to Jan. Ramala said, "Better that they sing at you, than I scream at you." Jan nodded in agreement, as she wiped the tears from her face. Ramala said, "Let me help you, sister." After that, Syn quickly went over to check on Ma.

Ramala and the Japha healers helped Jan, while San, Dan and all the men tried to fight their way through the emotional barrier the singing had built up in them. Just like the Hellcats screams, the singing only disoriented you for about ten minutes. After that, you were back to normal.

After everyone recuperated from the effects of the singing, Mangler, Ma, Dan and Syn were surrounded by Japha guards, San and his bodyguards. Ma was standing with the help of two Ra guards. San knew if serious fighting erupted, Ma would be an easy target. He looked at the singers, who were standing near Ramala, watching and waiting for hostilities to break out.

San motioned to his guards and said, "Hold your positions. Right now, they have the upper hand." Jan looked at San and said, "Have the guards move back. Let her go." San looked at Jan to see if she was serious. Then he motioned with his hand for them to move back.

Ramala looked at the two guards holding Ma and ordered, "Take her back and get her wounds tended to." Ma yelled "No! I'm not going back! I'll take my chances with my sisters at the monastery!"

There was a moment of silence. It shocked everyone that Ma would think the Japha would let her enter their territory, without killing her. However, as Ma looked around at Dan, Syn, Ramala and everyone else here, all she saw were the people who betrayed her by not telling her the truth about Yin's death.

With her leg busted up badly and with her other injuries, Ma didn't think she'd ever have the chance to kill San. Right now, she just wanted to die. She knew if she attempted to go north to the monastery and announced it to the Japha, that's just what would happen. So did everyone else.

Syn moved closer to Ma and said, "You can't be serious!" Ma looked at Syn with a betrayed look in her eyes and said, "I've never been more serious." Syn said, "I'm going with you!" Ma said, "No, you're not!" Syn replied, "Who's going to stop me? Certainly, not you!" Both girls stared at each other for a moment, before Ma said, "Fine, do what you want!" Syn said, just as animated "Fine, I will!"

San said, "What makes you think either of you will make past the Japha army to that monastery?" Ramala co-signed "And what makes you think I would give up two of my best female warriors?"

Syn looked at Ramala with angry pleading eyes and saying, "Look at her leg! At best, she may walk with a limp! She's done as an effective killer. As for me, I'm staying with Ma!"

Ramala could see that Ma was worthless to her, as a fighter. She also could see the determination on Syn's face that said she would die, before leaving Ma's side. Ramala also saw that San would probably use every Japha guard at his disposal to kill Ma and Syn. She saw Dan out of the corner of her eye. Ramala was disgusted with Dan for coming here. She still couldn't figure out why he did.

If Dan weren't here, Ramala never would have come. However, knowing if Dan somehow got himself wounded, or killed by the Japha, Ramala knew she'd be powerless to stop La from warring with the Japha.

Ramala was snapped out of her thoughts as she saw Danaaa bolt past her, look at Ma only for a second, before turning, in front of Ma, with her hands at a draw position next to her axes. Yin quickly moved next to Danaaa, on guard. Young Dan, Don and Ram moved next to Yin. Yin saw San and instantly became angered. He took a step towards San, before Young Dan slammed the flat side of his Hammer-Axe into Yin's chest, really hard, stopping him. Yin quickly looked at Young Dan. Young Dan looked at Yin as if he should hold his ground. Yin could see he'd have to fight Dan in order to get to San. Yin stood his ground, while staring at San.

Before Ramala could say anything, she heard the harshest tone she'd ever heard come out of La's mouth, when La yelled, "Somebody had better tell me what's going on, before I come to my own conclusions!"

La drew her axes in that same instant. The rest of the Hammer-Axes Six did the same. Ramala knew she had to take control, before La got out of control.

Ramala yelled to La, without looking at her "I thought I told you to stay at the caravan, unless I summoned you!"

The Hammer-Axe Six had been Ramala's personal bodyguards, as punishment for killing three of her personal bodyguards. Ramala brought them along with her and told them to stay with the elephants.

La knew there had been a serious battle here and was still caught up in the moment, when she yelled, "I'm your personal bodyguard! I'm here to protect Daddy . . . And you!"

Ramala turned and looked at La, who was staring at San and his bodyguards. She also saw the rest of the Hammer-Axe Six on guard, ready to attack, at the drop of a dime.

Ramala paused and then sternly said "Just who, in the Hell, do you think you're yelling at?!"

Before La could respond, Danaaa yelled, "She's not yelling at you, she's just yelling! She always yells, whenever she wants! You already know that!" Then Danaaa face got a look of confusion on it, as her lower lip went crooked on one side, where it began to shake, as she stared at the Japha guards in front of her.

Upon hearing Danaaa yell, Ramala slowly turned and saw that strange, but familiar, look on Danaaa's face. Baby was past angry, she was cross!

There was a second of silence, before a short, but painful burst of laughter from Jan, broke it. That was followed by Syn's laughter. Ma even giggled a little.

However, Ramala wasn't laughing. Jan saw that, right away. She also saw Ramala's children still on guard. Jan definitely wasn't going to let San's, or any Japha guards attack Ramala's children. Jan ordered, "Guards, move back!"

She paused for a moment, while wincing in pain. She then smiled at Danaaa and said, "There's been a terrible mistake. My guards thought we were being attacked, when all Ma and Syn were trying to do was go north to the monastery."

Danaaa, remembering when guards came into her sleeping room, yelled, "Guards are always doing something they're not supposed to!"

Jan said "The guards were doing what they thought was best. Thankfully, everything has been cleared up. Ma and Syn will be allowed to go to the monastery, unharmed. As long as they stay there, guards won't make the mistake of thinking them a threat."

Jan had done what was best to preserve her alliance with Ramala and the Hellcats by pardoning Ma and giving permission for Ma and Syn to go north, through Japha territory, to the female monastery. San only looked at Jan for a moment. He peeked at young Yin, before motioning to his guards and walking away.

Everyone relaxed a little, except for Danaaa, Yin and Ram. They were still on high alert. Although, somewhat relaxed, La knew she hadn't been told the whole story. She could see that both Jan

Robert Davis

and Ma were wounded. La knew she had to be respectful, so she lowered her head to Jan and said, "If our guards can take Aunt Ma to our healers, we can have them work on her wounds."

Jan nodded in agreement. La yelled for Ali. Not ten seconds later, Ali and twenty of his guards came running up. La ordered them to take Ma to the Ra healers. She then turned to Jan and said she was concerned about young King San and his siblings and wanted to see them. Jan nodded in agreement and had Japha guards lead the Ra children. After the Ra children left, Jan smiled, shook her head and said to Ramala "She's just like you!"

The Ra children were led to the double elephant plat formed enclosure that housed the Japha children. Once the Japha children were told they had visitors, they walked down the ramp to greet them. The first thing the Ra children noticed was the sad looks on all of their faces. The second thing they noticed was that none of the Japha boys had their weapons attached to them.

La hugged and consoled the young Japha girls, first. San Jett was next to walk up to La looking to be consoled. La gave San Jett a reassuring look, while putting both her hands on his shoulders. A split second later, La backhand slapped him, with the returning open hand slap across San Jett's face. She then plowed her fist into his stomach, grabbing him and throwing him to the ground, while landing on top of him, all in one motion. La grabbed both his wrist and pressed them hard on the ground, while using her weight and leverage to pin San Jett's body to where he couldn't move.

Japha bodyguards quickly pulled their weapons. The Ra children pulled their weapons and went on guard against the Japha. Teesana and Sania took off running like two bolts of lightning. Jeb just stood there shocked at this turn of events.

La yelled, "Everyone put away your weapons!" The Japha guards weren't taking orders from La and said, "Let him go, or we attack!"

La looked down at San Jett and said, "I'm not going to harm you. Tell those guards to back off, so I can talk to you." San Jett angrily stared into La's eyes, for a moment, before saying, "Guards, put away your weapons! We're just talking!"

The Japha guards took one step back, but didn't put away their weapons. Their job was to protect the Japha children. La didn't have a weapon drawn, but if she made one false move, the bodyguards would attack.

None of that was lost on La. Once the immediate danger of being chopped to pieces by San Jett's bodyguards passed, La looked down at San Jett and sternly said, "You're the young King of Japha yet, in this very difficult time, you hide, crying with the children! Your job is to watch, protect and make good decisions for your family. That's what Kings do!"

La's face and voice softened just a little when she said, "I know this is a very hard time for you with what's happened. Still, you have to be strong. When I let go of you, go get your weapons holster and put it on. A King should never be without his weapons! Then you keep your mind occupied with what's going on in your camp."

La paused for a second, staring at San Jett. She said "Oh, and remember, don't be angry and try to fight me, because I'll be forced to beat you senseless, in no time flat. I don't want to do that, because I really like you. Besides, we're going to be working together for a very long time."

After La said that, Jan and Ramala had just broke through the guards to see what was going on. Ramala yelled "Ramala, get off of him, now!"

La got off San Jett, watching his every movement. San Jett stared at La while getting up. He looked at Ramala and then at Jan, before saying "She wasn't doing me harm. She's just a little rough, sometimes. That's her way of showing how much she really cares."

San Jett surprised everyone, even La, by giving her a hug and then leaving. Jan asked, "San Jett, where are you going?" San Jett looked at La and Jan, before saying "To get properly dressed." San looked at his brother Jeb and said "Come on, let's go."

Danaaa moved quickly towards Jeb, ready to pummel him. La saw Danaaa and yelled, "Baby, no!" Danaaa looked at La, before looking at Jeb and yelling "But, somebody needs to teach him how important it is to wear his weapon, too!" La responded, "That's enough! I think he already knows."

Danaaa stomped one foot and then the other, in protest. She yelled, "Now, I can't even teach him a lesson, when I know it'll be a good one he'll remember for a long time! I just know it!" La said, "Just get over here!" Danaaa walked, in a huff, over to La. When Danaaa got to La, she forcefully turned her body and head. Danaaa's ponytail slapped across La's backside. La quickly countered by grabbing Danaaa's ponytail and yanking violently down on it. Danaaa just looked at La and smiled at her. La threw her elbow into Danaaa's side, only to have Danaaa quickly do the same to her.

La was about to forget ruling protocol and put her sister in her place. Ramala saw that and said, "Alright girls, don't get started! It's time to go!"

Shaya meekly said "Mother, please allow us to meet with Aunt Jan and uncle San before we leave." Ramala paused a moment, just because she wasn't use to Shaya requesting anything. Ramala said, "I'll allow it, if your sisters can remember how to follow protocol." Ramala gave both La and Danaaa a stern look and said, "Can you?" Both girls chorused "Yes, Mother."

Even with that, Ramala could see that her daughters were itching to fight each other. Ramala said, "I'll escort you, just in case I have to remind either of you." Both girls knew that meant some instant physicality from Ramala if they didn't act right.

The meeting was held near the platform on the elephant that housed San. Both San and Jan were surprised to see San Jett and Jeb, along with their two sisters at the meeting. La wasn't. She and San Jett exchanged a smile that wasn't lost on anyone there.

Shaya begged La and La was encouraged by her advisers to let Shaya talk on occasion. La was dominant over Shaya and didn't see her as being a threat. Therefore, when La knew it wouldn't be wise to try to bully, or dominate someone, she would let Shaya do the talking. That way, if there had to be a compromise it wouldn't look like La was the one doing it.

San wasn't in the mood to see the Ra girls. Jan convinced him it would be wise to do so. Besides, Jan told San, it would only be a minor inconvenience. San looked over at Jan. He knew she'd pester him, until he agreed, so he did.

When San-Jett heard there was going to be a meeting with the Ra girls, he begged his father if he could be present. San agreed. San-Jett showed up to the meeting with his brother and two sisters. It surprised both San and Jan that all of San's children were dressed, complete with their weapons holsters, even the girls.

When San asked them why they had their weapons holsters on, San-Jett replied "You just never know when you might need them." San couldn't argue with that. Besides, it was starting to look like his children were focused on something other than their mother's death. San thought that was a good thing.

San was sitting in his throne chair, near his plat formed Elephant. Jan was standing next to him. The Japha children were next to Jan. After getting situated, they didn't have to wait long before the Ra children, accompanied by Ramala walked up. All of the Ra lowered their heads, out of respect and after getting the same respect from the Japha, the Ra girls took a couple of steps forwards.

San wondered what these young girls could possibly have to say to him. He decided that he would be cordial, until, when or if he heard something he didn't like.

Because they weren't told, it surprised everyone when Shaya spoke, instead of La. Shaya looked directly at San, when Shaya softly said, "Uncle San thanks for giving us this audience. It's good that we can talk in light of trying circumstances. I don't want to waste time, so I'll get right to the point. It's about Aunt Ma. We know she's not perfect and has made many mistakes in her life. Still, we love her. If any harm comes to her, we would be beside ourselves with grief. There's no telling how we would react."

San was listening to Shaya's soft soothing voice. It was nothing like Ramala, or La's. Shaya's voice made you want to listen and even though San knew there was somehow a threat in what Shaya said, it didn't offend him. He thought that strange, but kept listening.

Shaya was saying, "We checked her wounds. Her leg is broken. Even when it heals, she's done as a fighter. With that being said, all she wants to do is go and live in peace at the monastery where she was raised. Aunt Jan has agreed to let this happen. It would mean the world to us if you would allow this to happen. I beg, of you . . . ."

La grabbed Shaya's arm, pulling hard, until Shaya was facing her. La sternly said, "We don't beg for anything!" After only looking at La for a second, Shaya pulled her arm away from La and looked back at San as if nothing had happened. Shaya collected her thoughts and then said in a calm voice "Grant us this one favor and allow aunt Ma safe passage to the monastery and that no harm will come to her. Will you allow this favor, uncle San?"

San, as well as everyone else was impressed with Shaya's little speech. Even though he wanted Ma dead, it didn't seem so important after hearing Shaya speak. San thought that if Ramala could speak to people like that, she could have built her kingdom without spilling one drop of blood.

San also saw the Ra children looking emotional about their aunt Ma. San could see La trying to put on her best face, without looking like this was an ultimatum. San could see in La's eyes, it was just that.

He thought that they might even get themselves killed trying to protect Ma. He knew that wouldn't be a good thing for the Japha. But, amazingly, it wasn't just the sound logic alone that decided San's decision. Shaya's voice and words did it.

San forced a slight smile on his face, as he looked at Shaya and then at La, saying, "I will allow this." San looked at La, because despite Shaya's speech, he knew whom he was really dealing with.

San's decision brought relief to all of the Ra children. They momentarily forgot about ruling protocol and thanked their uncle San profusely. Even La was caught up in the moment. Ramala smiled and watched the whole scene, wondering how long San and Jan would wait, before finally having Ma killed. She hoped long enough that whatever story they made up would be believable to her children, Yin and Syn, Jara.

After the meeting, the Ra girls went and stayed with Ma. The Ra boys went to see their father, who was with their mother, in her covered platform. Dan and Ramala had been talking, until they heard their boys coming. Once there, Young Dan got straight to the point. He said, while looking at Ramala "With your permission, the Hammer-Axe Six will escort Aunt Ma to the monastery, insuring her safety. Once we've done that, we will return to Ra territory."

Ramala looked at her sons and Yin. All of them were teenagers, except for Ram. Ram and Danaaa would be teenagers in just over a year. Ramala thought it would be La that requested this. She was proud that young Dan was taking a more active leadership role. Ramala turned her head and peeked at Elder Dan, with a slight smile on her face, conveying how proud she was of her oldest son. She then looked at young Dan and said, "I will allow this." Dan got a big smile on his face. He said "Thanks, mom!"

Then he remembered his father was here. Young Dan composed himself and lowered his head to both his parents, out of respect. The other Ra boys did, also. They left after that.

Ramala stood up and looked at Dan. Before their boys came, Ramala questioned Dan about why he didn't tell her he was going to stop Ma from getting herself killed. Dan didn't think about saying anything to Ramala. Once Syn told him she suspected Ma was going to avenge Yin's death and asked him to come, they got Mangler, a few guard and left. That was the gist of it. That's what he told Ramala, but she was offended that she wasn't informed, beforehand.

After giving his short explanation, which he thought was going above and beyond what was called for, Dan decided there wasn't anything else he could say, so he wasn't going to. Dan knew Ramala was getting upset that he wouldn't, so he watched her closely, as she got up and looked at him.

Ramala walked over to Dan and slowly sat on his lap. She put her arms around him and said, in almost a whisper "See, even your son knows it's best to inform me what's going on. It's not that hard to do, you know."

Dan said, "He's required to, because he's your son. I'm not going to run up and tell you every little thing I do." Once Dan said that, he thought, maybe, he could have said it better. It was too late for that.

Dan could feel the sudden change in Ramala. Her soft, but firm body, stiffened against his. Dan had been through this drill with Ramala enough times to know something was about to happen.

Ramala roughly pulled back from Dan, turning and letting her elbow hit Dan on the back of his head as she moved back. She yelled, "You're a shit for brains asshole! You make me sick, with your ignorant stupidity!"

Dan could see his Queen was building herself up for a good fight. Dan decided to give it to her. He grabbed her roughly by her waist. Ramala, not wanting to be controlled by anyone, forcefully pulled away and stood up. Dan stood up, not letting Ramala put any space between them. Ramala tried to use leverage to get to a better position in which she could strike Dan and teach him a lesson for his stupidity.

Dan realizing this, quickly pulled on Ramala's wrist, just as she smashed the elbow of her other arm into Dan's ribs. In that same instant, Dan's free hand moved quickly between Ramala's legs, slowly rubbing between them, while stretching her other arm towards the arm of the chair in front of her.

Ramala smashed her elbow into Dan's ribs again, while struggling to get her other hand free. When she couldn't, she whispered sternly "What do you think you're doing?!"

In Ramala's split second of confusion, Dan quickly grabbed Ramala's other wrist and forcefully put it, along with the other one, on the arms of the throne chair. Now having Ramala bent over the chair, Dan said "You've known me long enough to know what's about to happen!"

Ramala did know. For all her aggressiveness towards Dan, the only time she could force herself to give in to him, was when she knew he was going to give her something she couldn't stop herself from getting from him, anytime she could.

After Dan said that, Ramala firmly grabbed the arms of the chair, with her hands and then sternly whispered, "The guards will hear us!" Dan said, while taking his hands off Ramala's wrist and removing the clothes covering her perfectly round butt "Not if you keep quiet."

With concern in her voice, Ramala whispered "But, you know I can't do that!"

As Dan slowly entered Ramala, he said, "You can try." Ramala knew it was on. So, with a steely resolve Ramala determined she could keep quiet, if she just gave it give it the old college try!

Not three minutes into it, Dan, knowing all the right spots to hit in Ramala, started hitting them with reckless abandonment. Sometimes slow and then sometimes fast. Ramala kept her mouth shut, taking what Dan was dishing out, by breathing through her nose and keeping her mouth shut.

Ramala loved it. However, as her breathing became elevated Ramala couldn't get enough air, into her lungs, through her nose. Therefore, breathing just through her nose wasn't an option, anymore. Ramala opened her mouth and started taking short quick breaths, to better deal with Dan's thrusting. Dan detected that and decided to turn it up a notch.

While taking a deep breath, Ramala was hit with a thrust that felt so good, when she exhaled, she made a low continuous moan, that conveyed the pleasure she was feeling. With every powerful thrust after that, Ramala's vocal chords told an emotional story of the rollercoaster ride she was enjoying. The pitch and volume increased with every passing moment. In other words, she was screaming and didn't care!

After about forty minutes, Dan backed up off Ramala. Ramala turned around slowly, with a half-crazed look of lust on her face. Dan realized this wasn't over, yet. He was right. Ramala wrestled Dan roughly to the floor. Once there, she got on top and started riding him, as she'd done on so many occasions.

Ramala rode Dan, with him thrusting upwards from beneath her, until she erupted in a screaming orgasm. Her legs and arms gave way, and she fell, lying on top of Dan. After a moment, she forced herself, unstably, back on her hands and knees and climbed off Dan. She lay next to him, looking at the roof of the platform, while taking back control of her breath.

Now, that the deed was done, Ramala thought about how out of control she was. She was sure the guards and everyone else heard her. She just knew it! So, even though she wasn't as pissed at Dan as she was before, Ramala said with a hint of embarrassment in her voice, "You're still a shit for brains asshole!"

Dan was already reaching for his clothes, when he said, nonchalantly "I know. I'm the shit for brains that's got you on your back and loving it." Ramala didn't say anything, because she knew Dan was right.

Once Dan was dressed, he looked back at Ramala. She was sitting on the floor staring at him, with her arms wrapped around her knees, smiling. At certain times, things Ramala did reminded Dan of his daughters.

For some reason, right now, Ramala reminded him of Danaaa, the way she was looking at him. He wasn't going to ask her why she was watching him, or what she was thinking. That could possibly ruin his chance for a clean escape.

Dan smiled and got a return smile that said job well done. He left after that. After Dan walked down the ramp, he saw Ramala's maids rushing to go and help make the Queen suitable for presentation. They always did that, after one of Dan and Ramala's sex-capades.

Ramala instructed her children that once they escorted Ma to the monastery, it was imperative that they turn around and get out of Japha territory as soon as possible. They all said they would. After that, Ramala went to see Jan. Jan smiled, when she saw Ramala and said, "You let everyone know that you were getting it really good."

Ramala hadn't realized her screams of pleasure had reached clear over to the Japha camp. She said, "I told Dan that would happen! But, you know him, he just wouldn't listen!" Jan laughed, until the pain slowed her laughter.

When the Ra girls heard their mother howling in pleasure, it warmed their hearts. That was one of the signs letting them know their parents were getting along, well. After witnessing some of their parent's fights, it always made the Ra girls euphoric when their parents were getting along.

The Japha caravan left, shortly, after that. The Ra girls rode on a phant with Syn and Ma. The Ra young men rode on phants next to the one the Ra girls were on. Ali, Bo, Hoban, Elite Guards surrounded the Ra children as they followed the Japha caravan, north.

The trip to the Monastery was uneventful. Once they got there, Jan and her bodyguards met with the Nuns. After a short period of time, Jan had her guards summon Ma. The Hammer-Axe Six escorted Ma and Syn to the front gate of the Monastery, where the Nuns were waiting.

Everyone hugged and it was an emotional farewell. After everyone composed themselves, La stared at the Nuns and said sternly, with her eyes glossed over with moisture "Know that if any harm comes to my aunt Ma, I'll start by destroying this Monastery and everyone in it trying to find whoever is guilty! If I don't find them here, I'll keep going, until I kill them all!"

Danaaa quickly pulled her Axes, putting one in front of her, just below her eyes, flat, with the blade pointing at the Nuns. The other Ax was straight down at her side, just behind her leg, with the Hammer side facing forward.

Shaya, who normally had a soft pleasant look on her face, didn't. Once La started making her threat, Shaya's stare became cold and callous, conveying that something ominous would indeed happen, if they didn't heed La's words.

Ma was slightly shocked, but didn't say anything. Jan was stunned, but not surprised that La would make such a threat. Jan saw Ramala's girls staring at the Nuns as if they were on the verge of attacking them. She knew she had to say something, before La did.

However, it was Syn who yelled, "Girls, mind your manners!" That shocked the Ra girls, because no one would dare yell an order to them, except for their parents.

La turned her back to the Nuns, flinging her cape, letting everyone know that she was upset, as she walked away. Danaaa spun her Axes one super-fast revolution, before slamming them in their holsters. She then looked at Syn and did a quick lowering and raising of her head. Danaaa turned and followed La.

Shaya, who normally would instantly follow La, stared coldly at the Nuns. She didn't break her stare, until she heard La's voice say "Enough of this, Shaya! Come, let's go!"

Shaya broke her stare on the Nuns and looked at Syn. Shaya's face had instantly turned soft. She smiled at Syn, then slowly lowered her head and raised it in the same manner. Shaya turned and yelled, "Wait for me!" as she bolted towards La and Danaaa. Once there, Shaya roughly forced her way between La and Danaaa, even though she didn't have to, because there was more than enough room for her.

That didn't bother La, or Danaaa. They knew that just meant Shaya was upset. After her show of displeasure, Shaya moved close to La and leaned on her shoulder. La was instantly annoyed by that. Still, she didn't stop Shaya from doing it.

As the Ra girls were heading back to their caravan, San-Jett came running up. He stopped in front of La. San-Jett said, with a smile on his face "I just wanted to give you one last hug, before you go." La smiled at San-Jett, letting him know she would allow this. Shaya and Danaaa moved aside.

San-Jett moved close to hug La and all of a sudden, plowed his fist at La's stomach. La moved to the side, while grabbing the arm that San-Jett was swinging at her, pulling him towards her, wrapping her other arm around his neck from behind him. Then, all in one motion, La let go of San-Jett's arm and neck, putting both her hands on his back and pushing him forward. Before San-Jett could take his second step, La plowed her foot into his back, sending him stumbling forward.

San-Jett quickly turned around with a smile on his face. He saw La's face was frantic and serious, as she screamed, "Baby, No!" San-Jett's eyes quickly darted to Danaaa, who's axes where just moving back away from him. In that split second he wondered how close those Axes came to him, before they started moving backwards. He watched as Danaaa slammed her Axes back into their holsters. Danaaa looked at La for a second and then took a couple of steps back from San-Jett.

Seeing he'd barely avoided being cut to pieces, San-Jett tried to hide the slight nervousness in his voice, when he said, "Man, she's really fast with those Axes!" La said, "You don't even know!" San-Jett peeked at Danaaa and then looked at La. He said, "How did you know what I was going to do?"

La turned and looked at Danaaa, checking her mood, before turning back to San-Jett and saying "I just knew it." San-Jett curiously looked at La for a moment, before turning to leave. He said, "See you, later." La said, "See you." Shaya moved back close to La, leaning on her shoulder and saying, "I think he likes getting roughed up by you." La said, "He just likes me. That's the best way he knows how to show it."

Now Shaya was up to speed on what was going on here. Danaaa was already up to speed from formulating her own thoughts on earlier events. She thought that if Japha, San kept liking La this way, sooner, or later, her axes were going to catch up to him, before La stopped her.

Danaaa took a quick peek a La that La noticed. These two watched each other, constantly. Danaaa, to se if she could gain some kind of advantage on La. La, to make sure she could catch Danaaa, before Danaaa did something, La considered, crazy.

Because of all the beatings La had put on her siblings, in the past, she had to watch all of them very closely, in order to guard against retaliation. La saw that same, sneak attack move that San-Jett tried, several times over by one of her sisters and two of her brothers. Shaya and Ram learned by seeing what happened to the others that La dished out extreme physicality, when you attack her. That's why San-Jett never had a chance with his attack on La.

CHAPTER 14

By the time they made it home, Jan's nerves were shot from dealing with the whining from the Terrible Two. Jan knew it was the wrong way to think, but she couldn't help feeling animosity towards Tara for putting her and her family though all this pain.

Once Jan reached her palace, Jan's oldest friends and top advisers were waiting on her. Mia and Nina were already briefed, by messengers, about Tee's death. They made sure Jan was comfortable and then they told her that the Elder member of the Tat clan passed away, in his sleep, two days ago. This shocked Jan. She asked Nina and Mia to make sure the Tat had what they needed. They assured Jan that had been taken care of. They also assured Jan they would see that San and his children were taken care of. Jan knew that would happen once they made it home, but it was good to hear it.

All of this had almost been too much for Jan. Nina and Mia could see that and suggested that Jan see Healers and then get some rest, before she did anything else. Jan didn't put up a fight. It was times like these when her girls meant the most to her. Jan let herself be led off and she got some much needed rest.

After sleeping most of the next day, only getting up to check on San and his children, Jan sent messengers to the Tat compound, asking if it was a good time to see them. It had almost been a week since their Elder's death and passing away ceremony. The Tat were ready to receive visitors.

Up to this point, Jan had always met with the Tat Elder number nine. The younger ones never talked much, if at all. Jan was invited to have first day's meal with the Tat and after breakfast, they would converse.

There were only nine Tat left. All were highly advanced in their mental and spiritual skills. At twenty-one, Taz was the oldest and now elder of what was left of the Tat clan. Tone and Tamyika were twenty years old. Tonia was nineteen. Tre was sixteen. Tanya was fifteen. Tani was twelve. The youngest and most spiritually powerful was the eleven-year-old Tat, Tira.

Tira Tat was able to communicate with other in their minds, almost from birth. Because Tira was so good at it, she hardly spoke and had to be trained to speak, while having a conversation with others.

The Tat Elders were made aware of her advanced skills and put her under the tutelage of Tat Elder number nine. Tat number nine was to keep the other Elders informed of the progress of young Tira. Tira loved to learn and often would take the teachings of Tat Elder number nine a level further than he thought possible.

By the time Tira was five, she was a master of mental manipulation. Mental manipulation is the process of entering someone's mind, without their knowledge and influencing their thoughts to actions that you make them, without them knowing. Tat Elder number nine had a hard time keeping Tira disciplined in not controlling the actions of others. Still, his number one student was a quick learner and for all the advanced spiritual skills she had, Tira was very disciplined and would heed the warnings of not abusing her abilities.

By the age of nine, Tira was so far advanced, she had learned to open doors to other dimensions. Once Elder number nine was aware of this, he strictly forbid Tira to do it, unless he was present to help guide her through the process and explain to her where she had traveled.

Back then, at the age of nine, Tira, although disciplined, still had some of the inexperienced traits of a nine-year-old girl. One of those traits was curiosity. That coupled with the fact that she knew she was more advanced that her counterparts, made Tira push herself to the limits of her abilities.

One day Tira decided that she would travel in her mind and follow her guest spirit through some of its memories. This is a very tricky feat, because spirits live in the past, present, future and sometimes in between time, which is where the different dimensions are. As advanced as Tira was, her guest spirits were also advanced. In addition, because Tira's level of spirituality was so high, it didn't take long for her guest spirits to learn Tira's human functions. Remember, as we learn and use our guest spirits, they also learn the ways and uses of their hosts. (Spirit Awareness 101)

Therefore, even though Tira was highly in tune with her guest spirits, she didn't know what all they were capable of. How could she? She was only nine years old. Still, Tira was emboldened by her advanced level of spirituality to try something on her own.

Tira left her conscious mind and hitched a ride with one of her spirits. She traveled back and forth through time, until she was at the doors of several dimensions. Tira had never gone this far before, so she didn't know what door to open. They all looked the same to her, so Tira picked one.

Tira opened the door to a dimension that astounded her so much, that she stopped in her tracks at the doorway of this dimension. Upon opening this door, Tira saw that it looked like she was on another world. It was dark, except for the lighting of the stars, which made the landscape very bright. She could see a barren dirt like field, with giant black marble like statues of men far off in the distance. Tira blinked once in wonderment at the size of the giant statues, but when her eyes opened from just one blink, the giant statues had moved closer, covering half the ground between herself and them.

Shocked by that, Tira blinked again. This time the giant statues were even closer. Now she could see the faces and they seemed to be staring at her. Another blink and the statues were now right over Tira, with angry faces, reaching down for her with giant stone hands. Tira was frightened tremendously, but was aware enough to know that every time she blinked these statues moved to action. In her terror and panic at the statues reaching for her, Tira's eyes closed, in a slow motion blink. Before she opened her eyes, Tira was snatched backwards out of the entrance of the doorway, by someone she couldn't see. She looked, as Tat Elder number nine moved in front of her and quickly slammed the door to that dimension.

The Elder turned and looked sternly at Tira, letting her know that he was displeased with what she'd done. Tira only looked at her Elder for a second, before being transported to where her body was and into consciousness.

When Tira opened her eyes, she saw the other eight young Tat surrounding her. She looked to her left and saw the Tat Elder slowly opening his eyes, turning and looking at her.

Without speaking, using her mental powers, Tira thanked all of her fellow students and her Elder for helping her find her way back. The Elder, while still looking at Tira, spoke to her, using thought, asking her "You've been taught how dangerous it is to go where you went, yet, you still went. Tell me why your discipline failed you in this instance?"

Tira's mind spoke to the Elder, saying, "Because I told myself that I could handle whatever I came across. I told myself that I knew better than what I was taught by my Elders. I was wrong and was blessed to learn that valuable lesson, without being harmed."

The Tat Elder responded in thought "Learning a lesson taught can often save you from the tougher lesson of actually going through something you could have learned, by adhering to lessons taught. Some lessons that you force yourself to learn, on your own, are hard to come back from, completely. Sometimes you never come back."

Tira knew how blessed she was to make it back. Still, she let her curiosity get the best of her. Her thoughts asked the Elder "What were those things?"

The Tat Elder simply replied "Something you don't come back from!"

Tira lowered her head out of respect to her Elder. She knew he was telling her that she wasn't ready for that lesson, yet. Tira was sure the Elder would instruct her about what she saw when the time was right. That time was not now. Back then, Tira didn't know that lesson wouldn't come from this Elder.

Although, Tira was more advanced than the other advanced Tat students, she had to use her mental disciplines to fight her immaturity, as well as her sometimes overwhelming curiosity.

At breakfast with the young Tat, Jan felt slightly uncomfortable as memories of everything that happen on her trip to the House of Ra flooded her mind. She knew the Tat were going through her memories. Jan decided if that's what the Tat wanted to do, she wasn't going to protest in any way. If the Tat didn't like what they saw, she would deal with that as best she could.

After breakfast, the Elder of the Tat clan, Taz spoke. He said, "You and yours will rule the North, for a very long time. We like it here, so we'll do our part to make that happen as easily as possible." Jan smiled, lowered her head slightly, then got up and left. She heard all she needed to hear.

Besides making attacks on Yin's House of Hell, the Shinmushee would attack and slaughter any small groups of Ra guards they could catch off guard. The open plains in the Ra territory were some of the most dangerous areas for Ra guards, outside of the Southern jungle. Wana's Warlords were in charge of keeping the plains safe. They found that they needed to keep most of their guards to protect their strongholds.

At first, these Warlords would send guards and scouts to patrol areas of the plains. They realized they were losing guards at a rate that they weren't willing to let Wana, or her Hellcats cousins know about. Therefore, these Warlords only fiercely protected the immediate area where they and their family lived. Soon, they even stopped sending guards out on patrol. They needed every guard and scout, just to maintain their immediate positions.

Ramala gave Warlord Benobu and other Warlords land outside the main city of Ra, past the Lake. She and Wana knew they would hold that land and protect it, because their families lived there. All of the Warlords, including Han and the Warlords in and around Wa province, knew how important it was to them and their family's position in the House of Ra, that they control their territory. It was outside of those areas, where rebels from every faction could roam almost effortlessly, unless they saw one of the larger Ra patrols, which they would avoid. The smaller Ra patrols were usually attacked and slaughtered.

The Hellcats were aware that there had always been rebel opposition in, what they considered sparse areas of their kingdom. For them, that was too much for their liking. Several times the Hellcats made plans to rid themselves of rebel activity, by sending their Butchers to quell all rebellions. So far, that hadn't worked. In addition, because of the deaths of the Butchers Backir, Catismallianne, or just Cat and Yin, the mystique of the Butchers being unbeatable was gone. Now, everyone with a vendetta against the House of Ra and the Butchers, wanted to be known as the person who killed one of the Butchers.

The Hellcats only found out how bad things were on the open plains, because some of their messengers were coming up missing. None of their Warlords, outside the city of Ra, all the way to Yee province, could tell the Hellcats what happened. That's when Wana, after consulting with Ramala, ordered a meeting of all the top Warlords in the House of Ra.

All of these Warlords were told to leave their captains and guards to control their areas and only to bring their bodyguards for their personal protection. The Hellcats didn't want all of their Warlords, with all of their forces, in the main city, all at once. That could possibly be disastrous, if the Warlords decided to stage another rebellion.

The Ra Warlords knew how dangerous the plains had become. They had messengers go north to Yee province and present Han with a plan that would get all of them to the main city safely, without incident.

The plan was for a large contingency of Han's guards to escort Han and the other Warlords to the safety of the Lake, at the most northern part of the main city. They would camp there, until Han and the other top Warlords returned, to be escorted to their individual strongholds. Han heard the plan and didn't see how the plan went against the wishes of his Queen, Ramala, or her Hellcat cousins.

Although, the Hellcats found out the Warlords found a loophole in their orders, they didn't take it as a sign of disrespect, especially since the Warlords left all of their guards camped, just beyond the Lake.

On the day of the meeting, at first days meal, La sat in her seat, thinking about the past seventy days in which Ramala had La and her sibling following each of the Hellcats around as part of the Hellcats personal bodyguard detail. Most days they would guard Ramala, but Ramala wanted them to have different experiences as bodyguards, so sometimes they spent most of the day guarding Tara and other days with Wana.

It didn't bother the rest of the Hammer-Axe Six, because they viewed it as training. And even though La was learning a lot about the placement and positioning of bodyguards, she didn't like being one. La just saw this as her mother wasting La's time, when La thought she could be doing something else. La peeked over at her mother, only for a second. She knew her mother would read intent on her face if she stared longer than she did. It wouldn't be long before this bodyguard nonsense was over. Then, La would have more time to do important things, like bossing people around.

La looked over at her father. Now that La was maturing, she could see that he really was the womanizer that her mother always complained about him being. La's love for her father made her ignore that fact, as long as she could. Danaaa's unusually keen sense of smell let her identify the scent of every woman she smelled on their father, no matter how well he cleaned up before he came home.

Danaaa never failed to reveal to La what woman her father smelled like that day. That news always sickened La, even though, over time, she wanted and expected Danaaa to tell her every time Danaaa caught the scent of another woman on her father. La loved her father, but hated that he had this affliction for women, as La called it.

Ramala watched all of her children this day. It amazed her that all of the boys, although watching their environment, paid close attention to Young Dan's every move and somehow acted, accordingly. Ramala could see that Dan had the Ra boys performing strictly to the protocol he set forth.

Ramala looked at Ram. She was surprised when her girls told her about the way Ram protected the Ra, Anne. Ramala got to see firsthand that Ram was comfortable with Anne, who did most all the talking, when they were together. Ramala thought that this girl probably had seen Ram close to his worse and was still willing to befriend him.

That's when she decided to interview Anne, in private, without any of her children knowing about it. After the interview, Ramala decided that Anne would most likely be the best candidate to be Ram's mate.

Ramala wasn't going to tell her children about that. She was going to let Ram and Anne's relationship continue, under the watchful supervision of herself and Anne's Elders. Since it wasn't formally announced that Anne was chosen for Ram's mate it gave Ramala the option to end it, if she found a better mate for Ram.

It was different with the girls. Shaya and Danaaa would watch everything and everyone in the room. Both girls would report to La anything they didn't think she saw. In tune with every movement La made, Shaya would sometimes stare at La, until she was sure she could read La's intentions.

Danaaa and Ram had superb field vision. Field vision allows a person to look directly at something, while seeing everything else in their field of vision just as clearly as if they were looking directly at it.

Danaaa would look straight and used her field vision to look at La and everything else, while figuring out what La expected of her. Danaaa also watched Shaya. Shaya always knew what was going on with La, even if Danaaa didn't. For Danaaa, reading Shaya could sometimes prevent a fight between Danaaa and La.

With Yani and Tammy, it was different. La wasn't as strict on them, but she still expected them to do what she wanted them to do. La handled the Terrible Two with Shaya and Danaaa. All La had to do was look at the Terrible Two and then look at Shaya as if she was annoyed with them and Shaya would call the girls to attention and instruct them on what to do. Most of the time they would listen, knowing that the next step was Danaaa's physicality, which would put them on track. Because they were young and sometimes didn't care to listen to Shaya, they got physicality they never saw coming, but somehow always came, from Danaaa. Ramala looked over at Tara and saw her studying all of the children, much in the same way she was.

The meeting with the Warlords of Ra was in an outdoor horseshoe shaped courtyard. All of the Warlords sat around the sides of the courtyard, while the Hellcats and Elder Dan sat at the open end, facing towards the middle of the courtyard. The Ra children were standing, at attention, next to their parents.

Once everyone was seated, La moved forward, just before Ramala stood up to address the Warlords. As La walked forward, Shaya and Danaaa quickly moved to her sides. Ali, La's top Warlord, quickly moved to the left of the Ra girls, one step back, while Hoban, La's top henchman, moved to the right of the girls, a step behind them, just as Ali had done. La was smart. She knew the routine of meetings like the back of her hand and planned this for days, once she found out about the meeting.

All three Hellcats watched, as it seemed, La was taking over the meeting. In the past Ramala would let La have her say, after Ramala did. In Ramala's eyes, the Queen talks first, unless she orders someone else to!

La yelled "Get down on your knees for your Queen, Mother, Hayee, Ramala!" Although, everyone had already been on their knees when Ramala entered, they thought it a good idea to do it a second time.

La, her sisters and her whole entourage, turned, faced Ramala and then got on their knees. Ramala, although pleased, gave La a slight look, before looking out over the crowd and saying "You may rise."

Once given that order, La and her entourage turned and faced the crowd, as everyone else took their seats, again. Ramala stood up and walked forward to the front of the throne area. She looked around the courtyard, making eye contact with all the Warlords, as she did.

Ramala's face was arrogant and full of displeasure, when she said, "All of you have been given Land to protect in my name. It seems, so far, you've managed to do that. Even so, who here can tell me why some of my messengers have gone missing?"

No one came forward, so La, while looking at the Warlords, said "Queen, Mother, I don't think they know. The House of Ra has a lot of territory. These Warlords have their hands full, protecting the areas they can. Still, something has to be done so our messengers can freely travel. I'm the one who's going to do something about it. Thanks to my Queen, Mother, I have acquired bodyguard skills that will help me insure that our messenger service be restored to the highest level."

This was the most respectful La had ever talked, while addressing a crowd. She only did it because of her group of advisers, which included her grandfather Roe, Shaya, Tania and several others. They suggested she try a calmer approach and if she didn't get the level cooperation she expected, she could use her usual standard of threatening orders. La reluctantly agreed.

She was still talking, saying "With the help of my brothers and sisters, along with our Warlords, Special Guards and Bodyguards, I will make this happen. I will also deal with the Lawlessness that prevails in the less guarded areas of Ra. That includes dealing with the rebels and those Shitmushee.

'We will be traveling through all of the territories occupied by you Warlords here today. Wherever I decide to rest and have supplies restocked, I expect to be given all the respect and cooperation that I, your Queen, deserves. When I'm done, everyone throughout the land of Ra will respect the wishes of their Queen, Mother, Hayee, Ramala and their young Queen, me, the Ra, Ramala."

La paused long enough to let everyone know that she hadn't made a mistake in calling herself the Queen. Then she continued with "You will still be responsible to follow protocol set forth by your Queen, Mother, Hayee, Ramala. However, you will also be responsible for the protocol set forth by your young Queen, me! That's very important, so don't forget it!"

La paused, as she stared around the courtyard looking for any hint of opposition. She had been as nice as she could before her arrogant streak started manifesting itself.

La was charging herself, ready to go into an arrogant tirade, when she heard Ramala say, "Alright La, I'm sure my Warlords and everyone else here understands the level of cooperation you expect from them. And since you're taking on a task that none of them seem to be too eager to jump at, I'm sure your efforts will be more than appreciated."

Ramala continued talking, making sure that all of her Warlords felt, at the least, a bit uncomfortable about the fact that they didn't volunteer to do this themselves. The other two Hellcats watched Ramala. It seemed to them that she wasn't affected by La referring to herself as the Queen. It also surprised everyone when Ramala said that she expected nothing less than the full cooperation of everyone in the quest the Number One Princess was undertaking.

CHAPTER 15

Back in the jungle, the Wa were living amongst the Shinmushee. The older Wa survived a battle with the Ra children in Yee province, in which they were captured, put in a dungeon and ridiculed by the Ra children, who were much younger than they were. They barely made it back to the jungle, after a hellish battle with the Ra guards, in which only four of them survived. Yaya was the Wa girl that grew up in the House of Ra, with the Ra children. She was the only one of the older Wa, who wasn't trying to think of a way to kill the Ra. Everything the Wa saw of the Ra children told them that would be near impossible to do, at this time.

The younger Wa, who were left in the jungle that time didn't have a firsthand account on how tough the Ra were. They were anxious to do something. They noticed the older Wa weren't as enthusiastic, as before, about leaving the jungle and going after the Ra. They told the younger Wa that they needed much more training, if they ever hoped to succeed in hunting and killing the Butchers, or the Ra. After time passed, the older Wa still refused to make a plan to go and kill Butchers. The younger Wa saw being told they needed more training, as an excuse for doing nothing.

There were eight young Wa. All were distant cousins. Junzee was the oldest at nineteen. Tay, Boku, Zandu and Chet were all seventeen. The Young Wa girls Jami, Uma and Gia were all sixteen.

Jami was tall and had tight muscles on her athletic frame. Her skin was very dark brown. Her hair was in two ponytail braids that hung down over the front of her shoulders. Jami was a natural athlete and took to fighting very well. Jami had a calm demeanor, because of her strict upbringing at the all-female monastery.

Uma was shorter than Jani, but taller than Gia. Uma was slim, but deceivingly powerful for her size. She was dark skinned, also. Her hair was in two braided ponytails, just like Jami and Gia's. Uma was mostly quiet, unless her cousins engaged her in conversation. She always watched everything, looking for the unexpected, because most of her life, that's just what happened.

Gia was slightly shorter than Uma. She was very dark. Gia had a powerfully built, thick frame. She was the quickest and best fighter of the Wa females. Gia had a very positive bubbly attitude. Sometimes she would talk, nonstop. Gia always found a positive in every situation. She felt blessed to have made it this far.

Tay was as dark as brown could get. He was average height for a man. He had good weight but wasn't the size if a brute. Tay was in excellent fighting shape. He was strong, fast and powerful. He had a playful attitude. Tay liked to joke around, but could get serious, instantly.

Zandu was as tall, dark and big as Tay. Everyone called him Zan. Zandu was an angry young man because he witnessed most of his family being killed. He hated the Butchers, the Hellcats and the Ra with a passion. Zandu had very good fighting skills.

Boku was slightly shorter than Tay and Zandu. He was slim, but not skinny and very muscular. Boku had excellent fighting skills. He was strong and quick. Boku was easy going, until it was time to fight.

Chet was about the same height as Boku. He had medium brown skin and a slightly thicker build than Boku. Chet's muscles were chiseled. He was very fast, strong and had good power. His fighting technique was the best of the Wa. Chet was also easy going, but he hatred of the Ra.

The Young Wa spent their time training in the art of fighting and spent part of their days learning from the Elder Shinmushee on all aspect of life. They had a Shinmushee Elder that taught them about the plants, bushes and trees that grew in the jungle and how they were used in everyday life. One teacher taught them protocol on treatment of others in formal and non-formal settings. Another teacher taught them how to track their movements when traveling in the daytime by landmarks and by the moon and stars at night. The Shinmushee teachers taught the Wa these things and more. One day, Gia, being fed up, learning things she didn't think that important, asked in frustration "Why do we have to learn all of this stuff, anyway?!"

Her teacher responded "Because, one day, or another, you'll need to use everything you learn here." Gia was young and looked at the old teacher like that was something she expected him to say. She continued her training, as she always did.

In the evenings after training, the Wa would have dinner with the Shinmushee of all ages. When everyone was done eating, one of the Elders would address everyone, telling them a story, they either made up, or a story from the past. The stories were very exciting, but always had a lesson buried within them. Everyone loved the stories that the Master Storytellers told. After telling the story, the Elder storyteller who told the story and other Elders present, would talk to and get the opinions of the younger people to gauge their level of understanding. The Elders also gave them insights into the story that the younger ones hadn't come up with on their own.

This was one of the many ways the Elders taught and instilled the knowledge of life situations to all the Shinmushee. The Storytellers back then were called Tellers of Life. Thousands of years later, some of the stories they told were known as African folklore.

Yaya loved these stories and couldn't wait, until most of the day's chores and training was over, so she could hear another story. As much as Yaya loved the stories, she also enjoyed the fact that at these times she felt accepted by the Shinmushee. She was allowed to join in the question and answers sessions, after the stories. The Elders were very kind to Yaya and were patient with her, helping her understand parts of the stories she hadn't.

Yaya thought about training in the House of Ra. She was trained in fighting techniques and drilled on how to interpret a situation to see if it was dangerous, or not. Everything she was taught in the House of Ra was done as an exercise, or training lesson. There weren't any question and answer sessions. The Ra instructors expected all of their student to strictly adhere to protocol concerning the lesson and not disrespect their teachers by asking questions. Yaya was taught that if she did it the way the instructor taught her, even if she didn't understand it, she would be successful.

Yaya learned that even when she didn't understand some things, she did what she was told according to the protocol of that lesson and was mostly successful every time.

Now, here in the Southern Jungle, Yaya still had teachers that were strict in training her, but she also had teachers that let her question them and give her opinions. Yaya loved that, because she never had it, before.

She also thought about different ways she was taught in the House of Ra and in the Southern Jungles of the Shinmushee. Yaya wondered if teaching was done differently in all different cultures, even though you might learn some things that were the same and some things that were different. Yaya thought it would be good to learn from as many different cultures as possible, just to see if she would enjoy it.

Yaya was snapped out of her daydream when China called her. It was time to clean up the eating area and then get ready for sleep. Yaya smiled at China and started doing what she learned to do, from the first day she came to the Southern Jungle.

Later, that same evening, when the girls finished preparing themselves for sleep, China started telling Yaya some things the Shinmushee hadn't told her. All of the Wa girls watched Yaya's reactions, as China spoke.

China told Yaya that the Ra, led by the young Queen, princess Ramala and her siblings have been moving through the plains setting up checkpoints and making it hard for the Shinmushee scouts to move around and get information that could lead to successful ambushes.

China said, "The only way to move around the plains was to blend in with one of the tribes that roamed the plains. The Ra under the rule of the princess Ramala didn't pressure the roaming tribes like her mother's warriors did, in the past. The Young Princess and her Warlord brothers stopped the Queen's warriors from abusing these tribes and taking their women, making them their personal whores, while putting the young men into slavery.'

'The tribes still were responsible for giving services and goods to the Queen, but it seems the young Princess has taken over all of the plains leading up to and including Wa and Yee provinces.'

'At first, our Shinmushee brothers tested the forces of the Young Ra Warlords who call themselves The Hammer-Axe Six, by engaging them in battles. They found out the Hammer-Axe Six and their warriors were near impossible to deal with. The Shinmushee were forced to move back towards the Southern Jungle. The Ra kept clear of the Jungle but have many checkpoints, where warriors heavily patrol those areas facing the jungle."

Yaya had been listening, intently. This was the first information she had about the Ra since she and her Wa family members barely escaped Yee province with their lives. Yaya wanted to hear more about her Ra brothers and sisters.

China told Yaya that after being tested, repeatedly, the Ra had now been in control of the plains for a little more than six moons, or months. She said that the Ra sent messengers to the Shinmushee messengers, telling them that they wanted the Wa and their big sister Ya to come and meet with them to discuss getting some of their ancestral land back. China stressed that fact the Shinmushee messenger was very clear in his stating that the Ra messenger referred to Yaya as being the big sister to the Ra Princess and her Warlord siblings.

After saying that, China asked Yaya "You still seem to have favor with the Ra, even though you've been here quite some time. Everyone here knows you know more about the Ra than anyone does. What we can't figure out is why you haven't told us the layout of the main city. You haven't even told us any of their weaknesses that we could exploit. Some wonder if you're a spy for the Ra!"

Yaya kept her eyes fixed on China's, while she felt the stares of the other Wa girls burning into the side of her face. Still, Yaya said nothing. After giving Yaya a chance to say something, China said, "The Shinmushee and our Wa family wanted to interrogate you on these matters. I begged them to give me the chance to talk with you and get you to come clean and tell us everything about your involvement with the Ra. If I can't get you to talk, they'll use whatever techniques they deem necessary."

China's eyes conveyed the seriousness of the situation to Yaya. Yaya wondered how her Wa family would react if she said nothing. She also wondered if the Shinmushee considered her a spy would they try to kill her, or kick her out of the jungle. That would put her right into the hands of the Hellcats, Tara and Wana, who would kill her, first chance they got. Yaya was Queen Hayee, Ramala's adopted daughter. However, the Hellcats Tara and Wana wanted Yaya killed for disrespecting the Hayee clan, by rejecting a Hayee male chosen to be Yaya's mate.

China startled Yaya back to reality by saying "You have to say something! Whatever you say won't be as bad as saying nothing!"

Yaya felt trapped. Her mind went into Butcher survival mode. Right now, the only weapon she had was the knife she always carried on her inner thigh. Her other weapons were hanging on the rack, down the hall. She didn't want them so she could use them on someone, Yaya wanted them so she could leave and avoid further questioning.

China had given Yaya more than enough chances to talk. Now she was fed up. China turned away from Yaya and said, "If that's the way you want it, that's fine with me! Now, you're on your own!"

China started walking towards the other girls, when Yaya yelled, "Wait, I'll talk!" China slowly turned and looked at Yaya. Yaya looked down at the ground, for a moment. When she raised her head back up she told China and the Wa girls a few more things that she knew they couldn't use against the House of Ra. However, since it was more that Yaya had ever told them, China and the others listened, intently.

China had Yaya tell her story to the male Wa and then to the Shinmushee Elders in the area. Yaya looked at all the different faces and their reactions when she told her story. Some faces looked understanding, while some had a slightly hostile undertone. They questioned Yaya, but didn't get anything more than what she'd already told them. Yaya hoped La really was going to give her family some of their land back, because she could see it would only be a matter of time before she had to leave the Southern Jungle, for good.

La and Dan begged for guard, warrior and attack Elephant support from Wana, until she gave in. Of the forty-five Special Guards La put thirty-five as Warlords over their own settlements across the plains. Each of those Warlords were given Guards, Warriors, Elephants and messengers, along with everything necessary to create and hold a settlement. Every warrior, guard and attack Elephant, that Wana could spare, was protecting these settlements. Backed up by Wana's forces, as well as the Hammer-Axe Six, these new Warlords were to hold these territories in the name of the Number One Princess, for the Queen of the House of Ra, the Hayee Hellcat, Ramala.

Once everything was in place, La and Dan waged a bloody campaign, hunting and destroying Shinmushee and rebel activity in the plains, between the settlements. The tribes that roamed the plains were given the mandate that helping the rebels would get their families eliminated. La was strict on her mandate and had to be stopped by her advisers, early in the campaign, from wiping out a tribe that helped some Shinmushee escape to the Jungle. Other than that, the tribes of the plains were under the protection of La, the Young Queen of the House of Ra.

It only took the Hammer-Axe Six and their Special guard a little over a year to make the plains safe for travel. In the time, that La and her siblings quelled rebellion in the plains. Wa province became their main base of operations.

La's core group of advisers was her grandfather, the Hayee, Roe and her main fighting instructor, the Hayee, Deen. Tania and

Shaya were amongst others. When La was hell-bent on enforcing her protocol, only one of her advisers could circumvent La's rule. That was Shaya.

Shaya would, in cases where she thought it necessary, change La's orders from kill at will, to watch and report the next infraction. La would say nothing when Shaya changed her orders. She knew that after giving a second chance to a tribe, Shaya wouldn't give them another. Still, as young as Shaya was, most of the tribes would ask for an audience with Shaya and La's advisers, knowing that Shaya had the most influence over the ruthless Young Queen.

Shaya would always go and discuss every conversation the Elders of those tribes had with her with her grandfather Roe, before she made a decision, one way, or another. The Hayee, Roe was most helpful in influencing Shaya's decisions.

Even with that, there was no mistake who controlled the plains north of the lake, all the way through Yee province. It was the young Queen Ra, Ramala.

Queen Hayee, Ramala and her Hellcat cousins, Tara and Wana, were so pleased with the progress made in the plains, that they gave La and Dan more leverage and control over Yee Province, too. Of course, the Hayee, Wana closely monitored her niece and nephew as they took on more and more ruling responsibilities. Wana would travel the plains, with her Elite Guards, inspecting the settlements and provinces in Ra territory. She was always surprised, as well as proud of the level of security.

Young Dan was still Warlord over the Six Lower Houses of Ra. He was pulling double duty, helping La in the plains, while running his own territory, with the help of the Warlords of each of those Lower Houses.

Now, the Warlord Dan and his twin sister, the Number One Princess, controlled all of the Ra territory, outside of the main city of Ra and the Lake, in the name of their mother, Queen Hayee, Ramala.

Wa province, the stronghold of the Hammer-Axe Six, was where a meeting was set up with the Wa survivors. One of the sticking point to the negotiations was that the Wa, with it being so few of them, didn't trust that the Ra wouldn't use this meeting as an opportunity to eliminate them. For protection, the Wa wanted Shinmushee Butchers escort them to the meeting.

La was dead set against this. Wana had already warned the Ra children that the Shinmushee Butchers were the toughest enemy she knew they might face. Wana warned if they ran into them, the Ra girls should scream, freezing them and then take their heads. Under no circumstances were they to engage them physically, unless absolutely necessary.

Young Dan, being the three time Hammer-Axe Champion, was battle tested during the earlier campaign to clear the plains. Dan was unbeatable with the help of his Warlords, along with Danaaa and Ram. At only sixteen, Dan's fighting ego was always looking for a challenge.

Dan argued with La and the Ra advisers to let the Wa bring the Shinmushee Butchers as protection. If they started trouble, Dan was sure he could deal with them, until his sisters blasted a scream. After a while, La gave in. Still, she insisted that Dan only let a limited number of Shinmushee Butchers be present. They could bring more regular Shitmushee warriors if they chose to. La wasn't the least bit worried about regular warriors. Dan was good with that.

All of the guest, which were the Wa and their Shinmushee protectors, were seated, and then surrounded by a couple hundred of the toughest Elite Guards at La's disposal. The Wa sat in front, closest to the throne area. Yaya was in the front row.

The throne area about fifty feet away. Dan and La's Warlords stood on both sides of the throne area. There were six singers kneeling in front of the throne. After everyone was seated, drums beating signaled the arrival of the Ra.

The Ra walked to the throne area, two by two, with Dan and La leading the way. Dan and the Ra boys all sat down. The Ra girls just stood in the throne area looking at the crowd.

The Wa and the Shinmushee looked at the Ra girls. La was between her sisters, holding on to Danaaa's ponytail. Shaya was standing very close to La, with her head leaning on La's shoulder. All the guest thought that strange behavior, except for Yaya.

After looking over everyone, the Ra girls stared at Yaya. Yaya smiled at her younger Ra sisters. Shaya and Danaaa smiled at Yaya, until La pulled on Danaaa's ponytail and slightly bumped Shaya. La arrogantly looked at Yaya, letting her know who was in control, as if Yaya didn't.

La looked out over the crowd once more and ordered "All Wa stand that I may see you." All of the Wa slowly stood up. When they did, the Ra, as well as all of the Royal Court studied each of them.

La asked, "Is this all Wa?" After a short pause, Yaya said, "All but the youngest five are here." La asked, "Why are they not?" When Yaya hesitated, China said, "Our youngest five stayed behind, just in case we don't make it back alive."

La thought that was a very smart move and wasn't offended by China's words. La, looking at China, said, "As everyone here knows, Ya use to be our big sister." No sooner than La finished that sentence, both Shaya and Danaaa forcefully chorused, "She still is!"

It only took La a second to regroup, before she continued. La, trying to be diplomatic, said, "As you can see, my sisters and I still have love for Ya. With that being said, I made a promise that all Wa would dwell in the land of their ancestors and have free travel throughout the plains. As young Queen of the House of Ra, I have made this so. Anyone who attempts harm to any Wa will answer to my blades and those of my Executioners.'

'For this, the Wa are required to protect their land in the name of the House of Ra and reveal any plots against the Hellcats, as well as the Ra. To seal this deal, each Wa must pledge their loyalty, by saying this I will do."

La stood and waited, but there was only silence. La was trying to be reasonable, but it looked like the Wa weren't being appreciative. La sounded annoyed, when she said, "I have been a most gracious host, have I not? However, you do not respond to my request. Am I to take this silence, as a sign of disrespect?"

China said "We mean no disrespect young Queen. It's just that we have become close to our Shinmushee family. The Shinmushee and the House of Ra have been warring with each other in the past. We don't want to be trapped in the middle, should hostilities break out."

La looked at the Shinmushee, before looking back at China and saying "I don't care about your associations with them, just as long as you stay neutral if we have a dispute with them. We don't need your help dealing with those Shitmushee!"

La had been advised not to use her favorite word for the Shinmushee. She was told to refer to them as the jungle people. La was a little agitated that things weren't going her way. La was doing well, until her last sentence. Her favorite word wasn't lost on the ears of the Shinmushee.

Yaya could feel the tension rising from the Shinmushee behind her, even though she was looking forward. Yaya said, "I agree, under those circumstances." China was next to agree, with the rest of the Wa agreeing after that.

When the last Wa agreed, La held her hand forward. Hoban and Ali moved closer to La, to better protect her against a surprise attack. Ali motioned to the Wa to come forward. He told the Wa what was expected of them. La could see as each of the Wa walked up and kissed her hand that they really didn't want to do it. La didn't care about their discomfort. Part of the high for La was getting someone to do something for her, even though they didn't want to.

After the Wa went back to where they were seated, La looked back out at the Shinmushee, with arrogant contemptibility. Shaya saw La and put her hand on La's arm, just as a reminder that La promised not to purposely provoke a fight with the Shinmushee.

However, looking at the Shinmushee reminded La of all the times her father had to leave her and risk his life fighting them. She thought she should give them a slight warning, at the least. La said in a voice less harsh than normal "Those of you that are Butchers, not warriors, from the Southern Jungle please stand, so that I may address you."

To the surprise of everyone, all of the Shinmushee stood up. La's lower lip slowly hung crooked on one side. This was a trait that all Queen Ramala's girls inherited from her, when they were extremely angry, hurt, or cross. Ramala's lip would hang crooked on one side, only when Dan would hurt her feelings like no one else could. Of course, Danaaa's lip would go crooked when she got extremely angry, to the point of being cross.

La felt she had been nice enough to allow the Shinmushee to come to the plains as protectors of the Wa and as her guest, only to have them deceive her by bringing, not just a few, but all Butchers to this meeting. That's why La's lip went crooked.

Without knowing it, with her lip still crooked, La said almost in a whisper, "All of you are Shinmushee Butchers?" That was the first time anyone could remember La calling the Shinmushee by their right name.

It only took La a second to regroup. La mustered up the nastiest tone she could, when she said, "You jungle people have caused trouble for the House of Ra in the past! Look at me, the Young Queen of Ra and know that I control this territory! You go back to the jungle and tell your masters if they cause me any trouble, I'll kill every Shitmushee, until there are no more!"

The Shinmushee Butchers looking at La knew they were being baited into battle. They knew the three Ra girls were screamers. They also saw the six unarmed girls kneeling, watching them in front of La. They didn't know these girls were singers and assumed they were screamers, too.

The Shinmushee Butchers knew they were at a military disadvantage. If they attacked, most likely, they all would be killed. Therefore, they continued doing what they came here to do. Watch the Ra for any weaknesses they could use in the future.

La stared at the Shinmushee and could see that her threats weren't enough to move them into action. She was done playing nice. Right now, all La knew was she wanted these Shinmushee dead. Then, as if on cue, Danaaa's hands went to a quick draw position, next to her axes. She sternly said in her whispering voice "Just holler charge!"

La, sinisterly, said, "I've got something better in mind!" Dan, upon hearing that, said "Alright La, step aside, I've got something to say."

La stared at the Shinmushee, while waiting for Dan to come forward. Why would Dan give her such an order in front of an enemy? She was slightly confused, wondering what Dan would say.

La quickly turned sideways, staring at Dan, while keeping an eye on the Shinmushee. Dan stood up and looked into La's angry, annoyed eyes. While walking pass La, Dan whispered to her "Calm down and get control of your wits. That's how you figure out the best thing to do."

Dan and La locked eyes for a moment after he said that. La had the curse of her mother's fury, only worse. It was sometimes hard for her to control it. When Dan said that, although La was still angry, she challenged herself to find a level of control suitable for the situation. Still, La reserved the right to act a stone cold fool, if she thought it necessary!

Dan looked at the Shinmushee, smiled and then said, "My sister is straight to the point and there's no doubt she'll do exactly what she said. Still, we are not to that point, yet. I've heard many tales about the skills of the Shinmushee Butchers. You're the best the Southern Jungle has to offer. I admire that."

Dan paused and slightly lowered his head to the Shinmushee. Protocol says that La should be poised in all situations. However, Dan was testing her, by embarrassing her in front of her enemy and then giving them praise.

La's lip went even more crooked on one side, after Dan lowered his head to the Shinmushee. Her arms stiffened, straight down at her sides, as her fist balled tightly. She was slightly leaning forward towards Dan, as if his next words would determine if she would have to knock him back to reality.

Shaya, seeing La was close to losing it, grabbed La's ponytail and lightly pulled on it. La turned and stared at Shaya, just as Dan began to speak again. Dan continued with "I ask that the Hammer-Axe Champion from the House of Ra have a fair competition with

Robert Davis

a Butcher from Shinmushee, one on one." La yelled "What's this nonsense?!"

Danaaa immediately stepped to Dan's side, grabbed his arm, pulling him towards her, looked him in his eyes and slowly shook her head no. Dan smiled at Danaaa, and then with that same smile on his face, looked back at the Shinmushee and said, "That's me, you know!"

When Dan said Hammer-Axe Champion, the Shinmushee Butchers looked at all the Ra guards to see who looked to hold that title. When Dan said it was him, they thought it a joke, until they saw the arrogant look of confidence on Dan's face.

One of the Shinmushee Butchers stepped forward and said, "We don't compete. We cut well. That means you'll get cut well." Dan said, "I'm also Warlord Faster Cut. Cutting well is one thing. Being a Faster Cut is another. If you're that good, I'd like see it!" The Shinmushee Butcher had been taunted. He said, "We will oblige."

Room was made for the two combatants. The rules were simple. The match would be over, when one combatant conceded defeat. All of Shinmushee Butchers looked like well-built fighting machines. No one could figure out why Dan was doing this. He was warned repeatedly not to do this, but each time Dan refused to listen.

One of the Shinmushee Butchers stepped forward. Dan studied the Butcher he was about to fight. He could see this man was powerful and in his prime fighting years of between twenty-five and forty-five. Dan pegged him at about thirty. That meant he was close to his peak in strength, speed, power and stamina. Dan was snapped back into reality when the Shinmushee Butcher pulled his axes. Dan immediately pulled his Hammer-Axes and started circling the Butcher, staying from being directly in front of him.

The Shinmushee Ax has a blade on both sides. Adrenaline was pumping through Dan's whole body in anticipation of what this fight would be like. Dan knew his defense would be tested, if this Butcher had any skills. The Butcher watched Dan, without attacking.

Dan decided if the Butcher wasn't going to attack, he was. Dan struck with lightning fast efficiency. He was striking high and low, swinging both his axes at their targets, at the same time. The Shinmushee Butcher blocked Dan's axes, but Dan was very quick and countered off the blocks, twisting his axes off the blocks, and charging them back towards the Butcher's vital organs. The Butcher managed to move just out of the way of one of Dan's sneaky counter-attacks off a block and was hit hard on the back of his shoulder by the Hammer side of Dan's other axe.

If Dan had used the blade side of his Hammer-Axe, the Shinmushee Butcher would be well on his way to a bloody death. However, Dan was young and this was a game to him. The Shinmushee Butcher was a grown man, giving this battle the seriousness it deserved.

It shocked, as well as angered, the Butcher that this young man was able to get a clean strike, so early in this battle. Now it was time to teach this young man a lesson his siblings would never forget.

In the instant Dan's Hammer came off his shoulder, the Butcher turned around swinging both his axes where Dan was. Dan managed to move out of the way of one, but had to block the other. He realized the power of this Butcher as her went stumbling backwards after the block. The Butcher instantly closed the distance between himself and Dan. Now, he was swinging both his axes, at the same time, at Dan, forcing Dan to make quicker decisions on blocking and evading his axes. Dan was completely on defense, now.

Both the Butchers axes were coming at him so fast, it was everything Dan could do to avoid them. Even when Dan would tuck and roll, or do a couple of flips to create some distance, the Butcher was always there to greet Dan with some nifty ax play. It seemed the Butcher's axes were getting as close as they could, without actually cutting Dan. It wasn't from a lack of trying by the Butcher. This was a tribute to Dan's defensive skills. Still, the Butcher managed to get in a couple of glancing blows in on Dan. The Butcher increased the pressure on Dan. He twisted his blade off Dan's block and with the flat side of the blade forced Dan's ax downward. Then the Butcher sent his axes flying as Dan. He was surprised that Dan was quick enough to bring the flat side of his ax up, just in time to block and dodge axes that would have split Dan's chest wide open.

The Butcher was persistent in his attack and forced Dan out of position by pressing hard on Dan's blocking ax. The Butcher was already at a side angle on Dan when he did a super fast spin, with the blade of his ax coming towards the back of Dan's neck. Without an ax to block, even if Dan tried to move his neck out of the way, the Butcher still had a clean shot at mortally wounding Dan on the back his head, or his upper back.

Then came a short sharp, but violent shriek from Danaaa. That shriek disoriented the Butcher enough to slow his axes just enough so Dan could get low. The Butcher's axe whizzed over the top of Dan's head. The Butcher still had good enough position to get another clean strike at Dan, but was hit by two more shrieks, that were followed up by a powerful scream from La. Shaya screamed after La did. Dan was disoriented and all of the Shinmushee Butchers were frozen still. Through Dan's hazy fog, he heard La yell "Kill them all!"

Dan, while still unstable, yelled "No, stand your ground!" That stopped the guards, but La and Danaaa had their axes drawn and were charging towards the Shinmushee Butchers. Dan jumped in front of his sisters, and after several blocks, La and Danaaa backed away, staring angrily at Dan.

La screamed "Are you INSANE!?! If Baby hadn't screamed, he would have taken your head clean off! So, why stop us from finishing them?!!"

Only for a second, did Dan let himself think about that ax coming at his neck. Then, he said to La "Even still, don't kill them. After all, he did beat me in a fair competition." La said, more animated than before "A fair competition! That's what you call fair! You don't try to take someone's head in a fair competition!" Dan said, as a matter of fact, "You heard him. They don't compete, they cut well."

La stared at Dan, not saying a word. Now, she wanted to take his head clean off with her ax. La moved her ax up, pointed it at Dan and said, "You make jokes, when you could have been killed! Then what?" Dan saw concern and fear for him in La's eyes, so he stared without saying anything. La paused only for a second and then said, "Sometimes, you're so stupid, you make me sick!" Danaaa turned to La and with both hands open, palms up, exclaimed "But, I'm Stupid!" La looked at Danaaa and said, "That makes two of you!"

Danaaa quickly looked around and then looked back at La. She was confused. She didn't see another one of herself, anywhere!

La looked from Danaaa, to Dan. She said, "They'll be regaining movement soon. What if they still want to cut well? You've already proven you're no match for them!" La's words cut Dan deeper than any blade she could have swung at him. His eyes went down from hers as he reflected on how soundly he was beaten.

Then Shaya said, "I have an idea on how we won't have to kill them!" Shaya summoned the six singers. Then she smiled at La and said, "Watch this!"

Shaya started walking towards the Shinmushee with the singers right behind her. When Danaaa saw Shaya moving towards the Shinmushee, she quickly moved to Shaya's side, with axes still in hand. Dan moved to Shaya's other side.

La watched from where she was. She didn't feel the need to address these Butchers. To her, after almost killing her brother, the sharp edge of her ax blade was the only thing La had for them. Of course, only after she rendered them motionless with a powerful scream.

The Ra boys moved a little closer to where Shaya and the singers were. After seeing what happened to Dan, the Ra boys thought Shaya was getting a little too close to the Butchers. She was close enough to them now, that it was making Don nervous. Just as he was about to warn Shaya, she stopped. She looked over all the Butchers and could see that some of them were starting to regain movement. She also saw something that surprised her.

Shaya didn't let the surprise show on her face, when she said, "You Shinmushee did well in your respectful behavior, making sure no harm came to the Wa. It was most unfortunate that my Brother bated you into a competition. As a Butcher, you did what you had to do to win. We did what we had to stop you from harming our brother. Although my sister, the Young Queen of the House of Ra is very offended by your actions, no Ra blood was spilled. Normally, we would collect your heads, while you were unable to move. It didn't get to that point, because my brother, the first born King of Ra decided to spare your lives."

As Shaya was talking, some of the Shinmushee Butchers had fully regained their movement. The singers behind Shaya started up with a soulful hum that drained any tension right out of the air.

Shaya paused for a second, when the singers started up. She continued with "Your job with the Wa is complete. Leave here and go back to the Jungle in peace. If you plot otherwise, that would be most regrettable."

The Shinmushee Butchers were going to carve and cut the Ra well, once they'd regained movement. What surprised them was that even though a lot of them had earpieces in, some were rendered motionless. Others, who had earpieces in were disoriented and thought they might get the others killed if they attacked. So, they just pretended to be frozen. When Shaya got close, she saw the ear plugs and that's what surprised her.

Now that the singers had softened up the aggressiveness in the Shinmushee Butchers, they thought it best to go back to the jungle, report what they'd seen of the Ra and plan their next move. They only looked at each other for a moment, before leaving. Once they'd turned to leave, Dan yelled, "Hey, thanks for the lesson!"

The Shinmushee Butcher that almost took Dan's head, half turned and peeked over his shoulder at Dan out of the corner of his eye, before turning back and continuing with his comrades.

That Butcher wondered how the young man thought he was giving him a lesson, when he would have taken his head clean off, if those annoying screams hadn't stopped him. The Butcher thought how lucky Dan was to have his sisters there. He also thought that young King is very reckless. He won't live long like that.

Dan gave orders that those Shinmushee Butcher were not to be attacked. All of the Hayee guards, Elite guards and Special Guards were thrilled with that order. None wanted to fight a Shinmushee Butcher, unless it was absolutely necessary.

They watched as the Shinmushee Butchers disappeared off into the distance. While the other Wa kept their distance, Yaya walked up to Shaya, smiled at her with pride as she said, "How did you learn to talk like that?" Shaya shrugged her shoulders, as if she had no clue. Danaaa answered Yaya, while looking at Shaya, yelling, "She only does it when she wants to! Nobody ever knows when it'll be!"

La had walked over when she saw Yaya talking. Danaaa leaned on La's shoulder and yelled "Most of the time, Shaya just does this!" La quickly moved the shoulder Danaaa was leaning on, pushing her and saying "Quit playing around!"

Danaaa gave La a silly look. La looked over at Shaya and saw that she was more interested in talking to Yaya, than leaving. La said "Ram, Yin, Don, stay here with Shaya. Baby, you come with me. We're going to get some rest."

Danaaa looked at Shaya and Yaya only for a moment, before running over and joining La. As they were walking, Danaaa noticed, right away, they weren't headed towards the sleeping quarters. She looked curiously at La. La never looked at Danaaa. They just walked, until they got to where Dan was.

While healers were attending Dan's wounds, his bodyguards made a perimeter around them. At first, Dan didn't know that he'd been roughed up so much by the Shinmushee Butcher. When he went to get cleaned up, he realized he had bruises on his arms and midsection. Dan's bodyguards saw that and called for the healers.

La folded her arms and angrily stared at Dan, letting him know she was displeased with him. She moved closer and examined Dan's wounds. Once she'd done that, La stepped back and said, "I hope that was enough to satisfy your curiosity!"

Dan tried to put on his poker face that said he wasn't bothered or concerned by what happened. Truth be told, the more Dan thought about it, the more it bothered him that he could be the Hammer-Axe Champion of Ra and be beaten so soundly.

In the coming months, a settlement was set up for the Wa. The settlement was near the stronghold of the Hammer-Axe Six, which was in Wa province. Each of the Wa had a home built for them. They had storehouses, and land allotted to them for growing food.

In addition, in that time, La warmed up to Yaya and they became close, like sisters, again. La even went as far as to give Yaya favor, on orders from the Number One Princess, in all of the House of Ra. La also made sure her Guards and Elite Guards got word of that to Wana's Guards and Warlords. This meant that Yaya could travel anywhere in the House of Ra and no harm would come to her, under the threat of being beheaded by La's Executioners. All Hayee and Ra that she came in contact with also would give her hospitality. Still, the Hellcats Wana and Tara were exempt from La's orders.

Yaya tried to get La to become closer to her Wa family, but La would only see the Wa in formal settings, or at gatherings. When the Wa were invited to a gathering, they were given strict orders not to approach La. La's bodyguards had orders that no Wa should approach her without having it arranged and approved well in advance. Not even Shaya could get La to budge on that.

Six more months passed before Queen Hayee, Ramala summoned her children to the main city of Ra. The Ra waited until they got two more messages to come to the main city. The third message was an ultimatum from Ramala saying that if word didn't come to her that they were on their way, she would personally come and get them herself. She told the messenger to emphasize they really didn't want that. Even with that, it took the Hammer-Axe Six more than another six months to return to the city of Ra.

CHAPTER 16

Ramala, although, angry with her children, was anxious to see them. Because they took so long getting back, Ramala ordered that no one greet the Ra when they entered the city, until after they met with the Hellcats. Once the Ra entered the city, guards instructed them where they were expected.

The Hellcats and Elder Dan were all seated in one of the great halls of the palace. Yani and Tammy were also seated at the same table impatiently, waiting, anticipating, seeing their brother and cousins.

The Hammer-Axe Six walked in, lined up, lowered their heads and raised them, before looking at their parents. It had been well over a year since Ramala last saw her children. She stared at and examined each of them, without saying a word.

All of the Ra were dressed as if they were ready for battle. The girls had on everything from their chest, elbow and wrist protectors, to their fingerless padded gloves. The only thing they didn't have on them was their axes. They had them put in the corner of the room, when they walked in.

At seventeen, Dan looked like a hardened warrior. His muscles were chiseled and the look in his eyes was that of a Butcher. Ramala didn't see any of the playful boy, she use to always see, in him.

La's eyes scanned and read everyone in the room, until they got to Ramala. Then she stared at Ramala. Ramala watched her oldest daughter, closely. La looked like a predator, looking for any weakness she could exploit. Ramala could also see La's attitude was as arrogant and aggressive as she'd ever seen.

Ramala refused to get into a staring match with La, so she slowly moved her eyes to Shaya. Once Ramala and Shaya's eyes met, Shaya quickly looked away from Ramala. Shaya's eyes went from Ramala's to Elder Dan's and then away from his to Tara's eyes. Her eyes moved from Tara's eyes to Wana's and then back to Ramala's.

After only looking at Ramala for a second, Shaya looked down, turned her head and nervously looked at La. Ramala thought Shaya's behavior meant that Shaya knew about something La was planning and that Shaya didn't want to give it away.

Don was just as big as Dan and almost as muscular. He seemed to be hiding something, just as Ramala suspected Shaya was. She wondered what it would take to have Don telling everything, like he use to, when he was younger and under pressure.

Ramala looked next to her nephew Yin. He looked just like his father, only younger. When Yin saw his aunt Ramala looking at him, he smiled at her. Ramala saw that trademark evil grin Yin inherited from his father.

Then there was Ram. Even though Dan was four years older than Ram, Ram was bigger. He was very muscular, but still had a healthiness that said he didn't miss any meals. Ramala noticed his eyes still hadn't changed. They still looked like there was someone, other than Ram, staring out at you. She refused to stare into Ram's eyes for too long.

Finally, Ramala looked at Danaaa. As Ram was to Dan, Danaaa was every bit as tall as La, but slightly thicker. She was very muscular and if it weren't for two budding breast poking through her clothes, her body would still look like that of a boy.

Looking into Danaaa's eyes, Ramala could see a stressful turmoil going on, that Danaaa couldn't hide. She looked a bit more mature, but still had her childlike demeanor. Danaaa stared right into Ramala's eyes. Ramala was going to find out what was going on with her Baby, just not right now.

Ramala realized with Ram and Danaaa just barely being thirteen years of age, all of her children were now teenagers. Whether they wanted to be, or not, Ramala knew teenagers were troublesome. She snapped out of her daydream and said, "Alright, all of you can relax."

As soon as Ramala said that, Danaaa and Shaya ran over to where Elder Dan was. He stood up just in time to have his two youngest daughters pulling a tugging at him. Danaaa surprised Dan by opening her blouse, revealing her bare breast and yelling "Look a here Daddy! I'm almost a grown woman, like La and Shaya!"

Almost everyone in the room, simultaneously, yelled for Danaaa to close her blouse. None of the Hammer-Axe Six were surprised by Danaaa's actions. Once her breast came in she was proudly showing everyone, until La and Shaya put a stop to it. Ramala smiled at Danaaa, shaking her head at how crazy her Baby was.

Elder Dan looked over at La. She'd only walked halfway to him and was standing there, like she was waiting on him to come to her. Once she saw he wasn't, La slowly sauntered over to her father. Dan grabbed La and gave her a big hug.

Ramala motioned for her boys to come to her, while Tara and her daughters fawned all over Yin. Even though it was a little embarrassing for Yin, he enjoyed it. Maids brought over a young baby boy. Tara said, "This is your brother, the Ra, Yinsanjett. We call him Jett." after Tara said that, La and her sisters ran over to see their new cousin. Even the Ra boys curiously walked over and stared. No one had to tell anyone who the father was. Little Jett looked like the perfect mix of Tara and King Japha, San.

Once all the greetings were over, Ramala said, "Some think that your actions, since I last saw you, makes you heroes. Some think you were out of line. I'm going to find out the truth, here this day!" Ramala asked her children to explain their behavior over the last, almost year and a half that they'd been gone.

La and Dan did all of the talking. Like most teenagers, they told the story of what happened in a sort of fairytale way, conveniently leaving out certain parts of the truth, while shoring up other parts, in order to put themselves in a better light.

None of the Hellcats were buying anything Dan and La said. They had spies everywhere. This included some of La's most trusted

Special Guard. Of course, La didn't know that, yet. Still, there were a few things the spies dare not tell the Hellcats, for fear of theirs and their family's lives. They knew now that the Hammer-Axe Six were back in the main city, some of these things would become known.

One of the first things happened halfway through one of Ramala's sentences. All of a sudden, Danaaa slouched back in her chair, looked at La, put her feet on the table and yelled, as if all of this was an annoyance to her "How much longer do we have to listen to this?!" That shocked everyone.

Ramala, immediately, yelled, "You'll listen, until I'm done!" Never looking at Ramala, Danaaa yelled "I wonder when that's gonna be!" Ramala's anger was so inflamed that she had to pause, because her heart skipped a beat.

In Ramala's pause, La yelled "Baby, get your feet off the table! You know you can't act like this, at home!" Danaaa slowly slid her feet off the table and slammed them on the floor. Elder Dan sternly said "Danaaa, that's enough!" Danaaa barely gave Elder Dan a look that said she was bored with all of this.

Ramala looked at Dan and said "She's been gone a while and thinks she can act and talk like a heathen!" Ramala looked back at Danaaa and said, "Well, if that's how you want to act, then that's how I'm going to treat you. Get over here, NOW!"

Danaaa stood up, folded her arms about her chest and stared at Ramala. Ramala jumped out of her seat and screamed, "I said, NOW!" Danaaa started walking towards Ramala, with her arms still folded. Just as Danaaa got to Ramala, while still looking her in her eyes, Danaaa said in her whispering voice, "I think it's best if you not try to hit me. I'm tired, so just send me to my room!"

Now that Danaaa was a very young teenager, she was becoming more in tune with the woman she would become, even though she still had most of her childlike qualities. Danaaa had always spoken her thoughts. Now, she sometimes would be brutally honest, without regards to how others would take it, just like her mother. She also, sometimes, didn't choose the right words to say what she thought, just like her father. Being the advanced version of her parents, Danaaa did both things better and worse than either of them.

Ramala didn't understand Danaaa's words like Danaaa meant them. She took it as a disrespectful threat from Danaaa, when Danaaa was trying to convey that it might be better to send her to her room than to slap her.

So what did Ramala do? What she always does in a situation like this. She sent an extra fast lightning slap at Danaaa's face. Danaaa ducked just out of the way.

Ramala was surprised when she missed. Ramala quickly moved her other hand to grab Danaaa, so she would be sure to hit her next time. Danaaa moved her shoulder just before Ramala's hand got there. Now, angrier and more determined than ever, Ramala, after several more attempts to grab Danaaa and missing, went into an all-out assault on Danaaa, throwing punches.

Elder Dan knew Danaaa was in danger of being seriously hurt if Ramala connected with one of those blows. He stood up and was about to warn Ramala that she was going too far, but stopped in his tracks. Dan was amazed at the reflexes of his youngest daughter. She was avoiding Ramala's every swing, not blocking any of them, with her arms still folded at her chest!

Ramala wasn't impressed by this. She was determined to put Danaaa in her place. Whatever that meant. So she added more pressure by throwing in a few well-placed kicks. Even though Danaaa avoided them, both Tara and Wana called to Ramala to stop. Ramala almost had Danaaa cornered, and wasn't about to let her get away with this act of defiance.

After five lightning fast kicks, Danaaa was set up to where there was no escaping Ramala's next move. Danaaa looked to be off balance, crouching, from avoiding those kicks. Ramala's hand came down fast over Danaaa's head. Danaaa twirled low with her back facing Ramala. Danaaa threw both her hands crossed over her head, blocking Ramala's hand at the wrist, between both her wrists, while looking at La and sticking her tongue out at La.

That was a split second snap shot that everyone saw, except for Ramala. Ramala tried to grab Danaaa's wrist with the same hand that was blocked, while launching a powerful kick to Danaaa's back. Danaaa moved her hands clear of Ramala's reaching hand. At the same time, Danaaa jumped up onto the edge of the table, just out of the reach of that kick, aimed at her back.

Then, all in one move, Danaaa launched herself into a back flip off the edge of the table into the wall behind her. She pushed off the wall with her legs, rocketing back towards the table, catching the edge of it with both hands, while tucking her knees to her chest, flinging herself under the table. Danaaa sliding on her feet came out on the other side, turning into a standing position, staring at Ramala.

Everyone, including Ramala, was so astounded by what they'd seen that no one moved, or said a word. They just stared at Danaaa. That is, until Danaaa yelled "But I already told you, I don't want to be hit!"

That snapped Ramala out of her daze. She launched herself in Danaaa's direction, only to be caught and restrained by Tara and Wana. Elder Dan moved between the Hellcats and Danaaa, for extra support.

Tara looked at La and Shaya, yelling, "Get her out of here, before your mother kills her!"

La and Shaya ran over to Danaaa. Just before, they reached for her, Danaaa turned facing La and yelled, "Don't touch me! You already know I don't like to be touched!"

Now, La and Danaaa were staring at each other. La didn't care about what she'd just seen Danaaa do. La was fed up with Danaaa and about to put her in her place.

Then, it seemed like out of nowhere, Shaya jumped in front of Danaaa and pushed La backwards, with good force. La stumbled backwards, until the table behind her stopped her momentum. La braced herself on the table with her hands, while staring at Shaya, looking for an explanation.

In a voice that neither the Hellcats, or Elder Dan had ever heard from Shaya, Shaya yelled at La, "Don't touch her! You know how Baby gets! She doesn't like to be touched, at this time!"

Even more surprising to the Hellcats and Dan was the fact that La just stood there and didn't move against Shaya. Shaya's stern face turned soft as she looked at Ramala and said in a soft voice "Mother, please forgive Baby. It's close to her cycle and she gets very sensitive, easily aggravated and very ornery." Young Dan interrupted with "You mean she gets crazy!"

Shaya's head snapped around and she gave Dan a hard stare, before turning back to Ramala and softly saying "Baby's tired from the trip home. After a short nap, I'm sure she'll be more cooperative."

Before Ramala could stop herself, she'd already nodded to Shaya that it was all right to leave. Shaya grabbed Danaaa sternly by her shoulders, stared at her and said, "You need rest! Come, let's go!"

Danaaa relaxed and let herself be maneuvered around the other side of the table, away from Ramala. La turned to join her sisters and was greeted by Shaya half turning and yelling at her, "You stay here! I'm not going to deal with you two fighting, all day long!"

La angrily yelled back to Shaya "You'd better stop yelling at me, or else!" Shaya quickly said in a less forceful, almost pleading voice "Alright, I will!"

That seemed to calm La a little. Still, La said, "You make sure you stay with Baby, until she wakes and then both of you find me, right away!" Shaya nodded her head that she would, then left.

When Danaaa and Shaya reached the doorway, a guard looked in and said, "Is everything alright my Queen?" as he looked in Ramala's direction.

No sooner than he said his last word, Danaaa drove her fist into and through his chin, twisting and driving her fist at the same time, snapping the guards head and neck in the opposite direction he was first facing. The force from the punch made the guard's one leg go out in front of him, like the kickstand of a bike, while the heel of his foot tried to balance him. On unstable legs and probably already unconscious, the foot on the kick-stand leg did a half moon circle, going from left to right, just before the guard went crashing to the floor.

He was out cold. Danaaa, while being restrained by Shaya, yelled at him "Don't be yelling in my face!" Shaya sternly said "Come on, let's go!" Danaaa, once again, let herself be lead away by Shaya.

Young Dan and Don looked at each other and said in unison "Twenty-Three Ski-doo!"

Young Dan came up with the term Ski-doo after seeing Danaaa knock several guards out cold, using the technique of driving her fist through and twisting it at the same time, into the lower jaw, almost at the chin.

Danaaa's counter-attack teacher Deen taught her that technique. Once she mastered that technique, Danaaa used it indiscriminately. Danaaa got so good at it that every time she used it on someone they did the kickstand move.

Once Dan saw that, he was so amazed, that every time Danaaa did it, he would say she Ski-Dooed someone.

Being the scientist he was, Dan wanted to test his theory and see if it would indeed happen every time. Dan had Danaaa knock out twenty-three guards in a row and to his surprise, it happened every time. After that, anytime Danaaa used that technique, Dan and Don would look at each other and yell out 'Twenty-three Ski-doo!'

Once Danaaa left the room, it seemed, everyone took a deep breath and relaxed a little. Tara's daughters, Yani and Tammy ran over to Ramala. No one had to guess that Ramala was these two girls favorite aunt. That didn't bother Wana, or Tara, with Wana being Shaya's favorite aunt and Tara being La's favorite.

Yani and Tammy seemed to be so traumatized over what happened that Ramala was now consoling both of them. At times, Tara didn't like the way Ramala spoiled her girls. It seemed the more Ramala spoiled them, the more Tara's girls needed it. Tara also resented the fact that her daughters would do anything Ramala asked them to do, while she would have to sometimes fight and wrestle with them to get them to do simple tasks.

Tara finally said "Alright girls, that's enough." Ramala, always ready to defend her nieces, smiled at Tara and said, "They're fine.

They're keeping me calm." Tara said, "In that case, you're going to need them. Your girls are really something. Can you believe Danaaa?" Wana said, as a matter of fact "If she gets any worse, you're going to have to keep her in a cage." Tara said in an astonished tone "Wa, don't say that!" Wana looked at Ramala and said, "Don't act like we didn't see what we just saw. I'm just saying!"

No one could argue with that, so they just changed the subject. The conversation went on, with the Ra telling some of, but not all of their adventures. Everyone was having a good time, with Yani and Tammy playing and pestering their brother and cousins. Yani and Tammy asked that they be excused for a bathroom break. Tara nodded that they could. Most everyone there wanted to get rid of the pestering Terrible-Two, if only for a few moments. That is, everyone except Ramala, who enjoyed every moment of her nieces antics, regardless of what they were doing. Time seemed to pass quickly.

Danaaa was having a peaceful rest when she heard something. Her first thought went back to when guards tried sneak up on her and her sisters. Danaaa realized she left her axes on the wall in the eating room. Still, she had her gutting knife and the small blade on the inside of her thigh. Danaaa sniffed the air. Once she caught a scent, she cautiously walked out into the hallway.

Once Danaaa got out into the hallway, she saw her two cousins, the Terrible-Two, leaning on the wall. When they saw, Danaaa come out of her room they turned and faced her. Danaaa stopped at a safe distance from her cousins, wondering why they were here.

She found out, right away when she saw Yani on guard, while Tammy started talking. Tammy pointed her finger at Danaaa and said, "We'll not stand idly by, while you disrespect my Queen Aunt! That's why we're here! We're going to teach you a lesson you'll not soon forget!"

As Danaaa listened to Tammy, she watched Yani closely. Danaaa knew her two cousins very well. Yani was the older and the more physical of the two, while Tammy was a big talker who wasn't afraid of some physicality. Just as Danaaa had anticipated, right after Tammy's last sentence, Yani attacked first, with Tammy joining in a second later.

Although younger, the terrible-Two fought ferociously against Danaaa, but to no avail. Danaaa had a soft spot for the Terrible-Two, so she was stern, but merciful in her beating of them. After beating them into submission in that hallway, Danaaa put them both in headlocks and dragged them back to the dining Hall where everyone else was.

When Danaaa walked through the doorway of the dining Hall, she slung both her cousins in front of her. Tammy instantly took off towards Ramala. Yani, with the audience of her mother and favorite aunt Ramala, got beside herself and turned angrily back towards Danaaa. Danaaa gave Yani an open hand slap that set her up for the returning backhand slap. Yani stumbled a bit and once she caught her balance, ran to Ramala. The Terrible-Two, at Ramala's side, glared at Danaaa swearing, to themselves, the next time would be different.

Right after that, Danaaa looked around the room and had a surprised, but fearful look on her face. La shocked everyone by yelling "Where's Shaya?!"

Danaaa, with palms open, facing upwards, shrugged her shoulders. Ramala looked at La and said, "Why look so panicked? She never goes too far from either of you. I'm sure she's close by."

All of the Ra children looked at each other with concern. The Hellcats, as well as Elder Dan, thought that to be strange. Then out of the silence, came moaning cries of pleasure, from a distance. The grown-ups all smiled to themselves, knowing some young woman was really getting it taken to her. Then as the moaning and cries escalated into a form of pleasurable begging and unintelligible verbiage, everyone recognized whose voice it was. It was Shaya!

Hearing those cries of passion was more torturous than anything Elder Dan had ever heard. Ramala was also very upset, to say the least.

Ramala jumped out of her seat, leaning towards and giving La a death stare, with both hand on the table. Elder Dan slammed both his fist of the table as he stood up and gave the same death stare to

Dan. Elder Dan turned and angrily looked at his Hammer-Axes leaning against the wall. In Elder Dan's mind, there was only one way to deal with something like this.

Ramala saw Elder Dan and yelled, "No Dan, please, let me handle this!" Since Ramala begged him, which was the way Dan heard it, he looked away from his Axes and back to Young Dan.

Both La and Dan felt so much pressure from the stares they were getting from their parents that they leaned back in their seats. Ramala, slowly, but sternly ordered, "Find her and bring her to me! And bring me the head of . . . ." After a short, frustrated pause, she continued with ". . . Of whomever you find with her!"

All of the Ra jumped out of their seats. Ramala yelled, "Wait!" They all stopped, turned and looked at her. Ramala looked at La and said, "You stay here!" Then, Ramala turned to Dan and said, "Whoever you find with her, don't kill them! Take them to the dungeon. I'll deal with them, myself!" After a quick nod that they understood, the Ra took off.

After hearing several more of Shaya's passionate howling, Ramala fell back in her chair. She covered her ears, looked at La and whispered sternly "I suspect this isn't the first time this has happened! You tell me, how did this happened?!" La told Ramala what she thought she could, without signing her and Shaya's death warrant.

A short ways into La's explanation, Ramala yelled "What about you?!! Are you . . . ?!" La frantically shook her head no. Ramala looked over at Elder Dan and could see he was very disturbed by what he was hearing, to the point that he stood up, grabbed his axes and walked out of the room. Ramala knew if Dan happened to run into whoever was with Shaya, she would never see them alive. Of that, she was sure of!

Before today, hearing a woman's passionate screams was one of the biggest turn on for Elder Dan. Right now, his stomach was so sickened by what he heard, he wondered if he ever wanted to hear these sounds again.

After Elder Dan left the room, Wana and Tara walked over to Ramala. They tried to console her. Even though La was telling them, all Ramala, or any of them could think was 'How could this happen?'

Ramala and her Hellcat cousins weren't naïve in thinking something like this couldn't happen. It's just that they thought they'd taken all the necessary precautions to prevent this from happening.

All the Ra girls, as well as all the girls in the Hayee hierarchy, were trained to save themselves for their chosen mates. They were watched and monitored closely to make sure they didn't succumb to certain urges. All the girls had maids, Elders and Bodyguards watching them, constantly. Even above that, Young Dan, as well as La were also on guard against this sort of activity. So, with that being said, how could this happen?

CHAPTER 17

While helping La and Dan clear the plains of rebel activity, at thirteen years of age, Shaya became aware of her strong sexuality. That led to masturbation when she was alone. No one knew about it. Not even La and Danaaa knew, although they were with Shaya most of the time. La began to notice strange behavior from Shaya. One night, when the three sisters were alone, La questioned Shaya. Shaya told La everything. It shocked La and Danaaa. La said to Shaya "Don't let it worry you. We'll figure out something." Danaaa turned from Shaya, to La and said "But, she's got an affliction!"

Before La knew it, she'd sent a lightning fast backhand slap at Danaaa. Danaaa barely avoided it by quickly moving backwards and falling against the wall behind her. La gave Danaaa a death stare. Danaaa, not knowing when to leave well enough alone, opened both her hands, palms facing up and whispered, "Well, she does!" La quickly said "Not another word from you!" La and Danaaa stared at each other. La to see if Danaaa would defy her, by saying something. Danaaa trying to figure out if she had anything else to say.

Just about almost the same time Shaya was going through that, Don was exhibiting mannish behavior on a level only the highest-ranking Ra, under La and Dan, could get away with. One day, as the Ra boys were headed to training, after mid-day meals, Don pointed out a group of teenage girls, also walking to their training session. Don looked at Dan, and said, "Watch this."

Dan's curious look was all the permission Don needed to proceed. Don veered towards the group of teenage girls. When the girls saw Don walking towards them, they smiled and lowered their heads, without stopping. Don sternly ordered, "Hold it! Security check!"

Every Guard within earshot of Don's voice turned and suspiciously looked at Don. Once seeing that Don was addressing these girls, the Guards moved closer, scrutinizing the girls.

Upon hearing Don's voice the girls stopped in their tracks. They also saw Guards moving closer and wondered if they'd done something to offend the Warlord Don, or their King, Dan. Don was ahead of his brothers and cousin when he reached the girls. He sternly asked, "Do you have any illegal weapons on your person?"

None of these girls understood the question. No weapon they could possibly have would be considered illegal. Every Ra and Hayee was allowed to carry weapons. All of these girls were Ra, because they were the same age, or younger than La and Dan and were born after the House of Ra was created.

Being a Ra meant that these girls had high rank. They had special privileges that their Hayee family members didn't and could get away with most anything, except for disrespect to the Hellcats, or the Hammer-Axe Six.

So, these girls were confused by the question. In their moment of confusion, Don further threw them off guard, by saying "Just as I suspected!"

He stepped up to one of the girls and patted her hips, just above her weapons holster, that held her machetes. Then, Don kneeled down and moved one hand between the girl's thighs. Her reflexes tightened her thigh muscles and she pressed her legs together. That stopped Don's hand before it could go any further. Don looked an indictment up at the girl and said, "What's this!"

The girl nervously loosened her thigh muscles, so Don could move his hand. She thought Don had discovered the blade strapped to her inner thigh. Most girls in this day had them there. She pleaded, "That's just my personal protection!"

Once Don's hand was free, he moved it further between the girl's legs, until he completely palmed one of her butt cheeks. Again, her thigh and butt muscles clinched and held Don's arm so that it couldn't move. Don looked up at the girl and she loosened her muscles, even though now her leg muscles twitched with every movement of Don's hand. Don quickly removed his hand from between the girl's legs, before anyone could consider his actions overly abusive, even though that's what they were.

Don then put both his hands under the same girl's armpits, trying to legitimize his earlier actions. He moved them around to her back, as if he was searching for something. After finding nothing on her back, his hands retraced their path, back through the girl's armpits, moving around to her chest. Don did a quick palm search of her breast. He stepped back and announced, "She's alright." Don gave the next girl the same treatment.

However, when Don went to check the third girl, she and the girl next to her went down on their knees, facing Dan. The last girl just stood there with her head lowered, looking, with angry eyes at Dan's feet. Her hands were very close to her machetes.

Up to that point, Dan and Yin had been enjoying Don's show. Now Dan could see that the girls on their knees were begging him to stop Don, without words. Dan saw that the last girl's actions said she'd rather be killed defending herself, than be humiliated by Don. Dan also knew all these girls were daughters of high-ranking Hayee Warlords.

The one still standing was one of La's cabinet members. Her name was Hesta. Dan knew her to be a very good fighter, with a temper. Dan knew all the training she had, up to this point, was the only reason she'd kept her composure this long.

Before Don made his next move, Dan sternly ordered "Don, that's enough!" Dan walked over, grabbed Don roughly by his collar, and pulled him away from the girls. Dan then took the hands of the girls on their knees and helped them to their feet. He looked at all of the girls and then shook his head as if he was disgusted with Don.

Dan said, "Sometimes my brother gets mixed up in what protocols he should be enforcing. You girls are some of the finest Ra produced by Hayee. In his haste, he has treated you less than respectful. That should never happen." Dan half turned to Don and said, "You own them an apology."

Don looked at Dan and saw he was serious. Don lowered his head and said "My deepest apologies." All of the girls lowered their heads to Don and then to Dan. Dan looked at all the girl and said, "We need not mention this unfortunate event to anyone, do we?"

All of the girls lowered their heads again and chorused, "As you wish, my King." Dan said "Alright, on to your next day's training." they lowered their heads again and left.

As they were leaving, the first girl Don searched nervously peeked at him. The second girl he searched looked directly at Don with a slight smile on her face, before the third girl pushed her forward. The next two girls had looks of curiosity on their faces as they snuck a peek at Don. The last girl didn't look at Don. Don was glad Dan stopped him before he got to her, because the look on her face said she would have tried to slice him to pieces with her machetes.

Dan snapped Don out of his daydream by saying "Come on, we've wasted enough time. Let's get to next training." Yin was still excited about what Don had done. He exclaimed, "That was great! How'd you think of that?" Don shrugged his shoulders and said, "I don't know, I just did." Yin said, "You should do it, again! Next time I'll help!"

Dan stopped and turned towards Yin. Yin and Don instinctively took a step back. Dan gave both of them a hard look and said "Don't you know those girls have high rank! If they tell anyone, that could disrupt our support amongst the up and coming Ra. I don't need problems like that!"

Dan stared at the two of them. He didn't have to stare at Ram, because Ram wasn't interested in girls, yet. Then, Dan's face got a little less serious when he said, "That was funny, though. If you're going to do something like that, pick girls with very little rank. And don't ever do it in public!"

Even though the teenage Ra girls that Don felt up didn't talk to their Elders about what happened, they talked amongst themselves and to other Ra girls. All of the Ra girls knew Don was second only to their King, Young Dan as the highest-ranking male in the Ra clan. A girl could do very well for herself, if she became the mate of, or even had the child of any one of Ramala's sons, or their cousin Yin.

So the two girls that had been fondled by Don became very popular amongst most all the Ra girls. So much so, that even the first girl who, was disturbed by what happened to her, started to enjoy the popularity that came with that unpleasant experience.

While Shaya and Don were dealing with adolescent hormone imbalances, La and Dan were busy solidifying their hold on all the territories in the House of Ra. Besides the open plains, La and Dan controlled the Lower Houses of Ra. They also had a complex structure of Warlords, officers, messengers and spies in all the main cities and provinces, carrying out their orders. When the young Ra Rulers wanted something done, all they had to do was send messengers ahead, saying that one of the Ra emissaries would be visiting and discussing whatever requests the Young King and Queen expected.

When these representatives came, they were expected to have the complete cooperation of their host. Every Warlord under the Rule of the Hellcats would rather deal with the young Ra emissaries, than deal directly with Young Dan, or La.

CHAPTER 18

Weeks later, after a rigorous first day's training session, the Ra boys were headed to first day's meal. The Ra boys and everyone else were catching Hell from Dan because of his defeat at the hands of the Shinmushee Butcher.

Not only did Dan increase his own training schedule, but he also increased everyone else's. Dan figured he probably wasn't the only one that would meet a Shinmushee Butcher in battle, again. He wanted everyone on his team to be prepared for that challenge.

Yin and Don were fed up with Dan pushing them to their limits all the time. Sometimes they just wanted to beat Dan, until he couldn't move. Only problem with that was, they couldn't beat Dan, even when all three of them attacked him at the same time. Young Dan was just that good.

After a short walk, they saw a group four girls. Three of the girls ran up to the Ra boys, lowered their heads and excitedly said "Security check!"

That was Don and Yin's cue to give these girls' bodies a thorough search. The girls giggled as this was happening. Several more girls came up, waiting for their turn. One girl walked up to Dan and said "My King, please honor me with a security check."

Up to this point, Dan had only enjoyed a good laugh, watching Don and Yin do security searches. Dan looked into the girl's eyes for a moment, before scoping out her body. Maybe she did need investigating. Dan thought it might be an insult to her, if he didn't check her.

Dan gave the girl a thorough body search that both he and the girl enjoyed. When he was done, she smiled at him and then ran over to the other girls. Dan turned to see Yin and Don deviously smiling at him, with approval. Ram just stood there, watching. None of the girls tried to get Ram to search them. They were too afraid they might be his next victim. Just like everyone else, they avoided Ram, without being disrespectful.

Every day, after first day's training, all of the Hammer-Axe Six had first day's meal together. On the way, their bodyguards and Dan's Warlord Bo met the Ra boys. Dan was quickly briefed on everything Bo knew.

The Ra girls always got to the eating hall first, because the Ra boys always took their time getting there. Ali and the Ra girls' bodyguards were with them. When the Ra boys finally arrived, they saw their sisters already sitting and waiting on them. Tania and Anne were sitting at the table closest to them, with some of La's other female advisers.

Dan saw La searching with her eyes, until she didn't find what she was looking for. A hint of disappointment flashed on her face, before she removed it and watched her brothers, as they came and sat with the Ra girls. Anne jumped to a standing position when she saw Ram, smiling and trying to get his attention. Both La and Tania cut their eyes in Anne's direction, without looking directly at her. Anne quickly sat down and meekly looked around the room.

After the Ra boys sat down, Dan looked at La. He knew she was searching for Bo, when he saw that look of disappointment on her face. La saw Dan staring at her and stared back at him. Maids and servants started bringing food in and placing it on the tables.

Everyone noticed La and Dan staring at each other without saying anything. Because it wasn't an angry stare, no one knew what to make of it. Ram was the only one who wasn't consumed by La and Dan's behavior. He was watching everyone in the room, while stealthily watching Anne. Anne knew Ram's attention was on her. She knew if she let on that she knew he was watching her, he would stop. Therefore, Anne pretended to be caught up in La and Dan's staring match.

Finally, Dan said, "I sent Bo to get the messengers we sent to Anduku. They'll be here shortly to tell us about the meeting." La took her gaze off Dan and nonchalantly said, "They'd better have good news. I never liked the Anduku, the times they visited, when we were younger."

Dan said, "You don't have to like them, as long as they're cooperating and giving us what we want. That's what matters."

La's eyes darted to Dan's and then quickly looked away. La didn't respond. La knew Dan was toying with her and checking her attitude. Dan didn't like that, even though Bo made a mockery of the interview for becoming La's mate, La was still smitten with him. La tried not to let it show. Because Bo was the best, the House of Ra had to offer, Dan made Bo his Warlord.

Dan made sure he kept Bo from being around La as much as possible. Still, there were times when Bo would be around La. If La pissed Dan off, Dan would make those times, rare. Dan was satisfied that La was behaving, appropriately.

Not ten minutes later, Bo walked in with the messengers. La only looked at Bo for a moment, before all of her attention went to the messengers. All three of them looked like they were beaten up, pretty good.

La looked away from them, with her head arrogantly high and sternly said "How'd this happen?!"

One of the messengers said that when they reached Anduku territory, a large number of guards met them. The guards asked them what their business was. The Ra messengers told the guards that their business was with the Elder Anduku, on behalf of the Warlord Dan and the Number One Princess Ramala. The guards ordered the Ra messengers to wait where they stood.

A short time later, a young man of just around twenty walked up to the messengers. He told them they could tell him anything they had to say and he would see if it was worth telling the Elders.

In their arrogance, the Ra messengers told the young man that the message wasn't for his review. That he shouldn't waste any more of their time with this nonsense. That they should be taken directly to the Elders of Anduku, at once!

The Ra messengers immediately received a stern and severe beating. After the beating, they were bound and gagged. Guards told the messengers, that it was being considered whether they would be killed for their disrespect. A short time later, they were released and escorted out of Anduku territory.

Of course, the Ra messengers cleaned that up a bit when they told La and Dan. The messengers made it seem like they begged to see the Anduku Elders and were beaten and sent away.

Dan was a pissed, but La was furious! La angrily said "Alright, if that's how the want it, then . . . . !" Shaya grabbed La's arm and gave her a stern look. La watched as Shaya stood up and ordered "Maids and servants, take your leave! Guards! Summon Hoban and the Elite Guards, available! When that's done, wait outside the building for further instructions."

La hadn't taken her eyes off Shaya the entire time she was talking. When Shaya was done, La turned and looked at the Guards, as if she'd given the order. The Guards, after looking at La, quickly left with the maids and servants.

Once everyone that needed to be there was, Dan stood up and looked out at everyone. He peeked at La, before looking out at everyone again and calmly saying, "Looks like we'll be visiting Anduku territory. They need to be shown how the Ra expected to be treated. Put together a caravan. We leave as soon as possible."

La sternly said, "I don't want my grandpa, or Master Deen to find out about this! I don't need them trying to talk us out of it!" Everyone nodded in agreement. La continued with "Also, I think it's time we test the trainees. Prepare Little Shit, the Chusee Two and the Behemoth. They're going with us." Everyone looked at La in astonishment, as if they couldn't believe what she just said.

La looked at everyone once again, before saying "Right, then, get it done!"

The reason La decided to let four of the undesirables come along was that they had made great strides in their training. The

Ra, Yosuetta was called Sue. However, because of her horridly putrid body odor, she was called Little Shit.

Little Shit's odor was so bad that you could smell her more than one hundred yards away. Within fifty yards, her odor made you instinctively move in the opposite direction. Within twenty-five yards, your eyes would water and your stomach would turn. Any closer than that and you were damn near incapacitated. In addition, to make matters worse, if she passed gas, that ramped up the smell tenfold.

At first, La cursed Shit's parents for creating such an entity. She wanted to put this girl and everyone's noses out of their misery by killing Sue. However, one day, La was trying to figure out the cruelest punishment she could inflict on some of her guards who weren't performing up to the level she thought they should. She didn't want to kill the guards, so she had to come up with something that would motivate them to work harder.

While thinking, she caught a whiff of Little Shit, who was way off in the distance. La told Shit's handlers to keep her as far away from La as possible. After being distracted by the smell, La got an idea. She ordered the underachieving guards to be placed in the dungeon for two hours. The guards gladly complied, thinking they'd gotten off easy. Then Little Shit walked into the dungeon.

Those two hours seemed like two years. After that, those guards were some of the highest achieving guards La had. It seemed that once the word got around that being put in the dungeon with Little Shit was a possible punishment, all of La's guards put extra efforts in training sessions. That's when La knew she had something special.

La wanted to test Shit's power, so she made her guards train one session a day with Shit at close range. At first, the guards could barely concentrate on their technique. After a while, they adjusted to the smell.

La forced Danaaa and Shaya, along with herself to endure that same training, at least, once a day. Danaaa and Ram had to deal with Shit twice a day. Once while in physical training and again later trying to identify other scents, as the powerful stench of Little Shit's smell permeated through their nostrils.

The Hammer-Axe Six watched as everyone filed out, on their way to put together the caravan. Shortly after that, they went to their next training session. The caravan was put together in less than a week. La's grandfather the Hayee, Roe and their main instructor the Hayee, Deen found out about the caravan being put together, from all the commotion around Wa province. They ordered a meeting with the Hammer-Axe Six.

Both Roe and Deen questioned the Ra extensively, to no avail. La and Dan insisted that they were going on a training mission and wanted to test themselves on adhering to protocol, without supervision from their Elders.

Roe and Deen suspected this wasn't completely true, but the Hammer-Axe Six stuck to their story. Roe talked to Deen later and convinced him that they probably didn't want to know everything the Royal Ra were doing. Deen still wasn't convinced his students weren't up to something. He conferred with and instructed the Ra children once more, and then left it at that.

The military caravan was ready to travel in three days. It was complete with the Ra Warlords, warriors, guards, bodyguards and singers. They had a host of attack elephants and plat formed elephants for everything from sleeping quarters to meeting rooms and everything in between. Once everything was set, the Ra were on their way early on the fourth day.

Everyone was excited about the expedition. The Ra girls chattered on about what techniques they would use and everything else, until they fell asleep, shortly after their mid-day meal.

Dan instructed the Ra boys, as well as their Warlords on what he expected from them. The Warlords in turn instructed the warriors and guards. The travel time to Anduku territory was four days. The military caravan set up camp about an hour away from Anduku territory.

Dan had a meeting with his Warlords and the Rulers of Ra. He said he didn't want to send an army into Anduku territory without consulting their Queen Mother. Instead, Dan said it would be best if they went in with a smaller force. La protested, saying they would be vulnerable to attack. Dan countered by saying that if they were attacked, they could teach the Anduku a lesson they would never forget and not be blamed for being too aggressive.

La looked at Dan for a moment, before her face lit up from the thought of what she could get away with, using that excuse. She quickly agreed, with a smile. Dan returned La's smile. Then Dan handpicked who would be going with him to talk to the Anduku Elders.

Dan picked the Hammer-Axe Six, Ali, Bo, Hoban, fourteen Elite Guards, five singers, five maids, five servants and six messengers. La and Shaya thought they needed more than just fourteen Elite Guards. Dan told them that's why they were bringing the singers. The singers could accomplish just as much if not more than Elite Guards. La thought she had enough firepower with this small group, so she was good with that.

At first daylight, they headed for Anduku territory on foot. Danaaa, who always walked beside La, let everyone know how close the Anduku scouts were to them, by catching their scent.

Anduku guards had been spying on the Ra caravan, once it was close to Anduku territory. Now that the Ra were traveling in a smaller group, they saw more groups of Anduku Guards watching them.

As the Ra entourage was about to enter Anduku territory, they were met by a large group of Anduku warriors. Ten Anduku stepped ahead of the others and waited as the Ra walked closer. Although relatively young, to the Ra, they were dressed as if they had high rank. The Ra also identified that their eyes had the look of hardened killers.

The ten Anduku watched the Ra, as they got closer. They had a spotter with them that could see Ali, Hoban and Bo seemed to be the biggest threat. They weren't worried, though. They also identified the fourteen Elite Guards they assumed were warriors. The Anduku didn't see enough to cause serious concern. Still they watched them, closely.

Their spies told these Anduku everything they could find out about the Ra. They knew the females they were looking at were either singers, or screamers. The Anduku put in earplugs and most of their warriors had metal shields to help deflect the sound.

The Ra entourage stopped and the Hammer-Axe Six stepped forward with Ali and Hoban next to the Ra girls, while Bo was next to Dan. The ten Anduku could see one girl holding the end of the girl's next to her ponytail. The girl whose ponytail was being held stared indirectly at them with her hands in a draw position next to her axes. They all peeked at the spotter, with smirks on their faces, wondering if they should consider the brat looking girl a threat. At this point, the spotter wasn't sure.

La quickly scanned the ten men, before saying, "I'm your young Queen Ramala. You must be my escorts. I'm here to see the Anduku Elders. Lead me to them, right away." The Anduku wanted to be respectful, so one of the ten Anduku said "Young Queen, right now, the Elders are . . . Indisposed. Maybe we can help you."

La stared at him for a moment, before saying, "The only way you can help is by doing what I requested of you. If not, you're no use to me. And what is this talk of indisposed? To me that means we'll have to find them on our own!"

Not wanting to look bad in front of his men, that same Anduku offered up a little more information to appease the young Queen. He said, "There's a transition of power going on. It's personal family business. I think it best if we send messengers letting you know a better time to visit."

La's face instantly became angry, as she stared at the man talking. Didn't this man know that she was trying to be nice? She was done with that, now. La yelled "Who told you to think?! Right now, I don't even like you!"

Danaaa yelled, "Holler charge!" La pulled on her ponytail. Danaaa angrily peeked at La and then turned her attention back to the men ahead. La stared at the man she'd been talking to and said, "After I make an example out of you, I'll see how cooperative everyone else can be!"

La's words angered the Anduku she was talking to, as well as the other nine with him. His face got stern and had a steely resolve that said he was ready for whatever. La turned her head and looked at Hoban and Ali. They both knew she wanted an example made of that man. Dan saw that and ordered, "Hold it!"

Everyone froze in place. Dan walked forward. As he did, he looked at La. Dan could see she was agitated by his actions. Still, he moved ahead of her and said, "This situation looks like it can be easily resolved. I suggest a simple contest. You, or anyone you choose, against the Hammer-Axe Champion of Ra. That's me, you know! If Anduku wins, we leave. If Ra wins, you lead us to the Elders."

The ten Anduku looked at Dan to see if he was serious. Dan stared at them with an arrogance that said he was. The Anduku looked at each other. They weren't going to lead anyone anywhere, no matter what happened in any competition. The one who'd been speaking said, "Sounds fair. Let's do it."

La walked up to Dan and said, "This wasn't part of the plan!" Dan said, "Yes it was. I just hadn't told you, yet." They stared at each other.

La was on this expedition to show the Anduku they needed to do whatever she requested. Dan was here to test his skills against the best combatants he could find.

La didn't care whether Dan lost this competition, or not. She was still going to do what she came here to do in the first place. La said, "Fine, do what you want!" then she stepped back.

Dan took another step forward and waited on his opponent. He was disappointed when it wasn't one of the ten Anduku ahead of the rest. They looked to be better killers than the man who walked up. Still, all of Dan's teachers from his parents to Deen always told him to never underestimate an opponent. Therefore, Dan studied this man and took in everything he could about him.

Dan could see that the man he was facing was taller and more muscular than himself. His weapon of choice was the Hammer-Axe. Most of the Anduku were using Hammer-Axes. That was enough information for now. Dan would learn more about this man, once the battle started.

As always, whenever he got the chance, Dan wouldn't wait on his opponent. He would always attack first. This time was no different. Dan charged at the Anduku, swinging his axes, but not totally committing himself. He wanted to see what the Anduku had. Dan found out, right away.

The Anduku moved out of the way and sent lightning fast strikes at Dan. Dan counter-attacked, but nearly had his head took off by the Anduku's ax. Dan ducked and countered off another move. This time he was almost split open about the chest.

Dan realized he was facing an opponent that was using a very deadly style. This Anduku used a counter, counter-attacking style. Every time Dan counter-attacked, so did the Anduku.

From the first strike Dan attempted on the Anduku, the action was continuous. Both Dan and the Anduku were determined to put enough pressure on the other to make them make a mistake that would cost them their life.

Nevertheless, they didn't call Dan the Faster Cut for no good reason. Dan could shift his fighting to a higher level of speed, without compromising his offensive and defensive techniques. After five minutes of feeling the Anduku out, that's just what Dan did.

The Anduku tried to adjust to Dan's speed. He was still countering, but his defense couldn't match Dan's speed. Dan caught him with a hammer shot to the shoulder. A few moments later, he caught him with a hammer shot to the chest. Then three consecutive shots from Dan's hammers backed the Anduku up to a regrouping position.

The Anduku and Dan stared at each other, both realizing Dan was better. Still, the Anduku's pride would not let him concede defeat. He charged himself and attacked Dan.

Dan countered off the Anduku strikes. Once he was sure of the opening, Dan avoided the Anduku axes and with lightning fast strikes, smashed his hammers into the Anduku's shoulders and chest, again. Before the Anduku could react, Dan smashed one hammer into the Anduku's knee and sliced his shirt open with the Ax in his other hand. Dan quickly backed up from the Anduku to a safe enough distance, watching him closely.

The Anduku saw his shirt was split open, exposing his chest and stomach. He took a step and stumbled, almost falling over from the pain shooting through his knee. He was beaten and this time he couldn't mount a respectable attack. He knew if he tried, he would be at the mercy of this young man before him. He turned and looked at the Ten Anduku behind him. They motioned to him that he should take his leave.

Dan looked at the ten Anduku. They didn't look like they were ready to honor the terms of the contest. Dan knew La was going to slaughter these men at the first sign they wouldn't.

Dan said, "That warrior was pretty good. I know you were only testing me, before you sent out my real opponent. I'm good with that. You men look very tough. I'm hoping it's one of you, unless you have someone better."

La was about to put an end to Dan's antic, but thought better of it. The way Dan had been acting lately, La didn't want to take the chance he might put her in her place, using his higher rank. She knew if she really wanted to, she could start a fight with Dan that would stop this nonsense. A fight with Dan could cause him to give even more orders, out of spite. She didn't want that, either. La decided to let Dan have a little more fun and then it would be her turn to toy with the Anduku.

Dan's arrogant taunting angered the Anduku. They looked at each other. They were going to give the young man what he wanted. One of the ten stepped forward. Dan knew, right away, this fight was going to be much tougher that the last.

The man Dan was facing was taller than he was. He was chiseled from his neck down to his feet. Even though he looked to be in his young twenties, Dan knew this man was a serious killer. Adrenaline raced through Dan's body in anticipation of this fight.

He didn't have to wait long, because even though Dan always attacked first, this time, the Anduku did. Dan was instantly put on defense. The Anduku was so fast, Dan couldn't use his counter-attacking techniques, until he was sure he wouldn't be cut to pieces.

Dan had to avoid the first five swings from the Anduku. The Anduku closed the gap between himself and Dan. Dan had to block the next seven swings with his Hammer-Axes. While blocking, to save his neck, Dan was trying to create some space so he could regroup and mount an attack. The Anduku wasn't having that. He kept high heat on Dan with his axes.

Things got very serious when the Anduku's axes shredded most of Dan's shirt off in a lightning fast volley of swings. The Anduku, while not stopping, was amazed at Dan's defensive skills. Most warriors he fought would have been carved to pieces, by now.

For the first time in his life, Dan knew he was in serious trouble. His pride wouldn't allow him to let anyone know he needed help. Dan hadn't made one offensive move and he hadn't even thought to try one. Right now, his defensive skills were being tested like never before.

Even though the Shinmushee Butcher had put a thorough beating on him and probably would have killed him, if the fight had gone longer, this was nothing like that. This was the Hell of Axes continuously coming at you from all angles. All Dan had to do was make one mistake and he knew he was dead.

That mistake came after twenty more nonstop swings of the Anduku's Axes. The Anduku used his power to bully his axes past Dan's defense. In a split second, Dan realized the Anduku would, at least get a clean slice at him. Dan moved his axes to best defend his neck and chest. Then he hoped for the best, as he desperately tried to get out of the way.

In that same instant, Dan was pulled backwards by Ali, while Bo's axes blocked two kill shots coming at Dan. Bo and the Anduku went hard at each other. Dan stood back and watched as the Anduku couldn't bully and manipulate Bo's Hammer-Axes as he'd done with Dan's. Although Dan was faster, Bo was much more powerful than Dan.

Bo put in some real work with the Anduku and had him backing up, on defense, after only five minutes. Just when it seemed Bo was about to finish the Anduku off, Dan yelled "Alright Bo, that's enough!" Bo disengaged the Anduku and backed away from him.

The Anduku wasn't done. He looked like he would rather die than be defeated. He stared at Bo. Bo took another two steps back, because of Dan's order, but stayed on guard after seeing all that.

Then, La made a subtle, but obvious movement with the hand that was holding Danaaa's ponytail. She raised it up in the air, presenting the ponytail to everyone.

La stared at the Anduku who was charging himself to attack Bo, again. La said, "Back yourself up and stop this nonsense, or I let my Executioner deal with you. She's High Pressure. What she can do, you don't even know!" Danaaa put her hand in a quick draw position next to her Axes and yelled "I Chop I . . .!"

La yelled, "Alright, Baby, he got the message!" The Anduku looked at Danaaa and was sure the Ra were toying with him. Bo, knowing Danaaa, moved back even further.

Dan quickly gestured to the Anduku, warning him "Hey, you beat me fair and square. You win. Besides, she's right. So, it's best if we negotiate."

The Anduku wasn't in the mood to negotiate with Dan, or the young girls. He wanted another chance at Bo. This time, he was sure things would be different.

The Anduku said, "I don't have time to play with children! Besides, I'm not done with him, yet!" as he pointed his ax at Bo. La's smile had a crooked smirked, when she said to the Anduku "You're done, you just don't know it, yet!" then La let Danaaa's ponytail fall from her hand.

The second La let go of Danaaa's ponytail, Danaaa marched straight for the Anduku. She quickly pulled her axes. The Anduku turned towards Danaaa. He didn't take her seriously, until he saw the determined look on her face.

Danaaa marched right up to the Anduku. She was met with a powerful swing from his ax. Because of the force of the swing,

Danaaa could only partially block it with the flat side of her ax, at an angle. That deflected the power of the blow, slightly sending Danaaa spinning away from the Anduku. As she was spinning away, she extended her ax slicing into his forearm.

The Anduku was already swinging at Danaaa with his other ax, just as she stumbled away, trying to catch her footing. She launched herself towards him, just under his ax, tucking and rolling past him. The Anduku swung his ax again, but Danaaa quickly moved behind him. In an instant, he was turning in the opposite direction, swinging his ax where Danaaa was, behind him.

Danaaa jumped in the air, flipping up and over his ax, barely being missed by it. She extended her arm and her ax sliced halfway through the side of his neck. As soon as her feet hit the ground, Danaaa flipped back toward the Anduku, slicing the rest of his neck from his body, as he was falling to the ground. When Danaaa's feet hit the ground, she was facing the rest of the Anduku. She spun her axes on super-fast revolution and slammed then into the holster on her waist. Her hands were at her sides in a quick draw position, with her fingers lightly touching the top of the ax handle.

Just getting past the shock of seeing this young girl ruthlessly slaughter one of their own, the other nine Anduku all drew their axes. In that same instant, Danaaa pulled her axes out of their holsters. She quickly moved the ax in her left hand down to her side, ax blade pointing backwards. In the same motion, the ax in her right hand came up just below eye level, with the blade pointing towards the Anduku.

Then, as if out of nowhere, Yin appeared at Danaaa's side with both his axes draw. Both blades, at chest level, one on top of the other, pointed at the Anduku. Ram was on the other side of Yin, just as fast, with his axes drawn. The ax in his left hand was just below eye level, with the blade pointing forward at the Anduku. The ax in Ram's right hand was down at his side, just behind his leg, with the ax blade pointing backwards. Ram had the exact same stance as Danaaa, but only with the opposite hands.

The Anduku saw these children looked like they meant serious business. It made them pause for a second, because they'd never seen a fighting formation like this one, before. They also saw two young teenagers with their hands very close to hammers in a vest around their chest, behind the three out front. The other reason they paused was they found it hard to believe how quick the young girl almost effortlessly killed one of their skilled Anduku. They looked at their Spotter. The Spotter looked worried, like they were at a disadvantage from what she'd already seen. The Anduku turned their attention back to the Ra.

After a short moment, their minds told them that these were only children standing in front of them. Their minds also told them, what happened to the last Anduku could never happen to them. They all stepped away from each other, giving themselves ample room to maneuver.

Dan saw that and ordered, "Hold it! Stand your ground!" La peeked at Dan and then walked behind Danaaa. She grabbed Danaaa's ponytail and with a crooked smirk on her face, La said, "What she did, just now, is nothing compare to what these three can do together." La presented Danaaa's ponytail to the Anduku and said, "If you need more convincing, let me know. All I have to do is let go of this, again. What happens after that, you don't want to know!"

La was trying to build a fate in the minds of the Anduku greater than what really might happen. The crooked smirk came off La's face, but she still looked serious when she said, "Right now, all we want is for you to explain why we're not being led to the Anduku Elders. Just talk to me and we can continue to be allies, as you are with my Queen Mother. Besides, we're going to find the Elders with, or without your help. Make your choice!"

The Anduku stared at La for a moment. Then they looked at each other. After another short moment, the Anduku agreed. They told La that the reason for not taking her to the Elders was that there was a civil war among the Anduku families.

They said a group of fourteen young Anduku headed a large group of young Anduku that wanted to run the territory more aggressively. The Elders didn't agree. The young Anduku continued to meet and plan on how they could achieve their goals. The Elders decided to put a stop to the meetings, first by forbidding them. When that didn't work, they sent their Warlords to disperse the meetings. That's when hostilities broke out.

Most all of the Warlords were over forty. They didn't anticipate that most of the guards in their charge under the age of thirty would side with the young Anduku. Even with that, their stubborn warrior mentality wouldn't let them compromise. Even though they were outnumbered, they were still protecting the Elders. Although they were now pinned down, they were giving the young Anduku a hellish battle that had turned into a stalemate. The young Anduku controlled most of the Anduku territory. Still, they couldn't take over the portion of the main city that the Elders and their Warlords controlled.

They said that now there were only thirteen young Anduku in charge, because of the Anduku Danaaa killed, earlier. Nine of the ones in charge were here and the other four were maintaining military pressure on the Elders and their Warlords.

After hearing that, La and Dan looked curiously at each other for a moment. La looked back at the Anduku and said, "Sometimes, Elders just can't see all that the younger generations have to offer. Take me for example. I'm the Young Queen of Ra, Ramala. All of you have heard of my mother, Queen Hayee, Ramala. Being that this is the House of Ra, I've decided that as the young Queen, I need to find out who is ally to me. Those that are not will find it hard to survive."

La paused for a moment and then said, "I will see the Elders of Anduku and end this stalemate, if all of you pledge your unwavering support of me. Then, I'll only recognize you as the rulers of Anduku territory. Now, I'm trying hard to be nice. That's not how I normally do things. I'm trying something new. Don't make me regret it!"

One of the Anduku asked, "How do we know they'll agree to that?

Danaaa incredulously yelled "She's the Number One Princess, Queen Ramala!" La said, "That's right!" La brought herself down, just a little, enough to say, "Don't concern yourself with such things. Just take me to your Elders. I'll do the rest." All of the young Anduku leaders agreed. They took the Ra to the outpost where the four young Anduku in charge were headquartered.

CHAPTER 19

The Ra were introduced to the four young Anduku leaders that they hadn't met, yet. Only one was a female. In fact, she was the only female of all the thirteen young Anduku leaders. She also was the first to notice her cousin wasn't here. When she asked where he was, one of the Anduku explained what happened. At the end of his explanation, he told them that the Ra Executioner exhibited speed and skill that was remarkable.

Even though the four had heard the story of what happened and all of the Anduku that witnessed it confirmed what the Anduku talking said, their anger had them looking at all the Ra to see who this Executioner was.

One of the Anduku who witnessed the killing saw them looking. He pointed to Danaaa and said, "That's their little Executioner. Don't be fooled by her looks. She's instant death on two legs." They stared at her for a moment longer. La was getting impatient. She held up Danaaa's ponytail and said, "Do they need to be convinced?"

One Anduku said, "No, they're just curious. Everything's fine. We'll take you as far as we can and I'm sure you'll know what to do, after that."

Several of the Anduku got the four young leaders out of La's sight. They knew there would be trouble, because of that Anduku's death, if they didn't. La didn't care about that. All she knew was the Anduku were cooperating, once she showed them who was boss!

The Anduku showed the Ra which way to go and then held back. The Ra walked a short distance before they saw a heavily guarded checkpoint. They walked right up to it. Ali announced who they were and that they'd come to have audience with the Anduku Elders.

One of the guards said he would see if the Elders would receive them. When the guards said that, the look on La's face changed and she instantly became impatient. Dan saw that. He put his hand on La's shoulders and whispered "You're doing a pretty good job, here. I haven't had to change any of your orders in a while, now." La quickly turned and looked at Dan after he said that. He smiled at her. La didn't smile. She looked back at the guards. This was serious time. If the guards kept her waiting any longer, La was going to show everyone just how serious it was.

It wasn't long before guards came out, followed by a Warlord. The Warlord walked up and looked at the Ra. He knew exactly who was who. He'd seen all of the Ra before when the oldest twins were about six years of age. Even though they were older, they mostly looked the same.

The Warlord lowered his head and then raised it. La gave him a favorable look. He said, "Times are very difficult, as you can see. If it pleases the young Princess, I will have food and drink prepared. After that, we can talk about why you're here."

The Warlord was being very respectful because he'd dealt with Queen Hayee, Ramala, before. He thought it best to amuse the Princess, as not to offend his Queen and have her come here personally.

La liked that this Warlord knew how to show the proper respect with his actions and words. She said, "Why I'm here, I'll tell you, now. I need to talk to the Anduku Elders, as soon as possible."

The Warlord said, "It might be a few days, before you can see them, if that. Right now, they are conferring on the situation concerning the rebelling Anduku. But, if you want, I'll do my best to help you in any way."

La looked at the Anduku Warlord as he talked. Before he was done with his first sentence, La interpreted him as saying he wasn't going to do what she'd asked of him. La let her eyes go slowly down to the Warlords feet. Then she slowly moved them back up to his eyes and said, "It's important that you understand what I tell you, because I'll not say it, again. You go make ready the Anduku Elders so they can be addressed by their Young Queen. I'm growing more impatient as time goes by. I'm trying to be nice, but I can be very difficult when I want. Believe me when I say, you don't want that!"

La gave the Warlord a hard stare that made him a little uncomfortable. His uncomfortably came from the fact that this young girl sounded just like the Queen Ramala he met a few years back. He remembered a few of his fellow Warlords lost their lives, before the others realized it was what Queen Ramala wanted, when she wanted it. That experience was degrading and very unpleasant to say the least.

As he and La locked eyes for a moment, he decided not to do what he really wanted. That was to pull his axes and split this young girl and her sibling into pieces. Instead, he took a big gulp, swallowed his pride, lowered his head and then said, "As you wish . . . . Young Queen." The Warlord left, after that.

La was impressed! Her grandpa and other advisers were right. If she explained herself clearly, she could use her calm voice, instead of the threatening one she was so use to using. She was going to use more of this technique. Right now, La was very proud of herself. So was Shaya. Even though Dan couldn't believe La was being so calm, he didn't think it would last for long. Nevertheless, Dan was impressed that it lasted this long.

A few minutes later, guards came and escorted the Ra to a large dining area. The guards said that food would be served and the Elders would be out shortly after that. This was hospitality, so the Ra had to accept it.

Food was brought out and served. Danaaa and Ram walked around the table sniffing every food item there. These two could detect poison, with their noses, even if it was tasteless and odorless. No one knew how, or why they could, they just could.

After examining and smelling all of the food and drink, Danaaa and Ram looked at La and gave a favorable nod. All of the Ra sat down, ate and enjoyed the food. Right after they finished, a troop of guards walked in and stationed themselves around and behind the Ra. They were followed by a large number of Warlords who posted themselves in front of and around a throne area that was in front of the room. Lastly, a group of fifteen old men walked in and sat on the throne chairs.

The Anduku Elders were very old and they wore tan animal skin that covered their shoulders down to their feet.

The Ra all lowered their heads out of respect. The Elders inspected the Ra and then did the same. Before the Anduku Elders could ask, La said "You're probably wondering why we're here." the Elders nodded that they were. La said "Seems our messengers can't visit you without being beaten. That can't happen. Whatever is causing problems needs to be fixed."

One of the Elders stared hard at La, before saying "Those young men who brought you here are the problem. They're reckless behavior is causing a split in our family. We're taking steps to get them back in line."

La didn't like that last sentence. She looked at all the Elders, ending with the one who spoke and said "Steps aren't good enough. I need this taken care of, right away, so you can do I want, done. Now, here's what's going to happen!"

The Elders were shocked at the bold directness of the Young Queen. She told them, as of now, all the Anduku Elders were her Advisers in this territory. La also told them that the Young rebelling Anduku would be her military hand here. The Elders would be responsible for training the very young and adhering to protocols La set forth. After that, they could continue their family traditions as they'd always done.

La told them that the teenagers and the rest of the Anduku military would be under her direct orders. That if the Elders did their part, they would have no trouble out of the rebelling teenagers.

The Elder who spoke earlier questioned, "So you've already negotiated this with our youngsters." La quickly said, "I'm not here to negotiate with them, or anyone else! I'm here to tell everyone here what I need done! All I need to know is if you're ready to cooperate, or not. Your decision will determine what happens next!"

That same Elder said, "We'd like to hear from Queen Ramala that she has given charge of this territory to the Young Queen." La said, "She's got nothing to do with this! You need to know is that things you do for me might be different from the things you do for her. No matter what, I expect whatever I need, it gets done."

The Anduku Elders studied La and the other Ra. After a moment of silence, the same Elder said, "We will agree to your wishes if you stay with us seven days and learn Anduku customs. That might help you get the best use out of the Anduku."

La looked at all the Elders. She didn't think they understood what was really going on here. La charged herself for action. She looked down and then slowly looked back up at the Elders. La's face was full of fury. She was interrupted by Shaya pulling on her arm. La quickly turned and gave Shaya a hard stare. Shaya turned from La and faced the Elders. Shaya smiled at them and announced, "We agree to those terms."

The Anduku Elders looked at Shaya while she was talking, but turned their attention to La, after Shaya was done. They knew La was in charge. La tried not to show she was annoyed. As she looked from Shaya to the Anduku Elders, a crooked smile came on her face. She gave a nod that said she approved. The Elders ended the meeting shortly after that. They had their Warlords show the Ra several buildings allotted for their stay.

La ignored Shaya, until the Anduku guards were gone. Ali, Hoban, Bo and the Ra guards checked out the building where the Ra would be staying. Once they were sure they were up to standards, they let the Ra enter. Everyone got comfortable. La turned to Shaya and gave her a hard stare. Shaya meekly looked at La, wondering why she was getting attitude, even though she knew. Once La established her dominance over Shaya, she said, "Be very careful you don't say something to others that I don't like."

Shaya meekly nodded in agreement. La stared at Shaya for a moment, before her look softened. She turned towards the Ra boys and said, "Looks like we'll find out how these Anduku live." Dan, who was slouching on a pillow looking up at the ceiling, said "It might not be so bad." La looked over at Dan and said "Yeah, if you can stop yourself from getting into fights, every chance you can!"

Dan looked at La for a second and then looked back at the ceiling. He wondered why La would say that, when she already knew he was going to do that.

The week went quickly for the Ra. They learned a lot about Anduku customs. They met with the rebelling Anduku and worked out an arrangement with the two opposing sides. Everything was going smoothly. Dan even got to spar with some of the top Anduku Warlords. The Ra girls were glad Dan was getting training, without putting his life in danger.

The Ra girls also were surprised that it was very interesting learning another culture. When the week was done, they were just short of wanting to stay a few more days.

Early in the day that the Ra were leaving, the Anduku gave them a large first day's meal. All the Elders, Warlords, as well as the young Anduku attended. After that, the Ra prepared to go.

As a sign of respect, some of the young Anduku escorted the Ra to the edge of their territory. The trip was uneventful. When the Ra got to the edge of Anduku territory, the Anduku warriors said that the young Anduku military leaders were on their way to say their farewells.

The Ra waited a moment before they saw six of the young Anduku who were now in control of the military. One was the only female and the three that had to be lead away after finding out about the death of their cousin. The Ra noticed that, right away.

Bo, Hoban and Ali walked up and created a barrier in front of the Ra. La, not wanting the Anduku to get the impression that she saw them as a threat, ordered the Ra Warlord to move aside.

The young Anduku walked up and lowered their heads. They wished the Ra a safe trip home. They lowered their heads, again. Each of them looked at Danaaa before walking off. Everyone saw that. Dan told everyone to be on guard against attack. Then the Ra entourage began to move towards the main camp.

About halfway to the main camp, the guards detected movement ahead in the brush. The guards alerted the Ra Warlords. Then one of the guards yelled out "Spears!" just as a hail of spears came at the Ra from in front and on both sides. The guards went into a frenzy trying to block as many spears as they could. Hoban, Ali and Bo tried to block the spears the guards missed, but some got past them. The Hammer-Axe Six went on guard, got good spacing and blocked the rest of them.

Volley after volley of spears rained down on the Ra entourage. Several guards were killed while blocking spears meant for the Ra. Ali yelled to everyone that they had to move forward, or eventually, if the spears didn't stop coming, they'd all be killed.

Dan and La motioned that they agreed. That's when Shaya screamed out. La quickly turned towards Shaya. La would have been killed if Dan and Bo hadn't saw her and blocked spears aimed at her.

Shaya had a gash on her thigh from a glancing spear that missed its mark. Right after Shaya screamed she stumbled right into the path of several more spears. With severe pain coming from her leg every time she put weight on it, Shaya was only able to block one of the spears coming at her. An axe blade whizzed in front of Shaya blocking several more spears. She was instantly snatched off her feet and secured in Hoban's left arm, while he ferociously fought off spears coming at himself and Shaya with the axe in his right hand.

La had only looked at Shaya for a moment before her rage went rocketing out of control. She bolted in front of Dan, unprotected, bent her knees and took in as much air as possible. Dan's heart skipped a beat when he saw what La had done. He saw spears heading in her direction and he didn't have time to block them all. Even still, he took off diving towards La, determined to block as many as possible.

Then came the most horrific scream Dan had ever heard come out of his twin sister. Within a second of La's scream, Danaaa let out a short, powerful sonic shriek. Immediately after that, Danaaa quickly bent her knees and took in air. She then let out a scream that intertwined with La's. The combination sent everyone to their knees, even those behind the two screamers.

When La's scream hit the open air, it moved forward in a blasting sonic wave. The scream slammed into the oncoming spears and instantly exploded the wooden poles of the spears, leaving just the metal spear tips moving forwards. Danaaa's powerful shriek punched into the metal spear tips, vibrating the molecules in them, slowing them down. Once Danaaa let out her best full scream, mixed with La's scream, the spear tips, while vibrating even more, went downward and fell into the dirt a few yards in front of La and Danaaa. Once the screaming stopped, no spears came towards the Ra. Dan, who was laying on his side on the ground, with his Hammer-Axe in hand, still a bit disoriented, marveled at what his sisters had done.

Dan wasn't the only ones astounded by what they'd just seen. The Ra guards' eyes were staring back and forth from the spearheads on the ground to La and Danaaa. They slowly repeated that, until they were shocked back into reality by La pointing towards the brush and screaming, "I want their heads, NOW!"

The Ra guards raced towards the bushes, at the sides of the road, while the Ra bodyguards created a safe perimeter. Dan quickly got off the ground. He saw La looking around, surveying the damage. Three guards, two bodyguards, one Elite guard and one singer were dead. La's eyes connected with where Shaya was. Some of the singers were attending to Shaya's wound. La quickly moved towards Shaya when she was violently snatched backwards, by someone roughly holding her arm. Her instincts had her axe moving to gut the person who had her arm. In that split second before her axe blade met skin, she saw it was Dan. La's axe quickly moved back to her side.

Dan and La stared angrily at each other. Dan yelled "Why would you jump in front of spears without protection?! You could have been killed! Don't you know how scared I was for you?! Don't ever do anything like that, again!"

La roughly pulled her arm out of Dan's hand. She pointed her axe at Dan's hand that grabbed her and then she pointed her axe at Dan's face and yelled, "Don't ever do anything like that, again! You could have just been killed, you Stupid Rhino's Ass!"

Dan was ready to go into an angry rant, but La turned, dropped her axes and ran towards Shaya. Dan took in an angry breath and then let it out. He was really pissed that La put herself in danger like that. Dan looked around and saw the Ra Warlords on guard. He then made his way over to Shaya to make sure she was alright.

La understood why, but didn't care that Dan was upset at her. It served him right that he got a good dose of his own medicine. Every time Dan recklessly challenged one of those Shinmushee Butchers, or an Anduku Warlord and was getting his ass kicked, La's heart was being trampled on. Maybe this would shock Dan into thinking about how she felt, for once!

Even though Dan didn't know, La knew her special scream would stop those spears. She didn't think she was in danger, at all. La wasn't going to tell Dan that.

Dan joined Don and Yin who were standing close to Shaya, watching La and Danaaa console Shaya while her leg was being wrapped, tightly. Dan only stood there for a moment. The more he looked at Shaya, the angrier he got. Dan looked at Don, Ram and Yin. He ordered, "Alright, La and Danaaa are taking care of Shaya. Let's check the perimeters so we can get back to the main camp!"

Dan was very strict on his Warlords, guards and bodyguards ordering them around. Normally, Bo and Ali handled security issues. Dan was pissed and did not think his people had done enough to protect his sister. He was making sure something like that wouldn't happen, again.

Once Shaya's wound had been attended to and she was safely back on an Elephant, the Ra moved back to the main camp. Once everything settled, Dan called a meeting for the Hammer-Axe Six. All of them were there, except for Shaya.

La looked at all of them. She could see anger in their eyes. She said, "If they want to play rough, that's what we'll give them!"

several guards walking up interrupted her. The Hammer-Axe Six turned to see eight guards, two of which were carrying Shaya, who was sitting on a throne chair. Six of them got on their knee, while the two carrying Shaya marched up to the Hammer-Axe Six and sat her chair next to La. The two guards quickly moved back to where the other guards were and got on their knees. Everyone was shocked to silence, because Shaya looked very regal to all of them. La missed none of that.

Although, La was sympathetic towards Shaya, because of her wound, La stared angrily at Shaya and said, "How is it that you come here in my throne chair, as if you're the Queen? Be very careful that you don't overstep boundaries! And didn't I tell you to stay and get some rest?"

Shaya smiled meekly at La and said "Don't be silly. Everyone knows you're the Queen. It's just that I'm not supposed to put pressure on this leg. Besides, how can you have a meeting without me?"

La said, "This is something that doesn't concern you." Shaya's voice was serious when she said, "Whatever it is you're talking about, or planning, if it concerns you, it concerns me! Besides, I might be able to help." The rest of the Hammer-Axe Six chorused "No you can't!"

Shaya exclaimed, "Fine, but I'm not going anywhere!" La and Shaya stared at each other. There was rarely a confrontation between these two that La couldn't win. La felt it was time to put Shaya in her place.

Before she did, Dan said "Alright you two, enough of this nonsense!" Both Shaya and La quickly turned and stared at Dan. Dan said "La, back to what you were saying. Or do I need to take charge, here?"

La stared at Dan as she said, "Guards, take your leave!" The guards quickly left. Without breaking eye contact with Dan, La said, "It's simple. When first day comes, we're going to hunt down those less than ant shit heathens that attacked us. Pack as much food and water on you person as you can carry. All of you need to have two sets of your sharpest Hammer-Axes. Two at your waist and two strapped to your back. Shaya's staying here at the main camp. Our bodyguards, Elite guards, warriors and the singers will protect her. She's not to leave this camp, under any circumstances, unless things have gotten to the point that she has to head to the main city. Under no circumstances is she to come in search of us!" La turned, stared Shaya in her eyes and said, "Is that understood!"

Shaya meekly pleaded, "Yes, I understand!" La said "Good!" La looked at Dan to see if he had anything to add. Dan said, "Early next day, we have serious business to attend to, so be ready. Everyone get some rest."

The meeting ended at that point. La stood in front of Shaya, extended her hand and said, "Come, stand on your good leg." Shaya, while looking La in her eyes, took La's hand and did just that. Once Shaya was standing, La moved behind her and sat in the throne chair. La said, "Sit." Shaya sat on La's lap. Danaaa yelled "But, where am I supposed to sit?!"

La said, "There's not enough room here." Danaaa pressed her lips tightly together, while looking at La and Shaya. Lastly, Danaaa looked at the throne chair. Danaaa bent her knees and launched herself into a flip, over La and Shaya, feet landing, facing forward, on the back of the throne chair.

Both La and Shaya looked up at Danaaa. Danaaa, while balancing herself, looked down and yelled "But, there's enough room for me up here!" Shaya shook her head and said, "Baby, you're so crazy!" La had had enough of this. She looked away from Danaaa and yelled "Guards!" Guards quickly ran up. Four guards lifted the throne chair and marched the Ra girls to their sleeping quarters.

After a good meal, the Hammer-Axe Six decided to go to sleep, early. Ram fell asleep at the dinner table, right after he finished his meal. Dan had to bully Ram, just to get him to his sleeping platform. While dragging Ram, who was half sleep, to his sleeping platform, Dan told him "Make sure they pay dearly for harming Shaya. And remember whatever you do, be careful and don't get caught!"

Ram was walking, stumbling in a half sleep daze. Dan couldn't tell if Ram heard him, or not. All Dan knew was most times when Ram went to sleep early, he disappeared in the middle of the night and a headless body was discovered sometime in the next day.

Early next day, before the sun came up, Dan woke up and was surprised to see Ram was still sleep. He was a little disappointed. Dan just knew Ram would kill a bunch of whoever did this to Shaya, in the middle of the night, while they slept. Dan guessed there was no telling what Ram would do, or when he would do it.

CHAPTER 20

Early when next day came the Ra had breakfast. They all packed water and food for their journey. La filled the pockets on Danaaa's vest with close to twenty cookies. Danaaa looked into La's eyes trying to figure out why La was doing that. La saw Danaaa staring at her and said "I expect we will have a difficult and long day. Whenever you feel you need to, eat as many of these cookies as you want. I need you to do your very best to make sure these people understand to never try anything like this, again!"

A confused look came on Danaaa's face as she yelled "But, if I do my very best, mommy's gonna be angry with me, just like last time!"

La took Danaaa by her shoulders and said, "What's worse, what they did to Shaya, or mommy getting angry and putting you in a dungeon?" Danaaa didn't answer. La paused and then said, "Baby, I expect my Executioner to perform with High Pressure, today! You make them pay for what they did to Shaya! Do you remember what they smell like?" Danaaa squinted her eyes and then nodded that she did. La said "Good! Time to deal with this properly!"

Dan decided that it would only be the Hammer-Axe Six, plus Ali, Hoban and Bo going on this mission. He said a bigger force would be spotted right away. If they couldn't catch whoever did this by surprise, Dan wanted them to think they had the advantage. They would travel a ways by Elephant, with a few guards and go the rest of the way on foot.

All three Ra Warlord protested, saying it was too dangerous. However, since La was angry and wasn't listening to reason, she agreed that Dan's plan would work. The Ra Warlords knew they would be tested, with only three of them protecting the six Ra.

As soon as they left the camp, Danaaa fell asleep. La told Dan that Ram would have to pick up the scent, until Danaaa awakened from sleep. Dan looked at Ram. Ram pointed and that's the direction they went.

They rode for about forty minutes, before it was time to go on foot. Danaaa still looked groggy. Danaaa kept trying to find a spot on the ground to go back to sleep. La wondered how good Danaaa would be if they were attacked, right now. After seeing Danaaa wasn't going to walk on her own, La had Hoban throw Danaaa over his shoulder, like a sack of potatoes. Danaaa's arms hung towards the ground as they walked. This was the first time La wondered if this really was a good idea.

They walked for another twenty minutes, with Ram leading the way. He stopped, looked at Dan and at La. Ram pointed, and said in his low deep voice, "That's where they are."

Upon hearing Ram's voice, Danaaa instantly was awakened. She jumped from Hoban's shoulder and walked over to La. Danaaa sniffed the air. She looked in the direction Ram had pointed and nodded in agreement.

Everyone turned and saw Ram walking off on his own. La sternly said "Ram, be careful!"

Ram turned and looked at La, for a second, before continuing on his way. Yin said, "I'll go with Ram and keep an eye on him." La somehow knew Ram would be all right on his own, but said, "Alright, go!"

Yin hustled and caught up with Ram. Ram turned and gave Yin a long hard stare. Yin said, "You know I only said that so La wouldn't try to stop you. I'm not here to stop you, or anything. I just want to help you get whoever hurt Shaya. Don't worry about me, I can handle myself."

Yin knew how to read Ram's questions without Ram saying a word. He told Ram everything Ram needed to know. They both walked off. Yin was a little nervous. He knew wherever Ram was leading him, if he wasn't at his best, he wouldn't live to tell about it. Yin followed Ram a short distance, until they came to a group of about five trees, surrounded by bushes and heavy undergrowth. Ram stood behind one of the trees, leaning with his back against it. He pointed to the tree next to him and said, "Stand there like me. Don't move."

Yin only looked at Ram for a second, before he got behind the tree as he saw Ram doing. Yin and Ram would look at each other from time to time. Each time Yin looked over at Ram, Ram put his finger up to his lips, letting Yin know not to say a word. Yin saw that Ram was relaxed and didn't seem to mind waiting. Yin wondered how long they would play this waiting game.

Now that they didn't have Ram and Yin, Dan walked over to Hoban, Ali and Bo. He ordered them to protect La at all cost. Dan said if they were somehow separated, it was their job to get La back to safety. Dan said he and Don would protect Danaaa. All three Ra Warlords asked Dan if one of them could protect him. Dan said he, Don, and Danaaa would protect each other. The Ra Warlords looked at Danaaa and figured that might work. Still, they were going to do their best to protect all of the Royal children, without looking like they were disobeying Dan's orders.

La gave everyone a stern look and said, "Let's take care of this!" they started walking and after a couple of minutes, they saw a small group of warriors approaching. The Ra walked, until they saw the warriors stop a short distance away.

There were ten of them. Seven had axes and three had two spears each. One of the axmen said "Right on time, just as they said you'd be. Follow us, there are some people who want to meet you. Don't give us any trouble, or things might get rough for you."

La's lip was hanging crooked on one side as she stared at the warriors with hatred in her eyes. She said, "One of you good for nothing piles of ant shit hit my sister with a spear! That was bad enough. Now you stand before me and talk as if I even care what you say! Well, at least, your friends won't have to listen to your stupidity much longer, because they'll all be dead!"

La and Danaaa charged in a sprint at the ten warriors. The Ra Warlords raced to get in position to protect the Ra girls. Dan and

Don jumped forward, with Dan engaging the warriors, while Don pulled two hammers from his vest. Both of Don's hammers were instantly flying through the air, towards the men with spears. As soon as he released those two hammers, Don quickly grabbed two more and sent them at the spearmen.

La and Danaaa reached the warriors at the same time. The warrior's axes came flying at both of them. La ducked one swing, intended to split her neck open and blocked another ax coming from the other side. Danaaa avoided an ax swing by moving closer to La and hacking off the arm of the warrior that missed La's neck. La spun her axes off the block and sliced them through the chest and neck of the warrior in front of her. Danaaa turned her back to La so she could address the warrior she'd avoided earlier. She dodged him and swung her axes low at his hips and legs.

Coming off the double strike with her axes, La jumped into a flip over Danaaa, striking down at the warrior attacking Danaaa. That warrior brought his axes up to save his neck from La's axes. He had his mid section split open and one arm taken off, by Danaaa. Without stopping, La and Danaaa quickly moved to the guards closest to them, putting the same heat on them.

More warriors charged at the Ra, until they were surrounded. Still, Dan, Danaaa and La moved forward offensively. Bo fought protecting La side, while Ali and Hoban fought protecting their backs. Don was holding his own on Dan's side.

The Ra pushed forward, chopping and slashing a path through the warriors. This went on for a little over a half hour. They finished off the last of the warriors just as they were coming up on a clearing. The Ra and their bodyguards were shocked at what they saw. There were Six Anduku standing with about fifteen Shinmushee Butcher. Behind them, for as far as the eyes could see were multitudes of Shinmushee warriors.

Danaaa reached in her vest pocket and pulled out a cookie. She shoved it into her mouth. Danaaa quickly ate two more cookies, while looking at the warriors ahead of her. La and Dan looked at each other, after seeing Danaaa. They both reached in their food pouch and gobbled down as much as they could, before drinking water. Ali announced, "Seems there's just as many behind us, too."

La looked over at Dan and said, low enough only for him to hear. "I told you this was a bad idea! I knew we should have brought more guards!"

Dan was in shock at what he was seeing. La brought him back to reality when she said that. He knew she'd said no such thing and that was her way of telling him she was nervous about what she was seeing.

Dan smiled at La when he calmly said, "We'll take care of these, just like we took care of the ones before them." Dan turned and looked at the Ra Warlords with a serious face and said, "No matter what happens, Bo, Hoban and Ali, you get the Number One Princess back to safety. Is that clear?!"

All three chorused "Yes, my King!" Dan looked at La and said "Good enough?" La nervously nodded that it was. Dan said "Good, because here they come. When they get here I want you to say something that will let them know we're in charge." La peeked at Dan, while keeping an eye on the oncoming army. She wondered if Dan had a plan. La said, "What are you going to do while I'm doing that?"

Dan said, "First, I'm going to enjoy whatever you say to them. Then I'm going to carve a path right through these Shitmushee, back to the caravan."

La nodded in agreement. When she turned back, the Anduku and the Shinmushee Butchers were close enough that she could see their faces. La saw that four of the six Anduku were the ones who stared at Danaaa before they left. La also saw Anduku and Shinmushee warriors carrying what looked like large round shields. Once they put the object on all side of the Ra, La figured out what they were.

The first one to talk was the Anduku girl. Her face was angry and her voice was harsh when she said, "If you scream the sound reflectors will send that vibration back at you magnified. So, I wouldn't try it if I were you. The days of the Ra coming into Anduku territory is over! We're tired of being puppets for the

House of Ra! We have friends from the southern jungle that are willing to help rid us of you!"

The girl then looks at Danaaa and says, "You killed my cousin! For that, all of you die!"

Before La could say anything, a volley of spears was flying at her. She quickly pulled her axes and charged forward, while blocking the spears. Danaaa and the Ra Warlords bolted forward to catch up with La. A split second later, so did Dan and Don.

The Ra never made it to where the girl and the other Anduku were standing. Anduku warriors poured around their leaders and attacked the Ra. The Ra chopped and slashed their way through the warriors for close to an hour before the Anduku warriors moved back.

La could see the female Anduku staring at her. La yelled to her "You didn't think those warriors would be enough to stop us, did you? It's only a matter of time before I get to you! And when I do, you'll wish I hadn't!"

The look on the female Anduku's face was still angry, but not as confident as before. She stared at La for a moment and then said "Alright, something else!"

Right after the girl said that, twelve Shinmushee Butchers walked up. They had metal sound reflecting shields in one hand and axes in the other. La knew if she screamed the sound would reflect back on them, possibly disorienting the three Ra Warlords. She didn't have long to think about that, because six of the Shinmushee Butchers attacked, immediately. The other six Butchers moved into positions, trying to catch the Ra unprotected.

La saw that the only advantage she had was that she had two axes and a ponytail, to the Butchers one axe and a shield. La was very crafty. She baited the Butcher by spinning one quick revolution to the right and then sending both her axes to the right side of the Butcher's body, while the metal ball at the end of her ponytail went flying around the left side at his head. Because of the angle of La's axes, the Butcher had to use his shield to block the ponytail. He avoided the inside swing of La's ax, while blocking the outside ax with his own.

The Butcher countered off La's swing and sent his ax crossways at her chest. La flipped her entire body over his swinging ax, slicing into his arm, while the subtle movement of her head sent her metal ball rocketing at his skull. He managed to avoid the metal ball, just as La's feet were hitting the ground and her axes were already moving towards him on his right side. The Butcher masterfully blocked both axes in one swing, but was hit on the side of his neck with La's metal ball.

Seeing that when she was on his side, she had the advantage of having two axes and a metal ball going against one ax, that's where La stayed. She ran and positioned herself, while the Butcher tried to turn in order to have his body squared up so he could use both his arms for battle. However, La was really fast and attacked quickly, as soon as she had the advantage. She'd managed to slice the Butcher up pretty good, before two more attacked her from her right side and from behind her.

Danaaa was using the same tactics La was using, but with much more efficiency. That got her triple teamed a few seconds, before La. Once Bo saw La was being triple teamed, he forced his fight towards her, as did the other two Ra Warlords. The three Ra warlords were immediately double-teamed.

Meanwhile, La was dancing, dodging and swinging her axes for all they were worth. Normally, La would slack on her defense, to get to a better offensive option. This time she couldn't. Every time La avoided one ax, she had to look for and avoid several more. She was still managing to send her ponytail rocketing at the Butchers, keeping them somewhat on guard.

Then, without warning, La felt a powerful tug on her scalp. That could only mean one thing. Someone had her ponytail! La managed to keep her balance and fight as she felt another strong pull on her scalp. She knew the Butcher who had her ponytail was somehow wrapping it up, pulling it and moving closer to her from behind.

Before she anticipated the next strong tug on her scalp, La took a step backwards, while plunging both her axes behind her, hoping she'd hit pay dirt. She knew she had when she felt both her axes slow down from the resistance on slicing into flesh. La instantly pulled her axes back forward, as she ducked under a swing from an ax that would have taken her head off, at the neck.

La sent both her axes backwards and over her shoulders back into the Butcher behind her. Again, she felt her axes go into and then come out of flesh. Still, the Butcher behind La refused to let go of her ponytail.

La had to take a step back, because the Butcher behind her had wrapped up her hair to where she was leaning back against him. La panicked. She could see the other two Butchers moving fast into position with axes swinging at her.

La moved out of the way of the first axe as it went by her and into the Butcher behind her. She blocked down hard, with both axes, blocking the swing from the other Butcher. Then came another swing that La had to avoid by lifting her entire body over the axe, using her head and neck muscles to raise herself. That's when the Butcher holding La's ponytail succumbed to his wounds and fell to his knees. La was bent backwards from his weight, before she used her neck and leg muscles to lift up the Butcher behind her and stabilize herself. She had to avoid swings by both attacking Butchers.

The Butcher who had La's ponytail wrapped around his arm slumped towards the ground, only being partially held up by the strength of La's neck muscles. La used her legs and neck muscles to stand and hold up the weight of the dead Butcher behind her. Now La was grounded and couldn't run. There was no way she could stand up to the power of these two Butchers swinging their axes at her.

La saw the first of two swings coming at her. Both were powerful enough that she would have to use both her axes just to block one. La decided she wasn't going to die from the first one and sold out, blocking it down into the dirt on her right side. La knew her left side was exposed. So, at the same time she tried to move her neck out of the way and hoped the ax coming at her, wouldn't hit a vital organ.

Then came the violent clang of axes on her left side. Someone saved La from being split open. La recovered enough to protect herself from another powerful swing. Then she felt the weight of the man holding her ponytail reduced to almost nothing.

Now La was able to maneuver. La danced out of the way of two more axes coming at her. She swung her ponytail around and saw it still had the man's entire arm, up to his shoulder, attached to her ponytail. Someone managed to hack it off. La beat the Butcher with that severed arm attached to her ponytail, until blood got in his eye. In that split second that he couldn't see, La split him open several times over.

When she was done, La quickly looked around. She saw Ram and Don finishing off a Butcher, while Yin was helping Ali, and Hoban finish off another two Butchers.

Another volley of spears came and all of them were blocked. After that, another group of warriors attacked. After close to an hour, they disappeared back into the tall thick bushes.

Dan looked at Don, who had barely held his own, in a hellish battle with a Shinmushee Butcher, earlier, before Yin and Ram arrived to help. Don's eyes were still blazed with adrenaline, mixed with the stress from the intensity of the continuous battles.

Dan walked over to Don and put his hand on Don's shoulder. Dan gave Don a reassuring look, before saying, "You did good! No one said it would be easy. Just concentrate on technique and stay sharp. That's how we make it through these battles."

Don nodded that he understood Dan. Although, Dan's words calmed Don a little, he was still on edge and stressed, after quite a few life threatening close calls with a Shinmushee Butcher. Dan looked at Yin and Ram. They were high from battle, but didn't seem as affected as Don did. Don walked over to Yin and Ram. Dan saw that Danaaa was all right, so he went to check on La.

La saw Dan quickly making his way over to her. La felt someone else moving towards her from behind and quickly swung her axes around. She stopped her axes a foot away from Bo's neck.

Bo moved closer to La with a concerned look on his face. He checked her for wounds. After not seeing any visible wounds,

Bo stared down into La's eyes and said "My deepest apologies for getting over to you so late. Next time I'll do better, protecting you. Are you harmed, at all?"

La didn't answer. Instead, she just stared at Bo. She realized it was Bo that saved her life, earlier. Her mind raced back to the fear she felt when La was sure she'd be split open.

After seeing La in a half trance, Bo moved closer and put his arms around La for support. La's arms dropped to her sides and she all but melted into Bo's arms. La still hadn't spoken, or stopped looking into Bo's eyes.

In an instant, La felt Bo's arm quickly release from around her. She stumbled a little, until she got her footing. Dan had snatched Bo's arm from around La and was staring angrily at Bo. Danaaa was also standing there with her arms folded staring at Bo. La was so caught up she didn't even see where Danaaa came from.

Dan strongly ordered, "They seemed to have retreated back into the bushes! You'd already know that if you weren't over here playing around! Now, go check the perimeter!"

Bo lowered his head and then did as ordered. Dan slowly turned to La, indicting her with a hard stare. La innocently said, "You told him to protect me, at all cost! When he does, you scold him! I just don't get it!"

Dan looked from La to Danaaa. Danaaa was unwrapping the severed arm from La's ponytail. When Danaaa was done, she showed La the arm, before tossing it to the ground. La said, "That was a close call."

Danaaa got a sad look on her face and said in her low voice "Yeah, but I would have gotten there sooner if that less than Shitmushee hadn't cut open the pocket on my vest holding my cookies. I caught all but two of them, before they could fall to the ground. The two Shitmushee that were trying to chop me trampled the two that fell on the ground. After I secured my cookies in another pocket, I chopped those two to pieces. After that is when I came and helped you!"

La couldn't believe what she'd just heard. La's face got angry and her lip was crooked on one side, when she said "You were worried about cookies, when I could have been killed?!"

Danaaa curiously looked at La's lip as she said, "You couldn't have been killed because you're here, now!"

Danaaa had barely gotten the last word out of her mouth, before her head was twisted to the left, from a lightning fast backhand slap from La. Danaaa's hand quickly moved to her face, as her head jerked back around towards La.

In that same instant, Danaaa hit La with a lightning fast open hand slap. That was immediately followed up by another lightning fast slap from La to Danaaa's face.

Danaaa took one stomping step towards La and then balled her fist up at her sides. La stared a dare at Danaaa. Dan quickly stepped forward in between is sisters and said "That's enough you two! We already have enough problems as it is! It's getting close to dark. We have to find a safe place to camp for the night."

Dan looked at both of his sisters, who hadn't moved an inch. Danaaa whispered while staring at La "You're still here, but those two cookies are gone, forever!"

Dan grabbed Danaaa's arm and said, "Forget about those cookies! They'll be others, once we get home!" Danaaa solemnly said, "Not like those, there won't." Dan said, "You're so Stupid! I don't even know why I try to talk to you!"

La turned away from Dan and Danaaa. She could feel where Danaaa's hand hit her face. Danaaa's slap was light and harmless, but the damage had already been done. La was going to wait for the right time and make Baby pay dearly for that!

Dan looked away from Danaaa and saw Don, Ram and Yin staring at him. Dan calmed himself. He said "It's a good thing you two showed up when you did. Where were you, anyway?"

Yin's eyes lit up with excitement. He said "We were . . . .!" then Ram's head jerked around and he gave Yin a stare that everyone saw. Yin knew Ram was staring at him, but Yin wouldn't look at Ram. He knew Ram didn't want him to tell about their top-secret mission. Yin said, "We were thinking you might need help, so we waited and caught them by surprise!"

Dan and La looked at Yin and then at Ram. They knew they weren't going to get any more information, but didn't care. As long as Ram kept showing up in time to help, that was all that mattered.

The Ra were viciously attacked for three more days, almost nonstop. The attacks would only stop at night, but would resume early when next day came. On the third night, the Ra and their Warlords were tired and hungry. The last of their food was gone and they were at least a half days journey back to the caravan.

They were also dirty from sweat to the point that they could smell themselves. It didn't bother the Ra boys that much, but this was the first time that La and Danaaa had gone this long without bathing. Before this, they'd not gone a half day without bathing. That put the Ra girls' nerves on edge.

CHAPTER 21

It was a star filled clear night and the sky was a deep rich blue. The moon was three quarters full and gave half decent lighting. Every few minutes a breeze would push by, rustling the leaves in the trees they were sitting next to. Everyone appreciated those timely breezes.

Dan and the others were sitting near a fallen tree stump that was wedged against a tall tree. La sat next to Dan. She was irritated by everyone's smell, including her own. She looked at Danaaa, who'd walked over by the Ra Warlords, guarding the perimeter of this small camp. Torches lit the perimeter of the camp. Once in a while Danaaa would let out a short sharp sheik. It kept the predators rattled. That and the torches kept animals away from the camp. They could still hear the sounds of different animals, in the distance.

La was hurt that Danaaa would leave her in peril, while she secured cookies. That's what La got from what Danaaa said. However, Danaaa didn't explain herself, correctly. Once, Danaaa perceived La was in danger, she rushed over to help.

When Danaaa had her pocket sliced open and went after the Shinmushee Butchers, it was before the Butcher grabbed La's ponytail. Since La didn't know that, she was harboring bad feelings towards Danaaa.

Danaaa was over by Hoban on the perimeter of the camp. She sniffed the air several times, before going over to where Ali and Bo were station and doing the same thing. Once Danaaa was sure she didn't smell trouble she turned towards her siblings.

When Danaaa turned around, she saw Ram, Don and Yin talking. Dan was sitting, leaning against a tree looking at her. To Danaaa, Dan looked tired and like he was thinking about something. She knew she'd never figure out what, so Danaaa looked down at La. La was lying across Dan's leg, on her side, propping her head up with her hand, staring at Danaaa.

Happy that there wasn't any smell of danger, Danaaa had a smile on her face when she and La locked eyes. Danaaa stopped in her tracks. The smile quickly left Danaaa's face, when she saw La staring angrily at her. Danaaa could feel La's anger and wondered why it was directed at her. That made Danaaa pause for a moment. Then Danaaa thought back to the day's earlier events to see if she could determine why La was looking at her in anger.

Danaaa's mind went back to when the Shinmushee Butchers attacked them. The Shinmushee Butcher that attacked her looked mean and nasty to her. He also smelled like old sweat, mixed with dried bile. Danaaa was appalled. If this man wasn't going to try to clean himself, he deserved to die.

That's when the Butchers axes came at Danaaa. Adrenaline surged through her body as she barely avoided a couple of well-placed ax swings. Now, with adrenaline pumping through her body, Danaaa started seeing everything moving in slow motion, even though she wasn't.

Danaaa countered and played with the Butcher to the point that another Butcher also attacked Danaaa. Even though they looked to be moving in slow motion, they were good enough that Danaaa had to concentrate on not getting cut. Finally, one Butcher trapped Danaaa and when she barely avoided him, the other one was close enough that the edge of his blade lightly sliced across her vest, splitting it open.

While avoiding a return ax swing, two cookies fell to the ground. They were trample under foot, in the heat of the battle. Danaaa wasn't going to let that happen to the others. She caught the remaining five cookies, while avoiding the two Butchers ax swings.

The two Butchers were so amazed by that they looked at each other, before attacking, again. That was all the time Danaaa needed. She quickly stuffed the other cookies in another vest pocket. Once she'd done that, Danaaa attacked.

This time she wasn't the girl avoiding swings from axes. She was coming forward, right in the path of the axes, moving at the last moment, counter-attacking with great accuracy. Danaaa quickly polished off those Butchers. That's when Danaaa turned and saw a Butcher grabbing La's ponytail. Danaaa charged towards La, but was intercepted by a Butcher, swinging his axes at her.

Danaaa carved this Butcher to pieces, with some nifty counter-attack moves. When she was done, she saw La's ponytail was wrapped almost up to her head. Danaaa raced to help La. She saw Bo moving in front of La blocking several swings from axes. That's when Danaaa jumped in the air and came down with all her might, slicing her axe through the shoulder of the man holding La's ponytail.

Danaaa's mind went to La not appreciating her help and slapping Danaaa across her face. With all the reflecting Danaaa had done, she still couldn't figure out why La would do such a thing. So, guess what? Now, Danaaa was angry, too!

Danaaa walked angrily towards La. Danaaa announced in her loud angry voice "I'm tired and I need sleep!" La glared at Danaaa and said "Well, don't come over here!" even though both La and Danaaa knew that's exactly where Danaaa was headed.

Dan pulled hard on La's ponytail. La jumped and turned, all in one motion, facing Dan giving him an angry look. Normally, the only two men allowed touching La's ponytail, and live to tell about it, were Elder Dan and young Dan. However, after having her tail wrapped up earlier, La was sensitive to anyone touching her ponytail, right now.

Dan saw all that in La's eyes. He didn't want things to escalate out here, so he said "Queen Ramala, get a hold of yourself! There's no time for foolishness! If we get off track, we might not make it home!"

La stared at Dan for a moment. She said "Fine!" then La jumped to her feet. Dan said "La!" La looked back at Dan and said, "I'm going to check the perimeter! I'll be back, shortly!"

La started walking away. Danaaa went to follow. La stopped, turned and went on guard. Dan ordered, saying "Stupid, get over here and lay down!" Danaaa looked at La for a split second then turned and looked at Dan. Dan yelled "Now!" Danaaa stared into Dan's eyes. He looked serious, so Danaaa slowly moved towards him and got down on the ground next to him. She turned on her side and stared at La.

Before La could stop herself, her feet started moving her towards Bo, because that's where she wanted to go. La knew Dan was watching her. She could feel it. Therefore, La walked over to Ali, first. She talked to him, while stealthily peeking at Bo and spying to see if Dan was watching her.

Then La went over to Hoban and repeated the same dance. After that, La walked over to Bo. Bo saw La coming over and knew this meant trouble from Dan. He refused to look at La. La knew Bo saw her coming over to him, but still he wouldn't look at her. That bothered La a little. When she got to Bo, La stayed a respectable distance as not to provoke Dan.

Whenever La got around Bo, there were so many thoughts in her head that she would get confused about what she wanted to say. There were the things she wanted to say but couldn't. Then, there were the things she was supposed to say, but didn't feel it was enough.

La went to her safe place of giving orders, so as not to look as weak for Bo as she felt on the inside. La arrogantly said, "I expect this area is secure." Bo said "Yes, my Queen, no signs of trouble." La said, with less arrogance in her voice "That was good work earlier this day."

Bo didn't look at La when he said "Next time I'll do better, my Queen." The fact that Bo saved La's life and still thought he should have done better fueled the fire of La's crush on Bo. Before La could stop herself, her heart melted and she said in the softest voice Bo had ever heard come from La "I know you will."

Bo was caught off guard by La's soft voice and the tenderness in it. Bo turned his head and looked at La. As soon as he did, he felt heat on the side of his face that he knew had to be Dan staring at him. Bo quickly turned his head back towards the darkness, beyond the campfire.

La saw Bo's reaction. She felt they made a special connection at that moment, but knew Dan was watching. Even though she didn't want to, La walked away from Bo and over to where Dan was. La decided she was going to play nice with Dan to get him to ease up, when she was around Bo.

La only looked at Dan for a moment, before looking at Danaaa. La moved behind Danaaa and got close to her. La threw the end of her ponytail over Danaaa. Danaaa grabbed it and closed her eyes. La grabbed Danaaa's ponytail and wrapped that same arm around Danaaa. Dan relaxed and thought it was about time La listened to his reasoning. La's move calmed Danaaa and put Dan's mind at ease, just as La planned.

La had only been there with Danaaa for a few moments, before she noticed Danaaa was squirming. La thought Danaaa was having a bad dream, so she rubbed Danaaa's shoulder, trying to soothe Danaaa. After a few moments more, Danaaa sat up. La quickly sat up and reached for her ax, all in one motion. La looked in Danaaa's eyes, waiting for Danaaa to reveal the danger.

Dan and the other Ra boys all grabbed their axes and looked around the camp. Ram slowly got up and looked at Danaaa without touching his axes. Yin noticed that and thought it strange.

A moment later La caught a scent. She grabbed Danaaa by her shoulders and looked her square in her eyes. La sternly whispered "Food! Is that what this is all about?!"

Danaaa's eyes were glazed over with moisture. She frantically whispered to La "But, I know somebody's eating a good meal, when we're not! I just know it!"

La angrily said, "I told you to eat bugs and shrubs! That should hold you over, until we can find food! Don't you think I'm hungry, too? Right now, we're in survival mode, so toughen up and get with it!"

Danaaa squinted her eyes and said, "So, you want me to toughen up, huh? Alright then, I'll show you tough!"

Dan couldn't believe his eyes. Did either of his sisters think he was going to put up with this nonsense out in the field, at night?

Dan warned both his sisters who were facing each other. Danaaa said, while looking into La's eyes "I smell Shit." La could smell herself, but didn't think it warranted Danaaa's description. La said "It must be you, because it's not me!"

Danaaa got a confused look on her face then sternly whispered "But I didn't say I smelled you, I smell Shit!" as she pointed towards the darkness. La curiously looked where Danaaa was pointing. A moment or so later, La smelled a vile odor and knew where it was coming from. La looked Danaaa in her eyes and said, "It's Little Shit!" Danaaa immediately said "But, I already told you that!"

Everyone stood and watched the darkness, until their eyes began to water. They pinned their noses and began to breathe out of their mouths. Shortly after that, out of the darkness appeared Little Shit, the Chusee Two, Anne and the Behemoth. After that, Six Elite Ra Guards appeared, carrying large containers of fresh water and food.

Anne bolted past everyone, until she got to Ram. Ram was a second away from pulling his ax, but decided to give Anne the benefit of the doubt. Anne stopped on a dime in front of Ram. They both stared at each other for a moment, before Anne pulled out a cookie. She said, "Here, take this." as she handed it to Ram. Ram snatched it and shoved most of the cookie into his mouth, as Danaaa stared in wonderment, at the cookie she would never have.

Anne said, "I thought you might need that. What have you been doing? I know, there's no telling. Shaya made us bring food. It was scary coming all this way. I don't know how Cha and Dee (The Chusee Two) knew where to find you, but they did. Neither Man, nor beast came close enough to bother us, thanks too little Shit." Anne continued talking Ram's ear off, while he watched the others Anne came with.

The Behemoth was carrying two huge sacks full of food. He sat one sack on the ground, while shielding the other sack with his tree trunk of an arm. La wondered if she ordered the Behemoth to drop the other sack, would he fight to the finish, before doing so.

La and everyone else was shocked back to reality when the Ra, Chamany Choppers, or Cha started spraying her report, indiscriminately. Besides the spray, every word that came out of Cha's mouth was accompanied by the sound of her teeth chattering like a typewriter, as the top ones violently slammed into the bottom ones.

Her brother, the Ra, Lookatdeese Choppers, or Dee, sprayed his comments between her sentences. His teeth, much bigger than his sister's, made an even louder chattering noise. The sight of the two of them were so appalling that the usually quiet Ram pulled his axes, pointed one at them and said in a booming deep voice "I'm taking their heads!"

Anne put her hand on Ram's ax handle, lightly forcing it down. She said, "Don't harm them. If it wasn't for them, I wouldn't have been able to give you that cookie. You know I made it myself. You did like it, didn't you?"

Ram slowly turned and looked at Anne. He nodded that he indeed enjoyed that cookie. With that, the Chusee two were safe, for the moment. Ram was lost in another round of Anne's nonstop rambling.

Although, horrific to watch, La, Dan and the Ra Warlords had to admit that the Chusee Two were a wealth of information. They told of all enemy positions around the Ra. Cha told La that Shaya had large numbers of Elite guards and regular Guards brought from Yee and Wa province to strengthen her position at the caravan, to better support the Ra's advanced force. Cha also said Shaya sent them with food, because she was worried that she hadn't heard word from Dan, or La.

When they were done, La almost stopped herself from asking, because of another round of chattering and spraying, but she had to know. La asked "And what of Shaya? How is she doing?"

Immediately, both of the Chusee Two went to their knees and said, spraying saliva into the dirt "We dare not say?"

Just as La was about to question them further, Anne said, "She's toying with the guards" La said "I can see that much! She's been giving them orders, without consulting me!" Anne gave La a curious look, because she didn't think La understood what she meant.

Dan, who was inspecting the food, said, "It's a good thing she didn't consult you. Otherwise, we wouldn't have this food." La had to admit to herself that Dan was right, so she let that go, for now.

After a good meal that night, early in the next day, before sunrise, Danaaa woke up before everyone. She lightly removed La's arm from around her and then carefully released her ponytail from La's grip. Danaaa looked down at La to make sure she hadn't awakened La.

After that, Danaaa looked at everyone else, seeing that they were still sleep. She then walked to the perimeter of the camp where she saw Ali, on guard. Ali turned to see Danaaa stealthily walking towards him. Danaaa put her finger up to her lips, warning Ali not to say a word. When Danaaa got close enough to where only Ali could hear her, she whispered "I'm going to kill enemies of the Ra. Follow me not, nor tell them that Danaaa has left, until well after she is gone. No one will witness what I shall do."

On many occasions, Danaaa had come to Ali and talked strangely to him, in the third partly, like this. Ali did as he'd always done. He listened, followed instructions and then told the other Ra that Danaaa had left, well after she was gone.

Hoban, Bo and the Elite guards were still sleeping. Ali was the only one to see Danaaa leave. Shortly after Danaaa left, Ali woke Hoban and Bo. He immediately told them what happened. Hoban went over to Dan and La. They both jumped to attention, upon hearing footsteps coming towards them.

After seeing Hoban, La realized Danaaa wasn't there. La quickly jumped up and looked around. She looked at Dan and said frantically "Baby's gone! We have to find her, now!"

Hoban looked at Ali. Ali asked for permission to speak. Once given permission, he told La Danaaa left a short while ago. After Ali was done, La could see he had mixed feelings. La assumed Danaaa probably threatened Ali. La stared at Ali for a moment and then quickly reached for her axes. She said "Any time Baby leaves without my permission, I expect you'll tell me, immediately. We have to find her, right away. If she's harmed, I blame you!"

La turned her back to Ali and looked at Dan who was getting Don, Yin and Ram, as well as the others, ready to go. A little later, Dan went over to Ali and gave him a reassuring look. Dan said, "La's just concerned. She'll be alright when we find Baby." As soon as they were ready, the Ra went in the direction where Ali saw Danaaa go.

Meanwhile, Danaaa moved quietly towards the enemy positions, ahead of her. When she came out of the Forrest, to a clearing, she could see a Shinmushee camp. A few Shinmushee warriors saw Danaaa, just as she saw them.

To Danaaa, it looked like they'd just finished a first day's meal. Some of them still had the fruit they were eating in their hands. Danaaa looked at the fruit, thinking they were lucky to have a meal, because she hadn't, even though she wasn't hungry, yet.

The Shinmushee warriors quickly looked behind Danaaa at the tree line she'd come out of. They were trying to see where the other Ra were. After realizing Danaaa was alone, one of the warriors alerted the others, who hadn't seen Danaaa. Another warrior asked Danaaa "Who the Hell are you? And you've come here, for what?"

Danaaa had never stopped moving forward from the time she came out of the trees. She pulled her axes. Now, she was almost in striking range. Danaaa said, "It's Dan Jinn-Eco! She's the Immaculate Degenerate, High Pressure the Executioner, but I Chop I! She's here to collect Shitmushee heads! Why else would we be here?"

Confused only for a second by the way the young girl was talking, the Shinmushee warriors found her words offensive. They quickly pulled their axes, moving into position to attack. Once they had their axes, was when Danaaa reached the first Shinmushee warriors.

When Danaaa got within three yards of the Shinmushee warriors, she charged at them, with both axes in hand, as fast as she could. Danaaa managed to kill over thirty Shinmushee warriors, before seven Shinmushee Butchers showed up and watched her for a moment. After that, they attacked.

As Danaaa was slaughtering the Shinmushee warriors, she saw their Butchers watching her. She thought that if they were going to just watch her kill their warriors, she was fine with that. Nevertheless, it seemed just as she finished off most off their warriors the Butchers attacked her.

Danaaa concentrated as the four Butchers attacked her. Her field vision helped her keep an eye on the other three that were close by spying and waiting on the chance to strike. As always, when Danaaa's Jinn was with her, she saw everything moving in slow motion.

Even with that, these Shinmushee Butchers were putting enough heat on Danaaa with their axes that she had to be very careful to make the right decisions in avoiding the continuous ax swings coming at her. Occasionally the three Butchers spying on Danaaa would take a swing at her, barely missing her.

Danaaa wasn't strong enough to block axes from men as strong as these, without leaving herself venerable to them bullying her through the manipulation of her axes. Danaaa had to purely rely on dodging and avoiding ax contact, at all cost. Still, even though she couldn't mount an effective counter-attack, Danaaa managed to get a non-lethal slice in on the Butchers here and there.

After about twenty more minutes of fighting, the Shinmushee Butchers stopped attacking. They stared at Danaaa in disbelief that she hadn't been cut to pieces, yet. They circled and watched Danaaa closely, looking for anything they could take advantage of. While they were doing so, Danaaa slowly turned with them, intently watching their every move, while on guard with her axes.

Danaaa smiled and then her eyes darted past the Butchers, before staring back at them. All of the Butchers noticed that and a couple of them looked in the direction they saw Danaaa looking. They didn't see anything, so they focused back on Danaaa. A couple of seconds later, they heard the clanging of axes in the distance and knew there was a battle nearby. A second later, all seven Shinmushee Butchers attacked Danaaa. Danaaa did everything she could not to get cut well!

When the seven Butchers attacked Danaaa, the voice in her head told her to do exactly what it said. Her voice told her move by move how to avoid the first two axes coming at her. Danaaa then moved towards three more axes, only to be told to jump up and over the Butchers in a tight ball with her axes at her sides.

Danaaa felt the pressure from powerful ax swings pounding off her axes on both side of her body. As soon as the Butchers axes moved from hers, Danaaa swung her axes outwards as hard and fast as she could. She felt the resistance of flesh, just before she landed.

Danaaa then dived to her left, straight into a tuck and roll, again, barely avoiding being sliced open. After coming out of the roll, instead of standing up as usual, Danaaa reversed the tuck, roll, and started swinging her axes, slicing open one Butcher's thigh and another one's stomach.

Danaaa stayed close to the last three Shinmushee Butchers sprinting circles around them, while slicing and dicing them, here and there. The three Butchers swung wildly trying to hit their target, but failed miserably, because of Danaaa's quickness. After Danaaa finished off the last Butcher, she watched him as he fought to breathe. While watching Danaaa stare at him, the Butcher took a few more breaths. Just before he took his last breath, Danaaa looked down and whispered to him "But I already told you, I can swing an Ax, real fast! I Chop I!" Danaaa turned around to see the Ra staring at her in disbelief.

When the Ra and their Warlords finally made it to where Danaaa was they saw her masterfully carving up the last two Shinmushee Butchers. The Ra knew they were Butchers because of the way they were dressed. The Ra were frozen still, watching in awe of Danaaa's skills. They didn't move, until she turned and looked at them. That's when La bolted over to Danaaa.

When La got over to Danaaa, she frantically looked Danaaa over for signs of wounds. Danaaa said in a voice that La didn't quite recognize "She's unharmed."

La quickly looked into Danaaa's eyes. La was startled and jumped back, because she saw eyes that weren't Danaaa's looking at her. La screamed, "Baby, what's wrong with you!" in that same instant, Danaaa's eyes changed back to the eyes La knew. With concern in her voice, La yelled "What just happened?!"

Danaaa curiously looked at La and said, "I killed some Shitmushee Butchers and warriors that would have killed Don, if I hadn't got them, first."

La said, "How do you know that?" Danaaa said, "I just knew it! That's why I told myself to come here. Then I said some really funny things. I almost laughed, but I told myself not to. After that, I told myself how to chop them up good! I Chop, I Chop, I Chop I . . . ."

Dan said, "Alright, I Chop I, you did good work here." Dan looked around for a moment. Danaaa said, "I know where more of them are!" Dan said, "Good, lead the way!"

(HAPTER 22

That day the Ra surprised the Anduku and Shinmushee by slaughtering them in droves. The seven Shinmushee Butchers and their warriors, that Danaaa killed, had moved ahead of the other Shinmushee forces to attempt a sneak attack on the Ra.

The day before, they had identified Don as the weakest fighter for the Ra. They were going to attack with their warriors and separate Don, attacking him with two Butchers. They knew they could kill him in that scenario, and probably would have.

However, Danaaa's Jinn-Eco knew this and sent Danaaa to destroy them. Besides being the Executioner for the Ra, Danaaa was also High Pressure the Executioner for the Jinn-Eco.

Later that night, after the Ra went to sleep, Ram stealthily got up. He looked at each of his brothers and La, before looking at Yin. Yin thought he heard Ram's voice and slowly opened his eyes to see Ram looking down at him. It startled Yin on the inside, but he tried not to let Ram see it.

Ram put his finger up to his lips to let Yin know to be quiet. Then Ram motioned for Yin to come with him. Yin quietly got his axes. He looked at La and Dan. They were deep in sleep. Ram grabbed Yin and motioned for him to follow.

Ram and Yin went to the perimeter of the camp, where Hoban and the six Elite Guards were posted. They turned and looked at Ram and Yin. Ram looked at each of them. Everyone knew Ram as the accepted serial killer in the House of Ra. Even though he was a young teenager, you really didn't want to get on Ram's bad side. That means never questioning Ram. Heck, you hoped he didn't know you existed!

Hoban and the Elite Guards all lowered their heads. They waited until Ram and Yin was gone, before raising their heads. Hoban and the Elite Guards went back to watching and protecting the Ra.

At first Yin didn't say anything. He just followed Ram, happy that Ram invited him on one of his secret missions. After walking a short distance, in the pitch black of night, Yin knew Ram wasn't going to offer up any information, so Yin said, "I know we're probably going to kill some . . . ."

Ram abruptly stopped, turned and stared intensely at Yin. Ram slowly put his finger up to his lips, again, without taking his eyes from Yin's eyes. Yin nodded slowly that he got it. Ram turned and started walking, again.

Ram would stop and make Yin stand in a certain place. Yin would do it, only to see something dangerous, like a leopard, lions, or a pack of hyenas passing downwind of them. The predators never even knew they were there. Yin was astounded that Ram always knew where these animals were coming from.

They traveled a short distance further, before Ram stopped. Even though it was pitch black, Yin's eyes had adjusted and he could see things close to him. Ram grabbed Yin by his shoulders and positioned him where he wanted him to stand. Ram whispered, "Stand right here. Don't move from this spot. I'll be back." Yin knew three whole sentences, from Ram, meant this was important. Still, Yin asked, "What if you need my help? How will I know when to come?" Ram whispered back "You won't know. Just stay here. If not, it will be your own doing. I'll be back when I'm done."

Yin thought, 'Four sentences. Ram must really trust me!' Yin watched as Ram moved towards the light of the enemy torches. Soon Ram disappeared into the darkness. Yin stood there watching. He saw darkness appear were there was light from torches. He heard warriors frantically calling and yelling to each other. Then more torches went out, until all Yin could see was darkness where he knew the enemy camp was.

Seconds later, Yin heard the most blood curdling yells form warriors and guards that he knew Ram was slaughtering. The yells and screams were mixed in with clanging of weapons and the frantic calls from the enemy warriors.

Yin was nervous and felt he had to do something. He went on guard, raising both his axes and wildly looking around. Yin didn't want to just stand there, not knowing if Ram needed his help. It was a hellish forty-five minutes for Yin, until, all of a sudden, the yelling stopped and there was complete silence.

Yin hadn't moved an inch, but the silence had him shaking, nervously. He stood there not knowing what to do. Then a hand touched his shoulder. Yin swung his ax around, determined to meet the threat. Ram avoided several swings from Yin and then said "It's me, Ram!" After seeing the startled look on Yin's face, Ram started laughing in a sinister bass. Yin stopped swinging his ax as he watched Ram laugh. Yin nervously chuckled as he watched his cousin. Yin thought 'So, this is Ram!'

Earlier, after leaving Yin standing at the spot he designated, Ram headed towards the enemy camp. He saw several warriors and knew where the warriors were that he couldn't see. Ram moved near the torches, but out of sight of the enemy warriors. Ram picked up two rocks. He threw them, one at a time at the torches, knocking them over. The guard nearest the first torch found himself in almost complete darkness. Before his eyes could adjust, he was split open about the neck and chest. He managed to yell out for help. While warriors were checking on him, Ram ran towards the other torches. He managed to put out two more torches.

Ram attacked in the darkness, taking the heads clean off several more warriors, with surprisingly powerful and deadly accurate swings of his axes. Now the whole camp was aware that they were under attack. They all grabbed their weapon. Some of them searched the area, while others moved to protect the remaining torches. Ram threw rocks that knocked over two more torches, while a sudden strong wind that seemed to come out of nowhere, blew out the other torches.

Once there was complete darkness, Ram started chopping up the warriors that were near him. Some of the warriors killed each other in the panic of trying to protect themselves. Ram polished off the rest of them. Ram killed sixty warriors in a half hour. In the darkness, Ram saw four Shinmushee Butchers standing with their backs to each other, on guard.

Ram moved close to them without making a sound. Once he was close enough, Ram slammed his axes down, slicing through both thighs of one of the Butchers. That Butcher yelled out in pain, while the other Butchers swung their axes where they thought the intruder was. But Ram was not there. He had moved and was now behind one of the other Butchers. Ram drove his ax through that Butcher's back and into his heart. That Butcher immediately fell to the ground. Ram sliced up the other two Butchers that where trying to locate him in the darkness. After he was done, Ram made his way over to Yin.

Ram and Yin made it back to camp, pretty much in the same way they came. Ram led the way and warned Yin of danger, until they made it back to their camp. Yin fell asleep shortly after that.

The reason Ram was able to kill and not get caught, or even detected is the same reason that most serial killers aren't caught and get away for long periods of time. Serial killers have been studied for centuries. When most are discovered, they are found to have only marginal intelligence. So why do they go completely undetected for so long, before being caught?

Well, I'll only say this. A lot of serial killers, but not all, hear a voice in their head that they sometimes mistake for their own. It tells them exactly what to do in certain scenarios. When the serial killer does exactly what the voice inside their head tells them to do, they are virtually undetectable and unstoppable. They kill it seems, indiscriminately, without being caught.

The reason some serial killers are caught is that after a while they think that it's them and want recognition for what they've done. In other words, they think they're smart and are in fact outsmarting everyone, when they're really not.

Some of them start to leave clues, or even figure they can plan random acts on their own. That usually leads to them being caught.

(Now, don't go getting any ideas. This is just a fictional account created in order to make the story more interesting.) Besides, I was told to say this, because it fits into the story I'm telling . . . . Just kidding!

The Shinmushee Butchers now knew they had a problem that had to be dealt with. It was the two youngest Ra twins. Most of them hadn't seen them and didn't even know what they looked like, except from scouting reports.

Early one morning, they were discussing their options. They knew it would be tough, but didn't think it would be impossible. They continued discussing how they would proceed. Then, it seemed like out of nowhere, there was a commotion in the distance. That commotion was followed by clanging of axes and a few blood-curdling screams.

The Shinmushee Butchers quickly stood up. They only looked at each other for a moment, before heading in the direction of the perceived battle. They trotted at a fast pace, until they came upon the scene. They saw about twenty or so dead Shinmushee warrior bodies strewn about the ground in this area. As they moved closer, they could see several Shinmushee warriors, who seemed to be trapped by one girl, who was saying something to them. The Butchers looked around and didn't see any other enemy combatants. They moved even closer. That's when the young girl looked in their direction.

The Shinmushee warriors who seemed to be trapped bolted in that very instant. Still, the Butchers, with axes in hand moved closer to the young girl. Her body, although it looked to be in good fighting condition, wasn't intimidating. They looked at her face. It was one of the strangest things they'd ever seen. Her eyes were glossed over with moisture, but no tears fell from them. Her lower lip hung crooked on one side and was shaking where it hung crooked. That's when they heard the young girl yelling "And that's when they killed Kitty! They killed Kitty! Why did they kill my Kitty?!"

As strange as this was to them, all of the Butchers continued to position themselves around this young girl. They hadn't seen a dead girl on the ground anywhere that they might have identified to be this girl's fallen comrade, named Kitty. They quickly let that go. They were going to give this girl a quick trip to Heaven. None of them said a word, except for one. He thought it would be fun to taunt the girl, before they killed her. He said "And now you're going to die, just like Kitty. Whoever, that is?"

Danaaa turned her head slightly in the direction of the Butcher who spoke. Even stranger than everything they'd seen up to this point, the moisture in the young girl's eyes seemed to disappear. Her eyes became, instantly, crystal clear. A second later, she attacked. She started with the Butcher who spoke and didn't stop, until all the Butchers were dead. Just as always, she left one with just enough life in him to witness what she had to say. The one spoke, out of line, about Kitty. The young girl said to him "Now, that was for Kitty! Remember this, I can swing an ax real fast! I Chop I!" after being cut to pieces, and hearing that, the man wondered 'Who was this Kitty she speaks of?' and then he fell over dead. The young girl quickly turned and then walked away.

CHAPTER 23

Every time, just before first day came, Danaaa would find attack and kill small groups of Shinmushee Butchers. Whenever they saw Danaaa coming, one of the warriors who could identify Danaaa would warn the others by pointing and then yelling "It's High Pressure the Executioner! Hammer-Axe Six!" That same warrior would flee the scene immediately and that's the only way he lived to tell about it.

Along with that, Ram would kill groups of warriors at night, with the help of his apprentice Yin. No matter the security precautions, Ram always found a way to complete his mission of taking out one enemy checkpoint a night. The early first day attacks by Danaaa and the night attacks by Ram wore heavily on the Shinmushee warriors, as well as the Anduku.

When the Ra saw that the Shinmushee and Anduku weren't attacking, but were now trying to strengthen their positions against attack, the Ra went on the offensive. La and Dan reasoned that if they caught up with and eliminated the Six Anduku that started this attack, they could get back to their main caravan. With the help of the Six Elite Guards, although everyday was a battle of life and death, the Ra pushed forward and put pressure on the Anduku.

Shaya pushed La's larger force into Anduku territory putting further pressure on the Anduku. Shaya established a messenger and supply line to Dan and La that kept them with fresh Elite Guards, water and food.

A couple more weeks went by and two of the six Anduku leaders surrendered and negotiated the surrender of two others. La wanted all of them beheaded, right away. Dan refused, citing that could possibly stir up more support for the two they were still hunting. La didn't agree, so Dan had to have the four Anduku prisoners sent to and put under Shaya's protection, until this campaign was over.

Shaya pushed hard into Anduku territory. She had most all of the Ra army under La's control occupying Anduku territory all the way to up the Main city, without entering it. La and Dan were now searching through the main city with their forces to no avail.

The occupation was so complete that the Hellcats found out and got a sketchy story of what was going on. Ramala demanded that the Hammer-Axe Six end the occupation and return to the main city to explain their actions to her.

Since one of the two they were searching for was the female who threatened her and Danaaa's life, La refused to back off. La figured she had time to make one last desperate move, before Ramala was fed up and came after them.

La ordered a meeting with the Young Anduku leaders that hadn't rebelled against her. Once they showed up, La had them detained and then called more Elite Guards into the main city to hold them. La told them that they had just one day to have their people bring the two Anduku to her, or they all would be beheaded when first day came.

The Anduku refused to help. Dan knew if they killed these young leaders, they would never have the support of any of the Anduku, young, or old. Therefore, after dinner, Dan had the young Leaders released. La was beside herself. La decided when first day came she was going to get results in her own way and told Dan as much. Dan tried to reason with La, but got nowhere.

Dan had his Warlord Bo and several of the Elite guards escort him as he went and told the young Anduku that when first day came, the young Queen was going to do something drastic that he probably wouldn't be able to stop. Dan said if there was any way to resolve this, by then, they should. Then he left.

Dan and La were debating on how they were going to deal with their mother about what they'd done. They decided they were going to pin it all on the Shinmushee and the rebelling young Anduku. Just before the Ra were getting ready to rest for the night, Ali said the Anduku wanted to talk about how they could resolve this situation. La told Ali that the Hammer-Axe Six would meet them.

The Hammer-Axe Six were surprised when they went to meet the Anduku. The seven Anduku leaders had the two rebelling Anduku leaders with them. The female had her hands and feet tied, restricting her movements. The male stood there with her of his own free will.

La motioned for her Elite Guards to take a hold of the two. Once they were secure in their hands, La walked closer and stared at them both.

Anger that they tried to hide was evident on both their faces. They refused to look at La. The female said in a low voice "Just kill me and get it over with!"

La's smile was crooked when she said, "I told you it would only be a matter of time before I got to you. Still, this is not about you. Never has been and never will be."

La turned her back to the female and said, "I'm going to rest well this night, so I can think how best to make you pay for what you've done. Take her out of my sight!"

Early, when next day came, Dan and La were informed by Ali that several groups of Anduku requested meetings with them. The groups of Anduku ranged from the Elders and Young Leaders to the Warlords and common folks.

Dan and La knew they wanted to plead for the lives of the two Anduku prisoners. Both also knew if they killed this girl, they would probably have to kill many more Anduku. That didn't matter to La, she refused to meet with the Anduku, until after she dealt with the two rebels. After a lengthy debate with Dan, La got her way. The only reason Dan gave in was the attempt on Shaya's life and the openly defiant attack on the Ra after that.

After first day's meal, the Hammer-Axe Six went to see the prisoners. They were followed by large groups of Anduku, who begged for the lives of the prisoners.

The Hammer-Axe Six had their Warlords and Elite Guards secure the perimeter of the building that held the prisoners, for privacy. Once inside, La motioned for the guards to untie the prisoners. She then had them both given two machetes, each.

La paced back and forth as she said "Normally, I would just have you beheaded and been done with you. Today, I've decided to let you die of your own accord. You now have the chance to kill as many of us as you can, in one on one battles, until you're killed, or you kill all of us. What more could you ask for?"

Dan watched the prisoners as La talked. If either of them made one false move, he knew the other Hammer-Axe Six would shred them to pieces.

La continued with "Tell me, which of you wants to go first and who would you like to fight?"

The Anduku male, who was nineteen, said "We didn't turn ourselves in to fight. We did it so no more Anduku blood would be spilled."

He threw both machetes on the floor, lowered his head and said, "Do what you will with us." The female hesitated and then threw her machetes on the floor.

La quickly drew her ax and swung it around the girl, without touching her. The girl never looked up at La. After seeing that, La turned, put her axes in their holsters and looked at Dan.

Dan took the hint, as La walked past him. Dan walked forward and sternly said, "I would be in my rights to take both your heads, but I won't, this time. Still, both of you are sentenced to hard labor, until I see fit to send you back to your people. If you can accept this sentence without reserve, your lives will be spared. Can you do this?"

Both humbly chorused that they could. Dan had the guards take them away after that. La and Dan both looked at each other, conceding a job well done.

The Hammer-Axe Six met with the Anduku Elders, as well as the Young Anduku leaders. They set the roles for both groups that included a messenger system that was to be uninterrupted regardless of any situation. The Anduku were told that if these guidelines weren't met, the Hammer-Axe Six would be returning to get answers why it wasn't happening. La assured all the Anduku that they didn't want that. After the meeting, the Hammer-Axe Six made their way back to the main caravan where Shaya was.

It was early afternoon when the Hammer-Axe Six and their forces finally made it to the main caravan. Shaya was alerted by the forward guards and was waiting on her siblings as they entered the camp.

All of the Ra could see that Shaya was standing in the distance, without assistance. Danaaa, excitedly bounced around looking at La and then at Shaya. La was excited too, and even though she quickened her pace, La was not going to be seen running to anyone.

But it seemed La didn't have to, because as soon as they were close enough to make eye contact, Shaya took off running towards them. Danaaa tried to run towards Shaya, but was stopped by La pulling sternly on her ponytail.

La even tried to look a warning to Shaya to adhere to protocol and stop running. Shaya ignored La and ran right into her, hugging and squeezing La. La missed Shaya, so she let herself get caught up in the moment, squeezing Shaya tightly. Danaaa, Dan and the rest of the Ra surrounded Shaya, hugging her and showing her how much they missed her.

In the middle of this love fest, everyone noticed that Danaaa and Ram were sniffing Shaya. They then turning around, sniffing the air. They did it several times over again, before finally staring at Shaya, with a strange look on their faces. Shaya instantly got nervous. Upon seeing all this La looked at Dan and then at Shaya, before looking at Danaaa and curiously asking, "Why are you acting this way?"

Danaaa's eyes went from Shaya's to La's eyes and then back to Shaya's eyes, as she sternly said in her soft voice "Shaya smells like the stink of guards!"

Shaya nervously looked at La and quickly said, "My personal bodyguards have been helping me in the rehabilitation of my leg. I'm sure that's what they smell."

Danaaa said in a nasty, but soft voice, "It's not that kind of smell!"

Anne, who was standing a short distance from them, said "I told you that when we brought you the food."

La turned and gave Anne a stern look not to interfere. Anne took the hint and lowered her head. La turned back to Danaaa to get further clarification on the matter.

Just then, three guards Shaya handpicked for her personal bodyguards, while La was gone, walked up and stood nearby. Everyone was startled when Ram and Danaaa quickly pulled their axes and attacked the three guards.

Before Dan or La could say anything to stop them, the three guards were dead. Two of them being sliced almost in half and the third one beheaded. To the astonished eyes of everyone there, Ram went over and slammed his axes through the necks of the two dead guard on the ground removing their heads.

La screamed at the youngest twins saying "Have you two gone insane?! Why would you do such a thing? Tell me this instant, what's the meaning of this?!

Ram turned and looked at La. His face was angry still he didn't say a word. His eyes were scarier than normal, so La turned and looked at Danaaa for an explanation. Danaaa's eyes were angry and glossed over with moisture. Her lip was crooked on one side when she yelled "But, I already told you!!"

Danaaa's eyes darted around at some of the guards that were gathering around. She angrily stomped up to La with her axes still in hand, making La a bit nervous, at first. Danaaa stopped in front of La and then put her lips up to La's ear and whispered "I smelled those guard's stink on Shaya and I smelled Shaya's stink on those guards! It's the stink of sex!"

La got dizzy and confused for a second as Danaaa's words sank in. La grabbed Danaaa by her shoulders and stared her in her eyes for conformation. Danaaa slowly nodded her head up and down. La's eyes filled with moisture as she slowly turned her head towards Shaya. Once La and Shaya's eyes met, Shaya took off like a rocket running away. La and Danaaa were instantly in hot pursuit.

The rest of the Hammer-Axes Six followed, except for Dan. Dan looked down at the bodies, before ordering the guard to clear them, away. Ali and Hoban looked at Dan to see if they should follow the royal teenagers. Dan motioned for them to stay here and not let any of the guards follow, so that's just what they did.

Dan was still in shock from what he realized had happened. Dan knew when they returned to the main city of Ra, if his parents found out about this, at the very least, he and La would be dead. He turned and trotted in the direction Shaya and his sibling had run. Dan really didn't want to catch up to them, but knew he had to.

Meanwhile, La and Danaaa were in hot pursuit of Shaya and gaining on her, with everyone else close behind. Shaya stopped at a tree turning her back to it, facing a charging La and Danaaa. La and Danaaa stopped right in front of Shaya as the other Ra stopped and stood behind them, staring at Shaya. La stared at Shaya and angrily pleaded, "Just tell me they took advantage of you and I'll have their entire families wiped out!"

Shaya wanted to agree with La to make this all go away, but she thought about the guards families for a split second. In that split second, Shaya's head shook no.

Before anyone knew what happened La had backhanded slapped Shaya, returning with an open-handed slap and then returning with another backhand. La then slammed her right fist into Shaya's stomach and then connecting to Shaya's face with a punch from her left hand. La swung and connected with Shaya's face two more times, before Shaya went to the ground. La was immediately on top of her.

La drew back with her fist, but was tackled off Shaya by Dan. La violently swung her elbow at Dan's head, while positioning herself and getting off the ground, on guard, ready to pummel Dan.

Dan had barely avoided La's elbow and knew if he hadn't, he might have been knocked out cold from it. Dan gave La a look that said he was disappointed in her. He slowly got off the ground and looked at Shaya. Yin and Danaaa helped Shaya to her feet. Breathing heavily, La angrily looked at Shaya.

That's when La saw the damage she had done. It shocked La that she had done this to Shaya, so quickly, out of anger. Shaya's left eye was already swollen and closing. Her lip was busted, bleeding and also swelling. Shaya's right cheek and forehead was also bleeding.

Shaya snatched her arms away from Yin and Danaaa. She got down on her knees in front of La and looked up at La, with tears in her eyes. Shaya thought she deserved everything La had done to her and more. Shaya was ready to take whatever punishment La thought appropriate.

La stared down at Shaya for a moment. La's voice was choked up and filled with hurt, while her lip was crooked on one side when she said "You know mother will kill me, if she finds I let this happen! Of all things, why do this?"

Shaya pleaded, "I don't know! I don't know what's wrong with me! I can't stop myself! Finish me off, here and now! Please, take my head! I don't want to go home! Just kill me and get it over with!"

La's eyes started burning, as tears fell from them. For the first time she felt powerless. This was just too much to deal with. La was confused and found it hard to breathe.

Her stomach instantly knotted up in a fierce pain. La turned her back to Shaya, grabbed her stomach with one hand and covered her eyes with the other. Tears flowed down La's face as she broke down crying, uncontrollably. Right after La started crying, so did Shaya. Danaaa was confused and looked around for someone to do something. The Ra boys were shocked, because they'd never seen La in this condition, before.

Dan didn't quite know what to do, but knew he had to do something.

He took off his ruling cape and put it over Shaya's head, while picking her up off the ground. He looked at Yin and told him to take Shaya back to her private platform and have the healers attend to her. Dan then had Don take off his ruling cape and he put it over La's head. They took La back to her private platform.

La was torn up emotionally from the inside and was violently ill from what she'd done to Shaya and from what Shaya had done with the guards. The Ra caravan didn't move for almost two weeks. La wouldn't eat and was getting weaker by the day. Because Danaaa was in tune with La's feelings, Danaaa began to have some of the same symptoms La had.

Dan was concerned and tried everything in his power to get help for La. It wasn't until Shaya comforted La that La's symptoms began to fade. La slowly started eating, again. During that time, Shaya told La what led up to things getting so out of hand. Of course, Shaya couldn't give La and Danaaa the completely raw story, but still, it was bad enough. Upon hearing Shaya's story, both La and Danaaa needed a few more days to recuperate.

Once La was well enough to have meetings, Tania was the first to request to see La. La was pissed that Tania didn't get word to her about what was going on with Shaya. Now La had someone other than Shaya to take this out on.

La sent for Tania, but was told Tania had committed herself as a prisoner in the makeshift dungeon. Tania begged for La to come and see her, there. La went with Danaaa to the dungeon, while La's Warlord Hoban stayed and guarded Shaya. Hoban was told to keep everyone away from Shaya, except the Hammer-Axe Six, at all cost.

When La got to the dungeon and saw Tania, she saw that Tania was tied up and had her head covered. La hadn't ordered this and wondered who would dare to do so, without her permission.

The guards told La that Tania put herself in the dungeon, over two moons, or two months, ago. Tania told the guards not to release her, but to inform the Queen where she was, once the Queen returned.

Before, La finished questioning the guards Shaya walked up with Hoban and some Elite Guards. La glared angrily at Hoban. Hoban lowered his head and said "The Number Two Princess can't be stopped by the likes of me. When she decided to come to the dungeon, the best I could do was protect her."

La turned from Hoban and looked at Shaya. La said, "I thought I told you to stay, until I returned!" Shaya looked at La and said, "I thought it best that I come here." Shaya moved close to La's side. La took in an angry deep breath and then released it. She wasn't going to argue with Shaya in front of her guards.

La had the guards remove the covering from Tania's head. The moment they'd done so Tania looked at Shaya. She quickly looked away and into La's eyes, lowering her head, after that. Tania sorrowfully pleaded, "I have failed you, my Queen. Certain things I had no power to stop, or even get word to you. Please, take my head for all my failures."

La stared at Tania. Tania had never failed to get La information before this time. La asked, "If food and supplies got to me, how is it that you couldn't get a coded message to me?"

Tania said, "I tried . . . . but I wasn't smart enough to succeed. That's when I was . . . . I, I mean that's when I put myself here and decided to take punishment!"

La's head turned slightly to the side and her eyes went down from Tania's as she whispered "Shaya!" Tania heard La and pleaded frantically "No, my Queen! Please, let it end here with me! Take my head, I beg of you!"

While still looking at Shaya out of the corner of her eyes, La said, "It seems when I ask questions around here, everyone wants to offer their heads, rather than answer my questions!"

La looked back at Tania and could see the fear in her eyes. She knew Shaya must have threatened her, somehow. La could feel Shaya moving closer, leaning on her shoulder. La roughly moved her shoulder and took a step towards Tania. La said, "You are right in the fact that you have failed me, miserably!"

La motioned to her guards. They untied Tania and took her to her knees. La motioned again and one of the guards pulled back on Tania's hair, to make her look up at La. La said, "So you want to offer your head, do you? Well, I don't accept!"

La motioned for her guards to let go of Tania. Tania fell to the ground. La said "Your head is no use to me, unless it's attached to your body and working properly. I'm assigning ten of my most trusted guards to watch your every movement. They will not leave your side, nor will they let anyone get close enough to do you harm. Get out of my sight and get yourself cleaned. Return as soon as you are proper. I expect you to then serve me as well you've done in the past."

La pointed out five guards to escort Tania. They helped Tania off the ground and followed her as she went to get cleaned up. La looked at Shaya and pulled on Danaaa's ponytail. That meant it was time to go.

The Ra girls walked a little ways, before La motioned for their bodyguards to give them privacy. Once the bodyguards were gone, La turned and stared at Shaya. Shaya meekly said "What?" La said, "I'm not going to ask what else you've done while I was away. That's the past. I will say this. If you harm Tania, or purposely go against my orders for my people, without consulting me first, I will take that as a challenge to me being Queen of the House of Ra. And after seeing the mess you've created here, I will eliminate that challenge, permanently. I don't care how much it hurts me, later! Is that understood?!"

Shaya fearfully nodded that she did. La stared at Shaya for a moment, before saying, "Come, so I can get this caravan moving!"

I'm not going to waste time telling the watered down story Shaya told to La and Danaaa. I'm also not going to describe every detail of what really occurred, either. What I will do is give you a good picture of what really happened, with Shaya, while the other Ra were gone, fighting the Anduku and Shinmushee.

CHAPTER 24

When Shaya was wounded in her thigh by a spear, she was fifteen years old. She couldn't put any weight on that leg, at all. The Ra healers and maids used all that they knew to help Shaya's leg recover as soon as possible.

Still, for the first couple of days Shaya mostly stayed in her covered platform. She quickly became bored with that. With La and Dan gone, Shaya decided she could do whatever she wanted and she was in charge.

Shaya summoned her bodyguards. She had them bring La's throne chair to her. Shaya's bodyguards transported her in La's throne chair to the headquarters of the Elite Guards Dan put in control of this Ra military caravan. The four top Elite Guards in charge stepped out when it was announced that Shaya was here.

After lowering their heads, they looked at Shaya, waiting on her to tell them why she was here. They also noticed Shaya was taking her time looking their entire bodies over, before looking each of them in their eyes.

Shaya said, "What plans do you have to give support to your King and Queen, out in the field?" One of the Elite Guards said, "Our orders are to protect you and this caravan. If we don't hear from the young King and Queen in seven days' time, we move the caravan back to Wa province and alert Hayee, Wana of the situation."

Shaya looked at all four of them, again. She said, "They could face serious peril, by then. On who's orders are you to do that?" The same Guard said "Young King, Dan's orders." Shaya said,

"Who's in charge of directing this caravan while your King and Queen are not here?"

The Guards studied Shaya for a second. She had a mild disposition, but the guards knew she had a reason for being here. They could see she was sitting on a throne chair and pulling rank, so the guard who spoke earlier said, "That would be the Number Two Princess." Shaya said, "That's right!"

Shaya told the Elite guards that they needed to get food and water to the advanced forces. The Elite guards told Shaya how dangerous it would be to try to send enough guards to make sure the supplies got to the King and Queen, while protecting the caravan, but they would come up with a plan to do both.

Shaya knew they were right, but she also knew she needed to make sure her siblings had the proper support. Her thoughts were interrupted when she saw the behemoth and the Chusee twins walking by. The Behemoth was shoveling food into his mouth, as usual. He saw Shaya looking at him.

Even though Shaya wasn't a real threat to his food, the Behemoth moved the sack of food to the arm furthest away from Shaya, peeking suspiciously at her and then shoveling more food in his mouth with his other hand. Shaya shook her head, because she thought that was the most absurd thing she'd ever seen.

In that same instant, Shaya got the idea of who she could send and not compromise the safety of the caravan. She also reasoned that if she ordered more guards from Wa and Yee province, she wouldn't have to worry about the safety of her caravan. So that's what she did.

Shaya toured the entire caravan, including the perimeter defenses. She decided to change a few things. The first thing Shaya did was put five of the singers, one each in different perimeter outpost. Shaya put Tania, La's personal assistant in charge of maids and bodyguards to ensure the singers weren't taken advantage of, by lonely guards.

Tania's original mission from La was to make sure Shaya's recovery went well. Since La wasn't here, everyone had to do what the Number Two Princess asked of them, including Tania.

That same day, Shaya ordered the caravan to move a little closer to Anduku territory, so she could support her siblings with the Ra military. Once Shaya was satisfied with the way she set up the caravan's defenses, she went back to her platform.

Shaya had to be lifted off the throne chair. Her thigh muscle hadn't completely sealed itself, so Shaya couldn't put any pressure on that leg. Maids rushed up to help her. One of the maids had trouble supporting Shaya's weight and stumbled. Shaya was on her way to the ground, when her bodyguard caught her. He lifted Shaya up and supported her body.

Shaya felt the guard's strong arms wrapped around her. Her body was pressed against his as he lifted her up. Shaya was so caught up in her awareness of the guard's muscular body that she accidentally took a step on her injured leg. Shaya immediately collapsed on that side, grabbing and pulling herself closer to the guard for support. The guard pulled Shaya closer and wrapped his arm around her waist, taking most all of her weight off her good leg, also. The guard asked, "Are you alright, young Princess?"

Shaya was more than alright. Shaya was caught up in the sensation of feeling the guard's muscles and firm hold on her. Several of the maids saw that and moved to take over for the guard. As soon as Shaya realized that, she ordered the maids to move back. She scolded them for causing her pain. She told them that from now on she would have her bodyguards carry her, until she could walk on her injured leg.

Shaya gave them a stern look then dismissed them. She had her bodyguards carry her on to her platform and sit her on some cushions. Shaya dismissed all but the one who caught her, earlier. The other bodyguards hesitated, because it was protocol that no male be left alone with any of the high-ranking Ra females. The other bodyguards asked if Shaya wanted them to send for her maids, before they left.

Shaya told the bodyguards that she would summon her maids as she thought fit and she didn't need them, now. She also told her bodyguards that her orders shouldn't be questioned, but should be followed. Shaya told her bodyguards that it was very important for them to show her the proper respect, so she could give a favorable report about them to La and Dan.

The guards could see that the Number Two Princess could be as much trouble as the Number One Princess, if she chose to be. The only difference was Shaya didn't have to yell to get her point across. The bodyguards lowered their heads. They looked at the last bodyguard letting him know not to do anything against protocol and then they left.

After the other bodyguards left, the one who was left with Shaya was a little nervous. He knew if La and Dan found out about this, at the very least, he would have some explaining to do.

Shaya watched him the entire time, smiling, knowing that it made him even more uncomfortable. After another moment, Shaya said, "Come, help me up. I want to put my cape away." The bodyguard said, "I can put it away, so you don't have to get up."

The pleasant smile came off Shaya's face. She was still calm when she said, "Why would you think I'd want that? Why would you think, or do anything, besides what I tell you?"

Shaya shifted on the pillows and then said, "If you want to think about something, think about this. You're here in the private quarters of the Number Two Princess, all alone. If I were to scream out, my other bodyguards would rush in and you'd be killed, instantly. After that, most members of your family would be killed, also. To avoid any misunderstandings, just do what I say, without questions."

Shaya's bodyguard was shocked beyond belief at what he was hearing from her. Shaya smiled and then said, "Now, help me stand." The bodyguard moved over, put his hands under Shaya's armpits and lifted her up. As he lifted Shaya, she slowly rubbed her hands over the muscles of his arms. Once she was standing, Shaya wrapped her arms around the guard's neck and pressed the front of her body firmly against his.

The bodyguard quickly moved back, while still holding Shaya up. Shaya looked seriously into his eyes and whispered sternly "Careful not to offend me! I can be a lot of trouble if I choose to!" After staring at him for a second, Shaya smiled and said, "Now hold me closer, so I don't lose my balance and cause pain to my leg."

The bodyguard did as he was told. When Shaya's body touched his, she pressed even harder. Shaya moved her hands around the guard's back and shoulders, feeling all the muscles, there. The guard was very nervous as he held Shaya. He knew he was a dead man. What he couldn't figure out was, of all the Ra girls, why was the Number Two Princess acting this way?

Shaya pressed her hips on the guard. Although excited, it made her a little nervous. She stopped and quickly said "I'm bored. Put me back on the cushions." The guard did as he was told.

Shaya said in a low voice "Calm yourself. If anyone sees you, they'll jump to conclusions. Neither of us wants that. Also, it's best for you and your family if you tell no one what goes on between me and you." Shaya paused, looked away from the guard and then looked back at him. She whispered, "When the time is right we will experiment, further."

Shaya watched the guard. It only took a moment for his blood flow to return to normal. When it did, Shaya ordered him to leave and send in her maids. The bodyguard left thinking that Shaya had gotten him involved in something that would get him killed, eventually.

Anne, being almost as stealthily as Ram, heard most everything that Shaya said to her bodyguard. Earlier, when Anne saw all but one of the guards leave Shaya's covered platform, she snuck around back, found a place to hide and listened. Shaya was unaware that Anne heard her.

Even though Shaya didn't know Anne heard her, she thought it a good idea to send Anne with the supplies. Shaya remembered how Anne used to sneak around the city of Ra, undetected. She remembered that not even Ram was aware of Anne, at first. Shaya decided she didn't want Anne snooping around and telling La what she saw. Shaya didn't know it was already too late for that.

Shaya had already threatened maids on several occasions. They would rather deal with Shaya's nice personality, rather than the cunning, cold hearted other side of her. Even still, when all the maids came as the bodyguard requested, Shaya gave them a special warning about spreading rumors. She said that any rumors attributed to her personal maids were punishable by death. The maids got the message loud and clear.

Shaya was nice, but firm with the Ra Warlords. Everyone else she let know that there would be consequences for going against her wishes. Once Shaya had established that with everyone, she started her experimentation with her bodyguard.

Even though Shaya had given Tania the task of keeping watch on all of the singers, who were at five different security positions, Tania managed to find out about Shaya's private experimentation with her bodyguard, after the first time they were alone together. Even though Tania's spies told her no sex was involved, Tania decided she needed to put a stop to this, before La and Dan came back and took her head for letting Shaya get away with this.

Shaya was getting more and more comfortable with the male body with each of her experimental sessions with her bodyguard. This day, Shaya had her maids leave and summon that same bodyguard. It was time to learn a few more things!

Shaya was impatiently waiting, when Tania walked in. There was a look of disappointment on Shaya's face that was very clear to Tania. Shaya said "Speak freely, I have other business to attend to."

Tania lowered her head, before saying, "As respectful as I must be, I have concerns about why one of your bodyguards visits you unattended. My concerns led me to order him not to do that, again."

Shaya studied Tania as she talked. When Tania was done, Shaya said, "So you decide to give my bodyguards orders, without my consent. What did you hope to achieve, besides irritating me?" Tania said, "My intent was not to irritate you, young Princess. My hope is that you might adhere to protocol, when dealing with males."

Shaya said, "Careful what you say to me, that I'm not offended. I also advise you not send word of anything I do to La, or Dan. That could prove most unfortunate for you and your family. You do understand what I mean, don't you?"

Tania couldn't believe this was Shaya talking this way to her. She lowered her head and said "I understand."

Shaya said "Good! Now take your leave and send in my bodyguard you sent away." Tania lowered her head, again, before she left. Tania knew she was powerless to stop Shaya from doing whatever she wanted, but Tania wasn't going to help her. Tania never told Shaya's bodyguard to go see Shaya, so he didn't. Tania also decided she was going to get word to La about what Shaya was up to.

Shaya decided she'd let Tania get away with not sending her bodyguard as she'd ordered. But when the Warlords guarding the perimeter got word to Shaya about messengers that Shaya hadn't sent, trying to leave the caravan, the messengers were detained and Shaya was notified. They were interrogated and told that Tania sent them.

Shaya had Tania restrained and put in the dungeon. She gave orders that no harm come to Tania and that she be treated well. Shaya waited until the next day, before going to see Tania.

When Shaya walked into the dungeon, Tania could see Shaya was surrounded by all of her bodyguards and a few Elite guards. Tania wondered how La and Dan would deal with this new power welding Shaya, when they got back.

Shaya walked up to Tania and said, "I know you've been treated well, because those were my orders. But, now I have to figure out how to deal with someone who has gone behind my back, trying to feed my brother and sister information I deem incendiary." Shaya stared at Tania and said "What to do? What to do?"

After a moment, Shaya said, "I can't spend my time trying to figure out what you're doing. I can't have you killed, either. La wouldn't like that. Until I feel I can trust you, this is where you'll be. I'm sure you'll be out of here when La returns. And when La returns, you should think long and hard about why you say you've been here. Do you understand what I mean?" Tania nodded that she did.

Everyone at the caravan knew what happened to Tania. That made them extra careful in staying on Shaya's good side. That gave Shaya all the time she needed for her sexual experiments. That led to sex. After that, she had to have it.

Sex wasn't the only thing that Shaya seemed to have a knack for. She had increased the Ra caravan, with guards from Wa and Yee provinces, to a large military force. Shaya controlled all movements and advances of the caravan, with the help of the Warlords in charge. The Warlords met with and updated Shaya several times a day.

Shaya had her own spy and messenger system set up. They scouted all the Anduku territory ahead of the Caravan. That allowed the Ra military, under the command of the Number Two Princess, Shaya, to put a strangle hold on all Anduku territory, outside of the main city. It stayed that way, until La and Dan came back. Much to the surprise of the Warlords dealing with Shaya, while La and Dan were gone, Shaya gladly stepped aside and gave up control of the military. As far as the military was concerned, things pretty much went back to normal.

The Ra caravan was now on its way back towards Wa province. Travel was going well. Still, things weren't quite the same, with the Ra knowing what happened with Shaya. It was especially awkward at meals. The rest of the Hammer-Axe Six tried not to look at Shaya, while trying to look like they weren't looking at Shaya. All while looking at Shaya. If you think that sounds confusing, it wasn't half as bad as actually being there.

The Ra knew they had to keep information about the Shaya situation from getting back to the main city of Ra. La and Dan were worried that if their mother found out about Shaya, they would lose their Warlord titles. Not to mention the fact that Queen Ramala might kill them! Even though Shaya had threatened everyone earlier, La and Dan made it a Law, punishable by death, to talk unfavorably about any of the Royal Ra children.

Once the caravan got back to Wa province everyone relaxed a little. Roe and Deen reminded La and Dan that they should get back to the main city of Ra as soon as possible. That Ramala last messenger reported that Wana and Ramala were readying a caravan to come and see why they weren't on their way back to the main city. Dan and La sent several messengers stating that they were already on their way home. They left for the main city when next day came.

CHAPTER 25

Ramala dealt harshly with Shaya after La and Dan found her and brought her to Ramala. Ramala interrogated Shaya, as well as the rest of the Ra children in order to get as much information as possible. Ramala then dealt some harsh physicality to La and Dan. Dan dealt well with it because he was tough enough to take whatever Ramala dished out.

La was a second away from defending herself against her mother when Ramala stopped getting physical with her. La was almost eighteen and only let Ramala get away with this because of the utmost respect she had for her mother. Ramala saw that in La's eyes and knew that was the last time La would allow her to get physical with her. Ramala was good with that. She would have to think of another way to punish La if she had to.

The guard found with Shaya was beaten and tortured for five days. He was beheaded after that. Most all of the Ra and Hayee guards knew why the guard was killed. It was an unspoken truth that if anything close to what happened with Shaya, happened again, entire families would be eliminated.

Ramala also made sure that Shaya was not left unattended by herself. One of the Hellcats, or Shaya's sisters would be with heart all times. That kept Shaya from getting into any unsavory situations.

Because Dan and La took so long responding to their mother's request to return home, Ramala forbid them to leave the main city. Their daily activities were reduced to training and attending royal functions.

Spies told Ramala about all her children's performances during their battles out in the field. Ramala had heard about Dan's defeats. She increased his training. Ramala also made Dan spar with several brutes at the same time, several times a day, so that no one could overpower and bully his axes.

Ramala put extra pressure on La in training. La had to spar with multiple opponents, while others tried to grab her ponytail. It seemed that Ramala punished each of her children according to the weaknesses they showed while out in the field. The Hammer-Axe Six got tired of that after eight weeks of nonstop training.

Although, Ramala limited her children to the city, they had become more popular than ever. The Ra successes out in the field made everyone want to be on their team, or at the least associated with them. La and Dan didn't have to recruit spies, warriors, or guards, anymore. They were mobbed by Ra and Hayee of all ages looking to serve their Young King and Queen in some way, or another. Even the high ranking Hayee were seeking audiences with La, Shaya and Dan. Everyone was trying to solidify his or her position under the up and coming Rulers of Ra.

Don's mannish ways were known by most all women in the House of Ra. Once word of Don's security checks on the young Ra girls spread, it made Don very popular amongst the Ra girls looking to get the highest Ranking mate. All the extra attention Don was getting from these females embolden him to see how far he could go, without going too far. In his young mind, how would he know how far not to go, if he didn't see how far he could?

On this day, Ramala called for a family meeting, after the mid-day meal and just before afternoon training. When questioned by her children, she said they'd find what it was about during the meeting. This made La suspicious. She met with Dan after first day's meal, just before training.

La had been trying to figure out a way to bust out of the routine that Ramala had them in as punishment for not returning when she summoned them. So far, La hadn't. La told Dan this meeting was probably their mother's way of giving them more duties to waste their time. La was desperate and told Dan the only way she thought they could get their mother off their backs and let them go back to ruling the plains. As soon as Dan heard La's suggestion, his eyes lit up with enthusiasm, just as La knew they would.

When it was time for the meeting, La and Dan already knew the main reason why their mother was having this meeting. La had a network of spies that was second to none. Ramala, Tara and her children, along with Wana were all seated when two families walked in. A young female stood in front of her family, while a young man stood in from of his family. Ramala smiled and then announced that these were the proposed mates that she chose for La and Dan.

La and Dan had discussed how they would react when Ramala announced this news. Dan said they should be cordial and polite. La agreed they should do just that.

After Ramala announced La's potential mate, he walked up, lowered his head to the Hellcats and then to La. La looked over at Ramala. She then looked back at the male, with her nose raised high, barely acknowledging his existence. After that, Jay moved over to his designated area.

La knew who he was the moment she saw him. His name was Abujasony. Everyone called him Jay. He was two years older than La. Jay was tall and muscular, but not as thick as most warriors his age. He was known to be tough, but didn't get into many fights.

Jay was the grandson of Ramala's Warlord Hayee, Ray. La knew him because she always saw him training with the Elite Guards. She knew him to be in charge of over three hundred family bodyguards that protected Ray's immediate family.

Although, La knew he was good enough to compete, Ray never allowed Jay to enter the Hammer-Axe competitions. Ray did that so the Hellcats, La, nor Dan would recruit Jay as their Elite Guard, or Warlord.

Even though La knew Jay, she did not know a lot about him, because she didn't care to. Once La was told that Jay was to be left to his family's duties, he was of no use to La, so she left him alone. Seeing him here now, La was as unimpressed with him as she'd always been. Dan smiled because of all the mates his mother could have found for La, he actually thought Jay wasn't a bad choice.

Dan only thought about that for a moment. He was mostly focused on the female Ramala chose for his mate. After Ramala announced her, the female walked up and lowered her head to the Hellcats, next to the Hammer-Axe Six. Lastly, she lowered her head to Dan, but did not raise her eyes above his knees.

Dan watched her for a moment and was curious as to why she hadn't looked up at him. He wondered if there was some protocol that he wasn't aware of. Dan peeked at La and then looked past La to Ramala. Ramala didn't give him a look as if he'd missed something, so Dan turned back to the girl in front of him. He'd seen this girl before, but because she was a very distant cousin he perceived not to have high rank besides having the Ra name, Dan didn't know much about her.

This girl's name was the Ra, Natrinada. Everyone called her Trina. Trina was born and mostly raised in the territory that used to be the House of Hayee. When the Rulers of Japha decided to change the name of everyone living in Japha territory to Japha, is when Trina's family moved to the House of Ra.

Since Trina was two and a half years younger than Dan, even though she was born north in the House of Hayee, she was a Ra. Trina was dark, thin and slightly less muscular than many of the warrior females in the Ra clan. She had grapefruit sized breast and a pleasant face. Besides that, she was average looking for a Ra. Dan couldn't figure out why Ramala picked Trina out of all the Ra girls to choose from.

Ramala chose Trina for several specific reasons. The first was she knew most girls from Trina's family almost exclusively produced males. Trina was the only girl out of nine children and the youngest that her mother produced. Ramala thought that would insure that there would be several heirs to Dan's throne.

The second reason Ramala picked Trina was that one of Ramala's Elder female cousin that knew Dan suggested she might be a perfect match for Dan. Ramala interview Trina for several months, while the Hammer-Axe Six were out in the field. Ramala could see that Trina was smart, but humble. Trina impressed Ramala enough that Trina was here this day.

La knew Trina and thought if she applied herself more, she might one day be one of her advisers. However, in La's mind, that day was not now. La smiled at Trina because she thought she was nice enough to get along with, as a sister.

With that being said, Trina was still standing in front of Dan. Her family was getting a little nervous at the awkward silence between Trina and Dan. They tried to get her attention without calling loudly to her. After another moment of silence, one of the Elder females from Trina's family sternly called her name. Trina didn't move. Even though Ramala had announced Trina by name, Dan had forgotten, because he wasn't paying that much attention to Ramala as he was to Trina.

When the Elder female said Trina's name, that's when Dan remembered. In his mind he said 'that's it, her name is Trina!' as the light bulb went on in his head. In reality, Dan actually said aloud the last word in his thoughts, which was Trina's name. That's when Trina looked up at Dan. Her emerald green eyes caught Dan off guard for a moment, because he hadn't noticed them, until now. Trina smiled slightly then stepped back to her designated area.

After that, all of the families mingled. Jay and Trina talked with the Hellcats, Roe and other close members of Ramala's family. Dan spent time meeting Trina's family and learning their names. La was fawned over by Jay's family.

The meeting ended with the families showing their respects and leaving. Ramala had been watching Dan and La's reactions the entire time. She didn't want to push things, so she didn't ask them what they thought of their proposed mates. She told them they were late for their next training session and should get there, immediately.

La and Dan never got to meet with Ramala about their plans. Whatever La and Dan thought about their prospective mates, they didn't let Ramala know. They had their Warlords and advisers gather as much information about their mates and their families as possible. La and Dan said that they needed this information as soon as they were done with afternoon training.

On the way to their afternoon training session, they talked about what they thought about their mates and decided that they wouldn't let Ramala know, until after they had their talk with her. If they had to, they would use these mates Ramala picked as a bargaining chip to get what they really wanted.

When afternoon training was done and after they were cleaned up, Tania briefed La and Dan on both their mates. Anne was with Tania. La was use to Anne being around now, because Tania kept Anne around, training her in advisory protocol.

A short time later, Ramala summoned La and Dan for a short meeting. The rest of the Hammer-Axe Six were told La and Dan would meet them, shortly. Shaya didn't like being left out of anything that La and Dan was involved in. If Ramala wouldn't let Shaya attend the meeting, Shaya would find another way to find out what was going on.

Shaya had bodyguards bring Anne to her. Since Anne was under Tania's charge, Tania and her guards showed up with Anne to see what was up. Shaya could see that La increased Tania's guards to fifteen. It made Tania look important, if she already didn't.

Tania saw Shaya, Ram, Danaaa, Yin and Don, along with several Ra Bodyguards. Nowadays, you never saw Shaya without at least one of her sibling present. Shaya only stared at Tania for a moment, before getting to the point. Both Shaya and Tania knew they would be dealing with each other for a long time. Shaya knew she couldn't get rid of Tania, because of La. Tania knew she couldn't create friction with Shaya, because sooner or, later she would lose. They decided not to hold on to what happened in the field. After hearing what Shaya needed, Tania smiled and motioned for Anne to comply.

Shaya sent Anne to spy on Ramala's meeting in the palace. She sent Ram with Anne. Anne didn't say much to Ram as they walked towards the palace. Once they got into earshot of the guards, Anne went into a mindless rant that made the guards glad they didn't have to listen to what Ram was hearing.

With one long, stare from Ram the guards moved out of Ram and Anne's way, even though Ramala said she was having a private meeting. Once inside the palace, they looked at each other. Anne went one way and Ram went another way.

Anne slowly moved down one of the corridors of the palace. She listened for voices that would give her clues to where La and Dan were. Anne turned down a hallway and saw several maids walking towards her. It startled her for a moment, but she tried not to let it show. The maids had seen Anne on several different occasions and knew who she was.

What they didn't know was why she was in the halls of the Ramala's palace, alone. One of the maids questioned her. Anne said she was looking for Ram and that he said to meet him here.

The maids looked suspiciously at Anne. They didn't believe one word she said. Anne looked at the maids, for a moment, trying to figure out what to say next, or if she should just take off running. Before Anne made her decision, the maids lowered their heads and moved aside. Anne noticed one of the maids looking past her, before lowering her head. Anne turned and looked. Anne almost jumped out of her skin at seeing Ram standing right behind her. After Anne composed herself, she and Ram walked past the maids. After they'd passed, the maids quickly left.

After the maids were out of earshot, Anne turned and scolded Ram in a whisper that only he could hear, saying "Don't sneak up behind me like that! You scared me!" Ram stared into Anne's eyes with a hard emotionless look. Anne looked annoyed, but after looking into Ram's eyes for only a moment, Anne's look changed and was softer. She whispered, "At least, warn me!" Ram's stare didn't change. Anne turned and looked down the hall. She then looked back at Ram. After listening for a moment, Anne whispered, "I hear La and Jay, but I don't hear Dan. Is he even in there?"

Ram shook his head no. Anne whispered, "Alright, you go find them, listen to what there're saying and then tell me, later."

Ram nodded in agreement and then turned to walk away, while Anne turned back, listening to La and Jay. Not a second later, once realizing Ram didn't really talk enough to give a complete report, both Ram and Anne turned and looked at each other acknowledging that fact.

Anne threw open both hands, palms facing Ram and pleading in a whisperer said "Just go and listen! We'll figure it out, later!" Ram only looked at Anne for a second, before turning and disappearing into a side hallway. After watching, until Ram was gone, Anne turned and listened to the rest of La and Jay's conversation.

Ramala didn't tell La, or Dan that the meeting she set up wasn't with her, but was with their proposed mate. She only told La and Dan as she escorted each of them to their meetings.

Ramala told La that she would be meeting with Jay for a short time. When La got to her meeting room, she peeked at Dan and then looked at Ramala with a pleasant smile on her face. Ramala walked off with Dan.

Once they were gone, La turned and walked into the room. Jay, who was standing near a table, lowered his head and got down on one knee, as La walked into the room. La walked back and forth past Jay without giving him permission to raise his head. After another moment, La stopped and said, "You may rise."

Jay saw La standing sideways, not facing him. Her head was arrogantly high and he could see a crooked scowl on her face. Trying to defuse the situation, Jay said, "Looks like we're going to be seeing a lot of each other."

La turned slightly, not looking directly at Jay, saying "Don't get your hopes up about me and you. I'll go through this process, but really, I have other plans."

Jay said "Believe me, it's not like that. This was put upon me, just like you. I have other plans, too." after a short pause, Jay continued with "Don't take this the wrong way, but my plans don't include being your glorified personal slave. I just hope that whatever your plans are, I can help you succeed with them."

Jay's words made La turn a little more towards him. She studied everything from his body posture to his eyes to see if there was a hint of disrespect, which she could take offense to. La could read eyes like her father. The eyes are the window to the soul and they almost never lie. Right now, to La, Jay seemed sincere about what he'd said.

La walked over and sat down at the table. Without looking at Jay she said in a low voice, intended for privacy "Let's talk about what our goals are and see whether, or not we can help each other achieve them." After saying that, La turned and looked Jay directly in his eyes.

Before today, Jay never had to deal with La. He'd heard about most of the things she'd done. He also heard about her arrogance and how difficult she could be. His uncles, grandfather, as well as other Elders told him how to deal with the Number One Princess. His attitude and answers would not only affect him, but could be quite detrimental to the rest of their family, if he wasn't careful.

Jay was about to base his answer on those thoughts, until La turned and stared straight into his eyes. Jay saw, first hand, in La's eyes that she was indeed as ruthless and cunning as advertised. In addition, he saw that if he didn't give La something she needed, that he would end up a puppet, or dead and out of her way.

Even with all of that, Jay knew he had to speak with authority and conviction. So, Jay first talked about his goals and how La could help him, never saying what he would do in return for La. Once La saw that his goals had nothing to do with being her mate, the half-crooked scowl became a devious half-crooked smile.

After hearing, what Jay had to say, La told Jay that she would give him the freedom to achieve his goals. La also said that Jay should put on the best front for trying to be her mate. That his performance would determine the level of cooperation from her on allowing him to achieve his goals.

La never told Jay what her goals were. Instead, she said she would let him know what was required of him when the time was right. She said that he should try to keep up on House of Ra business, without becoming annoying to her. After that, La told Jay to make small talk, until Ramala came back for them.

Right after leaving La, Ramala took Dan to a meeting room at the other end of the palace. After seeing Jay, Dan knew he was going to see Trina. On the way Dan couldn't stop himself, so he asked his mother "Why'd you pick her?" Ramala looked over at Dan, who was taller than she was and said, "That's for you to find out. That's half the fun of getting to know someone."

Dan didn't feel like playing word games with his mother so he decided he would get to know Trina in his own way. Ramala smiled because she knew Dan's silence meant that's what he was going to do, just as she intended.

When they got to the room, Dan could see Trina with two Elder females from her family. Dan turned back to Ramala and said, for everyone to hear "Mother, take these Elders away. This is between Trina and me. Rest assured I will be most respectful."

Ramala was surprised by Dan's assertiveness. She was also very proud of the young King unfolding before her very eyes. Ramala smiled at Dan. She then looked at and motioned for the Elder females to join her. Ramala turned back and smiled at Dan, before leaving. She hoped that Trina was ready for whatever test she knew Dan would subject her to.

Dan paused before walking into the room. For a second, he thought he saw his mother slightly lower her head to him when he asked her to get rid of the Elder females. She'd never done that to him! Then Dan thought he must have imagined that. He put it out of his mind and focused on Trina, who was sitting in a chair, at a table, facing him. When Dan walked into the room, Trina got out of the chair and went to her knees, lowering her head.

Dan walked over, grabbed a chair, turned it towards Trina and sat in it. Dan sat back in the chair and studied her for a moment. He looked back at one of his favorite treats in a dish on the table, before turning back and looking at Trina. Dan said, "If that's all you're going to do every time you see me, I'm going to tire of you very quickly." Trina said, "As of now, this is out of respect for my King. Tell me, what greeting would please my King?"

Dan was slightly annoyed when he said, "Getting on your knees every time you see me won't make me respect you. It just shows me that you're like everyone else."

Upon hearing that, Trina's eyebrows furrowed a little before straightening up. She lifted her head and looked at Dan with her emerald green eyes shimmering in the light. That threw Dan off guard for a moment. He noticed that when Trina wasn't looking straight at you, her eyes didn't have the light and intensity that they had when she looked directly into his eyes.

A half smile appeared on Dan's face, before he could cut it short. In that, instant he realized that Trina saw he was caught off guard. Trina moved one leg in front of her and slowly lifted herself into a standing position. She said, "How would you have me greet you?"

Now that Trina was standing and looking down at Dan sitting in his chair, Dan could see those green eyes had taken a new shade that showed a level of control that made Dan uncomfortable.

Dan quickly stood up and looked down into Trina's eyes. This was much better! Now back in a position of authority, Dan arrogantly said, "Am I going to have to tell you everything you should do?" Trina, while looking up into Dan's eyes, confidently said "No, but you will have to tell me some things you like and don't like, until I get to know you."

Dan said, "That's why we're here, isn't it? Let's see how you get to know me. You're also going to see how I'll get to know you." Dan immediately moved closer to Trina putting both his hand on her waist. He let his hands move down to her butt, grabbed her cheeks and squeezed. They were surprisingly firm, yet soft. Dan liked that!

While looking into Trina's astonished eyes, Dan calmly said "Security check." Trina said, "You can make and treat me like a common whore, if you like. That's your right. Just don't be surprised if I act like what you treat me. And remember, in public, people will see me as a reflection of you."

Dan immediately pushed Trina away and stared at her. Was she calling him a whore to his face?! Dan slightly angry with himself because he knew it was immature to do and say what he said. He was embarrassed, because Trina had put him in his place with words. Dan needed to regroup so he turned, grabbed one of his favorite pastries out of the dish on the table and took a bite out of it. He turned back to Trina with, what he thought was a clearer head.

Dan thought Trina was being too smart for her own good. Dan wanted to show Trina that he was smarter than she was and in control. Dan said "Alright, so you say a Queen is a reflection of her King. If that's true, you know I'm tough and will take on any challenge. According to you, that means you have to be tough. So if you want me to allow you to continue this mating process, go to the dungeon, commit yourself and wait, until my guards come get you. After that, you will fight someone of my choosing so I can see how tough you really are."

Trina saw an arrogant smirk on Dan's face. She said, "I'll not do this thing you ask, only because it's childish and proves nothing! I don't wish to know you under those circumstances! I'll not be treated this way, even by a King! I'm going home!"

Trina quickly turned her back to Dan. Trina had just broken several protocol rules regarding a King. The most offensive one was turning her back to a King, in anger. This was not lost on Dan. He was angered even more, but needed a moment to swallow the pastry in his mouth. That's when Trina stopped just before she got to the doorway and said, "By the way, I made those pastries you can't seem to stop shoving into your mouth!" then she walked out.

In his anger, Dan yelled, "They're not like my mother makes them!" When Dan said that, Trina stopped for a second. She blurted out "You only wish your mother's were as good as mine!" before storming away.

Dan wanted to yell something else, but Trina was already gone. Dan was more embarrassed that he had to bring his mother into this, just to have a snappy comeback. He was even angrier with himself, because even though he said the pastries weren't like his mother's, he liked them better. Dan angrily looked at the pastries wondering if he ate another one would it be a victory for Trina. After another moment, he decided that since she wasn't here, she'd never know he ate the rest of them.

What neither Dan, or Trina knew was that one of the maids heard what she thought was Trina yelling out something about Ramala not being as good as her. The maid told guards and guards got word to Ramala. Before Trina made it home, she was detained and thrown in the dungeon.

Ramala was in the dungeon within minutes of Trina arriving. She watched Trina closely for a few minutes without saying anything to her. After that, Ramala left and told the guards not to do anything to Trina, unless she ordered it.

Dan and La met after their next training session. Dan told La he wanted one of La's female guards to challenge Trina in a fair fight. He said that the girl should beat Trina pretty good, but not kill her. La looked at Dan and said, "She's in the dungeon. We will have to do it before dawn. I'm pretty sure that's when mommy's gonna have her beheaded."

Dan was shocked. He looked curiously at La and said "She going to kill Trina, just because she refuses to be my mate?!" La said as a matter of fact "That and the fact that she said that mother could never be as good a Queen as she could. That girl must really be crazy to say something like that!"

Dan thought he might never get another one of those pastries, again. In his moment of weakness, he said to La, "She never said anything like that!" La seeing the sincerity in Dan's eyes paused for a moment and then said, "We'll have to act quickly in order to save her. Let's get to the dungeon, right away!"

La turned towards the dungeon and saw that Dan hadn't moved. She turned back towards Dan and could see that Dan wasn't quite sure how to proceed. La could see that even though Dan didn't want the girl killed, he didn't want to go to the dungeon. La said, "I'll go to the dungeon and pretend to be tough on her. She won't be harmed. You go clear your head. When that's done, you come back to me and tell me everything she said, earlier. I'll tell you how to deal with her, if you want."

Dan looked away from La. He looked around and then said, "Whatever, if that's what you want."

La said "That's what I want." then she turned and left with her sisters. La only said it was what she wanted, because she knew it was what Dan wanted. Now, La was going to see if this girl really was worth saving.

Dan looked at the Ra boys like they'd better not start questioning him, so they didn't. Dan said "Come on, we have better things to do than just stand around here!" It was after last day's training and break time for the Ra, so they really didn't have anything better to do, until dinner. They could see that something was bothering Dan, so they let it alone.

La sent for Tania to meet her at the dungeon. She wanted more than just her sisters' opinion on this. When Tania arrived, La saw that Anne was with her. It only slightly annoyed La, before she let it go. They all walked into the dungeon.

Trina had been in this dungeon for a little over two hours. The stench of the dungeon was almost unbearable. No one told her why she was here, so Trina thought Dan had her put here out of spite.

Although Trina was tied up and blindfolded, she could hear people coming into the dungeon. She hoped it was Dan. Trina was so angry she was going to tell Dan to go to Hell, if he thought she was going to be his mate.

Trina felt a female's hand taking the blindfold from around her eyes. When her eyes were uncovered, she saw that it was La who'd taken the blindfold off. Trina quickly looked around for Dan, but only saw the other Ra girls, along with Tania and Anne staring at her. All of the girls saw that.

La looked closely into Trina's eyes before stepping back a little. La pulled out her gutting blade and put it between Trina's cheek and the cloth covering Trina's mouth. La pulled back and the sharp blade effortlessly cut through the cloth. La put her gutting knife away and then looked back at Trina. La said "Earlier this day, you had a meeting with my brother Dan, the Young King of the House of Ra."

All the girls noticed when La mentioned Dan's name, Trina's eyebrows furrowed in a flustered contemplation and her head shook slightly.

La noticed that but never stopped talking. She was saying, "What happened in that meeting, I don't even know. So you tell me everything and don't leave out one detail. Believe me when I say your life depends on it, because it does!"

Trina told La everything that happened, leaving out nothing. La asked Trina to repeat what she said regarding her mother. Trina did, so, admitting she'd made a mistake, but was lost in her emotions, when she'd done so.

La stepped back for a moment. She looked at her sisters and lastly at Tania. La then turned and looked at Trina. La walked back and forth in front of Trina a couple of times, before saying "How is it that you impress my Queen mother enough to get the chance to become the mate of the King of Ra, but end up in a dungeon, only after meeting with him, once?"

Trina said, "I don't know why Dan had me put here! I think . . . ." Trina was hit with a not as powerful as it could have been backhand slap from La. La said, "Is this the best you can do? If it is, you're as good as dead! Don't you even care about your family? Why you're here, you don't even know. I can see that much in your eyes and by what you just said." La paused for a second, while looking at Trina, before saying "I'll tell you, then. Dan never had you put here. That was my Queen mother's doing. You were overheard by maids who misinterpreted your words. How stupid of you to make mention of my mother. Never do that, again!"

La paused for another moment, as she paced back and forth in front of Trina, all the while looking into Trina's eyes. La could see why Trina's green eyes shook Dan. They were enticing, yet powerful. She could also see this girl was emotional when it came to Dan. After studying Trina, La said, "Sometime today, after I leave, I'm sure my brother will pay you a visit." La stopped pacing and turned her back to Trina. She said, "Believe me when I say that your life depends on this next meeting, between you and my brother. Show me how smart you are by doing what's best for my brother. That's how you keep your head around here!"

La walked away grabbing Danaaa's ponytail and saying "Come, I've had enough of this nonsense!" Everyone followed La out of the dungeon.

Once outside, La saw a couple of Dan's guards spying on the dungeon. La sent Tania over to them with a message to tell Dan to meet La at their headquarters. Once they were gone, La told the guards to feed Trina and leave no evidence of that. She also told them that this girl could quite possibly be the mate of their King and should be treated as such. La also told them to tastefully tear Trina's clothes and put a whip to her, once or twice, in order to leave visible whelps on her. La said that it was imperative that Dan not find out that La gave these orders.

La had a meeting with Dan shortly after the guards told him. La had Dan tell him everything that happened, earlier, between him and Trina. Dan did just that. La didn't comment much, except to say, "You might have handled that a bit better than you did."

La then told Dan that she wanted him to set up some sparring sessions for Jay with some of the Elite guards, so she could watch and see his skill level. Dan agreed, but wondered why La didn't do it herself. After that, he went with the Ra boys to the dungeon to see Trina.

(HAPTER 26

Dan expected that La had Trina protected and feed. When he walked in the dungeon, it appeared Trina had been beaten. Dan ordered the guards and his brothers out of the dungeon. Dan stared at Trina for a few moments in disbelief. He ordered that one of his personal plat formed Elephants be brought to the dungeon, ready for travel.

Dan walked into the cell and looked Trina over, again. This had gone a little too far for his liking. Dan cut the bindings from Trina, lastly removing the coverings from her eyes and mouth.

When the covering came off Trina's eyes, they met Dan's. Dan searched her eyes for a second and was immediately embarrassed that things had gone this far. He looked away and, out of frustration more than anything else, said, "You wouldn't be here if you hadn't gone and said what you did about my mother's cooking!"

Trina couldn't believe Dan was still trying to save face. Therefore, in spite of her better judgment, Trina said, "I'm here because you treated me like trash and then insulted me! Now you're here doing it, again! My goodness, why are you even here? Just have me killed and get it over with!"

Dan paused for a second without looking at Trina. This wasn't how he envisioned this going. It's just that it seemed Trina wouldn't stop yelling at him! Dan took in a deep breath and calmly said "Things seem to have gotten out of my control. As King, I could have handled this better. I'm not here to fight with you. I'm just here to take you home. Whatever happens after that is not my concern. Come let's go."

Trina calmed herself after hearing what Dan said. Still she didn't like that last part about him not being concerned about her. Trina looked away from Dan, while moving closer, happy because she wanted to leave this hellhole of a dungeon.

Dan told his brothers he would meet them at the palace. He led Trina up the ramp and no sooner than they sat down, they saw Don's Elephant boarded by the Ra boys. Dan noticed that the Ra boys, along with Bo and his guards were following him. He knew they wouldn't let him travel alone, without protecting him.

On the way, Dan tried to act as if he wasn't paying attention to Trina, because he didn't want to start any unnecessary turmoil in front of guards that might force him to say, or do something he might regret later. One thing Dan did wonder was why he was taking this girl home, when he couldn't care less if he saw her after that.

Meanwhile, Trina was marveling at how luxuriously comfortable this platform was. It made the city look even more beautiful from her vantage point. As she was enjoying this, she noticed Dan sneaking peeks at her.

Trina thought about how even though Ramala might have suspected she said something less than respectful, Ramala didn't have her killed. Heck, she didn't even call Trina on it. That's was what Trina thought.

Ramala went to the dungeon to see if indeed she had made a mistake in picking this girl and would have to have her killed. After studying Trina, Ramala was still confident she'd made the right choice.

Then the Number One Princess came and paid her a visit. La even took steps to help Trina. Trina still couldn't figure that out. All she knew was that if she didn't put forth her best efforts, her family could be blamed. Trina didn't like Dan, because he showed her his arrogant side, first. Still, she had to be nice, until she could figure out a way to get Dan to keep her family out of harm's way, while getting Dan to end this courtship by pardoning her.

Trina looked at Dan when she thought he wasn't looking at her. Eventually, after playing a game with their eyes, they locked

eyes for a moment. Trina looked down and away. Dan watched her
for a moment after that and then looked away. As soon as he did,
Trina said in almost a whisper "Were my pastries really that bad?"

Trina already knew the answer to this question, by the way
she saw Dan stuffing them into his mouth. She just needed some
common ground to break the tension between them.

Dan looked back at Trina, who still was looking away. He said,
"I never said they weren't good." Trina turned and looked at Dan
with a glimmer of hope in her eyes as she said, "So you liked
them?"

Dan hesitated and then said, "Yeah, they were pretty good."
Trina smiled a little, before looking away and watching the
scenery.

It wasn't long before they were at Trina's family's compound.
Dan escorted Trina to the guards at the gate and then he turned
and left. Trina took a couple of steps, turned and said "Dan, see you
later!" Dan didn't answer. After seeing that Dan ignored her, Trina
turned and went into her family's compound.

Dan didn't slow his pace, or respond in any way, even though
he heard Trina. He didn't want to give this girl any false hopes. The
only reason Dan went to the dungeon and brought Trina home
was because he felt if he had handled the situation better, things
wouldn't have gotten out of control. Now that Dan had rectified
the situation, he was done with it. Dan didn't care to ever see
Trina, again. Besides, he never told Trina he would see her later, he
just told her he was escorting her home. So, that just what he did.

Dan and the Ra boys were late for dinner. Something that
Ramala didn't tolerate. When young Dan came in, the first thing
he did was lower his head to his father, mother and everyone else.
After that, Dan went over to Ramala and gave a full report on why
he was late. After he'd done so he said that he hoped his mother
would forgive him this time. Ramala slightly lowered her head to
Dan and said she would.

This time, not only did Dan see his mother lower her head
to him, but everyone in the room saw it, also. La's eyes squinted
for a split second as she looked from Ramala to Dan. She didn't

like what she was seeing. La straightened her face up before she thought anyone saw her. After seeing what she just saw, La knew it was imperative that she have that meeting with her mother that she planned, earlier. Right after dinner, La asked for a private meeting with Ramala. After Dan reminded her, La included him. The rest of the Hammer-Axe Six decided they weren't going to be left out, either. Elder Dan couldn't resist seeing what his children had planned, so he showed up just as the meeting got started.

Ramala looked at her children and Yin. They all looked like hardened Butchers. She was proud of the extra training she'd forced on them. A moment later, Ramala got right to the point. She looked at La and asked, "What's this all about?" La said, "As you know, I took it upon myself to clear the plains of the lawlessness that was prevalent there. I succeeded in doing just that."

Ramala said, "That's your opinion of what happened. Most everyone didn't agree with what you did, especially concerning the Anduku." La said, "If the Anduku want to dispute my intentions, let them. The fact remains that they made an attempt on Shaya's life. I would have been perfectly within my rights, if I'd eliminated their entire tribe."

Ramala was getting annoyed with La, so she said, "Get to the point."

La said, "Alright, I will. What would it take for you to publicly announce me as Queen of the House of Ra.?"

Ramala thought 'Over my dead body!' but she said, "You're not ready for that, yet. Be patient, your time will come." La quickly said "Surely there must be some criteria that you're using to determine this. What can I do to make this happen sooner, rather than later?"

Ramala said "Nothing. This isn't up for negotiation." La pushed further, saying, "I'm not negotiating, mother. Still, would you publicly name me Queen of the House of Ra if I put at your feet the entire territory of those retched Shitmushee?"

Ramala quickly looked at young Dan and then back at La. She knew he was in on this, but was shocked that La thought she could use that, as a bargaining chip. Ramala quickly recovered. Before she did, La and Dan saw a light in Ramala's eyes that said that was a prize possession that she would love to have.

Ramala said, "I wouldn't think of sending you to war with the Shinmushee. It's not smart to stir up that hornet's nest, until I'm sure we're ready. Not a moment sooner."

La stood up. She put both her hands on the table and looked down at Ramala. Before La could say one word, Ramala ordered "Sit down!" La said, "I do this out of respect for you mother." La sat back down in her chair. La then said, "Mother, I respectfully ask that if I crush the Shinmushee and hand their territory to you, will you soon after that, name me Queen of the House of Ra?"

Ramala looked at La for a moment and then said, "La, listen carefully to me. Now is not the time. Be patient. When you're ready, I may give you the opportunity you ask. As of now, this meeting is over." Ramala stood up. The Hammer-Axe Six did right after that. La said, "As you wish, mother." then the Hammer-Axe Six all lowered their heads, before raising them. They left after that. Elder Dan looked at Ramala and said, "You know she's going into the Southern Jungle with, or without your permission, right?"

Ramala looked at Dan and said "I already know that much. My job is to make sure she's ready when she does."

Later that night, all three of Ramala's daughters came to her sleeping quarters. Elder Dan and Ramala were lounging around, barely paying attention to each other. When the girls came in, Dan could see that they wanted some alone time with their mother.

Elder Dan was going to use this time for one of his personal missions. Dan got up and hugged each of his girls. Just as he was leaving, Ramala said, "Don't go too far. When they leave, I'll send guards for you."

Dan turned and looked at Ramala, before leaving. He knew that was a smoke screen to keep him a bay. Dan knew when his daughters showed up at his sleeping quarters with nightclothes on, they would be staying all night.

Once Elder Dan was gone, Ramala's girls joined her on her sleeping cushions. All three moved closer to Ramala as La began to speak. La talked in a whisper, only audible to Ramala and La's sisters.

She said, "Mother, as you found out earlier, Little Shit was skewed with a Shitmushee spear, while visiting the first Lower House with her family. She died almost instantly. To me, that's unacceptable. Whatever her shortcomings, she was a Ra. The Shitmushee will pay dearly for that.'

'Mother, also, I found out who killed Shamika and her sisters. Ram identified them by their scent that was in the air by the bodies. It was three guards from Warlord Benobu's clan. Warlord Benobu must have thought that would be enough to make the other Warlords rebel and overthrow the House of Ra. We barely averted that disaster. The same Warlord Benobu allowed Shitmushee Butchers and warriors to freely move through Ra territory under his control, for the sole purpose of trying to eliminate Dan and me.

Mother, you can rest assured that I will eliminate Warlord Benobu, right away. His family will be spared, depending on their level of cooperation."

Ramala said, "Even if this is true, Benobu is very smart. If he has support from the Shinmushee, he will not be easily captured. There's also the fact that if Ray finds out that Benobu had his daughters killed, he will war with Benobu. I can't have two of my top Warlords fighting. That would weaken the House of Ra. Also, by killing Benobu, you could possibly turn a lot of Hayee against me and your aunts."

La said "That's why no one will know that you have prior knowledge of my actions. I will eliminate Warlord Benobu for plotting against you and put the Southern Jungle at your feet, if you let me."

Ramala sounded and was genuinely concerned, when she said, "I hesitate, because if you fail, all of you could be killed and the future of the House of Ra would be in peril."

La whispered, "Mother, I assure you I will not fail. I have a spy system second to none. I also have Butchers ready to move on my command. There's no way I can be stopped. That's why I'm here, this night. Advise me, freely, in secret, or watch me do what I've said on my own."

Ramala paused for a moment and then said, "I can't be a part of any of your plans. However, as you are my daughter, I'm obligated to advise you as best I can. Alright girls, let's rest now."

Starting early, the next day, the Hammer-Axe Six and their forces trained nearly from sun up, until sun down. La and Dan had everyone associated with them training extra, without giving reasons why. Dan and La were training so much that they managed to convince Ramala to put off the meetings with their proposed mates, for now.

After the first week, Trina sent Dan some of her pastries. After the second week of not seeing Dan, Trina brought the pastries herself, but had to leave them without seeing Dan. By the third week, Ramala allowed Trina to bring the pastries to Dan, but she wouldn't allow Trina to stay. Dan accepted the pastries but, to Trina, seemed too busy to pay her much attention.

When the eighth week of non-stop training ended, Dan and La decided that the Hammer-Axe Six and their forces would scale back their training schedules, a little. That just meant making time for meetings and updates from their messengers and spies from the territories they controlled.

Dan and La ordered a meeting for after last day's training session at their headquarters. When La walked in with her sisters, she saw Jay sitting at a table with six guards from his family. She knew Dan had invited him, because she hadn't. Dan also spotted Trina sitting close to the front of the room, at a table with Tania, Anne and a few of La's closest female advisers. He knew La must have invited Trina, because he hadn't. They both only looked at each other for a quick second acknowledging that fact.

The first part of the meeting was Dan and La being updated, by messengers, on what was going on in all parts of Ra territory. Next, Dan addressed everyone. At the end, he said they had a guest at this meeting. Dan asked Jay to stand and come up to the throne area.

When Jay stood up, so did his guards. When Jay's guards stood up, Hoban, Bo and Ali moved closer to the throne area. Once they did that, a few of their guards moved closer to them.

Dan and La said nothing. They wanted to see how Jay would proceed under these circumstances. Jay only looked at La and Dan for a moment, before he motioned for his guards to sit down. La thought whatever Jay's shortcomings were, at least he was smart enough not to approach the throne area with guards in tow. La knew Jay's guards wouldn't get anywhere near the throne area, before they were slaughtered.

Jay walked up to the throne area and then got down on one knee. Dan said "Rise!" Once Jay did he looked at the Ra in the throne area with his head slightly lowered. When Jay looked at La, he saw that she barely acknowledged him. Jay then looked at Dan.

La had nothing to do with Jay being here. Dan was taking the lead in this meeting, so La was being patient, trying to see where this was going. That's why La wasn't interested enough to look directly at Jay. This was arrogance at its finest!

Dan studied Jay for a moment, without saying anything. That made Jay even more curious as to why he was standing in front of the throne area. Dan broke the silence by saying "My Queen mother has chosen you for the mating process, regarding my sister. With that comes many responsibilities and duties. As first born King it's my obligation to check you on the duties I deem important."

Now, La knew exactly where this was going. Her bottom lip went crooked on one side, revealing an arrogant smirk like smile. Even though Jay hadn't figured out what was going on, he didn't miss La's smirk.

Dan paused and then said "Your fighting skills will be tested, here today, against the best we have to offer." In the instant Dan finished his last word, Danaaa had jumped out of her seat, towards Jay and drew both her axes. Dan yelled "Sit down Stupid, I didn't say you!"

When Jay saw Danaaa's movement, the blade of her ax was already flying towards his neck, before his reflexes could move his hands to his ax handles. Once Dan spoke, Danaaa's ax blade retreated from within inches of Jay's neck with the same quickness.

She twirled her axes one super-fast revolution and slammed them back into their holsters.

In a huff, Danaaa back flipped, landing and sitting in the chair behind her. She quickly folded her arms about her chest and slouched slightly back in her chair. Danaaa peeked at both La and Dan, before looking forward, but not directly at Jay. Danaaa said in her soft voice "But, I wasn't going to kill him, if that's what you thought!" Neither Dan nor La said anything to Danaaa. They both just looked around the room. Everyone in the room was astounded at the speed Danaaa effortlessly moved and swung her axes.

Jay tried to play it cool, but his nervousness showed slightly after having an ax blade move that fast, inches from slicing into his neck, before he could move. His eyes had never seen anything move as fast as Danaaa. He'd only managed to grab his ax handles, before realizing Danaaa was landing in the chair behind her. He tried to stay focused on Dan, but his eyes moved to Danaaa's and then to her axes and back to Danaaa's eyes.

As soon as Jay looked at Danaaa, Danaaa, out of frustration, said in her yelling voice "But, you should already know, I can swing an ax real fast! You just failed your first test! If this was for real quick draw, your head would already be rolling on the ground!"

Jay lowered his head to Danaaa. He had a new level of respect for all the Ra. He'd heard about the Ra but never saw them in action. Jay wondered if the youngest of them was that deadly, how deadly were the rest of them?

Dan could see and was enjoying how Danaaa had affected Jay. Dan chuckled and then said "She is really fast, isn't she? She's High Pressure, the Executioner. If I send her after you, you're dead. Simple as that." Jay had no problem believing that. Dan continued with "But she's not who I had in mind. This is who'll be testing you."

One of Dan's best Elite Guards stepped forward. Bo and Ali motion for everyone to move back to a safe distance. Jay watched the Elite Guard coming and was attacked immediately. Dan could see that Jay was holding his own with the Elite guard, so Dan motioned for two more Elite Guards to join the fight.

Now that Jay was triple teamed, he ramped up his defense. He even managed to go on the offensive from time to time, keeping the Elite Guards at bay. Jay was getting roughed up, but not enough to slow him down. Dan let the match go on for a good half hour, before stopping it. Dan said "Not bad, but I expect better in the near future."

Dan dismissed everyone except for his and La's Warlords, along with Jay. La and Dan talked with Jay for a short time, before dismissing him. His guards were waiting on him outside when he got there.

After Jay left, Tania, Trina and La's other female advisers came back into the room. Dan waited to see who La had for Trina to fight. It surprised Dan when La told her advisers she would meet with them, later. When Trina left with Tania, Anne and La's other female advisers, Dan was a little annoyed. La could see it. Still, Dan half looked at La and said "I took care of my end of the bargain and roughed Jay up, so you could see how tough he was and if he might be good enough to protect you. So tell me, how much longer am I going to have to wait to see how tough Trina is?"

La looked at Dan and said "She's tough enough for you to have me do your dirty work!" La paused a quick moment and then said "I know you can think of better things than that for Trina. To have her beaten? Is that what you really want?" La waited on a response. Dan stared at La, because she was making this harder than it was supposed to be. He didn't think he had to think about this. Dan said "I can see whatever I decide, I'll have to do it myself!" La smiled and said "As it should be." La grabbed Danaaa's ponytail and all three Ra girls left. Dan hated when La was right and threw it in his face.

When Jay got to his guards, he looked worse than when they left. They wondered if he'd taken more punishment from the Ra, or were his previous wounds swelling. Either way they could see that Jay wasn't happy about what had transpired at the meeting. Later that night, Jay left the city of Ra with a couple hundred of his closest guards.

CHAPTER 27

It wasn't until next day came that everyone found out about Jay's fight at the meeting and Jay leaving the city. Ramala questioned La and Dan as to why they challenged Jay. Dan told her his reasoning and said that if Jay ran after just one battle, he couldn't be trusted to protect La, anyway. La told Ramala that, at least, she wouldn't have to pretend to like Jay, anymore. But La seemed agitated that Jay would leave when he was supposed to be acting like he liked La. It brought back memories of when Bo purposely messed up his interview so he wouldn't have to be La's mate. Only this time La didn't have a crush on Jay.

La sent her messengers into all the Ra territories saying that she wanted to know where Jay was. La even had her Special Guards and Advisers pressing for information about Jay, anywhere they could. As the day wore on, La was more and more agitated with Jay.

Right after last day's meal, Tania came to La and Dan and told them she found out Jay was headed towards Warlord Benobu's territory. Tania said word was Jay was seeking asylum there in secrecy.

La looked at Dan. Dan asked "So, what do you want to do?" La said "When next day comes, we leave for Warlord Benobu's. We'll see firsthand what Jay has to say for himself." Dan studied La, before saying unconvincingly "Yeah, right! He'll be lucky if he gets to say anything!"

La sent messengers to Warlord Benobu, telling him that she was coming to deal with Jay, personally. Also, that she didn't want

Benobu to let Jay know she was coming. La's messengers said she wanted it to be a surprise.

Dan had the Warlords under his and La's charge get rest and be prepared to leave early when next day came. Normally most nights the Hammer-Axe Six stayed at the compound they used for their headquarters. This night the Hammer-Axe Six stayed at Ramala's palace. They had a short meeting before bedtime.

That's when Dan told La that taking a smaller force to Benobu's House wouldn't be seen as quite the threat as if they took all of their forces. La, Shaya and Don all turned and stared an indictment at Dan. They remembered the last time he convinced them to use a smaller group and the trouble it caused. Ram, Yin and Danaaa were excited about Dan's plan. Danaaa didn't care what plan was used, but would side with La, if it came down to that. The Hammer-Axe Six were split on this issue.

Dan had been training extra hard and now thought he could meet any challenge put before him. He still needed to prove to himself that he really was the Hammer-Axe Champion that everyone was calling him. Right now, until he could prove that in battle, Dan didn't believe it.

La could see that Dan's recklessness hadn't ended. She stared at him as he came up with every scenario in which they would come out on top. La argued and showed all the flaws in each and every one of Dan's plans. Dan countered that no plan could ever be completely safe. He said that all the extra training had them much more prepared than last time. That Benobu and Jay had no chance against them. Dan said that if La and Shaya were afraid, they could wait with the rest of the forces, until to coast was clear.

La interpreted Dan as saying she was a coward. Being called a coward in the House of Ra is a direct and malicious challenge. That insult to La had her stopping herself from smashing her fist into Dan's face. Dan had succeeded in angering La, when all he was really trying to do was challenge her ego, in order to get her to agree to his plan.

La's eyes blazed in anger after what Dan said. Dan felt a little uncomfortable and watched La's every movement, after seeing that.

La said "You dare challenge me, like I'm one of your subordinates?!"
Dan, now a little worried by La's anger, tried to defuse the situation
by saying "Challenge? I didn't mean it like that!"

La stood up. Shaya, nervous about what was happening yelled
"La . . . . !"

La peeked at Shaya, before looking back at Dan. La said
"Alright then, how about this! If you're good enough to best me
and my axes, when first day comes, I'll go along with your plan. If
I best you, then we go with my plan!"

Dan said "I'm not going to fight you. No good will come of
that."

La's bottom lip went crooked on one side when she said in the
nastiest tone she could muster "If the chicken shit Hammer-Axe
Champion is afraid of his sister, I can understand that. Just don't
expect us to follow you into battle, knowing that!" Shaya screamed
"La, don't say such things!" But the damage had already been
done.

La hit Dan where she knew it would hurt most and it did.
Dan couldn't believe La would say something like that to him. In
his mind, there was no way he could back down now. Dan calmed
himself, never taking his eyes off La. He said "Ready yourself for
when first day comes. I'll give you what you want!"

La only looked at Dan for a moment and then she looked at
both of her sisters. La cut her eyes at Dan one last time and said
"I've had enough of this nonsense! Come, let's go!" La quickly
turned, flinging her cape behind her and leaving out of the room.
Shaya and Danaaa jumped up and quickly followed. As Shaya was
leaving out of the doorway she turned and gave a begging look
to Dan that he shouldn't do this. Everyone heard La's voice boom
"I said, come on!" Shaya quickly disappeared out of the doorway,
after that.

Once the Ra girls were gone, the Ra boys looked at Dan to
see if he was really going to fight La when next day came. Dan
could see the question on all their faces. He said "Quit looking at
me and get some rest! We have training when first day comes!"

That was code for 'Don't bother me, unless you want a beating this night!' The Ra boys took it as just that and didn't question Dan anymore with their eyes, or their mouths.

When next day came, the Hammer-Axe Six all met at first day's training. Dan had hoped La would come to her senses by first day's training. As he looked at her, he could see that she hadn't. La was more focused than ever as she did her morning stretches.

Dan didn't want to fight La, but couldn't think of a way to defuse the situation, without looking weak. He watched La for any sign that he could interpret as a compromise. But when La turned, picked up her axes and looked at Dan, he realized she meant business.

La, with a serious, ready for battle, look on her face, said "Do you need more time, or are you ready?" Dan, still looking for a compromise, was a little unsure of himself. Still, his ego wouldn't allow him to stop what he knew was wrong. Dan said "Ready when you are."

La raised her axes about chest high and instantly started rapidly turning in a circle, while moving closer to Dan. Dan watched as that weighted ball on the end of La's ponytail took flight after her first turn. He also saw her axe blades twirling at him like saw blades. In an instant La was within striking distance.

Both Dan and La's ax blades clanged off of each other, repeatedly as Dan blocked everything La threw at him, while dodging that weighted ball which seemed to come from all angles. Dan had never fought La when she was using her weighted ball. He was amazed at how she could fight with such ferocity and still have that weighted ball coming at you with pinpoint precision. All that made this a very intense battle for Dan. Dan was enjoying this battle more than he wanted to admit to himself.

After fifteen minutes of dodging that ball, while blocking everything La was swinging at him, Dan lost track of that weighted ball for just a second, while just avoiding having his neck split open by La's ax blade. In the split second that Dan was offended that La would dare, intentionally, swing her axes at his neck, he was hit at the top of his neck, right behind his ear with that weighted ball. Almost immediately Dan heard a bell like ringing in his ears. He also felt intense pain from the hit, although the ringing seemed to bother him more.

Now, as Dan maneuvered to a better position to keep an eye on that weighted ball, he was pissed! Off of a block of La's ax, Dan blocked the weighted ball with his ax and launched it at La's shoulder, while sending his ax blade at her chest. La had to block the ax strike and was hit hard with her own weighted ball. She winced in pain for only a split second, before she had to block another powerful swing from Dan's axes.

Dan used his power to bully his way past La's block and sent the hammer side of his ax at her chest. La avoided that by moving to her left and was shocked as the hammer of Dan's other ax smashed into her chest. That was followed by two more super-fast and powerful hammer strikes to La's chest.

Before she could regroup, Dan maneuvered and hit La with two more powerful shots to her chest. Even though La's had on her chest protector, she had the wind knocked out of her. Dan quickly knocked both of La's axes out her hands with his hammers. Before La could think, one of Dan's axes was at her throat. Dan smiled at La, letting her know she'd been defeated.

What came next, Dan never expected. La forced her throat into the blade of Dan's Hammer-Axe. Once Dan realized La was purposely moving forward he moved his ax backwards and away from La's throat. Still, before he could do that, the blade of his ax touched La's throat. That's when Dan saw two sudden flashed of light, followed by a brief darkness.

When Dan's butt hit the ground was when everything started coming back into focus. He saw Danaaa blocking swings from La's axes. Dan remembered knocking those axes out of La's hands. How and when did she get them back? Dan tried to get up, but was hit with a wave of dizziness that said he should shake off the cob webs of being clobbered, before trying to stand.

La had given Dan a lightning fast one, two combination, followed by a powerful kick that sent Dan flying backwards. La grabbed her axes and was advancing quickly on Dan, when Danaaa jumped in front of her, with her hands in a quick draw position next to her axes.

La was furious and that wasn't going to be enough to stop her. She swung the hammer side of both her axes at Danaaa, intending to knock Danaaa out of her way so she could get to Dan. La was shocked and amazed when both her hammer strikes were blocked by Danaaa's axes. She hadn't even seen Danaaa pull her axes out of their holsters!

La quickly got over that and attacked Danaaa with everything she had. Danaaa toyed with La, avoiding and blocking every one of La's ax swings. Both girls were startled by a loud, but familiar voice yelling "What the Hell's going on here?!!"

Danaaa stopped instantly, but La took one more swing at Danaaa, before turning sideways, still on guard against attack from Danaaa. Danaaa avoided La's swing by moving backwards. Danaaa stomped both her feet in protest that La would try such a sneaky move.

Before anyone could say anything else, La yelled "Dan tried to kill me! He nearly took my head off with his ax! Look here, see this!" La pointed at her neck. There was a thin cut where she'd forced her neck into Dan's blade before he could move it back. The cut was red and blood was visible. Ramala saw it.

Ramala quickly pulled her Machete and was headed for Dan with bad intentions. She said "Why, I'll teach you to . . . .!" Before Ramala knew what happened, all three of her daughters had her locked up to where she couldn't move.

La wanted to see Dan get in trouble, but didn't want him killed. She never anticipated Ramala would pull her machete intent on killing Dan. La screamed "Mother I was untruthful! Dan did no such thing! I forced my neck into his blade out of anger! Dan would never hurt me, you know that!"

After La said that, there was complete silence. Dan, who was still on the ground, looked from Ramala to La. Dan and La stared at each other. They both realized how crazy all of this was.

Ramala never intended on killing, or even harming Dan. She just wanted to put the fear of death in Dan. It was La's concern for Dan that broke her. Ramala now knew another one of La's weaknesses she could exploit, although she wasn't going to let La know she knew she could.

Ramala yelled "Unhand me this instant!" in that same instant the Ra girls let go of their mother. La went down on her knees and looked up at Ramala. Shaya and Danaaa did so after that.

Ramala sighed and shook her head in disappointment. She said "There's a reason why I told all of you to never use real blades when sparring with each other! I don't know what happened here and I'm not sure I want to. Right now, I'm very disappointed in all of you!"

Ramala paused, looked at Dan and said "Look at you sitting there with a swelling jaw and puffing under one eye. What are people to think when they see you like this? A King has to make better decisions, or he won't be a King for very long. I'm leaving now. Try to see if you all can do better than trying to kill each other, because next time I won't come, until I'm sure you're done. Then, that's when I deal with whoever is left!" Ramala turned and walked away.

The Ra girls slowly got up off their knees and looked at each other. They turned to see Dan walking towards them. Dan looked at La's neck, before looking into her eyes. He said "We have work to do. We need to make a plan we both can agree on." La nodded in agreement without breaking eye contact with Dan. She said "I think your plan will work."

Dan quickly said "We'll keep our other forces close enough to help, if need be." La looked at Dan's neck where that metal ball smashed into his neck. It was bruised and slightly swollen. La wasn't going to tell Dan and he never knew that at the last second when La saw her metal ball was going to connect, La managed to slow it down and change the trajectory enough, as not to smash it into Dan's scull. She knew Dan wouldn't have survived if she hadn't.

La slowly and gently touched Dan's bruised neck. She then looked him in the eyes and said "Let's never fight, again." Dan said "I think that's best." La said "So do I."

First day's meal was normal for the most part. Young Dan had to endure a few harsh stares from Elder Dan because of the fight between him and La. La also had to put up with Ramala having attitude with her, after Ramala saw the bruise on Dan's neck. Both survived and move to their next day's training sessions.

Before they split up, La and Dan advised each other. Dan told La that when she used her defense, along with her offense he couldn't find an opening to exploit. He said that once she turned completely to offense, she exposed herself and he was able to move in and gain the advantage.

La nodded as she thought about what Dan was telling her. Then La told Dan that if he quit playing around at the beginning of fights that he could be more effective and very deadly. She said that all his playing around usually gave his opponents a second chance and that's why he lost those battles.

La said if he'd given each of those fights the seriousness they deserved, she was sure he would have won all of them. That made Dan think back. Was he his own worst enemy, when it came to serious battles? If he had been in the past, he was determined not to be in the future.

Even though Elder Dan hadn't said a word to young Dan about the fight between him and La, young Dan knew he had to go and clear the air with his father. Dan decided to do that sooner, rather than later.

Dan, his brothers and Yin headed for their next training session. They were met by Bo, his guards and some of the Elite Guards. There was a short update from Bo on what was going on this day. Dan didn't have the need to know everything like La and Shaya. He just wanted to know the important things. Still, it was one of Bo's jobs to keep Dan well informed, so that's what he did.

Once Bo was done, Dan told Bo he was going to see his father. Dan said that he would meet his brothers and Yin after their training session. That's when Don said "We're going with you." Bo immediately started directing guards and traffic. Dan watched Bo and the Elite Guards taking their duties very seriously.

Dan looked at both his brothers. He could see they were going even if he ordered them not to. No sense in starting something you can't win. Dan nodded to Don and then said "Come on. If we hurry we might catch him still training."

They found Elder Dan training in one of his private facilities. They walked in and watched as Elder Dan was swinging his axes. This always use to be a special treat for Dan and his brothers. But it seemed that because they all were so advanced in their training, most of their father's techniques looked outdated and beatable to them. This worried them because they knew if they could think past their father's moves, there might be someone else who could, too.

Elder Dan saw his sons and Yin watching him. He showed them some of his techniques, but not his best. He knew they were here for more than just a show, so when he was done he walked over to them.

He stopped in front of them. When he did, they lowered their heads and raised them. Elder Dan looked at all of them, lastly at Dan and said "Alright, what now?"

Don, Ram and Yin all looked at Dan. When Dan realized that, he looked at Elder Dan with a confused look on his face. Before he could say anything Elder Dan said "All of you walk with me."

They followed Elder Dan to the far side of the courtyard. Once there, Elder Dan stopped, turned and looked at Dan. He said "I thought you were smart enough not to fight La. You'll never beat her. It's not because your skill isn't good enough. It's because you're not willing to go as far as it takes to beat her, but she'll always do whatever it takes to beat you. Anyway, that's not a win you want, so make sure it doesn't happen again. You understand what I mean?"

Young Dan said "Yes sir, I do." then young Dan's eyebrows furrowed with confusion as he looked away and said "It's not just La." Young Dan didn't have to explain further. Elder Dan knew most everything that was going on with his children. He knew because Ramala, La and her sisters were his personal spies and told him, whether he wanted to know, or not.

Elder Dan said "Son believe me, you're not the only man to have to deal with a woman. I've seen that Ra, Trina. Your mother really knows how to pick them! Still, from what I've seen, she's a good girl. Don't play games with her mind, or you'll turn her spiteful towards you. Trust me, you don't want that."

Elder Dan could see he was starting to lose Dan, so he said "Just remember this, if you treat her well, keep her guessing and try not to piss her off, you'll be just fine."

Elder Dan grabbed his shirt, slung it over his shoulder and looked at his other two sons and Yin. He said "The rest of you don't get too curious about women, too soon! They'll be plenty of time for that, later. Now go tell your sisters to come see me." they lowered their heads to Elder Dan and then did what they were told.

Whenever La was in the city and her father sent for her, she went to him, immediately. When Elder Dan walked out from getting cleaned up, all three of his daughters greeted him with a smile. All three gave him a hug and kissed him on the cheek.

La stared at her father, trying to see why he summoned her. She had several theories, so she decided to find out. La said "What's up Dad?"

Dan looked at La. She had light scrapes on her face and seemed a bit disheveled. La saw her father looking at her. Her eyebrows furrowed in reflection as she looked away and said "That Syn, Jara! One day I'll . . . . !" and then La looked at Dan. Dan smiled, because he knew La was lucky to be here to say that.

The Syn, Jara only stayed at the female Monastery with Ma for a few months, before returning to the main city of Ra. Once the Ra girls returned from the field, Syn continued to train them, as she always had.

The smile left Dan's face and he said "The Southern Jungle isn't the best place to try and conquer. That place is a death trap. Can't you find somewhere else a little less dangerous to play conquest?"

La dismissed her father with a smile and said "Daddy you worry too much. You know I'm impossible to deal with." Dan said "That's what everyone thinks, until they get dealt with." La stared at her father for a moment. She didn't think he was capable of understanding that she really couldn't be dealt with. La smiled at Dan and said "I'll be very careful daddy. If things get too tough for us, we'll come and get your help." Dan didn't find La's sarcasm funny. He said "Just be careful!" La said "We will."

CHAPTER 28

Earlier, before going to see their father, the Ra girls went to have their after first day's meal training session with the Syn, Jara. Syn had gotten word from Ramala that La and Dan were planning on going to the Southern Jungle. Syn watched as all three girls walked on to the courtyard of her training facility. They all lowered their heads out of respect and then start stretching.

Syn motioned for La to approach her. La noticed a difference in Syn's attitude. She seemed a bit harsher than normal. La wondered had she done something to offend Syn, Jara. La put that out of her mind, as her arrogance took over. After all, La was the Queen and Syn was nothing but her instructor. La arrogantly looked at Syn, trying to convey that to Syn without words. None of that was lost on Syn, Jara.

Syn watched La as La stopped at a respectable distance. La hadn't shown Syn the proper respect, yet. Syn stared at La, not saying a word to her. La, although very arrogant, was deeply rooted in protocol. La's upbringing overruled her arrogance and she forced herself to lower her head to Syn.

Syn watched La go through the turmoil of humbling herself. It was hard for Syn to believe the level of arrogance she was seeing from La. Syn thought that she would never meet anyone as ruthless and arrogant as Ramala. She knew La had beaten Ramala in the arrogant department by leaps and bounds. Syn took it as was her duty to bring the Young Queen down a notch, or two.

After La lowered her head out of respect to Syn, Syn said "So, I hear you're going into the Southern Jungle. That place is a deathtrap. It's no place for a Young Queen."

A monetary flash of shock came on La's face that Syn would know about her plans. La wondered who else her mother told of her plans, besides Syn. It didn't matter to La. She wasn't going to be deterred by anyone. In the same instant it showed, the look of shock was gone. It was replaced by a smirk on La's face that had her bottom lip crooked on one side. La said "Don't worry about me. My best fighting days are ahead of me, unlike some. I'm going to take full advantage of them, while I can. One day when I'm not as good and older, like you, I'll retire to the main city and live out my days. For me, that time is not now. Now let's get with the sparring. I have other things to do."

In her arrogance, La thought she was putting Syn in her place. She didn't realize the level of taunting she'd done. Syn had a calm cool demeanor on the outside, not letting La know that she'd gotten to her. But on the inside, Syn was offended by being called old, washed up and retired. That was Syn's interpretation of what La said. If the Young Queen wanted to get on with the sparring session, Syn would oblige. Syn smiled at La and calmly said "As you wish, Young Queen."

La thought that once she'd put Syn in her place, Syn was showing her the level of respect that she was use to. La calmed herself and was ready for her daily sparring session. La lowered her head, again, letting Syn know she was ready.

La started slowly circling Syn, looking for a weakness that would tell her what technique to use this time. Since La had yet to find that weakness, she just attacked first as usual.

La never held back in any fight she had. Her intentions were always to finish off an opponent as quickly as possible, with the deadliest techniques she could think of. So, that's just what she did when she attacked the Syn, Jara.

La moved quickly, but cautiously on Syn. When La was close enough she sent a barrage of lightning fast powerful punches at Syn's face. Syn moved out of the way of the first two, but had to block every other one. La was selling out, trying to connect. After at least twenty well placed punches coming from La, that Syn had to use total concentration to block and dodge, barely being missed by them, Syn saw an opening and counter-attacked. She gave La a powerful back hand slap to her face that sent La into a half spin, before La could stop herself.

La took two more quick steps back to a safe position. In her entire life, La had only been slapped by her mother and Danaaa. She slowly put her hand on her face where she'd been slapped. With the other hand La pointed her finger at Syn. La's eyes glared at Syn. Her lower lip now hung on one side and had a crooked scowl on it. In shock from what just happened, La growled "You'd dare do that?! I've never been slapped by the likes you!! You tell me now, what's the meaning of this?!!"

Syn calmly said "Is that what you're going to say when you meet a Shinmushee Butcher in the Southern Jungle? He won't care much about whatever you're saying and will probably carve you to pieces, while you're talking. Also, I would hope your defense would be much better than what I've seen here this day. Remember your training and use everything you've learned!"

La slowly lowered the hand that her finger was pointing at Syn. She then slowly removed her other hand from her face. La could see the play that was going on here. This was a lesson. A test, even. La was determined not to fail, this day!

After Shaya saw La get slapped, she already knew what it was. Shaya turned to Danaaa and sternly whispered "Go get mommy, this has gotten serious!" Danaaa never looked at Shaya when she whispered back "No Way! You're crazy if you think I'm going to miss one moment of this!"

Shaya bumped Danaaa hard and whispered "I'll be right back! If things get too serious, you try and stop it!" Danaaa still didn't look at Shaya when she whispered "But, it already is serious! You already know that! You saw that slap La took! You'd better hurry!"

Shaya gave Danaaa a hard angry stare, before quickly leaving. Danaaa watched Shaya leave, as well as Syn and La, all at the same time, with her field vision. To Danaaa, this was priceless. She was determined not to miss one second of it!

La balled up her fist and lunged at Syn with lightning speed. When she got into striking range, instead of punches, La sent a lightning fast barrage of kicks at Syn. The accuracy and speed of the kicks kept Syn from moving inside of them and counter attacking. Syn knew if she was patient, La would give her that opportunity, eventually.

It came about five minutes, and a countless number of kicks, later. Syn was impressed that La was able to keep up an offensive kick attack that potent, for that long. Now Syn was going to make La pay.

Syn moved inside of one of La's kicks. At the same time, Syn sent her fist rocketing towards La's chest. In an instant, Syn saw two bright flashes of light. Syn didn't know how, but realized that La had clocked her with two pretty good punches!

It took everything Syn had not to lose consciousness. In a split second, without actually seeing La, Syn sent three powerful kicks to where she last saw La. The last one connected solidly to La's chest, sending her stumbling backwards, trying to gain control of her footing.

Once La gained control of her footing she looked at Syn. Syn had recovered enough from La's punches that she was moving in on La. La made several exaggerated movements of her head and neck. La instantly had her ponytail with the weighted ball on it, spinning like a helicopter blade in front of her.

Syn stopped at a safe distance, while watching La. She could see through the spinning ponytail that La was crouched, looking at her, with her fist balled up on guard, while taking measured steps towards Syn. Syn had never seen La use this technique before. She studied it for a half second, before La attacked.

As Syn suspected, when La lunged, attacking her with punches, that metal ball came rocketing at Syn's scull. Syn could see that in La's anger, La was going to try to kill her in order to win. Syn moved just in time as the metal ball went whizzing past her ear. She found herself blocking everything from a very potent attack from La, in which La was using both her fist and feet, along with that dreaded metal ball, that was always rocketing towards her skull. It was everything Syn could do not to get her scull crushed.

La sent another barrage of kicks at Syn. This time Syn, Jara decided it was time to end this. She stepped inside of the kick and put her shoulder under and between La's legs. Syn lifted La off the ground, twisted and turning downward, sending La's body towards the ground. At the last second, La curved her shoulder where she was being plowed into the ground, rolling herself, while locking her legs around Syn and sending Syn crashing hard to the ground. Both Syn and La tucked and rolled away and back towards each other with amazing speed, while still low to the ground. Syn sent her kick to the side of La's head. She knew the affects this kick would have on La, but was resigned to the fact that this was the only way she could stop La.

But that kick never got there. La's foot got underneath Syn's leg and blocked upward on it. Immediately after the block, La sent that same leg at Syn. La's foot landed solidly on Syn's shoulder, sending her backwards on to the ground. Syn recovered by tucking and rolling away from La. But La saw that and went flying into a super-fast tuck and roll that had her right on top of Syn, as Syn was coming out of her tuck and roll.

Before Syn could get to her feet, she saw that La had landed and was sending a powerful kick down at her. Syn fell backwards, avoiding the kick by landing on her shoulder. La was still close enough and positioned herself to strike. That's when Syn pushed her body upwards off her shoulders, upside down at La, driving both her feet into La's chest, sending La flying backwards. Coming out of the air, La bent backwards connecting to the ground with her hands, continuing into several back flips that she hoped would create some distance between her and Syn in order to regroup.

When La quickly turned around, she saw that she'd done just that. Syn was staring at La on guard for attack. La was determined not to disappoint Syn. She moved quickly towards the Syn, while getting her metal ball in flight. La then heard "Ramala, enough!

Hold your ground!" It was the only voice that could stop La in her tracks. It was her mother, Queen Ramala!

La peeked out of the corner of her eyes, while still on guard against Syn. With her voice full of rebellion, La growled, bellowing from the bottom of her stomach "BUT, MOTHERRR . . . .!!!" Ramala sternly said "I said, stand your ground!" La turned towards Ramala and lowered her head. La had angry eyes and never looked any higher than Ramala's feet.

That's when Syn started walking towards La. La tensed her body and made a half turn towards Syn. Ramala sternly said "Laaa!!" La turned slightly back towards, but not all the way in Ramala's direction. La was highly on guard, at seeing Syn walking towards her and was ready to explode at a second's notice.

Syn only looked at Ramala for moment, before she started walking towards La. She was surprised at how good La had become. In Syn's mind, La was better than Ramala ever had been, or ever would be. La was so good that the only chance Syn had to beat La was to try and kill her. And when Syn tried that, she still hadn't, yet. Syn knew if she kept fighting La, she would have had to kill her. Syn was glad Ramala was there to stop the fight, because Syn wasn't going to stop it herself.

When Syn got to La she could see La was angry and very tense. Syn slowly and cautiously moved her hands up to La's shoulders. She gently rubbed them back and forth. Syn said "How proud I am of you, this day! You finally showed me something I knew you had inside of you, all along. You're an excellent fighter, but always strive to get better. Also, remember to show compassion for the opposition. Even when you move into the Southern Jungle. That's the difference between a ruling Queen and a great Queen." Syn could see that La hadn't looked up at her. La's eyes were angry, but not like before. Syn put her hand under La's chin and lifted her head until their eyes met. Syn said "You did well, today, Young Queen! Remember everything you learned today and build upon it."

La took a step back from Syn. She did a quick lowering and raising of her head, much in the same way as Danaaa always did. La then turned, lowered her head to Ramala and started leaving the courtyard. Ramala said, almost in a pleading voice "La!"

La peeked over at Ramala. La hesitated, without stopping. Since La could see it wasn't an order, she kept walking.

Shaya and Danaaa lowered their heads to Ramala and Syn. They both jumped up and bolted over to La. La went on guard when she realized someone was coming up on her fast. When she saw it was Shaya and Danaaa she paused and stared at them. Shaya moved close to La and put her head on La's shoulder. Danaaa was on La's other side. Danaaa grabbed her own ponytail and gave it to La. La only looked at Danaaa for a second, before taking it and turning towards the exit. All three of the Ra walked out together.

Both Syn and Ramala watched the Ra girls, until they were gone. Ramala walked over to Syn. Syn looked like she took some punishment in that battle. La had done more damage to Syn than Ramala could ever remember anyone doing. It had Ramala beaming with pride. So much so that Syn could see it. Ramala caught herself and said "Forgive La, she's young and full of herself. Still, she'll remember everything you taught her. You've done a great service training all of my children. There's practically nothing you can't ask of me and not receive it. I am truly grateful!"

Syn smiled at Ramala and said "She's gotten very good. Her one, two combination punch is outstandingly fast. If she keeps her anger in check, she'll be almost unbeatable." Ramala questioned "Almost unbeatable?" Syn looked away. She then looked back at Ramala and said "No one is unbeatable their entire life. The trick is to know when to stop fighting, before you get beat." Ramala nodded her head in agreement. They walked out of the courtyard, together.

Syn went and soaked in a nice hot bath. Her body was sore all over. Syn didn't realize how long she and La had fought, until it was over. They went for a little over an hour. No one had ever lasted that long with Syn, Jara. La was eighteen and Syn was twice her age. That made Syn wonder how much longer she could keep fighting at her highest level. She thought about Cat, Backir, Yin and all of the other fallen Butchers. All of them had warning signs that they didn't see, or ignored. After that, for one reason, or another, all of them were defeated in battle.

Syn told herself that even though she didn't want to, she'd probably have to take her own advice. Stop while you're unbeatable, because if you keep fighting, sooner or later, someone will beat you. Syn wondered how do you know when that time is? Was this fight with La a warning? Then she thought that it might be, when someone half your age gives you the best one on one fight of your life!

When the Ra girls left their training session with Syn, neither Shaya nor Danaaa said a word to La. They both knew she would be calm shortly, if they gave her time. That's when they saw the Ra boys. All of the Ra boys looked at La and saw she'd been roughed up pretty good. They also saw that she wasn't in the best of moods. They all knew that's when you don't bother La! Still, Dan had to catch and stop himself from saying something out of line.

La looked at Dan. This time Dan thought before he spoke. He told La that their father wanted to see her as soon as possible. Dan smiled at La. He told her he would see her at mid day's meal. Dan looked at Shaya and Danaaa, before walking away with the Ra boys. La thought Dan would have made an out of the way comment after seeing her condition. She expected it, but was glad when he didn't.

Later that day, Elder Dan looked at all of his children and Yin. He thought back to the time he spent in the Southern Jungle. He thought it best if he told his children everything he knew about the Shinmushee and their Jungle ways. He did just that at last day's meal and afterwards. It was a long night of listening, but the Hammer-Axe Six learned a lot about the Shinmushee from Dan's dealings with them.

CHAPTER 29

After getting supplies the Ra caravan was ready to leave early, next day, just before sunrise. Tania was going this time. She was staying with the forces that were going to back up the Hammer-Axe Six.

Trina was staying behind, but came to see the caravan off. Dan saw her, but didn't see any of her tasty pastries. He was disappointed, so he ignored Trina. Trina saw that and walked up to Dan. Dan barely turned, acknowledging her. Trina said "Have a safe trip." Dan, nonchalantly, said "One or two of your pastries would have been a nice send off." Trina said "Return victorious and I'll make sure you have plenty, my King."

Dan said "I always return victorious!" Trina smiled and said "I know." Trina moved quickly on Dan, embracing him with a firm hug. Dan could feel every inch of Tina's body that was touching his. Because Trina wouldn't let go of Dan, he slowly put his arms around her waist, holding her firmly. After another moment, Trina slowly backed away from Dan and smiled, while looking into his eyes. Dan smiled, only looking at Trina for a second, before walking up the ramp. He had to admit to himself that the unexpected hug from Trina was a nice surprise. But still, after all that, he still wasn't getting a pastry!

The caravan traveled all day and camped that night, still a ways from Warlord Benobu's compound. Everyone ate well. They went over the plan once more. They knew exactly what was expected of them. Dan checked and inspected everyone, including La. La also checked everyone, ending with Dan. Once they were sure everyone was ready, it was time for rest.

After a few days travel they could see Benobu's place far off in the distance. Early, before day came, the Hammer-Axe Six, Ali, Bo and Hoban, along with six Elite Guards that Ali begged La and Dan for, moved quickly towards the Ra territory controlled by the Hayee, Warlord Benobu. Even though they moved stealthily through patches of thick bushes, spread out in this area, Benobu's scouts spotted the Ra and alerted him. Before the Hammer-Axe Six got to the first checkpoint, Benobu knew exactly where they were.

The closer the Hammer-Axe Six got to Benobu's compound the more guards they saw. All of Benobu's guards showed the proper respect to the Ra. Benobu's guards wanted to escort the Ra, but the Ra declined saying being so close to the compound, they felt safe with all the guards being everywhere.

Benobu's territory was huge. He controlled an area south and west of the main city of Ra that stretched to just south of Wa province. Even with all of that territory Benobu stayed headquartered a few days travel outside the main city of Ra.

Now that they were at the compound the six Elite guards had to create a barrier around the Royal Ra. It seemed everyone was trying to get their attention, or just a closer look. Because of the large crowd it made a tense situation for the Elite guards, as the Ra made their way towards Benobu's main house. The Royal Ra enjoyed all the attention they were getting.

The Ra were watching the crowd and saw a commotion that seemed to be moving towards them. All of them readied themselves, without pulling their axes. What they had planned would work more in their favor if they were attacked, first.

Just then, a group of four girls broke through the crowd. The three Elite Guards in front of the Royal Ra quickly pulled their axes, aiming them at the females. La's voice boomed "Don't harm them! Let them through!"

The three Elite Guards turned sideways and peeked at Dan. Dan nodded for them to move aside. They did so, immediately. The four girls bum rushed La and her sisters, hugging them profusely.

All the girls parted enough to get a good look at each other. The Hayee, Kastacia, or Stacia, or Stacie as she was called, exclaimed "Look at you! Little La, looking all grown up!" La smiled at Stacia. She was happy to see her, too.

The Hayee, Stacia was a very tall, thin and muscular girl. She was darker than the Ra girls and older at twenty three years old. Her sister was the Ra, Zeelynn. Zeelynn was called Lynn. Lynn was shorter than Stacia, but was just as thin and muscular. She was sixteen years old. The other two cousins were Callie and Lana. Both were twenty years old. All four were Great Granddaughters of Warlord Benobu.

These girls protected the Ra, against their older Hayee cousins, when the Ra were younger. La and her sisters genuinely loved these girls. La and her siblings treated the other three as if they were also Ra.

The Hayee, Stacia said "All of Lynn's training has paid off. This day she's being promoted to grandfather's bodyguard! She's just that good!" La said "That's great!" as all the Ra looked at Lynn. Lynn looked at the Ra girls and said "It pleases me that you would come all this way for my ceremony." La, using this unforeseen opportunity to her advantage, said "I'm glad we could make it."

Stacia stealthily peeked around and then said to La "The ceremony starts shortly. We can talk afterwards, if that's agreeable to you." La nodded that it was. The four girls dragged the Ra girls along with them, while the Ra boys tried to keep up. They were led to a courtyard where the ceremony was taking place.

Lynn took her place with about twenty males and three other females. They were standing, facing Benobu and other Elders of the Benobu clan. Once the Elders saw the Royal Ra, they invited them to the front of the courtyard.

Benobu studied La and Dan as they walked forward. La and Dan did the same to Benobu. Benobu and all the Elders lowered their heads to the Royal Ra. The Ra slightly lowered their heads.

Benobu was pleasant, saying "It's always a pleasure when the young King and Queen visit. Let me know if there's anything that I can do to make your visit more enjoyable." La smiled at Benobu and said "I will." Benobu smiled at La and then turned his attention to the ceremonies.

La and her siblings were given front row seats. They watched as Lynn and the others proudly walked past. All three of the Royal Ra girls were very proud of Lynn. None more so than La. La would have had Lynn working as one of her Special Guards. Lynn was just that good. But Stacia requested that La allow her crew of four to serve their grandfather. In return, Stacia offered to be La's eyes and ears in the Benobu camp. That was an offer La couldn't refuse. Even though Stacia didn't know about her grandfather's involvement in Shamika's murder, she'd given La lots of valuable information over time.

Lynn didn't know her sister was a spy for La. She just thought they liked to communicate, through messengers, because of the distance between them. La saw how proud Lynn looked, but knew Lynn had no idea that soon, all Hell would break loose!

After the ceremony, La told Benobu she requested he meet with her. Benobu set it up for this very courtyard. He had some of his guards get rid of the crowd, while a large contingency of guards stayed in the courtyard close to him. Lynn was there with the other new bodyguards.

Benobu stood up and then walked over to the Royal Ra. When he did his bodyguards moved with him. Benobu saw that and motioned for his guards to move back to their positions. He then walked over to and in front of La and Dan. He got down on his knees and then lowered his head.

La was momentarily confused by Benobu's show of respect. Where he was she could take his head clean off and be done with this. Was this some plan of his to get her to do just that? La knew Benobu was crafty, so she wasn't going to take his head, before displaying his guilt before his entire family.

La said "You may rise." When Benobu did, La held out her hand. Benobu didn't hesitate when he took it and gently kissed it.

La felt the tenderness in which he held her hand and it confused her even more.

La regrouped and said "Benobu, I am concerned about your ability to control this territory given to you in the name of your Queen, my mother Hayee, Ramala. While in Anduku territory we were attacked by Shitmushee Butchers. The Shitmushee that we faced coming through Anduku territory was unexpected, but we understood that under the circumstances, it was what it was. But to our surprise we were attacked from our backside by the Shitmushee, also. It troubled my greatly because the only way they could make it north to our position would be to travel through the city of Ra, or your territory, or maybe go further west through Wa territory. Or they could have gone even further west and gone through Yee province. Three of these scenarios could not have happened without starting a war. So, Benobu, tell me, what have you to say?"

They Royal Ra watched Benobu as La said the charge against him. He was calm and as soon as La was done, Benobu motioned for his guards to bring his throne chair. Benobu sat down and then said "It troubled me also to find that Shinmushee had moved through my territory before I knew about it. The ones responsible for letting that breach happen have been dealt with. I take full responsibility. I offer my head for my short comings."

As soon as Benobu said that La stood up. When La stood up about twenty of Benobu's bodyguards ran to his throne chair and got down on one knee beside him. The Hammer-Axe Six watched the guards closely and was just short of action when they got down next to Benobu's chair. Benobu yelled "Back to your post!"

None of his bodyguards moved. One of them said "Grandfather, no disrespect to the young Queen but, we guard your life, as well as your head, with our lives!" once that guards said that, another fifty bodyguards joined the others by Benobu's throne chair. Then, Stacia, her female cousins and a bunch of her male cousins walked back onto the courtyard and over to the side of Benobu's throne chair. Stacia looked at the Ra girls and then looked at Benobu. She asked "Grandfather, what's going on here?" Benobu said, without taking his eyes off of La "Our Young Queen has some questions she needs answered."

Stacia had a confused look on her face when she lowered her head to Benobu. She move back and got down on one knee next to him. She looked in the direction of the Royal Ra, but no higher than their feet, as most all of the others on Benobu's side were doing.

The level of support Benobu had here didn't surprise La. She came here knowing that she might have to carve up a few of her distant relative to get to Benobu. She just didn't want it to be Stacia, or Lynn. But still, even though she didn't want to, La would do what whatever it took to get the job done.

Where La was standing she didn't think she was in immediate danger. La as well as her sibling felt that they could easily kill Benobu even with close to eighty guards next to him. La looked at Benobu and said "The assault on the main palace has been traced back to your family, as well. My mother pardoned your guards, but I know you had knowledge of it. What say you to this?"

Just as calmly as before, Benobu said "I did know about it. Only I was here and couldn't stop it before it happened. I also eliminated the culprits of that plot."

Danaaa jumped out of her seat and was next to La before La knew it. Danaaa lightly bumped La, while looking at Benobu. She yelled "Heeee's guilty! Holler charge!" Without taking her eyes off Benobu, La reached behind Danaaa and grabbed her ponytail. La pulled it slightly and said "Baby, enough, for now. Stand here quietly and let me have my say." Danaaa said in her whispering voice "But you already know guards aren't supposed to come into the palace! So, what are you waiting for?!" La screamed "Silence! You let me have my say, here." Danaaa stomped one foot and then the other. She crossed both her arms about her chest and stared at Benobu.

Benobu watched as Shaya jumped out of her seat and quickly joined her sisters, standing on the other side of La. Then Shaya did something she hadn't done in a while. She reached and took the end of La's ponytail. Once she had it, with the same hand she was holding the ponytail with she stuck her thumb in her mouth and leaned her head gently on La's shoulder, while looking at Benobu. La and Danaaa saw that immediately. La couldn't understand why Shaya would do that, at this time. It was such a shock to La that she didn't respond, at all.

Upon seeing La not respond, in the least bit, Danaaa turned, pleading to La with both palms open, saying "But you already know what needs to be done! She's practically begging you to slap her and you won't even do it!" that's when La growled from the bottom of her belly "I said, let me have my say!!!"

In protest, Danaaa stomped one foot and then the other. She put one foot forward and started tapping it repeatedly on the ground, impatiently, still with her arms crossed about her chest. While composing herself, La looked at Danaaa's foot and then out over the crowd, daring anyone to look like what they were seeing was strange.

Benobu was amused by the Ra girl and the slight smile on his face said as much. He'd seen some of this behavior when the Ra girls were younger, be didn't expect to see it at their present age. Right now Benobu wouldn't be surprised if the Ra boys got into an all-out brawl with each other, right in front of him, like he'd seen in the past. When La saw the smile on Benobu's face, is when she started talking, again.

La said "So you admit to incompetence?" Benobu shook his head and said "Young Queen, it's embarrassing that I found out about these incidents without enough time to prevent them. It's embarrassing, to say the least. But incompetence, now that's going too far." Benobu motioned for his bodyguards to stay in place. He walked closer to La and her sisters.

Benobu could see that La was on guard. Shaya looked as if she was daydreaming, even though she was looking directly at Benobu. He also could see Danaaa was studying him so closely that if he made one false move, she'd see it coming.

Benobu looked all three of them over with a proud smile on his face, before settling his eyes on La. With his back to his guards, Benobu said so only the Ra girls could hear him "It makes me proud to see my three nieces growing up. You know, I watched your mother and aunts grow up, too. I'm getting older and a lot of things in my own house, I can't keep up with. La, you're very smart and I know you'll make a great Queen. If I might make one suggestion. Don't put me on trial in front of our family. A lot of the younger ones are Ra. They love you, but they love me more. If you have me killed, all these warriors that could be fighting for you, you'll have to kill. What sense does that make, when they could be working for you? If you have to kill me, do it so as no one knows you had it done. If it's your wish that I die, I'll cooperate, completely. That's how you keep unity in the House of Ra."

La was dumbfounded and caught off guard by Benobu's words. Benobu was teaching La what was best to do, when she came here intent on killing him. Heck, he was even teaching her the right way to get rid of himself!

La loved to learn and Benobu had tapped into that. She could read people as well as her mother and father. To La, Benobu seemed sincere. Like her sisters, after hearing that, La didn't want Benobu dead. This all seemed to be some sort of misunderstanding, where their poor uncle Benobu was framed. That had to be it! La redirected her thoughts and was focused again, when she said "Don't worry, uncle Benobu. You're a great Hero in the House of Ra. Still, I will find those who tried to tarnish your reputation. Rest assured I'll make them pay!"

La then lowered her head to Benobu. Danaaa wiped the sweat from her upper lip and did a quick jerk, lowering and raising of her head. Shaya did so after that. Then all three of them rushed Benobu and hugged him. It was a tense moment, in which Benobu's bodyguards hesitated, just long enough to see that he wasn't being attacked. Benobu was shocked by the affection the Ra girls were showing him. He hesitated a moment, before wrapping his arm around the Ra girls.

A second later, everyone in the courtyard erupted into favorable chants. The tension in the air dissipated almost instantly. Everyone looked at each other. It was time to celebrate. A gathering and feast was set up. Benobu could see that and decided to leave. The gathering lasted well after daylight was gone. Most everyone at the gathering, including the Royal Ra, rested well into the next day.

The Royal Ra decided to visit cousins, uncles and aunt that they hadn't seen in a while. It was always great spending time with family. That took the rest of that day. After another gathering, the Royal decided to leave when next day came.

The Royal Ra had a late first day's meal. With all the partying, La and Dan hadn't had a chance to question the whereabouts of Jay. They were determined to get that done today. After resting from the meal, La sent Ali and Hoban to find out where Jay could be found.

The two Ra Warlords returned with escorts ready to take the Royal Ra to Jay. It had been explained that Jay wasn't going to come of his own free will. La and Dan were good with that.

The escorts told the Ra that Jay was held up south in Benobu's territory. They gathered water and food. Shortly after that, they were on their way. On the way, Dan was glad that La didn't summon the rest of their forces. He knew Jay and his men would be a challenge, but nothing they couldn't handle. It would be a great workout before they returned to the Royal caravan.

It was a few hours travel, so the Ra split the journey by having a mid-day meal before continuing to their destination. When they were close the escorts said it might be better to travel the rest of the way on foot. He said that if Jay and his men saw the Elephants they might stay clear and they would be chasing Jay and possibly never catching him. La and Dan agreed.

They traveled on foot for another twenty minutes, or so, before they saw a camp off in the distance. Everyone got into stealth mode. La told the escorts they should head back as so not to get involved. The escorts did as they were told.

Everyone huddled up as Dan gave last minute instruction. He told the Elite guards, Ali, Hoban and Bo that he expected there wouldn't be a repeat performance in which the Number two princess would be wounded. That they should protect Shaya and La at all cost. Hoban questioned "And Danaaa?" everyone looked at Danaaa, who was wiping sweat from above her upper lip with her wrist wrap. When Danaaa noticed everyone looking at her she said "It's sweat, is all it is!" everyone turned and looked back at Hoban. Dan said "You know Stupid is High Pressure, an Executioner. I think she'll be alright. But you can keep an eye on her from time to time. Try not to get caught up in watching, though." Dan looked at Danaaa. He could see she was just as ready for action as she always was. They stared at each other for a moment and then Dan ordered everyone forward.

The Hammer-Axe Six, Bo, Ali, Hoban and their six Elite guards spread out a little and stealthily moved through the trees and bushes, closer to the camp. There was a clearing ahead of the plains that they would have to crawl on their bellies, instead of walking, if they didn't want to be seen. So that's what they did. As they were crawling towards the camp on the flat grasslands, Ram and Danaaa stopped. Dan and La looked over at them to see what it was that affected them. A moment later, they heard a low rumbling sound, like a heard of animals but not as loud. Dan looked over at La, and in a split second they figured out what it was.

Everyone jumped to their feet and looked around. They saw thousands upon thousands of Warriors in the distance racing towards them, from behind and both sides. They looked back in front and saw Warriors charging from the camp they were sneaking up on.

The Warriors were closing in from all sides but their distance meant they wouldn't reach the Hammer-Axe Six for close to a minute and a half. La looked at Dan and with her lower lip crooked on one side and said "Benobu!"

Dan said "We don't know that, yet! Just concentrate on the situation at hand! Form a circle around Don and Shaya! You two stay put and only use your hammers when necessary!"

The six Elite guards formed a circle around Shaya and Don giving them lanes to throw their hammers. The Ra Warlords and the rest of the hammer-Axe six formed a wider circle around the Elite Guards in the inner circle.

With only about thirty seconds before the warriors arrived Dan looked at his Warlords as everyone was spacing themselves for battle. Dan made eye contact with Don, Yin and Ram. They weren't shaken by the situation. That made him feel better. Dan lastly looked at La, who was next to him. He saw she was ready. La looked at Dan. It was a look that said 'Let's do whatever it takes, so we can deal with whoever set us up!' the look in Dan's eyes gave the answer La was looking for. La took a step away from Dan and violently jerked her head twice. That sent her ponytail into the air, spinning.

The adrenaline in Dan's body was pumping at a level like never before. Dan wanted a highly charged battle in which his skills would be challenged to the max. He was going to prove that he was the Hammer-Axe Champion, this day.

Dan heard La say, almost to herself "Cut Faster MesoCyclone!" Seconds before contact with the warriors, Dan noticed that Danaaa had moved back into the circle with Don and Shaya and was sitting with her legs crossed, Indian style, on the ground eating a cookie!

Dan put that out of his mind and turned back to the business at hand. He could now see the faces of the warriors charging at him. All of them were Shinmushee. A second later, it was warfare at its most basic level. Kill, or be killed!

La jerked her head again and turned her entire body one revolution, just as the first warrior, reached striking range of her metal ball. He misjudge the velocity of La's rocketing metal ball and it smashed into the side of his head with so much force it sent him sideways and off of his feet. But because of the sheer number of charging warriors La had to rely on her axes, while stepping inside of most every swing at her, using her counter-attacking offensive style. La mortally wounded everyone in range of her axes, dishing out only one chop each, with devastating effects. Warriors were dropping like flies at her feet.

Dan, being next to La wasn't going to be outdone by La's mastery of her axes. He chopped and blocked everything in front of him with machine like efficiency. Everyone held their ground and withstood the first initial push on the front line. After that, the Hammer-Axes Six and their forces widened their fighting circle, forcing the warriors to stop charging and start fighting with a bit more strategy. That still didn't seem to help them.

Just as the battle started, two of the Elite guards in the inner circle had to run and fight in the void where Ram was. When Ram saw Danaaa sitting and eating a cookie, he walked over to her and reached out his hand for one. Danaaa stared at Ram for a moment, before reaching into her vest pocket and giving him two cookies. Ram took the cookies and sat on the ground with his back to Danaaa. Both watched the raging battles around them, while enjoying some tasty cookies.

It wasn't long before the Hammer-Axe Six, minus four, plus their Warlords had control of this battle. The Ra forces kept their circle moving southward every time Shinmushee bodies started piling up in the area they were fighting in. That way they always had clear ground to fight on, while the Shinmushee had to step over, or fight around the bodies of their dead comrades.

Even Danaaa and Ram, who weren't involved in the battles, had to get up off the ground and follow in order to stay in the circle. After eating his cookies, Ram put out his hand to Danaaa looking for another cookie. Danaaa looked at Ram like that was enough for now and they had serious business at hand. But still, Danaaa gave Ram another cookie. He shoved it into his mouth as quickly as he'd done the others. They both stepped over bodies, staying in the circle next to Don and Shaya, but still not joining the battles.

While walking, Ram put out his hand to Danaaa for another cookie. Before he'd completely extended it, Danaaa slapped Ram's hand away. Ram was only use to physicality from a short list of people. Danaaa wasn't on that list. Ram's eyes went slowly from Danaaa's hand to Danaaa's eyes. They stared at each other. Danaaa was the only person who could stare into Ram's eyes without being affected by how creepy they were. Ram's hands moved to the handles of his axes. While looking into Ram's eyes, Danaaa saw Ram's hands moving towards his axes, with her field vision.

Danaaa wasn't worried, though. She knew if Ram pulled his axes intent on using them on her, he would regret it for the rest of his life. However much longer that would be. She just knew it!

A few moments after they locked eyes Danaaa yelled "But I already told you, we have more important things to do than eat cookies all day! You're getting too old for this kind of behavior!"

Ram didn't remember hearing Danaaa tell him that, before now. In his split second of confusion, Danaaa said "Come on, quit playing around!" then Danaaa turned and started walking towards the front line of battle, where La and Dan were. Ram hesitated for a moment and then followed.

At the front line of battle the Ra forces were pushing the Shinmushee back. The Shinmushee parted and moved back, revealing about forty, or so, Shinmushee Butchers. Just as that happened, Danaaa and Ram walked past Dan and La, in the direction of the Shinmushee Butchers. Danaaa turned and looked at La. She said "Shitmushee Butchers, now it's my turn!"

Dan started to follow but La pointed her ax in Dan's direction. When Dan looked at La, she gave him a look that said wait. So he did. Everyone watched as Danaaa and Ram marched right up to the Shinmushee Butchers.

The forty-five Shinmushee Butcher saw the two Ra walking towards them, while the others waited behind. The Shinmushee had been spotting the battle and had already picked who each of them were going to attack. Their plan slightly changed when they saw two of the Ra walking towards them. It seemed these two might want to negotiate, or something. They were going to kill them and then proceed with their plan of killing the other Ra.

Danaaa and Ram stopped just short of the Shinmushee Butchers. Danaaa put both her hands on her hips and said "Go back to the jungle and hide so that we can't find you! That's how you keep your heads!"

This was a direct insult and was dealt with as such. The Shinmushee Butchers didn't say a word. Twenty Shinmushee Butchers spread out and circled around the two Ra, concentrating on them with bad intentions. Ram and Danaaa moved away from each other letting ten Butchers surround each of them. As they watched Danaaa, a silly grin came on her face. A second later, both Ram and Danaaa were attacked.

Danaaa instantly put High Pressure on the Butchers and commenced to carving up them up, immediately. With, at least fifteen axes coming at her every time she move, Danaaa sent one, ore two of the Butchers to the ground with a mortal wound. It only took Danaaa thirty minutes to kill those ten Butchers. When she finished off the last Butchers, Danaaa saw Ram's shirt get shredded, while he was showing off. Ram's close calls with those Shinmushee axes had Danaaa fearing for his life.

Ram managed to kill five Butchers inside of twenty minutes. When there were only five of them left, determined to send Ram to hell, he did something amazing. Ram slammed his axes into the holsters on his waist and commenced to artfully dodging every ax swing of these Butchers. Ram flipped, tucked and rolled. He did every type of maneuver just staying out of reach of the enemy's axes.

Then out of nowhere, one of the Butchers axes sliced open Ram's shirt, near his ribs, without touching flesh. In an instant, Ram had his axes out of their holsters and was carving up these Butchers. He finished them off as quickly as he'd done the others. When he was done, Ram turned and saw Danaaa angrily staring at him.

Ram stood there staring at Danaaa. Ram still didn't like that Danaaa slapped his hand, over a cookie. Not even his mother had ever done that! Both realized they hadn't put their axes back in their holsters, while facing each other. As they stared at each other, neither was going to do it, unless the other did.

As long as they'd lived, these two never had one fight. Now, both wanted the other to back down. But since neither of these two rarely backed down from anyone, they just stood there staring at each other. Danaaa said "If you were fighting somebody like me, you'd never be able to Artfully Dodge like that!" Ram said in a low deep bass "If we fight, you lose!" Even though Danaaa wasn't saying she, herself, would fight Ram, Ram took it as just that.

Danaaa, trying to clear things up for Ram, never broke eye contact with Ram when she said "But, I already know that! If we fight, and I beat you, I lose! And you'll have to kill me to win! But I already know you can't do that! I just know it! Because then you lose, too!"

The murderous Ram was torn between seeing if he actually could beat Danaaa, or would attempt to. Ram inhaled slowly and then exhaled the same way, while staring at Danaaa. It was a Mexican standoff between the Immaculate Degenerate, High Pressure the Executioner, Dan Jinn-Eco and the Dirty Degenerate, Low Pressure Assassin, Eco-Jin Ram!

CHAPTER 30

Danaaa started slowly circling Ram, while Ram just stood there not moving at all. If Danaaa made one move towards him, Ram was going to cut her to pieces. He would deal with the consequences, after that.

While that was happening the rest of the Hammer-Axe Six were in death battles against the other twenty Shinmushee Butchers who had moved past the Butchers who attacked Ram and Danaaa.

Don and Shaya watched, from the circle, as the battles started. They could see that the Shinmushee Butchers were trying to separate the Hammer-Axe Six into battles of their choosing. Because of their skills it was working. Dan, La, Hoban, Ali, three Elite Guards, Yin, and Bo were on the outer circle. All of them were double teamed with two Shinmushee Butchers, each.

Once that happened, Shaya and Don saw another Shinmushee Butcher attack Dan between Dan and La, forcing more distance between La and Dan. After that, three more Shinmushee Butchers moved in and attacked La. In no time flat, both Shaya and Don launched all of their hammers at the Butchers closest to La.

All of Don's hammers were blocked, but took some of the heat off La. It amazed Shaya that all but three of her hammers were blocked. Still, all of them made a huge impact in the battle.

Once La was attacked she had to use everything she'd learned up to this point. When she saw that it was Butchers moving in on her, La quickly tucked her ponytail away. She couldn't afford for a Butcher to get a hold of her ponytail. She knew she'd be dead soon after that. La managed to swing her axes offensively a few times, before being put completely on defense. She had no choice. It was either get out of the way of the axes, or get cut to pieces. La's moves were tight, exact and extremely evasive. She blocked when she had to and dodged everything else. Her counter-attacking skills kept the Butchers, at least careful, giving La just enough room to evade them.

But when La saw three more Shinmushee Butchers moving in on her, she knew her life was in serious danger. In that instant, La saw the Butcher in front of her slightly disengage her, as he started blocking hammers. La didn't hesitate. She went on the offensive, immediately. She put that Butcher who was blocking hammers down with two well-placed axe strikes. One to his chest and one to the side of his neck. La caught two more Shinmushee Butchers with mortal strikes, after Shaya's hammers plowed into the sides of their heads.

Even with that, La still had high heat on her and everyone one of her moves had to be her best. After the hammers stopped coming, La was once again doing everything she could to stay out of the way of axe blades continuously coming at her.

Don ran up and took on one Butcher. Another Butcher attacked Don and now both he and La were battling two Butchers each. Shaya turned just in time to see that the back side of the circle had been breached. She charged herself, pulled her axes and joined that battle, immediately.

Shaya and the three Elite Guards protecting her were instantly in a dog fight against two Butchers, hell bent on killing Shaya. That left the three Elite Guards covering the backside of the circle with one Shinmushee Butcher each to deal with. Right now, with Yin, Bo, Hoban and Ali all battling two Butchers each, no one could give help to anyone else. This was the most highly charged intense battle any of the Hammer-Axe Six and their Warlords had ever been in.

The slightest mistake could mean the difference between life and death. It also meant that if you were killed, someone else would have to deal with extra heat from the person, or persons who killed you.

When Dan was attacked by three Butchers he had to give this fight the seriousness it deserved and he did. Dan countered offensively off of every axe swung at him. His speed was amazing, but it was only enough to deal with the six axes coming at him from all directions. Dan went move for move with every swing of those Shinmushee Butchers' axes.

Dan managed to see, for a split second, that La was in trouble. He tried to force the action of his battle towards her so he could help, but was met with stern resistance. Dan peeked again and saw La disappear under the hammers flying past her. Dan knew if the hammers had been thrown to help La, she must really be in trouble.

In a fraction of a fraction of a second, Dan decided he was going to get to La, no matter what it took. Dan hard charged with an offensive flurry towards the Butcher in the opposite direction of La. The precision and lightning quickness of his ax strikes backed up that Butcher. With the same lightning speed, Dan turned and attacked the Butcher at his back. Once that Butcher backed off a little, Dan took two steps towards him and launched himself up and over him. The three Butchers all saw Dan's move. Each one of them moved into position to make Dan pay for this reckless move with his life.

The Butcher Dan jumped over brought both his axes, swinging upward to take off one, or both of Dan's legs. The second Dan took two steps and was airborne, so was the Butcher on his left side. That Butcher had his ax in motion to strike at Dan in midair. The Butcher who was behind Dan and was momentarily backed up took off running to meet Dan where he knew he would land coming out of the air.

As Dan went airborne he knew the Butcher under him would strike from below, first. Dan brought his knees up to his chest and swung the ax in his right hand under his feet blocking the swings from below. At the same time Dan moved the axe in his left hand in a blocking position and managed to block several swings from the Butcher in the air with him on his left side. The Butcher, who was quickly moving around to Dan, from the ground, was almost in position to be there when Dan landed. Because Dan jumped in the air before the Butcher that jumped in the air attacking him, Dan landed a second sooner. No sooner than Dan's feet hit the ground, he dove away from the ax coming at him from the Butcher that had run around trying to get in position to cut Dan. That Butcher was a split second late and although he still got a good swing at Dan, Dan was able to dive in the opposite direction to avoid his axes.

Now as the Butcher who was coming out of the air, feet were just hitting the ground, Dan was there with his most potent lightning fast swings of his axes. Dan was the Faster Cut and without the Butchers feet firmly planted on the ground, he couldn't use his power to stop Dan's lightning fast attack. He was sliced open several times inside of a second by Dan's axes.

Adrenaline was flowing through Dan like high octane jet fuel. He quickly turned around and had to block swings by the two Butchers behind him. But now Dan was on an entirely different level than before. He was hell-bent on getting to La and nothing was going to stop him. Dan's axes instantly backed up one of the Butchers, while the other was trying to keep heat on Dan. Then the one who thought he was helping was turned upon with a lightning fast flurry by Dan that left him slashed through the front side of his left shoulder and the upper right side of his back. Dan had to quickly turn his attention back to the other Butcher and sent his axes flying at him before turning back to the wounded Butcher with lightning speed. With his first two swings being blocked, Dan took that Butcher's head clean off with the third strike. In an instant Dan had turned and was engaging the last Butcher he was fighting. Dan was backing him up with some high heat and was moving in La's direction. That caught the attention of the Butchers fighting La. La was just as high on adrenaline as Dan was.

The split second of attention those Butchers paid to Dan cost one of them his life, courtesy of La's Axes. La Cut faster than either of those Butchers had ever seen before and soon after she'd killed the first one the second one was wounded and in serious trouble. La killed her second Butcher, just as Dan was finishing off the last one he was fighting. They barely acknowledged each other before attacking, entering in and changing all of the battles that were going on around them. It wasn't long before there were only a few Butchers left. A wave of Shinmushee warriors charged the Hammer-Axe Six, trying to save the few Butchers left. They and the Butchers left were cut to pieces.

After the last Shinmushee Butchers were killed, the Shinmushee warriors retreated towards the jungle. La and Dan watched the retreating warriors with their eyes still blazing from adrenaline. They searched and saw that Yin, Don, Hoban, Bo and Ali, who were all looking around making sure the threat of danger was really gone.

They saw Ram and Danaaa making their way towards them. They were a little confused because they saw Danaaa pick up a severed arm and throw it at Ram, only to have Ram bat it back at Danaaa with the flat side of his ax. Before the severed arm got to Danaaa, she'd pulled her axes and batted it back towards Ram. This time Ram knocked the limb to the ground with the flat side of his ax. La and Dan didn't know what to make of that and wasn't going to waste time trying to figure it out. The main thing for La and Dan was they both were unharmed. The fact of the matter was when Ram and Danaaa saw hundreds of Shinmushee warriors headed towards them that ended their Mexican Standoff, for the time being.

La and Dan also looked around staring at a sea of dead Shinmushee bodies and body parts, limbs, heads and guts, everywhere. The ground had pools of blood and bloody mud mixed with guts everywhere they looked. It was a scene of carnage that only some warriors ever get to see in a lifetime. Still, a scene like this never leaves your mind and is burned into your memory, no matter how many lifetimes you're removed from it!

Lastly, Dan and La saw Shaya and three Elite Guards standing looking down at dead bodies. La and Dan quickly made their way over to Shaya. They both visually inspected Shaya for wounds. She had blood splattered all over her cloths, but none of it was hers.

While still looking down and without looking at Dan or La, Shaya said solemnly "They gave their lives protecting me. These are great heroes of Ra!"

Before anyone could agree, one of the three remaining Elite Guards wobbled and then fell to the ground. No one had noticed the many deep slices all over his body, until he was on his back, looking up. His eyes slowly moved to La's face. They seemed to gloss over, looking in focus one second and looking as if they were fading the next. He said to La "Long live my Queen, the Ra, Ramala! I did my best to protect you my Queen and our family against . . . . those . . . .Shit . . . . mu . . . . shee!" then he exhaled his last breath and his head rolled over to the side.

La thought about how she always treated her Hayee family members a little less favorably than she did her Ra family members. Yet, here was a Hayee who gave his life for her. La was not only changed by that, she was changed by the level of savagery she had to bring out of herself in order to survive, here today. La was still smart as ever and still the young Queen, but now she was changed forever. In the last three and a half hour battle, La was transformed from an extremely good killer, into a Butcher.

In fact, the rest of the Hammer-Axe Six all became true Butchers this day, along with Bo, Hoban, Ali and the two remaining Elite Guards. Ramala's youngest twins were already natural born Butchers.

All of them stared down at the Elite Guard who'd just died, until they noticed two tears fall to the ground from La's face. La didn't wipe the tears from her face when she looked at Ali and said "Take these great heroes of Ra back to the main city. I want the proper respect shown to them for their service."

Stacia and Lynn came running up and stopped short of La. La quickly turned and stared at them. They both immediately lowered their heads. La didn't beat around the bush when she said "If I find out that Jay, or Benobu had anything to do with this, I'll have their heads!"

Stacia didn't move, but Lynn took a step back. That made La and the others focus on Lynn. Stacia saw that and said "La!" then Stacia caught herself and said "I mean, young Queen, it was grandfather who sent us here to help. Our guards fought the Shinmushee off, until they retreated to the jungle. Grandfather did what he could to help! You're wrong about Grandfather!"

La loved her cousins and knew if she killed Benobu, she'd have to kill Stacia and Lynn. La said "I hope you're right!" La said that because she didn't want to kill these two if she didn't have to.

Stacia needed this conversation to go in another direction, so she said "Grandfather told us to do whatever you needed done, in order to help." La looked behind Stacia and saw a couple hundred of Benobu's warriors waiting to be instructed.

La stopped herself from thinking about Benobu. If he was involved in this, she would deal with him later. Right now, she had more important business. La looked at Stacia and said "Have those guards take these great heroes back to the main city so that they can get the proper respect. Get us food and water for a few days journey. Also, go to my caravan and have Tania take the caravan to the lower Houses. Have her stockpile supplies and tighten security in all Ra strongholds."

Stacia asked "I will, but what about you La? What about you?" La said "First, me and the Hammer-Axe Six are going to find the Hayee, Jay and see what he has to say for himself. After that, we're going to the Southern Jungle to convince the Shitmushee to end their random attacks in Ra territory!" Stacia's face looked shocked and concerned at the same time. She said "La, that's too dangerous! You'll need an army!"

La said "Let me worry about that! You just make sure Tania gets my message!" Stacia said "She'll have it before next day comes." La said "Good!" Lynn stepped forward and said "La, let me go with you. I know I can help!"

La looked at Lynn. Lynn was good, but La didn't think Lynn would make it back alive, if she let her come. La said "You stay here and guard Benobu. Train hard at you techniques and one day

I'm sure you'll get a chance to do your part to help me. That time is not now." Lynn lowered her head and backed up.

La looked at Stacia and said "You find a way to keep things under control here. If not, I'll come back and I'll secure this territory with whom I see fit. It's best for everyone if that doesn't happen. Do what you have to. If you need help, send messengers and I'll make sure you have all the support you need to run this territory properly."

Stacia could see that La was giving her power to control this territory. La was retiring Benobu, without taking his title. But still, Stacia knew, from what La said that if she couldn't get this territory secured, La would blame her.

Stacia went over and started giving orders to the warriors waiting. The warriors dispersed, with some taking the bodies of the dead Elite guards, while others went to take care of other task.

La looked at Dan, but noticed Danaaa wiping, with her forearm, just under her nose, again. La asked "Why is your nose running?" Danaaa said "Nothing's coming from my nose, its sweat!" La only looked at Danaaa for another second. They let it go. La sternly said "Come here!" Danaaa cautiously walked up to La. La reached behind Danaaa and grabbed her ponytail. She then turned and looked at Dan.

When La said that the Hammer-Axe Six were going after Jay and then going into the Southern Jungle, Dan smiled inwardly. He was barely able to control himself. On the outside he kept a calm cool demeanor. Dan knew there would be more highly charged battles like the one they just had, or better. That's just what he wanted. Only now he didn't have to try to convince La of anything. La seemed dead set on it.

When La turned and looked at Dan, Dan looked around at his other siblings. He said "Everyone proved their worth today. Not a weak link in the bunch. Still, we have a lot of tough work ahead of us. Where we're going things will get a lot tougher. Keep your minds sharp and your techniques tight. After we get supplies, we'll move south, immediately. That way, there won't be much forewarning of our coming." La looked at everyone and nodded in agreement.

Shaya looked at everyone. She could see that they all had exerted a lot of energy in this battle. Shaya thought they all could use some rest, before taking on such a big mission. She didn't want to argue with Dan and La, who seemed determined to leave right away. Shaya whined, saying "I need to get cleaned and rested before I go anywhere! If you have to go now, you'll just have to leave me here, until you get back!" La and Dan looked at Shaya. There was no way that was going to happen!

Dan could force Shaya to go now if he really wanted to. But he thought if she's really that tired, what use will she be in battle? Dan looked from Shaya to La and said "Maybe we should rest. There's no telling when the next time we'll be able to." La looked from Shaya to Dan. She then looked back at Shaya before looking at Dan again and saying "You're probably right." La pulled on Danaaa's ponytail and they all headed back to Benobu's place.

Once back at Benobu's place. Stacia had the Hammer-Axe Six heavily guarded. The girls bathed in the most luxurious bathing houses here. It had a push cushioned lounging area near the bathing pool. There was also tables and chair set up in the next room for private dining. It belonged to Benobu's seventh and youngest wife. She gladly let the Ra girls use it, looking for favor sometime in the future.

All three of the Ra girls soaked, leaning back, in a large bathing pool, relaxing from this day's battle. The hot water pulled the soreness out of their muscles and also drained the stress of battle, away. They were so relaxed, none of them said anything, until Shaya broke the silence, saying "Doesn't this make you want to go home and forget all about the Southern Jungle?"

There was no way La was going to agree with that. La lazily turned her head in Shaya's direction and said "Enjoy it while you can. There's no telling how long we'll be out in the field." After that, there was no more conversation. All three girls were enjoying this moment for what it was worth.

Dan and his male siblings were also soaking away the stress of the day, in another lavish bathing house. None of them said anything, until Dan said "Rest well this night. At some point, on this mission, I'm sure we will be tested to our limits. When it happens, just stay calm and remember your training."

Everyone rested well that night and was up early when next day came. Benobu wanted to see the Royal Ra off, but Stacia told him the Royal Ra didn't want an emotional farewell, because they needed to be sharp. Benobu reluctantly agreed that was best. The fact was Stacia purposely kept Benobu away from the Ra. Stacia was going to keep Benobu away from them, until she was sure La wouldn't have him killed.

Stacia informed La that Tania had the Royal caravan on its way to the lower Houses of Ra. Stacia also told La that all the other orders that she's given were taken care of. Also, that if La needed anything else, all she had to do was inform her what it was. La smiled at Stacia, knowing she would make the most of her new position. The Hammer-Axe Six were given a short farewell then they headed south towards the Southern Jungle.

They were walking when Danaaa said "What are we going to do, if we run out of food?" La said "You know there is an endless supply of bugs and such. We won't starve, if that's what you're worried about."

When out in the field, La would soldier up and eat whatever she had to, without pause. Danaaa and Shaya would eat what they had to, but could only take it for so long, before they started complaining. La hoped the complaints weren't starting, already.

The Hammer-Axe Six had been traveling south for over an hour and hadn't run into any resistance. All they saw were Shinmushee scouts from time to time. La said to Dan "You would think they'd have attacked us by now." Dan calmly said "They're waiting until we are far enough away that help can't reach us. That's probably when they'll attack."

La nodded and said "We'll be ready." After lunch and four hours into the journey, they could see the jungle in the distance. They kept moving towards it. As they got closer, they noticed a thin layer of clouds covering the sun. They appreciated not being in direct sunlight.

The closer to the jungle they got, the thicker the clouds got. Then it started to rain. By the time they reached the edge of the Southern Jungle there was a steady soaking rain. They still hadn't been attacked. Now they didn't even see scouts spying on them.

When they entered the Southern Jungle, the canopy of trees caught a lot of the rain, but they were still getting wet. They could hear the low droning sound of the rain hitting the leaves of the tress, continuously. The light dimmed to that of just after the sun went down. They kept moving forward. After walking for a few minutes they started to hear thunder in the far distance. As they walked further the thunder got louder and they could see flashes of lightning.

All of a sudden, both Ram and Danaaa stopped walking. That made everyone else go on guard. La whispered, asking Danaaa "What?" then they heard a boom of thunder that was louder than the last. Danaaa motioned with her hand for La to wait, while she cautiously moved a few steps ahead of everyone. She motioned with her hand for everyone to wait. She took a couple more cautious steps and then Danaaa said "Something's coming!"

There was a bright flash of lightning and an even louder boom of thunder. Everyone turned, studying their surroundings, trying to see what was coming. La whispered "Baby, what is it?!!" Danaaa didn't respond to La. She just stood there concentrating on her surroundings.

Then, seconds later, without warning, a bright lightning bolt exploded on the ground about twenty feet in front of Danaaa, with an instant boom of thunder. Danaaa fell backwards on to her butt. They all could see a large ball of electricity on the ground where the lightning had struck. Inside the ball of electricity there looked to be a man made of electricity standing there. They could see his eyes made of electricity looking at them!

In a deep loud booming voice, Ram yelled "RUN!!!" then turned and took off running in the opposite direction. Shear panic ran through everyone at seeing Ram run. They never knew anything to ever spook Ram. Heck, Ram was the spooky one! They knew if this thing was enough to scare Ram, they didn't want to deal with it.

Yin did a big hopping jump in the direction Ram was running and then yelled "You heard him, come on!!" then Yin grabbed Shaya and La's arm pulling and dragging them as he took off in the opposite direction. La snatched her arm from Yin and screamed "What about Baby!" La turned and started taking air into her lungs, when she saw Dan had picked up Danaaa from behind and they were running back towards her. La was just about to let out her best scream, when she looked into the eyes in the ball of electricity. Upon staring at those eyes, La started going into a trance. La slowly started exhaling. Running in stride next to Danaaa, Dan snatched La up off of her feet, without stopping. Dan and Danaaa raced chasing the others. They ran at top speed, hurdling bushes and fallen tree trunks. La had come out of the trance she was in, while Dan was running, but since Dan was running like a mad man and La wanted to get away, she let him!

Everyone ran well past the canopy of the Southern Jungle, following Ram. No one stopped running, until Ram did. Ram didn't stop running until he cleared the clouds that reached just past the Jungle.

Once Ram stopped, and while breathing heavily, he looked up at the clear sky overhead. He then turned and looked back at the Jungle. Everyone else ran behind him, stopped and turned also. They all were breathing heavily, trying to catch their breath. That's when Dan finally put La down.

After staring at the Jungle for a few moments, trying to digest what they'd just seen, everyone started looking at each other for an explanation. Finally, La walked over to Danaaa and asked "What was that?" everyone turned and looked at Danaaa. Danaaa said "It was a lightning Jinn!" almost everyone questioned, simultaneously "A WHAT??!!!"

Danaaa said "But, I already told you! It lives from the clouds to ground in that part of the jungle. It can't go any further than that area it's in. But once you're in its area, it controls things and plays dangerous games with you that you probably can't win!" Danaaa looked over at Ram and said "That's why Ram ran!" Ram jerked his head around and looked at Danaaa. Then Ram looked at everyone else, challenging them to look at him, like he was scared. No one did, except Danaaa.

Shaya jumped in front of La, looking terrified. Shaya bent both her legs and cried to La "I don't want to do this anymore! Oh, please La, we can't go back into the Jungle! How can we deal with something like that? I'm scared! Please, I just want to go home!"

La glared at Shaya, but didn't slap her, even though she wanted to. After seeing what she just saw, La wasn't sure if Shaya might be right, this time. La looked away from Shaya and at Danaaa. La asked "How come you didn't tell us it was there, before we went into the jungle?"

Danaaa squinted her eyes, retrospectively, and said "That one's tricky! It hid a great distance away and then move in on us fast. By the time I knew what it was, it was already there."

La knew there wasn't any way she could deal with something like that. Her voice sounded half defeated and frustrated when she said "How can anyone expect us to go into the Southern Jungle, with those Jungle Jinns waiting to ambush us?!"

Danaaa said "We don't have to worry about that one. As long as we don't go into the jungle that it controls, it can't play with us. It's the only one there. It's being punished for being bad." La asked "How do you know that?" Danaaa said "I just know it!"

La looked at Danaaa for a moment and then she said "So what you're saying is that we can go into the Jungle, if we go in another way." Danaaa nodded her head in agreement. La looked at Dan to see if he was opposed to doing that. Dan was shaken, but not deterred. He gave La a slight nod.

La looked at Danaaa. She said "Baby and Fat Boy, we need both of you to tell us when there's something around that we can't deal with. Can you do that?" Ram voice boomed with bass when he said "I did!" La said "Well, can you tell us a little sooner than that!" they both nodded that they would at least try. That was good enough for La.

La and Dan got everyone going east. They would travel to the Lower Houses of Ra and then move into the Southern Jungle from there. Danaaa said she knew they could get in that way, without seeing the Lightning Jinn. She just knew it!

Everyone walked for a while, saying nothing. They were still in shock from what had happened, earlier. None of them knew what to make of what they saw. Quite frankly it scared everyone from the Ra Warlords to Dan.

Shaya leaned on La's shoulder as soon as they started walking. It calmed Shaya. It also calmed La. For the first time in La's life, Shaya leaning on her gave La a peaceful sense of normalcy. La needed that after what she'd just seen.

Then, out of nowhere, Danaaa broke the silence. She wiped the sweat from between her upper lip and nose with her forearm and then said "Ram said run and then he did! Then, we all did!" Danaaa erupted into side splitting laughter. They all thought about how they ran, with barely any hesitation. It tickled them. Everyone else slowly joined in, until they all were laughing. The laughing seemed to release a lot of the tension and fear from seeing the so called Lightning Jinn. Ram was the last to join in. His laugh was a loud, booming, slow sinister bass of a laugh. After hearing Ram, everyone got quiet and stared at him. A moment later everyone continued on, without talking.

It was a three day's journey to the Sixth Lower House of Ra, which was closest to them. Ali suggested that they camp for the night and continue when first day came. Everyone agreed and got good rest.

When first day came, Danaaa and Ram were startled out of their sleep. That put everyone else on high alert. They all grabbed their axes and looked around. La moved close to Danaaa and asked "What is it?" Danaaa whispered "They're hiding themselves, but we'll soon see them." La said "See who?" Danaaa didn't answer. La looked around and saw Shaya looking up at the sky. La quickly looked up, too. Upon seeing La looking up, everyone else quickly looked up.

It was a clear day with only a few puffy clouds so everyone quickly went back to checking their surroundings. La needed answers so she sternly whispered to Danaaa "Tell me, is it another Jinn of some kind?" Danaaa whispered "No, but I already told you, they'll show themselves soon enough!" After seeing the Lightning Jinn, La was nervous about what she couldn't see with her own eyes.

Danaaa turned and when she did Ram turned in the same direction. After that, everyone else looked in that direction. In the distance all of them saw ten people walking towards them. Shaya nervously asked "Are they walking Jinns?" Danaaa turned and looked at Shaya like that was the craziest thing she ever heard. Danaaa looked back forward and said "There're just people that are going to try and kill us, is all." upon hearing that, everyone pulled their axes. Their confidence was back in full stride. As they got closer Dan could see them better. They didn't look like serious killer to him. Dan said "It's only ten of them. I'm sure we can handle them. But, still, let's be careful!"

Now the ten strangers were close enough that the Ra could see them clearly. One of them was a huge brute with large axes. The other nine were dressed nicely, but didn't have weapons of any kind, that they could see. That had Dan and his people focused on the brute, while slightly monitoring the others.

The ten strangers stopped a safe distance. After a moment of silence, in which they studied each other, La asked "Tell me, who are you? And why are you here?" Nine of the ten took a step forward. They all said their individual names. When they were done, the oldest said "We are the Tat. We've come here to convince you not to go into the Southern Jungle. That will set off a chain of events that would be most regrettable. If we can't convince you . . ." Taz, the oldest Tat, motioned with his hand, presenting the ax man, saying ". . . this man will end it here."

This shocked the Hammer-Axe Six as well as their Warlords. The Ra Warlords had heard enough about the Tat to know they were very dangerous. The Hammer-Axe Six had been told everything the Hellcats knew about the Tat. They were also told that they were probably the most dangerous group they'd ever face. That if they came upon them to try to get as far away from them as possible.

After hearing what Taz said, all of the Ra started slowly backing up, one step at a time. La said "We have no quarrel with you. You're from the north, protected by the House of Japha. You need not be here." the Tat, Tone said "We don't need anyone's protection." the Tat, Tonia scolded "Tone, don't talk. That's not why we're here!" Tone looked at Tonia and then looked back at the Ra. Taz said "You're forbidden to go into the Southern Jungle. That's final. What have you to say to this?"

Before Dan could stop La, she yelled "Forbidden!" then La stopped herself from saying what she really was thinking, which was 'I'll not only go into the Southern Jungle, but when I'm done there, I'll go North and see why I've been pestered by the likes of you!'

Right after La thought that, she remembered being told these people could read thoughts. La stared at the Tat. Maybe they didn't read those thoughts. That's when Taz said "That's just what we thought you'd do. That's why we're here to end this now."

The Ra and their Warlords knew exactly what was meant by that. They all went on guard with their axes, all at the same time. The Tat stared at them. None of the Ra or their Warlords moved, after that. They all realized they couldn't move, at all!

The Tat used their thoughts to block transmissions from the central nervous system that controls movement. At the same time the Tat sent suggestions through the central nervous system to the muscles, stopping all of them from moving. The Tat watched as the Ra stood motionless.

The brute pulled his ax. When he did the Ra and their Warlords, struggled, trying to regain movement. The brute walked over to where the Elite Guards were. They were closest to him and furthest from the Ra.

Taz ordered "Wait! Come and start over here with the one they call High Pressure, the Executioner. She's the most dangerous one of all. Take her head first and continue with the others." The brute looked at Taz for a moment, turned and started walking towards Danaaa.

The Hammer-Axe Six were near panic upon seeing that. They were trying everything to move themselves, but they couldn't.

The two Elite guards tried to move towards the brute with the ax. Ali, Bo and Hoban struggled, as well. Yin thought about all be beatings he took from Danaaa when they were younger. He swore he'd get even, one day. Now, Yin wished that if he couldn't save Danaaa that this brute would take his head, first. Yin knew that wish wasn't happening when the brute walked past him on his way to Danaaa.

Where Don was positioned, he couldn't see Danaaa. Don stared at the brute trying to get his attention, when he walked by. He thought maybe if he could offend the brute he wouldn't have to hear Danaaa's body and head hitting the ground, because he'd already be dead. The brute never even looked at Don as he walked by.

Shaya could barely see Danaaa out of the corner of her eye. She struggled vigorously trying to move. When the brute passed Shaya she tried to scream, but couldn't. Her legs got weak and she lost control of them. Shaya thought she would have fallen to the ground but she didn't. Even though she lost control of her legs, someone else hadn't.

When La saw that brute turn and start walking towards Danaaa, she struggled even harder. She couldn't believe this was happening. La knew as soon as that brute took Danaaa's head, they wouldn't have to take hers, because she knew she would die at that very moment. La couldn't stop herself from thinking she would never have the chance she wanted with Bo. Nor would she conquer the Shinmushee. La quickly put both of those thoughts out of her mind. Baby was more important. La knew she had to help Baby, so she frantically struggled to move. Why couldn't she move herself?!!

Dan tried to calm himself. He knew there had to be a way to get out of this. He tried to think of everything, but when the brute passed him on his way to Danaaa, Dan's heart dropped a mile, in a half a second. Dan couldn't force himself to believe they all would be killed. He felt this was entirely his fault, getting everyone out here. He struggled like a mad man, just as the rest of the Hammer-Axe Six were. This time, it wasn't enough.

Ram was closest to Danaaa. He couldn't understand why he couldn't move. With all his stealth, hunting and killing abilities, Ram was unable to use them against this brute.

When the brute reached Danaaa, he looked at her. Then the brute looked at Taz. Taz nodded his head. Danaaa saw the brute the entire time with her field vision. But still Danaaa couldn't move. If she could, she would just chop the brute to pieces. She just knew it!

Danaaa couldn't figure out how to use her wits to get herself to move. From what she could see, La's and Dan's wits weren't doing much better. Danaaa remembered she didn't like wits. They were never around when she needed them, most. And she really needed somebody to use their wits, now!

As Danaaa watched the brute lift his ax, a strange calmness came over her. She somehow realized that wits weren't that important, anymore. Danaaa thought about her mother and father. She wished she could have seen them one last time. The next thing Danaaa thought about was all the people she'd chopped with her axes. It was funny to Danaaa, in a strange way, because now it was her turn to get chopped. Just like the people she chopped never had a chance, it now seemed to Danaaa that she was in the same predicament.

Danaaa wanted to close her eyes so she wouldn't have to see that ax coming at her, but she couldn't. So she just watched the brute and everything else she could see with her field vision. Danaaa quickly looked at Yin and each of her brothers and sisters. She wanted to remember everything about them and take it with her, wherever she was going, if she could. Then the brute reared his ax back. A shockwave of panic hit Danaaa, seeing that. Then the brute swung his ax, full force, at Danaaa's neck.

CPSIA information can be obtained at www.ICGtesting.com
Printed in the USA
BVOW010733121212

307931BV00001B/38/P